£10

34

ONLINESS

Onliness

A NOVEL BY DAVE SMITH

LOUISIANA STATE UNIVERSITY PRESS
Baton Rouge and London   1981

DESIGN: Joanna Hill
TYPEFACE: Garamond
TYPESETTER: Service Typesetting Co.
PRINTER AND BINDER: Thomson-Shore, Inc.

LIBRARY OF CONGRESS CATALOGING IN PUBLICATION DATA

Smith, Dave, 1942–
  Onliness.

  I. Title.
PS3569.M517305   813'.54   81-255
ISBN 0-8071-0871-5   AACR2

This book is dedicated to Billy Carmines, Billy Wren, Olen Evans, and Dave Crumette, friends in the darkness—

I've given you my onliness—

TIM HARDIN

—and pilgrimes were they alle

CHAUCER

ONLINESS

Changing the Guard

Chapel, Virginia, is not the kind of place that changes much. A fishing village isolated on a peninsula between Hampton City and York County (famous to tourists looking for the end of the Revolutionary War) and ordinarily having little truck with either, Chapel is older than both. You hear the same family names in Rooster Smith's store. Everybody is related to each other. Some would kill before they'd admit it. Children leave for jobs in Newport News and Hampton, even distant cities, but enough of them stay to be watermen like their fathers. They crab, fish nets, oyster, fix boats, get drunk, fight, go to church, have children, and die. They live on family ground in thin old houses and they sell land when they're desperate. They try to ignore the outside world and pay whatever costs the inside exacts. They speak little, and mostly curse. It's unlikely you'd go among them and leave unchanged. You can tell what life is by driving the narrow roads along creeks that cradle the hulks of dead boats, by clapboard buildings collapsing sleepily under honeysuckle, by cars dying of rust wherever you look. The people go on.

All this the black man explained patiently to the young red-haired man who was beside him. They both wore the blue and gray uniform of Virginia state troopers and leaned against the imposing cruiser that was parked in two weed-covered ruts. Before them what appeared to be a large chicken shack buckled its last joints. The black man had a belly and he wore reflector sunglasses, but his dignity was severe and his uniform natty. Gold sergeant's chevrons adorned his sleeves. He held his Smokey Bear hat in one hand. The other rested on his gleaming holstered revolver. He had come there to show the young trooper where the beat ended, but now they had been standing in the afternoon glare long enough to bring a shadow of sweat to the back of each man. Across the street there was a banging noise in the Chapel Garage and a woman shouted "Clifton!"

"Been years but I still think about it," the black trooper said.

"They really had a war here?" The young trooper put his hat back on his head and glanced uneasily around at the trees.

"Hell of a war. Most everybody forgot it by now. Them that would tell about it is mostly dead or lost, you understand. Funny how things fall out, too. Clifton got kids and me 'bout to retire. My place is right over there by the river. Got a boat and a net. Billy Carmines taught me. Good a place as any in the world to live."

"Who won the war?"

"Nobody. Nobody ever does win a war. Everybody always in a war, though. Keeps some alive. Hell, living is all by itself a war." The black trooper lit a cigarette, puffed, coughed, then ground it out.

"Lord I hope not," the young trooper said. His cheeks, even in the shade of his great hat, were pink as a baby's.

The black trooper had been staring at the ruins but now he stood straight and glared at the other man who watched himself in the reflector glasses.

"Time," the black trooper said. They got in the cruiser.

"And they still out there?" the young trooper said just before the black trooper hit siren and roared out Yorktown Road for the last time.

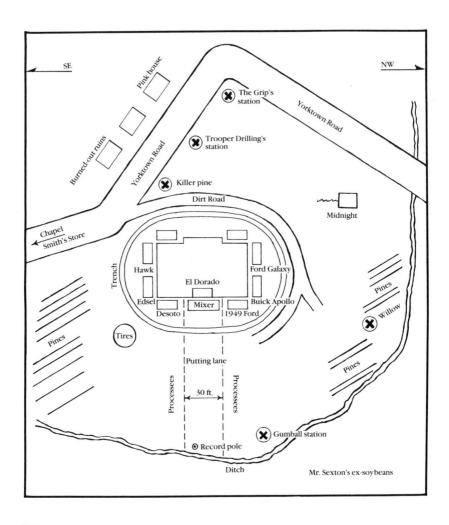

SE

NW

Pink house

Burned-out ruins

Yorktown Road

The Grip's station

Trooper Drilling's station

Yorktown Road

Killer pine

Dirt Road

Midnight

Chapel
Smith's Store

Trench

Hawk

El Dorado

Ford Galaxy

Edsel

Mixer

Buick Apollo

Desoto

1949 Ford

Tires

Pines

Willow

Putting lane

Pines

Processees

Processees

30 ft.

Pines

Gumball station

Record pole

Ditch

Mr. Sexton's ex-soybeans

The Map

4

CHAPTER I

The Pilgrimage

If only I had seen him, he thought.

Just once would'a been enough, he thought.

Billy Luke Tomson had never set eyes on his daddy that folks said he looked so much like. He stood there in the living room of his momma's trailer, looking at his momma lying drunk on the floor, and kept thinking those two thoughts, not once imagining what difference seeing his father would have made.

So far as his momma was concerned he was his father, which explained but did not ease the way she was always at him. People had told him it was hard to love anything as much as she had loved Big Jack. They said when his daddy died trying to save some little girls in a boat drifting off Kitty Hawk his momma had just locked in. She never snapped, she just locked in.

He picked up the picture of Big Jack and Katie Tomson that his momma kept on the keel piece of what she always called "the drowning boat" and looked close. At six-four, Jack Tomson was big but his bride was six feet even and when he looked at her he felt as if he saw his father. But he had never seen Big Jack, only this picture. And he usually saw it when his momma brought somebody in the trailer and said, "See this, ittas partn the keel onto that drowning boat what kilt Jack. That's me and Jack on top of things."

"Momma," he said. She didn't answer so he kneeled down to see if she was all right. She reeked of whiskey but breathed evenly, the breaths blowing the rug tufts that leaned in and out of her mouth. He rolled her so he got his arms under her, sucked air in, and squat-thrusted her up onto the couch.

"Girl," his momma said, then snored.

As he packed he remembered all the times he had searched out her bottles and broken them. At some point he accepted her drinking, so she drank more in defiance. She'd thrown him out of the trailer five or six times in the last two years. Once she'd pitched his daddy's seabag after him. He had known then that this moment was coming. Like his daddy he wanted to be Coast Guard so he might as well get on with it. Still, as he shoved in his clothes, he thought things might have been different if. . . .

His grandaddy Luther Miller met him at the highway. It was still cool but he could smell the ocean shifting toward summer. There were still tears in his eyes from where he had kissed his mother. Even drunk she had reached out and slapped him.

"Hurry up, boy," Luther Miller said. "Yore life is about to start."

They talked easily as Luther drove for the Currituck bus depot. His throat felt a little choked as he watched his grandaddy spit the brown Beechnut juice out the window.

"Don't act like a dog, boy," Luther Miller said. "Ain't I told you one year back she was crazy, daughter of mine or not? Possibly I tole you she wasn't the first to drink in her family, too." The old man rattled on while the car, never exceeding thirty miles per hour, crawled into the May night.

"If just once I'd seen daddy," Billy Luke said in a sudden silence.

"Not made a tinker's damn worth of difference," Luther Miller said, then spat. "He'd a tole you just as I've told you to get the hell away." Miller hesitated and squinted at his grandson for a long minute. "Listen, boy, I done knowed Jack all his life. He ain't had a player of getting them girls back and he knew it. Jack always known exactly what he was doing. Now I ain't just saying Katie and the whiskey made him go. I'm saying he was good as the Coast Guard has got and known what was what. Now you wait for that bus to Elizabeth City and go on and get sworn in. Go live *your* life."

"Yessir," Billy Luke said. He loved his grandaddy.

"Go to college if you can. Learn something."

"Yessir."

"Leave women alone as long as you can."

"Yessir." Billy Luke Tomson felt his face blush hot. How had his grandaddy known about that? A month had not passed since he had been accused of being the father of Tulip Gray's illegitimate child. The principal had called him into his office on his nineteenth birthday just to let him know what had happened and to assure him no one would hear outside those walls. By lunchtime the next day everyone was laughing about it and about Tulip Gray's stupidity. Didn't she know that Billy Luke Tomson had never even had a date?

"Well if you can stay away from women you'll be a better man than the rest of us."

They were quiet for a while and the boy watched the misty fields and thick pine trees of North Carolina slip by. The high moon made everything white.

"Boy for Christ's sake cheer up! You going in the Coast Guard!" Luther Miller said. He reached over and punched the boy affectionately. "One day you'll come back home and all the promises'll be made good and you'll have a little family and all. I'm old but I know some things."

"Yessir," he said.

It was foggy when Billy Luke Tomson stepped on the bus and he was sleepy so that he did not notice he had gone to Raleigh instead of Elizabeth City. An old woman riding next to him asked when he was born and he said November 19 and she oh-oh, a bad day to travel. He remembered that after he got off in Raleigh. The ticket salesman directed him to the Raleigh Recruiting Office. "Post office. Two blocks left, one right, basement," the man said.

Swinging his daddy's duffle bag on his great back, he walked into the post office and saluted a United Parcel Post man who was on coffee break. Without a giggle, the UPI man saluted back. When Tomson said he was ready to enlist the man said he had the wrong uniform and pointed down the hall at an open door. He thanked the man and, with his daddy's Sunday suit tugging at his armpits and crotch, he stepped to the door and halted at a desk.

"Jesus Mostus," the green uniform said behind the desk.

"Say what?" Tomson said, looking at the man's bald dome.

"Jesus H. Mostus," Staff Sergeant Kozywicki said. Then, "How the fuck big are you kid?"

"Six ten," Billy Luke Tomson answered, "but I don't weigh only 296."

"Jesus Mostus," the Staff Sergeant repeated. He walked from behind the desk and went behind Billy Luke and said "Hey, Ricco, get a load of this one."

Ricco did not bother to climb out of his swivel chair in the adjoining room. Instead he called "C'mere" and when Billy Luke Tomson entered that room he was handed a thick sheaf of papers.

"Fill 'em out and sign at the red x everywhere," Ricco said.

He was sworn in by a bored lieutenant with a catsup stain on his cheek, in a fake-panelled room full of gilded flags. On the Greyhound he heard a kid say that at least Fort Jackson would be on the East Coast. Tomson said the kid was wrong, since he was going to Yorktown, Virginia, where the Coast Guard trained.

"Jesus, you ain't only big as a friggin' elephant but also is as dumb. Boy they raise some dumb shits in the South. You are in the US of A's Army, friend," the kid told Basic Trainee Tomson. Everybody

8

on the bus laughed at the kid's hard little voice and the dummy who thought he was going sailing. They had a long ride and a quick, loud greeting, then fell fast asleep in their cots. Except for Billy Luke Tomson. He made no sound as he stepped to the little kid's bed or as he lifted the kid up by the elbows. Then there was only a soft snap and a long scream.

On the morning of Billy Luke Tomson's first day in boot camp, Aurelio Guiterrez Swartznik was medically discharged to Brooklyn, New York, and BT Tomson was assigned to the base disciplinary company. Here, his black cellmate said, he would get one sergeant personal-like who meant him to get his shit straight and keep it that way. He would never know how a sequence of arbitrary and random decisions, mistakes, and circumstances had led him to one of those men who, in a brief time, change our lives.

Staff Sergeant Roosevelt Franklin Davis stood five feet five in his spit-shined combat boots. His Smokey drill hat angled so low over his face that no man could verify he had eyes. His voice boomed and cut through the bars to Billy Luke Tomson. If BT Tomson had been asked he might have said it was a trick standing there, so unreal did everything seem.

"I will tame yore monstrous ass," SSGT Davis said. Then he threw open the door, walked into the cell, told Tomson to stand at attention, and when Tomson did the SSGT jumped up and punched him on the jaw. When Tomson woke he was lying in the sun in a great field of asphalt. SSGT Davis stood over him but did not look at him.

"I am one badass nigger sergeant. Boy, get up and do it quick," Davis said.

All day SSGT Davis walked Billy Luke Tomson around the parking lot. He had BT Tomson marching, halting, turning, counter-marching. He also had him heft and throw whatever he came to and had him run, jump, and sling things. SSGT Davis, it turned out, was the Fort Jackson track coach.

Billy Luke Tomson, the SSGT saw overnight, could put the sixteen-pound shot with extraordinary thrust. When he had marched the boy once more to the sea of asphalt and stood him in a brace, he said

"Trainee Tomson, I admire your style. Man shouldn't bust his fellow man like you done, of course. On the other hand, a man can only take so much. I'm gonna make a man of you."

They began to march again and suddenly Billy Luke Tomson saw they were in a huge green field and though he had never seen one he knew this was a track and field area. People ran on a dark circle and others jumped white frames. Some lay down and stretched. Some puffed and sweated. All seemed to have a distant and mysterious look on their faces.

"Tomson, you ever put the shot?" Staff Sergeant Davis said.

"Say shot?" Tomson answered, watching a small man in silk shorts go by.

"God hisself says SIR to me, boy. You forget, I must bust yo head." Sweat bubbled on the brown cheeks that Tomson could see.

"I asted you did you ever put the shot Tomson," SSGT Davis said.

Concentrating on remembering to say SIR, BT Tomson was slow to answer and another sergeant, unseen, slapped him on the side of the head, saying "Man aks you a question whale-shit."

If he had never heard of a shot or put one, Billy Luke Tomson knew what a slap in the head was and he returned it without thought, looping his thick arm in a backward arc that sent the unseen sergeant backward into a couple of silk-clad runners. All three went down in a tangle, the sergeant unconscious before he hit.

Sergeants Davis and Reymer held BT Tomson through so many weeks of extra boot training he was at last assigned to Davis and promoted twice. He also put the shot over 45 feet, a sixteen-pound shot. Sergeant Davis allowed that the twelve-pound shot was for boys and women. Then Sergeant Reymer said the U.S. Army didn't have room for the former and couldn't get enough of the latter.

Two years later, touring with the Army track team, Billy Luke Tomson took the All-Service shotput at Fort Belvoir, Virginia. That night he got drunk for the first time and found his way to a strip dive in the nation's capital. As he stood in line for a ticket the man before him reached back and touched something he should not have and Tomson, loosened by liquor, lifted and put the man over a

Volkswagen where a passing beer truck received him with a thump. Army investigators, having heard the victim was a homosexual, recommended a speedy for-the-good-of-the-service discharge. Discharge in hand, Tomson was told at the Coast Guard recruiting station that the Guard had a full quota. "Try the Marines," a fat chief told him.

He had no idea where he was going, had not even thought about it, but his direction was south. Only days before he had stood in scant track clothes in the Belvoir fieldhouse and now a light snow stung his cheeks. He was on the Shirley Highway below Washington where waves of semis rolled by and showered him with slush. They did not stop for the huge man with his thumb out. It was dark and he was too big if they had to handle him. Such men, truckdrivers knew, were everywhere in the land now. It was best to leave them alone.

He had been cold for a long time now. Snow crusted his eyebrows. To protect his head he had ripped open his Army cunt cap and jammed it on. He shivered and watched the taillights moving toward D.C. on the other side of the road. When he looked back a car was skidding toward him, its horn blaring. At last someone controlled the skid and the car washed past him, a woman waving from the passenger seat. Up the road no lights were coming at him from the darkness. He thought it might be just as good to go back to D.C. and would have but now there were no cars on that side. There was only the muffled silence of the falling snow. He would have to wait now. He blew on his hands and thought of putting the shot. That always pleased him. Then he thought of his grandaddy and that ride to Currituck. The old man had gone fishing in the surf, reached down for something in a wave and tumbled into it, according to an eyewitness. He wondered what his life would come to, where he was headed. So much, he thought, lay out there waiting to happen to a person and all of it unknown except one. Everybody died, he thought. Not yet, he thought, then saw the headlights crest the hill.

The panel truck stopped with hardly a sound. From the top of the hill its lights had flared bigger and bigger and he had a feeling about it. As he picked up his duffle bag he saw there were letters on the truck: ZUCOLD's Bowie Garage. The ZUCOLD was larger than the others. All the letters were painted in gold. From inside a hand reached out to him and he shook it.

"That is some mother handshake you got there, sport," Tom Zucold said.

"Name not sport," he answered.

"Bet me it ain't. Didn't think it was," Tom Zucold said as he picked up stuff from where there ought to be a passenger seat but wasn't and threw it in the rear, "else somebody fucked up on you long before this."

"Where you going?" Billy Luke Tomson asked, though the sudden wind took away everything but "going." Another time he might have carried on the argument about names but now he was cold and sleepy and he'd be anybody so long as he got a ride.

"Name must be The Grip," Tom Zucold said, and the man who stood in the snow and was named Billy Luke Tomson climbed up and into the rear of the panel truck. He was already The Grip.

"You crazy?" The Grip asked as he cleared a hole in the rear.

"Going? Where am I going? Question is where have I been. Been to Georgia, Vermont, Utah, the Oregon desert, Paris France, most everywhere you can think of, Grip," Tom Zucold said and accelerated back onto the highway. "Rode fine, too, won some they said was unwinnable. Lost some, too. You have a drink this night, son?" He held up a black pint, then swallowed from it.

"Crazy, Grip? Who ain't crazy? I know where I'm going. Been to D.C. for some parts to a 1958 Porsche Speedster, going home. Know where home is, too. No riddle at all when you programmed like me. But crazy, that's something else." The man had an enormous head and it bobbed when he took another drink.

"How big are you?" The Grip asked. Except for oncoming headlights it was absolute dark in the truck, not even a gauge light showing.

"Big enough to stomp the shit out of a snake when I got to."

The Grip wanted to ask how big that was but they were underway now and the steady ticking of the tires on tar strips and the hiss of slush made him grow sleepier. He pushed his duffle bag against the old man's seat and laid out on his back with his head on the bag.

"Oh shit it's something in our alley," Tom Zucold said and hit the brakes. "Hold on Grip."

He felt the panel truck slide and swerve and then heard a whining horn and Tom Zucold screamed into his rolled-up window "You crazy mother fucker."

"Say how big again," The Grip said and then was asleep

"Big enough to take you on and stomp snakes too," Tom Zucold said. "How big a man got to be, big as you?" When there was no answer he saw that his cargo was settled and sleeping and he drove steadily south. Once he snapped on a radio whose bulblight was out. It filled with static and a voice said something about Carolina and then named Virginia Beach and there was some gospel music. Tom Zucold assumed it was another Sunday Gospel hour so he dialed another station and got a preacher who claimed to be right then in the wilderness with Jesus.

"Shit," Tom Zucold said in answer. "He's in Waycross, Georgia."

He dialed more stations and all of them said something about Jesus and salvation. "You can't pick up a goddamn thing worth hearing on Sunday, you know that Mr. Grip? Man goes off driving through the wilderness, lays himself open to all kinds of evil and mayhem, and cannot get a lick of decent music to accompany his fate."

Tom Zucold talked of fate and history and home and Jesus and whatever else came into his mind until at last he saw the dirt road before the Bowie Garage and the sign across the street which said CHAPEL. Finally, his jaws aching, he said "We home," and turned off the ignition. The Grip did not hear a word, as he had heard nothing along the way. He was stretched out like a corpse between a Porsche block and a box of miscellaneous parts. He was dead to the world. Then Tom Zucold's dog began to bark.

CHAPTER II

The Bowie Garage

The sixteen-pound steel ball hit clay with a thump and rolled another ten feet. The Grip hefted again, pumping the shot in his right palm, then hopped and began his spin. He felt himself grow tighter with each put. He also felt the shots as they left his hand. He and Tom Zucold had made twelve of them from scrap fenders. Tom Zucold said fenders melted easiest. It pleased The Grip to be putting shots made from automobiles since he now not only lived among automobiles, he was learning to repair them. Indeed he had begun to dream about cars and even spoke a kind of car language. It seemed right that cars should be connected with the one thing he could do well, even if some of the shots were not quite round. And two weighed more than sixteen pounds.

He put another and watched it fall short. He had been steadily increasing his distance but today had fallen back and could do nothing to get himself on track. He tried to isolate his moving parts in his mind but he kept seeing the shot in flight. He had never made a great put and he wanted one badly. Twice in the last week he had sneaked into the high school library to check the world records in *High School Coach*. He was nowhere near them. But Tom Zucold had encouraged him after he began to see what he meant to do. He closed his eyes to try and remember his moves.

"Plan. Got to have a plan buddyroo. Do it all, if you can see ahead," Tom Zucold said.

The Grip turned and saw Tom Zucold standing in the rear door to the Bowie garage. He held two letters in his hand. "Say plan?" The Grip said.

"Cop come just now. Say he coming by anyway so he brung the letters. Something called the Citizens Committee of Chapel sent it. Asking all the peoples to help clean up Chapel. They after my processees is all. Other letter say I owing back payments on the Bowie Garage. They calling it to my attention."

"What you gone do?" The Grip said. Tom Zucold looked mashed.

"Do? Going to Hell, that's what. Cost money, what they say. Ittis my home, don't you see? Don't anybody see? Fuck 'em, that's what." Tom Zucold wheeled and went back into the garage, leaving The Grip wondering what a Citizens Committee was.

He picked up another shot and whipped it off only to see it smash into the windshield on a classic 1949 Ford. He had used hard body English but it had plunged in anyway.

"Got one," he shouted to Tom Zucold. There was no answer but he was sure he'd been heard. "Ford, 1949. Two door, black, no right side door." He ticked it off like an inventory item. He knew all of the cars, processees, as Tom Zucold called them, which formed the lane where he put shots. He had arranged each one in its place. He had cleared the ground of glass, bolts, beer cans, rusting parts, and had planted the grass. It had all been a mystery to Tom Zucold, who had scratched his head and watched. The Grip turned and went inside the Bowie Garage. Through the front overhead door he saw a woman drive off in a yellow Volkswagen convertible. Tom Zucold was walking back toward the Bowie Garage and he was counting money.

"Said got one. Ford, 1949."

"I heard you the first time," Tom Zucold said, pocketing the money. "Ain't much for fixing her rear end but every dime helps."

Tom Zucold walked in and sat down on the creeper and slipped back under the Plymouth Valiant with bad transmission seals. The Grip kneeled down by the door and said "What is Citizens Committee?"

"Boy, goddamned if I know," Tom Zucold said, and proceeded then to tell him. "Ittis always some people who ain't got enough to do so they got to get into doing for you. Seem like to me we is each programmed to do what we do best. Maybe what some people do best is bother. Maybe they part of the plan and we don't know it. Things work out, just the same." Tom Zucold sounded cheerful, The Grip thought, when it seemed that he ought to be otherwise.

"What do they want?"

"Hard as it is for you to believe," Tom Zucold said as he slid out from under the Plymouth, retrieved gaskets from the workbench, and slid back under, "they is people that thinks all them processees out there is naught but junk. Ittis some that has stopped here afore this and said old Tom ought maybe to clean up his curve. Look like a bunch of old ladies in flower hats and nothing to do is got bent on prettifying my property. They want everything modernized, what they call it. Can't stand nothing old. Probably cause they getting old." Tom Zucold banged and clattered and then banged some more. Then he said, "Course ittis some wants to put a shopping center in here and don't give a frog's spit what is pretty and what ain't."

"You gonna let them?" The Grip asked.

"Gonna stay free long as I can," Tom Zucold said. "We just wait and see what happens. Meantime I got faith. A man can do some things for hissef."

"Well I can heave some shots at 'em if they come around."

"Wrong."

"Say wrong?" The Grip said.

Tom Zucold scooted from under the Plymouth again and stood up. "Wrong," Tom Zucold said as he wiped his hands. "Is hard to see what Tom Zucold means maybe but things is laid out ahead of us if we got the sense to see how. A tick don't try to suck a fencepost. Bet me. Be foolish to cannonball them. Ain't in the plan. Move that Plymouth out in the yard. Time for lunch."

The Grip leaned back against the chain, his lunch pushing at the bottom of his throat, gritted his teeth and pulled to jerk the Corvette engine free. The chassis groaned and squeaked behind him. Tom Zucold tapped carefully with his ball-peen hammer but the engine didn't break loose and the chain cut into the muscle of The Grip's right shoulder. His face plumped red like a tomato with the pressure. Sweat dripped into his eyes and he wasn't sure whether he could hold on. He hissed through his teeth. It was excellent programming, Tom Zucold had reminded him.

"Seen him once in Memphis," Tom Zucold said from under the car.

The Grip's heart was pounding. Tom Zucold had said the engine would tug out just like a tooth so The Grip tried to imagine a tooth in his tow chain. Tom Zucold tapped harder, doing it crisply, doing it right. The Grip had learned from the old man you had to do things right, find the way. Before Zucold he hadn't cared how it got done so long as it was done. He hadn't been programmed.

"At's it, at's it," Tom Zucold said, "she's coming."

At last it gave, sounding like many nails pulled from boards, and The Grip walked the chain forward to the pulley wheel, then locked it. The engine swayed black and ugly above its hole. Oil spattered in the quiet.

"Goddamn, Grip. Thought you was gone pull the mother to Yorktown."

Because Tom Zucold had taught The Grip to listen more to how words got said than to what words were said, The Grip heard the pride expressed.

"Said he's in Memphis once," Tom Zucold piped from under the Corvette.

The Grip watched the engine, ignoring Tom Zucold. The oil had stopped dripping now. He could see the red oil pan and the dent in it. He thought it was gorgeous. It was going to be his. Was his. Tom Zucold had given it to him. It was mostly a wreck but Zucold could fix that easily enough, he was certain.

"Did not," The Grip said.

"Did not what, you ape?" Tom Zucold spit.

"Say he's in Memphis once. Said you *seen* him in Memphis."

The Grip moved to the engine pit and looked in. It was dark as a well except that at the bottom was a face like the Quaker Oats man's with a dirty beard. Tom Zucold squinted up at him, his eyelids working against the specks of falling dirt. What if the chain slipped, The Grip thought?

"Son of a bitch, you say," Tom Zucold spat.

"Say you seen him in Memphis."

"Think I don't know what Tom Zucold said?" Tom Zucold blinked. "Bet me." A wrench clattered on the concrete. Then the creeper shot out, narrowly missing The Grip's left leg, and Tom Zucold jumped off it.

"Let's go have a look and see who's saying what," Tom Zucold said as he brushed past The Grip and jammed a dead cigar into his small mouth.

The Grip followed him into the other half of the Bowie Garage, a room which Tom Zucold called their house because it was where the two of them lived. Before Tom Zucold it had been a chicken shack and sometimes the smell returned. Tom Zucold waddled over to the pot-bellied stove, pushed the cigar against it until it smoked faintly, then turned to stand in front of a poster taped to a window. Hard morning light luminously outlined a figure on the poster. The Grip stood beside Tom Zucold.

"Say he seen you in Memphis," The Grip said to the poster. There was no answer.

"Said you's in Memphis once," Tom Zucold said, his voice smaller than usual. Again there was no answer. Yet an answer had been given and both had heard it. Tom Zucold turned away to the Thunderbird bucket seat he had mounted on four stumped railroad ties. He climbed up and touched the electric switch that tilted his seat however he wanted it, making it hang forward so he was staring directly into The Grip's eyes.

"Said I seen him in Memphis once." And then, "Didn't though."

The Grip didn't know why this poster test worked, just that it worked. "Can't beat seeing the truth," he said.

"Don't matter," Tom Zucold said. "Truth is he is coming. I seen him in my head, how he moves, how he shoots, how he thinks. We just don't know when is all." He sounded more cheerful as he talked. "Bring me a beer would'ja and, say, you toted up how much we done saved? We got to be ready when he gets here."

The Grip stepped across the room to an ancient Kelvinator washing machine and lifted the lid under the wringing rollers. He took out a tall Blue Ribbon and a jar of Gatorade. Behind him the whirring of the electric motor hooked to the Thunderbird bucket seat told him Tom Zucold had changed his angle of vision. He had lived with the old man long enough to know such a change and a can of beer meant he was due for a lesson.

"Say how much?" The Grip said.

"Bet me. Man my age don't stutter."

"Five hunnert fourteen and twenty-two," The Grip said after a pause. He had not even had to look in the glove compartment which he had stashed in the wall by his bed. "Sixty-three due on Miz Sexton's Comet."

"Ain't nuff," Tom Zucold said.

"It'd make some payments," The Grip said as he tipped up the Gatorade and drained it.

"You still a small thinker, boy," Tom Zucold answered. "It's always more payments after the ones you pay. Man what thinks big looks to pay off debts. He wants to get free so he's able to walk about and admire the world. Ittis like that there," he said and pointed at a sign on the wall.

The Grip looked at the sign nailed directly over the open commode. In bold letters it said KEEP IT TIGHT, THINGS GO RIGHT. For a long time he had wondered if the sign referred to the commode handle or his craps or all the nuts Tom Zucold forever had him tightening. One day Tom Zucold had pointed and said "Strings."

"Strings?" The Grip said.

"Big as a goddamn LaSalle, had the best military training in the world, a young man, and you don't know fucking nothing about nothing. Boy, the body is naught but strings and fluids. Strings'll go flat quick as a beat-up double ply, mostly on curves," Tom Zucold had said.

The Grip stared at the sign but did not see the connection between strings which Tom Zucold had explained and Tom Zucold's refusal to pay mortgage payments. He knew he must wait. There was no need to ask for what Tom Zucold had meant to deliver all along. Tom Zucold, The Grip knew, not only knew an unnormal amount of things but was also willing to tell most people what he knew.

"Say ain't enough," The Grip repeated to get the lesson on track and over.

"Hell no," Tom Zucold said. "Sit down in your chair boy."

The Grip got one more Gatorade from the Kelvinator, it being a warm day, and sat hard in his Corvette bucket seat. Tom Zucold had said he would also mount the chair when The Grip had come to understand a few more things about the world but for the present the chair had to remain on the floor that was plain dirt seasoned with chicken droppings and covered by rugs taken from the processees.

"Everbody got a plan into him, see. Ittis like a hydraulic system in a car. Keep it tight, keep the pressure making it what it supposed to be and everything be fine. Plan is don't let things sag, don't loaf. Got to be what you are. Same thing true for human folks. Good beer," Tom Zucold said and swallowed hard several times. "Now once upon a time a young man wanted to ride horses. Hell of a rider. Work like a woodpecker carryin' shit out of the barn, carryin' straw in, such as that. One day a man come in a suit. Say, boy you too goddamn big. Say, don't come round here no more." Tom Zucold swallowed several more times.

"Mr. Grip, that was a true thing that man said. Was too big. Naught could the boy do because it was not in the plan for him to ride. Boy was then five-four and weight onefourtwo. Boy was me. I said Jesus Christ. No help. I said pray fool. No help. Said get off your ass and become yourself. Looka these, Mr. Grip."

Tom Zucold held up his hands and rotated them. The palms and underfingers were hard calloused, but the hands were long-fingered and frail like a pianist's and the skin was mostly smooth with scattered brown dots. The Grip looked at his fingers which were thick and blunt as cheap cigars.

"See I had hands because of the plan. How it is," Tom Zucold said. "I kin get them babies into holes thin as paper almost. Kin wiggle little nuts off that most need a magnet for. You can't hardly grab a tit with them mits."

A heavy look came into The Grip's naturally heavy face.

"Wrong," Tom Zucold said. "See what you thinkin'. Your plan seems like is to throw them steel balls. A man with my hands can't do that and I ain't seen no man do it better than you."

The Grip looked up into Tom Zucold's eyes. During all his lessons his eyes got sparkly and glowed like a hawk's that The Grip had seen once in a country fair and now Tom Zucold's eyes were flashing. The old man hit his tilt button and the Thunderbird chair leaned him forward so that he would have fallen out but for the safety belt. He hovered above The Grip and then said, "What you can do is what I can't, what maybe nobody ever born could do."

"What is that?" The Grip said.

"Life," Tom Zucold replied very softly.

"Say life," The Grip's thick lips mimicked.

"Monkeys in the house for Christ's sake," Tom Zucold spat and immediately hit the button to lean his chair in the opposite direction. "Surely that is why he is coming," he seemed to say to a dark rope that hung from the naked planks of the roof. Then he said to The Grip, "Didn't say life, said lift."

"Lift," The Grip said tonelessly.

"God bless," Tom Zucold said. "Boy you can lift and shove and push and tug and maul and shape when you like it. Way you are built. I got to work by what power I can use, electric and hydraulic and whatever. Lights go out I be sunk. What I do? I wait until a man come and say go on and work now. Make me hot to think of it. Go to take an axle offn a Maverick and get jack stuck, there I am. Waitin'. You can make things happen, force 'em. Thing is not to forget your plan. Worst thing is let your strings go slack and lug on you. But if you got them ready when they needed, why ittis life in spades."

The Grip was by nature a more practical man than Tom Zucold and if he saw the rightness of Tom Zucold's program he nevertheless had not taken his attention entirely off the immediate problem. "What we gone do about them payments?"

"Could pray," Tom Zucold said as he climbed down from his chair.

"Say pray?" The Grip said as Tom Zucold went out the door to the garage.

"Don't lift no Corvette engine. Won't patch up no fiberglass rear end, neither. Pay now, pay later. Question is how we gone pay. To do that we got to program and coordinate. You done seen what a four-speed is and you in neutral now. We got to get you in all the go gears. Gimme a half-inch," Tom Zucold said.

The Grip went to the near wall, took a wrench from a peg and walked to where Tom Zucold's boots stuck out from under the Corvette's rear end. When he said "Here" and tapped the side, a birdlike hand fluttered out and took the wrench, then said "Shit."

"See you think you are one lucky mother for this," Tom Zucold said and banged the undercarriage. "And you right. We lucky that fool let us have it, but ittis part of the plan."

The Grip thought about the man who had come to see the Corvette that had killed his only son. When the man had said he hoped never to see the rotten thing again, Tom Zucold had acted fast.

"Well," he had said, "ittis banged up pretty good and gone take some hard dust to get her to scratch."

"I beg your pardon," the man said.

"Will cost you a bundle to put it back on the road," Tom Zucold said. Then pointing at a sap stain on the fender, Tom Zucold said,

"Hard to imagine how that blood got all the way back there but it shows the damage don't it."

"Did you say that was blood?" the man said.

"Hit my tree pretty good," Tom Zucold said, "maybe good enough to kill it. Planted that when I was boy about the age of yourn."

"You said that was blood?"

Tom Zucold offered to take the car for the value of the tree and the man gave him a handwritten bill of sale on the spot. The investigating deputy sheriff and The Grip had dragged the Corvette into the garage yard while Tom Zucold handled this business.

"How that man hit that tree like this, rear first?" The Grip asked the deputy sheriff.

"Look like he must have come at that curve too fast and skidded around and into the tree so the tree snapped the kid right into the windshield. Only thing I can see," the deputy answered. He grinned, "Funny thing is it ain't the first one. Must be half a dozen since I come on the force."

The Grip had admired the wrecked Corvette that evening at dinner. Tom Zucold said it must be part of the plan and said it was his. He could own her and pay taxes on her. Tom Zucold said nothing was worth anything unless you had to pay the tax. The Grip remembered saying that it was sure a car to take a man somewhere in this world. Tom Zucold had asked him where he meant to go but he hadn't been able to answer. He had squeezed his face up tight to make some answer come but it hadn't.

"You hear what I said?" Tom Zucold said from under the Corvette.

"Say lucky," The Grip answered.

"Jesus save us. That was an hour ago. Said listen first, said we got to saw off this rear end second. Third we got to handle that engine. Course we don't do none of this iffn customers come in. Got to be ready for that."

"Check," The Grip said.

"Check? Bet me," Tom Zucold said as he wheeled out from under the car, then stood up. "I'm gone take a ride over to Carmines' Junkyard and see maybe if he got any wrecked Corvettes. Got to have something to put back onter this thing." He waited and when The Grip said nothing he added, "You can get back out there and throw them steel balls. Is in your plan."

The Grip turned and went out the Cadillac El Dorado door, then walked to the far end of the lane where he bagged his shots and began to arrange them for another round of putting. Standing at the door window so he could see The Grip, Tom Zucold said with more affection than heat, "Motherfucker give me an open face half-inch when I needed a closed, wouldn't you know?" The failing light of the afternoon shone full on this stumped figure who wore his usual white coveralls with an oval Esso patch speckled with oil. He had oil and grease in his white beard and great wiry hair for eyebrows so that he looked like an old beast who popped out of the earth or some kind of seed that had evolved wrong, oozing from sandy loam with its tendrils trailing. Flinging the wrench onto the concrete under the car, he jammed a baseball hat on his head and strode out to his panel truck that was parked by the killer tree.

The Grip straightened up and clenched his hands over his head so that his fingers locked palms up. He pulled as hard as he could then dropped into a half-squat so that every string in his body went instantly and visibly tight. He counted to one-thousand-ten and leaped up high. Trimmed to a hard 286 by Tom Zucold's programming, he felt himself slowly zeroing in on serious puts. As he worked out he tried to scan himself on the put that had got the 1949 Ford.

"Aimed it," Tom Zucold said. Only The Grip had imagined Tom Zucold's voice, for the little man was nowhere around. Indeed The Grip knew that if Tom Zucold had gone to Carmines' place he had had some hard drinks by now. That was mostly what Carmines offered his old friend.

Even though he knew he had only imagined Tom Zucold speaking, The Grip said "Did not."

He knew that he had, in fact, aimed the put. That could affect direction and distance. He knew that super performances came not when you tried to control an object but when you allowed yourself

24

to fuse its force with your own. You had to have a motion that, once started, allowed the body no choice but to complete itself. It began with a stance. Just as Tom Zucold had said, a plan. He did two more leaps, breathed for a few seconds, then walked out to the white stick he had planted in the middle of the lane. At seventy-five feet it was beyond a world record put. Maybe he would never reach it but at least he could see where it was. On his way back to the putting circle he stopped off and retrieved the shot that had lodged in the seat of the classic Ford. A mockingbird jeered him and seemed to swoop down at his head until he reached the circle.

He had no idea how long he had been putting. The lane was pocked with impressions from the shots and he was growing tired. He did not watch the time almost on principle. He was late or early, had always been so, and knew himself to be done only when his body stopped. He closed his eyes, palmed and hefted the shot to get the feel and rhythm, then told himself that it was absolutely the last shot he would put. When he opened his eyes, he had screwed himself into a maximum thrust position and he began the rocking that he hoped would finish in a great explosion of power.

It was cool already and the evening was going to be damp. Everything felt right as the shot took off. He thought that it would be a good one because his balance had been true. He had not slipped out of the ring the way he had so often in the past. As he let the shot go he felt as if he had slipped into another time. Leaves were sharp and bright above him. Nothing moved. He could see each blemish on the steel surface rotating slowly upwards.

But at the end of the lane a darkness was gathering and the sun seemed to have fallen, leaving that curious glaze of blue and gold light that sometimes dusk is. Yet the sun was an orange blaze off to his left and he saw that its flood scalded the twenty-four windshields and forty-eight headlights of the processees on his right. It was a terrible and ominous light that boiled from every surface before him, only to skid back across the green lane where thirty feet later it doubled and trebled its power at the headlights and windshields and chrome parts that quietly waited. So raging and glorious was this

light that he thought at first it could not be a mere light, even the
sun's. It flowed and pooled like a river. He reached out his hand to
touch it and his hand turned golden. Like a dog, he pushed his blunt
nose forward and sniffed it.

"What?" he said. "What?"

Now he looked again at the far end of the lane. There had been
some motion. Loblolly pine and sycamores and oncoming night made
a dark screen. He tried to look into the light at the left but could
not, blinked, and saw that out of the light a tiny figure had appeared.
It limped toward him until it reached a white stick he had implanted,
then it stopped. Wordlessly, it looked into his face. Then, still watching him, it pushed the white stick so that it vibrated and caused the
entire lane of light to tremble.

The Grip squinted. He had seen no face such as this one. He
thought it resembled the Chinese cook who had worked for Staff
Sergeant Davis, but not exactly and not enough. It seemed a wrong
face somehow, almost not a face so much as an oval of skin that
stretched like putty. The eyes were round and wide and, he thought,
very dark. The mouth was scarcely more than a scar but it was smiling. Whoever or whatever this was, it wore a shapeless white cloth
that had some kind of stain on the left breast.

He sank to his heels, as if he could see under the light. He rocked
and stared. It tried to speak and made a kind of noise. He wasn't
sure that he had actually heard it and thought maybe he had imagined it. He waved for it to come to him and it stepped forward
halfway and stopped.

"Say fire?" The Grip said.

The light was failing fast now and he was not much more than a
shadow. It stared at him, mouth open, but saying nothing. It turned
and looked at the stick, then at him again, then ran to the stick. It
pushed the stick once more, then darted into the pines and was gone.

"You say fire?" The Grip shouted. He blinked and rubbed his
eyes. Had he really seen anything?

"Hey, fire?" he shouted. He leaped to his feet now and broke for
the black screen of pine. When he reached it there was nothing, only

26

the smell of old oil which Tom Zucold had dumped for years in the bordering ditch. The Grip pushed through the trees to Miz Sexton's open field that was thick with short soybeans. It was as still and desolate as a battlefield before the first shot. Doves cooed, mosquitoes buzzed around him, and mist hung in the nickle blue light. He heard a door somewhere slam shut.

As he picked up the shots and put them in the Havoline box, The Grip said "Ittis a nigger girl." He thought that would make it real but it did not. Who, he thought, had ever seen a nigger girl like that? "Goddammit," he said, then turned back to the Bowie Garage. "It can't be nothing but a nigger girl from one of them houses across the street. Can't be." He did not notice that his last put had traveled fifty feet, the best of his life. Ahead of him the garage waited like fate, a seedy hovel of two large rooms for whatever chose to occupy them. It might as well have been a cave in the darkness. Still he leaned toward it. When he reached it he turned around. The lane now was filled with darkness. He could not even see the white stick he had planted. He felt adrift. If that unbelievable light was gone and if the nigger girl who obviously wasn't a nigger girl was gone and if his house was hardly more than a cave, what was real? Was he? Was anything?

"Godalmight damn," he said as he closed the Cadillac El Dorado door and locked it. Entering their house, he smelled chickens. He had mentioned to Tom Zucold that a man shouldn't live in a chicken shack.

"Man live in a house," Tom Zucold said. "Car stay in a garage. Chickens don't save automobiles and such."

He stepped forward in the darkness and tripped on Tom Zucold's creeper, falling and catching himself on the fender of his Corvette. It was darker inside than outside. He stood and said, "Godalmight damn."

Tom Zucold had made a table of some wooden crates and a door, a table which sat before the television in their house. The door obviously belonged to the back of the Bowie Garage and The Grip had asked about this one day.

"People these days steal whatever you got. Ain't no honor like used to be, Grip," Tom Zucold had said. "Put that door onto your house, you may as well hang a sign that say free anything you want. Ittis just no honor. Well, now, everybody knows a Cadillac is about the finest they is in cars and I figger that'd be true for a door too. Simple. Bolted me steel plates on and then hung me a Crimson Cadillac El Dorado door. Window come down real easy. You try it yet?" The Grip had thought Tom Zucold sounded sad but he knew a man could never be sure that Tom Zucold was what he appeared to be.

The Grip set his jar of Gatorade on the door table and slid his Corvette chair up close. He peeled out of his combat boots that were wet with dew and stripped off a green T-shirt, then his camouflaged fatigue pants. In only his puffing boxer shorts he snapped the television on and then sat before it. Though it was a color television, the picture came in black and white because Tom Zucold believed that color would only confuse their senses. Tom Zucold also refused to allow sound. At first The Grip had thought it silly but he was used to things now.

The Grip checked the Champion Spark Plug clock on the wall. It was time for TRUTH OR CONSEQUENCES. Tom Zucold tolerated no other show of any kind in the Bowie Garage and he watched this, so he claimed, only because he might see a way to win enough dough to be free forever. The Grip liked the jokes and Bob Barker. Though told not to laugh too hard, he often roared and this made Tom Zucold frown. The old man took the stunts seriously and he could not be distracted. Once he had made The Grip pretend to be a contestant with him. They had dressed themselves as angels and Tom Zucold sprayed them in some white latex that had gummed up the spray gun. The Grip had felt foolish and wouldn't budge from the garage. Tom Zucold had sulked. Now The Grip took a big drink of his Gatorade while he watched Bob Barker put his arm around a big-chested girl he was introducing.

Bob Barker fascinated The Grip. No one he had ever seen appeared so much in charge of everything, so poised, so charming, so successful. He had read books about how you were supposed to get girls, jobs, money and it all seemed to translate into the man on the screen. Somehow Bob Barker ran the universe if you once imagined that the stunts he conducted were only what happened to people everywhere all the time. The Grip knew that he couldn't be Bob Barker but he thought that if he watched closely enough he might see how to be more like Barker. Already he had noticed important details such as the fact that Barker's hair was always the same length and shape and the fact that Barker had an automatic grin and white teeth and the fact that Barker never aged a day. Without Tom Zucold's constant chatter at the television, The Grip was able to pay unusually close attention.

Even so, he found that he was exhausted. It was hard to keep up with the stunts. In one he saw that a woman danced with a gorilla in a downtown Los Angeles intersection. He was too tired even to discover what she had won. But the second stunt shocked him awake and he wished that Tom Zucold had been there to see it.

Bob Barker had just put two newlyweds together in a sealed back-stage room. The woman had been told she could get five one-hundred dollar bills to keep if she could manage to get them in her husband's pocket without his knowing what she had done. The camera zoomed in close as the woman began to kiss her husband and The Grip saw her slip the first bill in a rear pocket. Then Bob Barker's face appeared to announce a commercial. After the commercial, the camera went directly to the couple and just then the young husband lifted the woman's sweater and exposed her bare breasts. Then he bent and took one of them into his mouth. The Grip sat up straight in his Corvette chair. The camera cut to Bob Barker whose lips said "Those shits!" Too late The Grip had leaped up to tune in the color and bring back the sound. As he twisted knobs he heard a horn honking steadily and thought that it was another stunt, one that he would never see since his tuning had succeeded only in losing the picture altogether. But it was not TRUTH OR CONSEQUENCES at all, for just then the horn stopped blaring and Tom Zucold burst into the house, panting, to say "He is coming. I kept the faith and he is coming."

"That's right shithead. You can believe it. Don't believe me ask them niggers cross the street. Them's all my kin, you know. Course they'll keeck you out likely." The Grip did not have to be told that Tom Zucold had brought Billy Carmines home with him. Wild-haired and wild-eyed, in the fisherman's knee boots he habitually wore, Billy Carmines came through the door behind Tom Zucold. As soon as he was seated on the floor, leaning against the wall, he said to the darkness "Come on in, Pretty. We waitin' on you."

"Hi," the woman said as she appeared in the door and waved to The Grip. She was blonde and tall and pleasantly solid and he looked hard at her. "I'd like to stay Bill," she said, "but I've got a lot to do. Thanks for the help, hear." Then she was gone.

"That's Promise Land," Billy Carmines said. "She kin to me some-how but I keep forgettin' what. Good woman though. Wish I'd had the sprocket or whatziz she wanted."

"He comin', Grip," Tom Zucold said. He had climbed up to his Thunderbird chair and belted himself in. "For God, he is comin'."

"Say Promise Land?" The Grip said to Billy Carmines.

"You want me to fix you up with her? Jesus she's easy. Look just right for you, shithead," Billy Carmines said and laughed. "Here, have a drink and see if it don't set you right." Carmines handed him a mason jar of clear liquid and The Grip took a big mouthful down quick.

Tom Zucold woke The Grip early with his four stout strokes of a hammer against a frying pan. Tom Zucold said his mouth tasted like Pancho Villa's army had camped in it. The Grip held his head in his hands until he was sure it would stay on then splashed water in his face and dressed.

"Paper don't say a thing about him comin'," Tom Zucold said as he sipped his coffee.

"Ain't coming?" The Grip said.

"Did I say he wadn't coming, you ape? No I didn't. Said the paper

30

don't say nothing about it." Tom Zucold flipped one of the pages of the *Times-Herald* and continued reading. The Grip waited for his egg to boil. Overhead two banks of headlights, each bank holding eight globes on high beam, blazed down and filled the room with a painful light.

"How come paper don't know a thing like that?" The Grip asked.

"Paper don't know lots of things that is important until they done past. History know everything that is already happened but what do it know about what ain't happened yet? Think about that, boy. And think about that no paper never said anything about that boy cracking his Corvette against my tree did it? Why should it say anything about the Carolina Kid coming through to save me and you." The Grip could tell that Tom Zucold was heating up.

"Check," The Grip said.

"He coming all right," Tom Zucold said. "Billy Carmines told me and if ittis anybody knows what is going on ittis Billy Carmines. He coming and he ain't going to lose. He is a winner. Is a businessman, you might say."

"Say what business?" The Grip said. He pushed the last of his egg into his mouth, took his coffee mug and sat in the Corvette chair.

"People," Tom Zucold said. "And pool."

"How come you know so much about him?"

Tom Zucold touched the button on his Thunderbird seat so that it came forward easily with a soft whirr, then he stepped to the rug. He walked to a shelf by his bed, selected a cigar and lit it, then climbed back to his Thunderbird seat and put it in a three-fourths lean. He buckled himself in securely and the highbeams glinted off his buckle.

"I'll tell you what I know about the Carolina Kid, Mr. Grip. But might be you could stand to recall that some things is so even if you ain't seen them for a fact. Some things you got to see inside the way a bat sees a tree." Tom Zucold pushed the button again and the seat tilted forward so that if he had not been belted in he would have been thrown at The Grip's feet.

"Carolina Kid been around a long time. Yes sir, many moons.

Some say he make his own pool sticks. Say he cut 'em from special trees he grow up on a mountain in the Smokies. Cure 'em and trim 'em and fix 'em to fold up in a itty bitty bag so he can cart 'em around. Say lot of them he make he just burn right up seeing they ain't true enough. Say he can shoot the lights out. Say that everywhere he has been, fats and skinnies, blacks and whites, men and women, all of them say that." Tom Zucold paused to catch his breath.

The Grip got up and walked over to the poster of the Carolina Kid that Tom Zucold had taped to the window. "How big is he?" The Grip asked.

"You truly ain't learned gnat turds worth yet, have you?" Tom Zucold sneered. "Don't matter how big. Matters how you use it, how good you do with it. Like the French pussy say to the midget, ain't how big but how."

The Grip faced the poster and looked closely. There were so many details to understand once you started paying attention. Each one meant something, he thought.

"Does he work?" The Grip said. "For a living?"

"Goddamn you boy," Tom Zucold said and pushed the button to set himself upright. His curse was strong and warm, not mean, as if to recognize that The Grip had done exactly what he was supposed to do in a kind of odd catechism. "The Carolina Kid play pool mostly. But he been known to carpenter some. Cuts and nails and saws and sands and joins and builds. They say never was anybody do with hands what he can do. No hands in creation like hisn. Might say he's a kind of artist. Ain't anybody living ever touched him." Tom Zucold got down from his chair and walked to The Grip's side. Together now they stared at the poster in silence.

The Grip noted each detail in his mind, lingering carefully in a valiant and vain attempt to understand who had commanded Tom Zucold's intense loyalty and hope. He was, The Grip thought, clearly a gentleman. He was dressed in a style The Grip hadn't seen but it nevertheless seemed familiar and the clothes themselves were neat and clean. His eyes were small and round and very bright blue, Oldsmobile Marina Blue. Of course, The Grip reminded himself, that might have been altered by the photograph and touchup work. Tom Zucold had taught him that everything could be covered up. He had liked the Kid's eyes from the first and had often looked at them. There was a quality about them, a softness and a sharpness at the same time. He passed over the gray three-piece suit and looked again at the black and white alligator shoes. The Grip had balked at white alligator but Tom Zucold showed him they were dyed.

"Them suckers is real alligator, too. Would be even iffn they was blue," Tom Zucold had said.

The Grip had several times gotten up close to the poster because he hoped to see the pebble grain of the leather and tell for sure. Something had to be real, he thought. Now the sun was against the Kid's back and he looked very close but the sun did not help. It changed nothing and revealed nothing.

"Finest kind of gentleman," Tom Zucold said as proudly as if the Carolina Kid had been his son or he the son of the Carolina Kid.

There had to be something, some clue, The Grip thought, that would make him see or understand. He felt the presence of a mystery, an unanswered question. Something. All he knew was the poster made him nervous and yet he was drawn to it. He began again at the top. The derby was gray like the suit and insignificant. The face was washed out in the printing or bleached by the sun, he couldn't tell which. It was pale and lacked good distinction. There were dark hollows in the cheeks and under the eyes. The moustache drooped and was unevenly cut. Under it, the mouth puckered as if it had just tasted something sour. It was the light again, The Grip thought. He had looked at this face when it appeared to smile. He had seen it seem about to leap from the paper. At other times there was scarcely a face at all, as if it had fled behind the paper. He looked into eyes that were, right now, wet and shallow and hoped to see anything, but they remained blank.

"Goddamn thing could be two thousand year old," The Grip said. He could have said "birds fly" or "maggots eat dead men" and Tom Zucold would not have responded. He, too, was absorbed in the poster.

"He look like a man in a box," The Grip added.

"Ain't nobody like him," Tom Zucold said after a while. Then he turned and walked back to climb up in his chair. The Grip remained before the poster.

He began again. When he had traversed the length of the man he started to examine the rest. Below the figure he saw great gold letters that said: THE CAROLINA KID: WORLD CHAMPION. In smaller letters and farther below, it said *Ageless Master Undefeated Still, Welcomes Everyone.* Then in the lower right hand corner there was a gold shield with words printed one on top of another that said WORKSHOES, BIBLES, BEER. Way down at the edge of the paper, it said Rainelle, West Virginia. The Grip studied all the lettering in the hope there would be a clue but he found none.

"Jesus H., I do feel saved already," Tom Zucold said. "He gone play in lessn a month. Carmines say at the Virginia Beach Moose Hall."

"If he so hot how come he gone play at the Moose with all them fools?" The Grip had the feeling that it did not matter anymore what he asked, that Tom Zucold had been given all the answers. He had listened to Tom Zucold's voice to see that it did not betray doubt and it had passed all tests. The Grip knew that he could believe in the truth of the voice. Tom Zucold had made him see that early on. He also knew that he wanted to believe in what the Carolina Kid could do for them, wanted to believe there was a way to see in his pockets, pockets on new clothes, and new clothes gliding along in a sleek Corvette. If he had that, surely he would also have beside him a gorgeous girl, he thought. Maybe even Promise Land.

Tom Zucold hit the switch that turned his Thunderbird seat fully around so that he faced the poster and The Grip rather than the television. His whiskers were a pearl white under the highbeams and his forehead glowed pink. He looked suddenly fragile.

"Man who don't play with fools and freaks and weirdos don't have no game to play. What else is it? Who else going to put up money which should go to pay for baby formula and stitches for old folks, and them not even have a hand in what happens? But see, it look like the Carolina Kid know all of what gone happen before it does. Ittis programming and he is the best. Oh, he let it out ever so often that he has done got feeble, gone shaky in the hands, can't see them shooting lines no more. Some say he can't hold a stick. Them is the fools, don't you see. It is many a father and son seen him come down off that hill and he ain't been licked yet. What they say, anyhow."

"Who he gone play?" The Grip asked.

"Talked enough," Tom Zucold said. "Work to be done. We gone have to get some customers in here, get some cash, else we can't bet."

"Who he gone play?"

"Why you keep asking questions?" Tom Zucold snapped back. "I don't know who yet but I'll find out. Bet me."

The Grip turned and crossed the room and flipped three toggle switches on the wall. The highbeams winked out and the room filled with the soft blue light of a spring morning. Outside a mockingbird jeered loudly.

"I don't know," The Grip said. "He just don't look like so much to me." He knew the instant the words left his tongue he should not have said it but he had and there was no taking it back.

"Say what? What?" Tom Zucold leaped against his seat belt and hit the whirring button at the same time, straining to jump out of his chair until his tiny face had turned bright red. He was furious but could do nothing about it. "Say what? Say what," he repeated.

Finally The Grip went to Tom Zucold's chair and released him from the clutch of the seat belt. Tom Zucold immediately hopped to his feet in the chair so that he stood eyeball to eyeball with The Grip. "Godalmighty, you overgrowed rangotang. I hope you sure got more than you showin' because what you showin' ain't the sense it takes a hungry hog to get to the slops." He looked up into the rope and spread his hands out, then looked back at The Grip and said "Life ain't even put you in the throwing ring yet, has it? Boy you burn me."

Anticipating that Tom Zucold was actually going to throw a punch at him, The Grip backed up a step. Tom Zucold, without a word of warning, leaped onto the dark rope that hung from the roof. The Grip had seen him do this late at night once, when he had been sleepless, but he had said nothing. He had seen the little old man strain himself halfway up the rope, then glide back down. Again and again this had happened and not once had Tom Zucold made it past the halfway mark. Now, while The Grip stared open-mouthed, Tom Zucold whipped quickly up near the three-fourths point, then hung. He went neither up nor down. The funny thing was that he seemed almost to be talking to the roof.

"Say what?" The Grip said.

At just that moment Tom Zucold's automatic timer activated the cassette tape recorder that was hooked to four Blaupunkt speakers, one in each corner of their house, and "My Old Kentucky Home" blasted forth. When it ended a jittery voice announced they were off and described precisely who was off and just how they were doing. Tom Zucold had explained to The Grip that he considered this recording a splendid way to get each day started.

"Them's thoroughbreds," Tom Zucold said and pointed at the speakers. "You train with a thoroughbred you'll be programmed."

"Look like wasps' nests," The Grip said.

"You don't know the half of it, boy," Tom Zucold had said.

The Grip watched Tom Zucold cling to the rope while horses jostled in midair and sprinted for a finish line. When Nursery Flower cut past, Tom Zucold let himself slide to the ground.

"Time to get your Corvette out the way, sport. Ape that you are, God loves you and so do I. Still we got to make some money," Tom Zucold said as he pushed by The Grip and made for the garage.

"You'll never make it," The Grip said. Tom Zucold had already disappeared in the door but he would have had no idea what The Grip meant in any case, for how could he know that The Grip had already hugged himself hand-over-hand to the top of the rope where a hole the size of a pencil let in a light from the sky?

With the engine out, the fiberglass body of the Corvette weighed next to nothing and The Grip easily hoisted it with the chain, then lowered it on the Pontiac axles with its wheels and all. They pushed it out by the side of the Bowie Garage where Tom Zucold kept

Midnight chained up and Miz Sexton's Comet was in for a tune-up in a wink. It took The Grip only a few minutes to wirebrush the sparkplugs and re-gap them.

"Ain't using new?" he asked Tom Zucold.

"They good as new ain't they?" Tom Zucold said tediously.

The Grip knew very well that Tom Zucold was charging Miz Sexton for new plugs, and more. But it was not his business. He began to clean up her rotor cap.

"Slow down," Tom Zucold said. "We charging her by the hour. We gone charge everybody that way from now on. They don't give diddly squat about overhead and insurance and labor negotiations and all that a man's got to worry about. They ain't got no Citizens Committee wanting to tie a man's hands around his own property."

The Grip said nothing as he replaced the rotor cap. Tom Zucold had been off since he said he wasn't sure about the Carolina Kid. More than that, Tom Zucold had been acting a little strange ever since he had heard the Carolina Kid was coming. The Grip couldn't have said exactly what was strange but he knew that the old man was changing. Today he was just pissed off and it was not the first time that had happened.

"See you ain't knowing shit," Tom Zucold said. "Don't mean nothing personal you understand, just a fact. You don't know, for instance, that in business you got to keep a little something back. Just like in life. Don't show the other feller everything you got."

"Ain't what you doing. You cheating plenty, that's all."

"You dumbass monkey. You know what a paradox is?" Tom Zucold said.

The Grip went to the far wall, lifted the griplock pliers from a peg, and brought them back to Tom Zucold.

"What the hell these for?" Tom Zucold said.

Then Tom Zucold shook his head and said he meant paradox, not griplocks.

"P-A-R-A-D-O-X."

The Grip merely looked at Tom Zucold because he did not know what a paradox was.

"Damn if you don't look and act just about like a ape, Bozo,"

Tom Zucold said. "I could get me a ten-cent-a-hour wino in here and do more work than you. You don't even know how to break an egg."

"Can break an egg," The Grip said.

Ignoring him, Tom Zucold said "And you sure ain't no wino and ain't no ape. So that's a paradox. Way things are. Ittis why I ain't no goddamn jockey though I'd be underweight now with Volkswagens in my pocket."

"Can break an egg," The Grip said evenly. He had had enough now. "Can even break your head, I want to."

Tom Zucold looked back out of the Comet's engine well where he had just ducked his head, then said "Shitfire, I guess so." He began tapping something then and turned away.

The Grip felt it was now or never. He had been thinking about what might happen when they went to Virginia Beach but he had come to no decisions. He said quietly, "Say you ain't got no plan."

"Didn't I say what the plan was?" Tom Zucold said.

"Didn't say." The Grip waited for Tom Zucold to speak but he was silent. The Grip looked at the poster of the Carolina Kid but the poster said nothing. The tapping in the Comet's engine well went on.

"Ain't no plan," The Grip said. "I been knowing it."

Tom Zucold jerked away from the Comet, looked up at The Grip, and angrily said "Plan, you goddamn gorilla." Then he whipped out his baseball hat that said STARS on the front and jammed it on his head. He turned toward the door and stepped into it, then stopped. He stood silent for a long time.

"Known it," The Grip said. "Tom Zucold ain't never had a plan." He did not speak to anyone or anything in particular.

"Known what?" a feminine voice said. "Morning Mr. Zucold."

There not ten feet from where he stood The Grip saw Promise Land standing just inside the door to the Bowie Garage. She was wearing a sweatshirt that said VIRGINIA on the front and a pair of faded bluejeans. Her cowboy boots were scuffed and scratched but The Grip could still see that they were pink.

38

Before The Grip could speak Tom Zucold whirled around and said "Women ain't allowed in the Bowie Garage."

"Oh pish tush," Promise Land said and stuck her head just between Tom Zucold and the door frame. "You may scare that big boy here but you don't scare me." She leaned her head back and smiled at Tom Zucold, then looked into their house once more. "Sort of spartan, isn't it?"

"He don't know nothing about women," said Tom Zucold. He appeared to have flattened himself against the doorframe, as if he wished to get as far away from this woman as he could.

"Tell me what I don't know," Promise Land said. She stepped back and started for the front yard. "Charming I suppose." She stopped at the open door and looked back at The Grip. "I thought you might like to take a ride and get some air?"

The Grip knew that she meant he might like to escape Tom Zucold and he jumped at the idea. "Like that, like that," he said.

"Time is money. Don't waste either," Promise Land said and laughed. Then she winked at him and said "Come on."

He was surprised to see the pink Harley with the windshield and all the lights, but he liked it immediately. It made him a little self-conscious to climb up behind a woman who was half his size but after they were off The Grip thought no more about it. For the first time in months he smelled flowers and grass and pine. He saw the undersides and the shapes of things. He felt the body of the road and the land. They rode for hours, Promise Land chattering constantly. He scarcely heard a word due to the wind and the helmet that fit him too tightly, but he was not concerned. He had never been out with a girl in his life, much less on a motorcycle with one, and certainly not one who allowed him to have his arms around her all the time. He tried not to notice the hair that wisped under her helmet, its smell clean and fresh, unlike anything he could remember. When she swerved and still hit a pothole, his arms rose against her breasts and though she had said nothing he had still felt tight in his crotch and hot in his face.

Then she had turned off the highway onto country roads and suddenly they were flying, the road a black streak under them and the sky a blue blur that was interrupted only by skidding trees. He found himself slowly beginning to relax after a period of intense fear. He started to lean into the curves and hoped there would be more of them. A few cars passed going the other way. One waved and one honked at Promise Land. This made him feel odd and he squeezed her a little harder. As if in response to this, she accelerated so that low throb of the Harley rose to a kind of moan, then they slowed and she downshifted into a curve, hugged a bank under a pine, and suddenly shot out onto a long stretch that was a straight line to a wall of distant trees. She opened the Harley wide and after a few seconds shouted that they were over a hundred. Her hair whipped at the bottom edge of her helmet. The wind made his eyes water and he was just a little afraid but he wanted to go faster now, still faster. His skin tingled and he felt superalert as each tiny bump in the road passed up and through him.

Suddenly Promise Land began to brake and the Harley shuddered, tried to fishtail a little, then responded. They were slowing fast. The Grip sat up a little straighter and looked over her shoulder. Up ahead a man was pulling onto the road in a Volkswagen Beetle. Clearly the fool had either not looked for traffic or had seen them and pulled out anyway because it was only a thousand-pound motorcycle. On top of his bug, The Grip now saw, was some kind of animal or fish and it was tied front and rear.

"Look," Promise Land said to no one in particular. She was braking as hard as she could without skidding, downshifting and muscling the great handlebars.

"Gosh," she said. "That fellow's been fishing and got him a swordfish." She seemed to just about have control now although the motor was screaming with another downshift.

The Grip saw it coming and opened his mouth to warn her but he was too late by far. The man had at last seen them and had stopped in the middle of the lane. Promise Land had intended to spurt by without leaving her own lane, but now that was filled by another motorcycle and a young man who grinned and raised his fist as he sailed past.

Promise Land jammed the brakes now and the Harley's rear end started to skid toward the front. She yanked the front wheel in the direction of the skid and the bike seemed to right itself just as they came to the car; then The Grip heard the sound of rocks and felt the release. They were going sideways now, the motor roaring uncontrolled, and he saw in that slow motion vision one has before great danger the grassy bank that he knew they would land in. Then the engine was killed, Promise Land said "Goddamn Dick Bausch and japbikes," and they were airborne, flying, silent, light.

The Grip lay on his back and looked up into the cloudless sky. He reached to his head and his stomach went hard with fear. He could not feel hair or skin. It was something hard and shiny. What had happened? He sat up and then jumped to his feet and it was still there. He looked around and saw Promise Land kneeling with her hands in front of her. She was spitting blood.

"Ittis my head," he screamed at her. "What happened to my head?"

At the instant Promise Land looked up at him he realized that he had his hands on his helmet. Promise Land said, "Sweetheart I don't think you'd a needed it but that is your helmet you holding."

Neither of them was hurt much, they saw quickly. His knee ached a little but he knew that might even be from putting his shots. Her tongue was cut so that her words came out thicker and she had a patch of skin gone from her elbow. She had also lost the heel from one of her pink cowboy boots. The biggest damage was to the Harley and that was not serious. The fairing had been bent enough to interfere with steering but The Grip pulled and pushed it back to serviceable shape. At first the engine would not start but again The Grip did something and it turned over with blue clouds of smoke. Once they were sure it was all right, Promise Land cut the engine and they walked up the bank to the shade of a pine tree for a short rest.

"That was a swordfish on that Volkswagen," Promise Land said.

She had lit a cigarette and blew the smoke out in a great puff. "Gosh," she said, "that was actually a swordfish."

"Tom Zucold says it's a lot of fishing round here," The Grip said. He stared at the cigarette. He had seen plenty of smoking before and not just cigarettes but somehow it bothered him to see her doing it.

"Bet me it is," she said. "But ain't no swordfish right near here. Must be somebody went way out and is just coming in." She puffed and blew hard again. "Else it wasn't a swordfish at all. Way things were going there it could have been nearly anything. We were lucky my man."

"You done good," The Grip said. He saw that a butterfly had landed on her golden hair and he watched it. He felt almost as light and happy as he had during that instant flight on the motorcycle.

"Whole thing was probably damned Dick Bausch's idea, him and Goodwin. Goodwin once paraded a flock of giant sheep in front of me. But I got their number now." Promise Land stood up and brushed the grass off her jeans. "It is time to get rolling, friend."

They were nearly to the Bowie Garage when a siren went off so closely that The Grip felt it along his spine. Promise Land pulled the Harley over under the shade of some sycamores and got off, then walked back to the patrol car. She leaned into the window, The Grip saw out of the corner of his eye, pointing in his direction, then in the direction from which they had come, and laughed. The black policeman laughed too, soundlessly in the Harley mirror.

She let him off beside the killer tree at the corner of Tom Zucold's property. "We'll do it again, OK?" she said. But The Grip did not walk away, so she said, "Did you have something you wanted to say?"

He had never loved anybody except his mother and his grandfather. Now he thought he was in love but how was he to know? What was the proof? She seemed to him beyond doubt the most beautiful thing in the world. She was perched in the wide seat of her pink Harley like a statuette in a fountain and her golden hair curled wonderfully around her pink helmet. Her eyes were green as the sea and her teeth white as sand. He could tell from her pink boot that she had small and delicate feet and he liked that. But he also liked the fact that she was substantial in leg and arm, in bust and bottom. All these things swirled in his head not as words but as senses, smells, perceptions. He wanted to speak perhaps more than ever in his life but what to say? What words? And how should they be said?

"Fuck," he said.

"I beg your pardon," she said.

"Screw," he said, softly now. He understood that he had been wrong the first time. That word did not mean exactly and certainly not totally what he wanted to say. Even as he said the second word, he felt it to be wrong.

"Do it," he said. "I want." He spoke so softly that had Promise Land not been listening attentively she would not have heard him.

"You're sweet," she said, then leaned and kissed him on the cheek. She hopped up in the air, kicked the Harley into life, and roared down Yorktown Road. The Grip stood by the killer tree until she was out of sight, then shuffled toward the Bowie Garage, his face flexed in a wide grin.

"Wow, wow," said the melted face of the child from behind the far wall of the Bowie Garage. "Wow, wow," it said again, though it might have been "ow, ow" or even distinguishable words. In any case, its eyes followed The Grip and it spoke too softly for him to hear. When he disappeared into the garage it turned and fled under pines along Yorktown Road, leaving no sign that it had ever been there.

They had two tune-ups on Tuesday and one wheel cylinder job. Tom Zucold bitched loud and long all day. The Grip had seen the old man get into a bad mood but he had never stayed in one so long as this. And there wasn't any reason either. They were getting the business they had to have to save money for the big bet.

"Look to them what run this road that we is a bunch of brainless monkeys working here. Figure they can steal a old man blind is all,"

Tom Zucold said and dropped something into a bucket of solvent.

The Grip sat brushing spark plugs clean and looked out the main door of the Bowie Garage. He had a fine view of Yorktown Road around the big curve, especially down the road toward Chapel. He had been watching steadily for the pink motorcycle but he hadn't seen it. Once there had been the throbbing sound of the engine but he had been on the open commode and he couldn't get out fast enough.

"You ain't hear a word I'm saying," Tom Zucold said. He sat on the creeper at the naked axle of a Thunderbird. "Bout all you can think on since her is her. Damn shame too cause that Promise Land is one fickle bitch."

"Say bitch," The Grip said. He was echoing Tom Zucold, not hearing him, and had not ceased to watch the road where now Billy Carmines roared by, honking his horn as he passed.

"Bitch is right. And there goes one that ought to know. Carmines done been after her long as I remember. I'm not talking here for me, you understand. Trying to save you some trouble. She crazy, is all. Love you up one minute and gone the next. Man come along and spend everything he got on her and maybe she stay around until ittis gone and maybe she won't. Don't see what it is that gets a man to follow her around like a puppy. Course I might be getting old. Still and all, if she was to latch onto you then you got real trouble." Tom Zucold popped a dead cigar into his mouth and chewed the end.

"Trouble," The Grip said. He was trying to remember what her face looked like, its details, and could not exactly.

"Yessiree, boy. You get her and you get her idiot kid too."

"Check," The Grip said. He had not really heard anything Tom Zucold said, only the bitching tone, and he was responding the way a cow responded to a fly, automatically.

Then it was Wednesday and Tom Zucold was still bitching. And the cars were still lining up for service. It seemed to The Grip as if something must have happened to all the cars in Chapel at the same time. They had to fix a radiator on a Dodge, then a water pump on a Renault, and then transmission linkage on a Ford.

44

"Tell you everybody is just as greedy as the next one," Tom Zucold said. "Come down here for bargains. Dumb country shits go the other way. Country people go into cities to shopping centers to buy strawberries and corn from markets that get it from their neighbors. Stupid shit is what a man is."

"Say man," The Grip said. He had done such a good job on the spark plugs that Tom Zucold had given him a box of old plugs to brush and gap for future use. He brushed and looked down Yorktown Road.

"That's right, a man. Stupid because most of the time he know just what he is doing and can't stop himself. Think they is a bargain or he is suspicious somebody getting something he ain't and bingo he act like a ape. Why you got to have some faith. Faith ain't nothing but knowing what's what." Tom Zucold lifted the carburetor off a blue and white 1957 Ford convertible and held it up to the sunlight.

By afternoon they were assdeep in business, as Tom Zucold put it. The Grip had wirebrushed the sparkplugs from a Chevelle two door without air and then did the same thing to a Plymouth Satellite wagon with a stereo tape deck. Tom Zucold put down new plugs on each and every one of the bills. The Grip sat by the door and watched Yorktown Road. They got thirty-eight and sixty-six for the last two jobs.

"Don't figure it means anything," Tom Zucold said. "Of course it might." He had put on his baseball cap with STARS on the front when he had finished lunch and The Grip knew this meant something. Then he heard Tom Zucold singing something about Waycross, Georgia, and that, too, meant something. Late in the afternoon they were finished and about to close the door when a tractor chugged into the front yard.

It didn't take Tom Zucold long to show Jerry Moss that the dumb son of a bitch had thrown off his steering brace by more than eight degrees when he put the tractor into a storm drain. Tom Zucold refused Moss's offer to trade a pig and a pregnant pointer for his fee. He knew the dog was deaf and couldn't point a lick anyway.

Moss paid the twenty-four dollars in cash and when he left Tom Zucold said, "He'd skin your shorts off if you was to blink but it looks like God loves him bettern most."

"Five hunnert and seventy-three and sixteen," The Grip said. They were walking out to the end of the lane. He was putting a few shots now to loosen up and Tom Zucold, feeling he had worked hard, was just hanging around. A breeze crossed the lane where they walked and both smelled the thick scent of honeysuckle.

"Sweet, ain't it," Tom Zucold said. "Might can get five to one," he added. "Ain't no place and show in this. Ain't like horses. Deal come down to winners and losers."

"Twenty-five hunnert and some," The Grip said, hefting a shot.

"Got ten days yet. Might can figure more than twenty-five." He closed his eyes and held his head up so the honeysuckle could slide into his nose, then said "Might can figure a big five."

The Grip figured quickly that that meant a thousand to bet, a thousand they didn't have. He tried to figure how many tune-ups and water pumps and linkages that would add up to and it didn't seem possible.

Tom Zucold turned to face the Bowie Garage. His eyes were still closed, almost as if he were pointing at something high and far. Then he said, "Might be a big five."

The Grip cradled four shots in each arm so that they looked like over-sized silver peas and walked past Tom Zucold to his putting ring. His head was filled with numbers and spark plugs and fleeing images of Promise Land, whom he had not seen in days, and even pictures of well-dressed men that he had seen in a Montgomery Ward catalog in one of the cars they had repaired. He hefted the shot, balanced it, tried to clear his head of all the words, people, things, of everything, tried to just see the ball flying up and gleaming. It wasn't working. He now closed his eyes and looked at the ground. Maybe if he could imagine the pole going through his skull and his spine, exactly perpendicular to the ground, as SSGT Davis had taught him, maybe he could reprogram himself.

"Holy mother of monkeys," Tom Zucold shouted, so The Grip

46

opened his eyes and saw the old man standing in the lane and pointing at him. Before he could blink Tom Zucold had darted by him and into the Bowie Garage, slamming the El Dorado door so that the glass rattled.

When he reached Tom Zucold just inside the door to their house, he saw the woman curled up in the Thunderbird chair. She had a portable radio held up to her ear and it was playing rock music. But that wasn't the first thing he had noticed. He had first seen her slim and naked legs that ended in silver sandals and toes painted bright red.

"Ittis a goddamn woman," Tom Zucold said as he poked The Grip in the ribs. "Thassa goddamn woman for sure and she in my chair." Tom Zucold hawked and spit something that floated like a feather.

"See her," The Grip said. He was hefting the steel shot as he watched. Tom Zucold was flexing himself up and down on his toes like a spring and The Grip tried to think what he ought to do.

"One of 'em come in seem like all of 'em foller," Tom Zucold said lightly. Then, "She in my motherfucking chair. Don't want her there, Mr. Grip. Goddamn woman got to get out my goddamn chair."

Though she said nothing, the woman now slid her hand up and snapped off the radio, then with hardly any motion except a soft gliding hit the chair's normal position and finally started to slither out of the chair until she suddenly was on the carpeted floor and moving toward them. She yawned and the red tongue in her mouth made a pert little motion. When she stopped in front of them she seemed to sway as she observed first one and then the other.

Tom Zucold had stopped hopping now and stood fixed, rigid, never taking his eyes off her. "Poison," he said. "Ittis one of them that is poison."

"Long time no see, sweetheart," she said and blew Tom Zucold a kiss. Her lips were a darker red than The Grip had ever seen, darker even than Mercury Blood of Venus. Her hair was solid black and it shone like the sky at midnight, especially like the sky at midnight in the polished hood of a black 1949 Mercury. Her eyes were painted a metalflake green above and below.

"You know the woman?" The Grip said to the tiny statue beside him.

"Possibly, probably, maybe don't remember me," the woman said. "But any man got one of me somewhere that will turn his ass to stone soon as she show up." She closed her eyes and put one hand delicately over them, then said, "Name be Dick, no no it is James. That right? No, it is Bob. No, I know, it is Tom?"

"How you know that?" The Grip snapped. He had not seen that the woman was fishing.

"Woman in my business got to know things, sweetie. That's what they pay me for. My gosh you sure a big one. Let me take a look," she said and then twined herself around him with slow easy steps.

The Grip thought she looked like one of those women that Bob Barker was always hugging on TRUTH OR CONSEQUENCES. Except she really didn't look like them, or like anyone he had ever seen. How can this one be so different from Promise Land, he wondered. Women, he had always thought, were women, not very different from each other as men were. This one's hair was black and her eyes were almost Pontiac Grand Prix Almond, but not exactly. Her skin wasn't exactly Cadillac Ermine either. And those lips, well, the paint manuals just did not have a color like that. As she circled him, he thought *Mohair*. He wasn't sure what mohair was but Tom Zucold had told him that fine Cadillacs used to have it for seats. One of these days, Tom Zucold said, he'd find one of those Cadillacs and they'd spend days feeling mohair on their skins. The woman was the closest thing to mohair that The Grip could imagine.

"What you want?" Tom Zucold said, except that it was mostly a growl, flat like the dog Midnight's.

The woman stopped in front of him and blew a big pink bubble that she sucked back into a grin and The Grip said "Godalmight Jesus." Then he reached out to touch the iridescent T-shirt through which the woman's nipples exuberantly addressed him.

"Watchit fatso," she snarled and nipped out of reach. "Ain't no

48

tomater here, you know. Think this is some kind of fish market?"
It was odd but The Grip was sure her voice had changed. Now it
sounded old and ugly where before it had been young and glittery.

"What you want, devil?" Tom Zucold said. He had straightened
up to his full height now and had jammed on his head the baseball
cap that said STARS.

"One hand wash the other," she said to Tom Zucold. "You old
enough to know that Tom. Gimme what I want and you get what
you want. Deal ain't new. Ain't a man alive never heard of it."

"Godalmight Jesus," The Grip said. He was staring now at the
woman's flesh-colored short shorts. On one side at the bottom edge
it said CONFESSION and on the other it said PAYS.

"Look at him," she said to Tom Zucold. "Ever seen one more
prime? If he was a peach he be dripping juice. Look at him old man.
He can't wait to confess."

"Say confess," The Grip said. He was not sure what the word
meant so he said again "Confess."

"What the hell you think he got to confess?" Tom Zucold said to
the woman. "Ain't nothing to him yet, nothing to confess. How can
a man that ain't never done a goddamn thing worth spitting over
make a confession? Only a madman could of thought up such a
thing." Tom Zucold had started to hop on his toes again. He was
turning red around the ears too.

"Finest kind, Tom," the woman said, but she was looking at The
Grip and now she smiled so that he would swear for the rest of his
life that he had seen angels in her mouth. When he reached for her
again, she said "Don't be pawing me motherfucker. They sent me
here to do a job and I am going to do it but in my own time and my
own way. Merci don't take no shit from nobody," she hissed. As she
jumped back from his hand he heard something rattle even though
he saw she wore no necklace.

Tom Zucold had sent him to Carmines' Junkyard to pick up a part.
When he asked what he was supposed to pick up Tom Zucold told
him to stop farting around and go get it, that Carmines would know

which one. Now as he hunched over the steering wheel of the panel truck and shifted into third gear, he watched Carmines' place disappear in the rear-view mirror. Carmines had not known anything about any part. He drove slowly, thinking about the woman who was so different from Promise Land. Already he knew there was something about her, a hardness or an ugliness or something, that he feared and did not like. He couldn't be sure what it was. But he also knew that he wanted her. He had never thought about the future; one day at a time was enough for him. All he had ever wanted was to put the shot. Lately he had surprised himself by being interested in clothes that he saw in the Montgomery Ward catalog and in that Corvette that Tom Zucold was going to rebuild when he had time. He felt himself beginning to want things he could get only with money and to get money he had to think about the future. That was why Tom Zucold's programming was so important. He had even found himself standing before the Carolina Kid and hoping that he could believe. Slowly, it seemed to him, he was gathering enthusiasm. Now with Promise Land and the new woman swirling in his head, he felt more confused. Worst of all, he was feeling like leaving the Bowie Garage. He had nowhere in mind to go, it was only a vague sense, possibly just that he felt a little worn down by Tom Zucold's bitching, but it was still there. And he was getting nowhere thinking about it. He decided to concentrate on seeing himself put the shot and thought about that until he pulled into the Bowie Garage. He wasn't certain but he thought he heard Tom Zucold scream.

"Goddamn options killin' us all," Tom Zucold swore. The Grip might not have noticed him but for the tiny man's cursing. Tom Zucold had the hood of the bus raised just outside the door to the Bowie Garage and he stood on the wide front bumper, his head stuck into the heat and darkness.

"Carmines ain't got no part for me," The Grip said when he stood beside the bumper.

"Known it," Tom Zucold said. "You'll understand someday." He did not take his head from under the hood.

"Known it?" The Grip asked. Tom Zucold did not answer.

"Where that woman?" The Grip asked.

"Gone over there to them niggers on the other side of the road. Evil don't know color, take anything it can get."

The Grip ignored Tom Zucold's bitching. He had been doing it for days now and there was no reason for it. "What she go over there for?" As far as The Grip knew Tom Zucold never had crossed that street, nor had the niggers ever come on their side of the street. The Grip wasn't even sure why they were called niggers since they were just black people and not at all "badass niggers" like SSGT Davis was. Just down the road, on the other side of the Chapel town line, there were black people but nobody ever mentioned them. It was like they didn't exist.

"What she go over there for?" he asked again, his voice a little louder now.

"How the hell I know," Tom Zucold said in exasperation. "Said business, all I know. Maybe she kin to them. Maybe she hungry. She ain't nothing but trouble any way you cut it." He did not lift his head from the engine of the bus but still The Grip felt that Tom Zucold was watching him.

"Say you known her," The Grip said.

"Woman never seen me in her life," Tom Zucold shot back at him. Then after a minute he said, "Possibly met me somewheres. Maybe. Probably."

"Some bus ain't it," The Grip said. He had decided to change the subject. He wanted to know what Tom Zucold knew about the woman but he knew that he would hear from Tom Zucold only what the old man wanted him to hear. And he did not want his interest in the woman to be obvious.

"Shit," Tom Zucold said.

The Grip thought that Tom Zucold had said "look at it" so he did. It was no ordinary bus. It had started out as a school bus but now it had a special pearl paint. It wasn't Ford Ivory or Buick Cloud but a pure and essential white under which a subtle sparkle constantly maneuvered to be seen. He had seen something like this in a *Hot Rod* magazine he found in a 1955 Classic Chevrolet that they had stripped of chrome for a piano teacher. Only what he had seen was a chopped 1934 Ford coupe and it was maroon. The magazine had said the paint was made of crushed oyster shells and clear lacquer and you put it on coat after coat until it looked deep enough to put your finger down in it. Now he understood that you really couldn't appreciate the effect until you saw it in person. The best he had ever seen was a five-coat Cadillac Ermine, and that had stunned him.

He walked back along the bus. Its windows all were opaque smoked glass. The wheels he saw were brilliant chrome and the tires were enormous drag tires. But just over the wheel well, in crisp navy letters, it said THE CONFESSIONAL. And just under that was a silhouette of a woman praying.

"She praying," The Grip said. "By God, she praying." He heard a wrench drop against the engine where Tom Zucold was working. The old man said nothing that he heard, but he felt those crusty lips moving.

"Jesus," The Grip said. "Must cost her ten thousand and some."

"Souls?" Tom Zucold said. The Grip thought he said "balls," which was what Tom Zucold insisted on naming the steel shots, and though it was getting on toward dark he still had a little time left. As he passed Tom Zucold on his way through the Bowie Garage to the grassy lane, The Grip said "That woman praying."

"Bet me," Tom Zucold said. "Had better. She got bad trouble here." Then he wielded his wrenches and screwdrivers like a dentist until the sweat momentarily blinded him and he looked up and saw her leaning into the engine. He couldn't shake her from his sight. He had known she was the type to be trouble right off, even if he hadn't ever seen her before. At least he couldn't remember her. Now, he thought, he was having hallucinations and she was both inside him and outside. Women, he had learned all over the world, were nothing but a pain in the ass, some worse than others. He hadn't been busted from Master Sergeant Zucold to Private Zucold, then retired, for his soldiering but because of that woman in Paris.

"Jesus," Tom Zucold said and grinned. He hadn't thought of that woman or all that mess in a long time. Maybe it had been worth it.

"Won't help," the face in his vision said.

"Ittis you," Tom Zucold said and jerked back from her. It hadn't just been his eyes then.

"In the everloving flesh, Tom sweet thing." She disappeared from his view and he blinked then saw her on the ground. She was smoking a cigarette now. "So listen, man. I want outa here more than you want me out. Dig it? Ain't no profit here. Can't see how these hicks live, you know what I mean? Ask every one of them coon dudes they got any good dope and they look at me with them eyes like babies. I mean this is a sad place, man. So how fast you can fix it and what is the tariff?"

The Grip might have heard the woman shouting if he had not been concentrating so well on the put that he heaved almost to the fifty-foot mark. She accused Tom Zucold of robbery, called him every name he had ever heard and worse, and at last gave him the cash in advance he demanded. Then, saying she was out of cash, she asked for directions to the bank.

"Too late. Bank closed," Tom Zucold said. He was grinning now.

"Don't matter. Merci can find ways, you dig?" She wheeled quickly off and he watched her until she stood on the other side of Yorktown Road, her thumb out for a ride.

She had hardly stopped walking when a truck screeched to a stop beside her and she climbed in. The truck looked familiar and then Tom Zucold saw that it was Carmines' truck and then he saw that Carmines was driving it. He watched them wind out the gears until he could see them no more, feeling at first suspicious and then betrayed. He had counted on Carmines and now here he was riding that bitch around. He had known she was trouble. Maybe, he thought, this was some kind of trick by the Citizens Committee. Then he saw that the niggers across the street were all sitting in chairs on their porches. He was sure they were staring at him. They knew, he thought. That was it. Of course. But what did they know?

"I'll be goddamned," he said and pulled the Bowie Garage door down on the ground. Then he disappeared into the house. Night was coming on. It was still warm and mockingbirds jeered to each other from tree to tree.

The Champion Spark Plug clock said almost three thirty when The Grip got up. He was restless and sweaty. He kept dreaming about Promise Land and the other woman until the dreams became a tug of war and he sat up wide-eyed in the dark. After that he couldn't sleep so he had put on his pants and got a Gatorade. He stepped through the El Dorado door as quietly as he could, bending way down with care, and then easing the door into the frame. The lane was white with moonlight and a smoke of humidity filled the air. He had got almost to the white stick, half of the Gatorade gone already, when the blast of the shotgun lifted him off his feet. He was knocked down not by the gun but by his Army training.

"Don't move a goddamn muscle, you snake in the grass. I know she done sent you," the voice said. It was Tom Zucold. "Hee, hee, ain't nobody expect old Tom to take care of himself. Hee, hee. Ain't that old. Hee, hee."

The Grip thought he heard the sloshing of a bottle. He started to get up and Tom Zucold said, "You might think I can't hit you maybe. Hee, hee. Izz goods time trys any." There was a hard metallic click and The Grip knew that was Tom Zucold chambering another shell into the Winchester Model 12. He knew that this pump held five shots. He also knew now that Tom Zucold was drunk.

"Hey," a faint voice said then. "Hey white man, you all right?" The voice was coming from the front of the Bowie Garage. The Grip could see in his head the black man stepping closer to the Bowie Garage. He could also see now that Midnight had heard him coming and was waiting to leap.

"Watch that dog," The Grip shouted from the ground.

K-bam, the shotgun went off. The Grip heard its pellets spray against the far pine trunks.

"You come any further that's what you be getting too," Tom

54

Zucold shouted into the darkness at the voice. "I seen who's who. Citizens Committee gone have to try harder, hee hee."

Midnight started to howl now and The Grip heard Tom Zucold howling with him. There were no more words from the black voice. After a while the dog fell silent. Then The Grip saw that Tom Zucold had perched on top of the Studebaker Hawk. Beside the old man was a gallon jug and The Grip guessed that it was filled with moonshine. Tom Zucold was still singing, mostly howling, patriotic songs and military songs. Now and then he would stand up, tremble and sway a little, then point the shotgun at The Grip and say "Izz you move yous grass is ass."

The Grip tried once to tell Tom Zucold who he was but the old man was too drunk to understand and The Grip was afraid to move. He was in the open, no cover near. And once, after he had waited what seemed to him a long while, he had started to crawl slowly forward. "Trying fuckers," Tom Zucold snarled. Then the shotgun banged again. The shot pinged against the trees again but some of it hit the ground in front of The Grip. "Sling and ass," Tom Zucold said, then started to sing again.

The Grip laid his head on his arms. He was sure now that Tom Zucold would shoot him if he moved. But it pissed him off to have to take this crap from a drunk old fool. He thought about Tom Zucold. The old man was acting more and more crazy. What was going to happen next? The fool had him believing almost in a piece of paper that was taped to the window of a falling down chicken shed. He would have laughed out loud except that he might startle the fool into shooting again.

I ought to leave, The Grip thought. He hadn't actually thought those words before and they seemed hard to him. Then he thought there was no reason why he shouldn't leave. The old man had been good to him, there was that. But he had worked, too, done what the old man asked him to. But somehow he felt he was not doing right if he left. He owed the old man, he thought. Then he thought, maybe, but crazy is catching. It's possible to get really crazy from being with crazy friends. He was thinking about that when someone said "Psst."

"Psst, hey you," the voice came again. It was a whisper but strong.

There she was, the woman from the bus, behind the nearest pine. She was on her hands and knees, her head just sticking out from behind the trunk. Her face was very pale in the moonlight. He started to lift himself up.

"No stay down dumbshit," she whispered hoarsely. She motioned with her hand for him to stay down and he saw that each of her fingers glinted with a ring. "Niggers say he has done this before. Say he probably kill you if you move. Dig it? You want a joint?"

"Say joint?" The Grip answered and heard Tom Zucold stop wailing. He turned his head and watched the little figure on top the Studebaker. After a minute he saw that Tom Zucold was singing again and turned back. Right by his elbow was a cigarette that had funny twisted ends and a pack of matches. The Grip did not smoke because he knew that it would hurt his shotputting but he thought it was a good time to have a cigarette now. What else could he do? He put the cigarette in his mouth and lit it and took a deep puff into his throat, the way he had seen SSGT Davis do it. It burned and he coughed it back up.

K-bam, the shotgun went off again. "Seen that. Seen it," Tom Zucold cried. Then Midnight let out a snarling string of barks, settled into a howl, and after a bit stopped.

The Grip rolled over on his back. He felt cool below his belt and touched his pants. They were wet. "Goddamn," he said softly. He had wet himself during the shotgun's last round.

He re-lit the cigarette and took a smaller puff. This one only made him cough a little bit. He kept his hand over his mouth to stifle the noise. Then he took another puff and hardly coughed at all. It was getting easier. Then he could puff without coughing and without keeping his hand on his mouth. He stared at the stars that were almost as bright as headlights. Many of them had electric colors as they zinged across the darkness. He felt that he could reach up and touch them. As he lay there he began to feel extremely light and then he felt himself whirling at the same speed the planet was whirling. He could actually feel the earth moving just as his science teacher back in North Carolina had said it moved. Just as suddenly he felt he could see the stars and they were small steel balls just like his shots.

"Godalmight," The Grip said.

He stared into the darkness where the steel balls were clearly visible now. They shined down on him. Someone, he imagined, had thrown those balls up there and they had just stayed there forever and would not once be thrown again. It made him sad for whoever had thrown them up since there would not be the joy of doing it again and again and learning how to do it a little better each time. But try as hard as he could to imagine the thrower, he could not do it. He found it was harder to concentrate as he finished the cigarette and threw the last little bit off into the darkness. He wished he had more cigarettes like that. Then he felt himself drifting sleepily off into the darkness. He put his hands behind his head and picked out the brightest ball and watched it for a while. Just before he closed his eyes the ball turned into the face of Promise Land then became a ball again.

"Man ain't got but one chance," the voice said from the darkness.

"Bet me," Tom Zucold's voice said softly.

"No," was the last word The Grip said as he sank under the darkness that pressed down to send the breath out of him.

"Dig it," the woman said and darted from tree to tree until she had reached the door of her pearl-painted bus and had descended into its bowels. Tom Zucold, rocking slowly atop the Studebaker, went on singing. Across the street the rockers were still on porches.

It seemed to The Grip that something was leaping from tree to tree around the back of the lane, chattering and jeering, but when he opened his eyes and lifted his head to see it he could find nothing. He sat up and rubbed his eyes. Then he stood up. His large silhouette was indented in the grass. For an instant he wondered why he had spent the night in the putting lane, then he remembered Tom

Zucold atop the Studebaker. He hit the ground with a thump that knocked most of the air out of him. When he looked up there was no one atop the Studebaker. There was only the jug of moonshine, half full still.

After he had smashed the moonshine on a naked axle, The Grip shuffled into the Bowie Garage. He was angry now, remembering that he had been shot at and forced by his only friend to sleep on the ground. He meant to have it out, maybe even to leave, but Tom Zucold was gone. There was no panel truck parked in the front yard. The bus was right where it had been the night before and was no different except that curtains had been drawn all around. When he walked around to the back of the bus he saw Carmines' pickup truck but Carmines himself was nowhere around.

"Probably gone with Tom Zucold," The Grip said to no one and shuffled back inside the Bowie Garage. He stoked up the potbelly stove, fried two eggs, and made a large bowl of grits. Then he sat in the Corvette chair and began to eat. He had only about half the grits left when he looked up and saw taped to the television screen a Bowie Garage work order with red magic marker all over it. He reached forward and pulled it free and read it.

WOMAN WANT OVERHAUL STOP COMPLETE STOP COST SIX 100 AND 50 STOP SHE SAY GO STOP CAN MAKE BIG FIVE STOP GONE TO GET PARTS THAT CARMINES AINT GOT STOP CITIZENS COMMIT- TEE SENT RANGER LAST NIGHT STOP PLACED MAN UNDER ARREST STOP SHOTS FIRED STOP PRISONER GONE THIS MORNING STOP SUSPECT COLLABORATION BY WOMAN STOP WHAT THE HELL YOU SLEEPING ON LAND FOR STOP DO NOT GO ON BUS STOP WOMAN ORDER STOP SHE IN THERE WITH SNAKES SHE SAY STOP BE ALERT

SSGT TOM ZUCOLD

The Grip went before the poster of the Carolina Kid. For a few minutes he stared and was about to turn away when he saw that the hard morning light was spearing through the small figure's dark pupils. How could he have missed this? He had not missed it. It had not been there. He watched the thin ray of light through each pupil. His body began to feel pleasantly responsive. He grinned and thought about putting some shots. Then he thought of Tom Zucold and the last time they had watched TRUTH OR CONSEQUENCES together. He looked up Tom Zucold's rope then looked at the television screen. He could almost hear Tom Zucold say "Hit that tv rangotang, ittis time for TRUTH." Then as the television picture cleared Tom Zucold said, "Just keep your eyes open." When The Grip turned around to look there stood Bob Barker with his arms around a giant black woman with enormous breasts. Tom Zucold had said, "Ain't many knows it but that nigger there is the devil."

The Grip went out into the lane and walked into a patch of butterlight that warmed his skin and made him forget how strange Tom Zucold had gotten. He moved into the putting circle and pantomimed a few puts to get his rhythm right. On one he went through a check-off to see that everything was in the attitude that it ought to be. "Knees," he said, "feet, spine, elbows, hip extended, flexed calf, thrust."

He felt very good. His body seemed lighter than usual, quicker, and he was so certain that he would put well that he chose the best six shots he had. Today all the puts would be with these shots, even if that meant more walking. He hefted the first one, coiled, then spun furiously and released. It dwindled and thumped at the forty-foot marker. Some sparrows exploded from the hood of a DeSoto. The Grip started after the shot, wondering what had gone wrong. Working quickly he put one after another until he had seen the last one fly short of the Studebaker's left front wheel, scarcely 49 feet. He was panting lightly as he went to retrieve the six shots.

It took only an hour of putting to clean his mind. He had worked himself up to 52 feet and he could go no higher. Still he strained and shoved and found himself shutting out everything save the texture of each shot and its arc in the blue air. He was getting programmed, no doubt about that. He felt it even into his great toes. After the second hour, however, there came a kind of pounding at his temples. By the third hour it became a kind of word. It seemed to The Grip to say "Love" but he wasn't sure and even if it did say that he didn't know what it meant or why it was said.

"What the hell you throwin' that ball fo?"

"Say what?" The Grip said. He had just released a forty-three footer and turned now to find a caramel colored young man watching him. The boy had a large comb and he kept pushing it up through a bushy hairdo that was already the size of a pumpkin. He wore a white T-shirt and faded jeans and a pair of Converse All-Stars. He was almost as tall as The Grip but much skinnier and his long arms ended in enormous hands.

"Say why you throw them steel balls fo?" The young man looked as sleepy as his speech.

"You a nigger?" The Grip asked. He did not mean it as an insult but as an observation. SSGT Davis had told everybody he met that he was one badass nigger and he liked to hear everybody else say that about him. The Grip had known hardly any other black people except those that SSGT Davis recruited for the Army track team. All of them became SSGT Davis' "badass niggers" to anyone that asked. Even The Grip had more than once shaken hands with a brother who called him an honorary white badass nigger. In fact, if the truth were told The Grip meant what he had said as a tribute.

"Call me a nigger motherfucker I'm a go up side you head. Next time you dead, dig it, even if I ain't but seventeen and you a giant." The young man had drawn up his fists to his waist but he had also stepped back prudently.

"Didn't mean nothing," The Grip said. "SSGT Davis said call him a nigger."

"Who this fuckhead name Davis?" The young man asked, but already relaxing.

It turned out that Clifton had been sent by Promise Land to tell The Grip that she missed seeing him. Clifton said he had been drinking a drink, just relaxing at Rooster Smith's store, and Promise Land came in, getting gas for that pink cycle or something, and anyway she said could he step on across the street sometime and let The Grip have this message and he said of course cause he is Clifton the King and no sweat except his momma said he better stay way from that crazy Tom Zucold who just as likely as not will take a gun and blow Clifton's head off but Clifton not 'fraid of no honky white man, special not some ancient dude, even if his uncle Lionel the Drill say that old honky got some reason and a rep too, and he tell Momma ain't no reason to worry cause he a stone dude himself and here he come combing his 'fro and what the hell but some bigass honky got to call him a nigger and all that might likely maybe start a bad war and all he want to know is what he throwin' them steel balls for anyway and he bet he can heave one 'bout a hunnert feet but oh sheeet they heavy man and he don't throw that boy more than a couple cars but look aheah you want to bet some dust on HORSE and probably you can't even dunk it I can no sweat and this bus woman got to be crazy wantin' to know any of us got dope and uncle Lionel find dope round us he take that shiny pistol and bang and no dope no us.

Clifton started to walk back toward the front of the Bowie Garage, then stopped and said "I like to met that Davis cat sometime. Sound like my kind of dude. Be cool Grip."

The Grip had gone to pick up the steel balls for one more round when Tom Zucold shattered the stillness with the bus airhorn. It didn't take long for the two of them to strip the front end of the bus and yank the engine out. While The Grip stripped the head off Tom Zucold fixed them a lunch of fish and grits. They had avoided the unpleasant subject of the woman who was apparently still in the back of the bus and technically therefore in the Bowie Garage. The Grip imagined at least that that made the old man sullen and morose. At last, washing his grits down with Gatorade, The Grip said, "Don't like the woman, why don't you send her somewheres else?"

"Don't like her ain't it," Tom Zucold said. He had already finished his lunch and now had his ratchet wrench on part of the grimy block. "Woman gone pay. Gone pay big. Such just don't happen along. Got to be part of the plan."

"Tom Zucold act like he can hardly stand it."

"Don't matter he can or can't. Kinda business a man gets in mean he might got to put up with what he can't stand now and again. Work don't know like and not like," Tom Zucold said flatly.

The Grip started to disassemble the carburetor.

"Besides she won't be having much to do with me. Ain't any of them want me. They all after you," Tom Zucold said.

"Godalmight Jesus," The Grip said and dropped the carburetor.

"No help," Tom Zucold said.

The Grip got up and wandered around the engine well that was now starting to resemble a large open mouth. He picked up a wire brush and then casually dropped it. He took a screwdriver and removed some screws from a part whose name he didn't know. Finally he wandered over to the El Dorado door whose window was down. He stared out into the putting lane. It was green and quiet and beautiful.

Suddenly the bus woman walked out from between two of the cars, laid a blanket down on the grass, then kneeled and took off the top of her bathing suit. Just before she laid down, she waved at The Grip.

"Jesus," The Grip said. He backed away from the window.

"Gimme a hand here will you?" Tom Zucold said as he tugged at the side of the block.

"Jesus Christ," The Grip said again.

"He ain't gonna do it you gorilla," Tom Zucold said.

"Ittis that woman. She's out there," The Grip said. When Tom Zucold did not answer him, he said "She near naked. Laying in the lane."

"Know it," Tom Zucold said sadly. "Been knowin' it." Then he pulled whatever the part was loose and it fell into his crotch and he screamed.

CHAPTER III

Fire in the Processees

Tom Zucold slept all night and all of the following day after he had dropped the hot manifold on his lap and burnt the top of his penis. The Grip had taken a day off and walked and driven Tom Zucold's panel truck all over Chapel. He'd gone down to the fishing docks at the Point and had eaten crabs at Crosby Forest's place and he had stopped at the high school to watch Coach Evans' track team practice. He had successfully resisted an urge to help out with the two shotputters who, so far as he could see, knew precious little about what they were trying to do. He'd even walked into the woods that Billy Carmines called the Big Woods. The man had said the name so that it both scared The Grip and tantalized him. He had found only the same pine trees and elms and sycamores that he could see from the road. It had been a long day and a weary Grip was glad to get back to the Bowie Garage and to sit in his Corvette chair and watch TRUTH OR CONSEQUENCES with Tom Zucold. They had seen one stunt in which people painted themselves up to be fruit and tried to hide in supermarkets and this led Tom Zucold to the subject of the woman's bus.

"It ain't normal to paint like that. Nothing but waste. Ittis stupid," Tom Zucold had said.

"We gone do my Corvette like that," The Grip answered.

"Gone do what to what?" Tom Zucold almost gagged on his fish supper. As soon as he stopped choking he took a dead cigar from his coverall pockets and popped it in and lit it. "Be goddamned. Bet me if we ain't both goddamned."

"Ain't nothing unnormal about pearl paint. Look pretty to me." He was too surprised by Tom Zucold's anger to be defensive.

"Maybe it ain't nothing you seen yet," Tom Zucold barked, "but you'll see soon enough. Or maybe you won't, which is worse." He puffed a small cloud over his bed, then took out the cigar and pointed and said, "You gone paint that stuff onto that Corvette over my dead body."

"Everybody got to go sometime," The Grip said. He meant it to be funny but Tom Zucold looked like he had been slapped and The Grip knew he ought not to have said that.

"And you just proved you just as normal as the next son of a bitch. Teach me to hope," Tom Zucold said.

They were up early the next morning and after a short breakfast of grits and milk, they were out of eggs, went to work on the bus engine. Whatever Tom Zucold took off he gave to The Grip who then wire brushed it and dipped it in solvent and then hung it on the wall rack to dry. Tom Zucold was solemn and said little as he worked. The silence gave The Grip time to think about the woman he had seen out there in the lane. But he also was thinking about Promise Land and how he'd like to pick her up in a lime metalflake Corvette. He felt real good because he could see some details of his future now. He had been awake when Tom Zucold had started

64

banging the frying pan because he had been dreaming that he was going somewhere very important. But just as he was about to find out where he woke up. Then he had lain very still hoping the dream would ignite or at least spark out the place, but it hadn't. He had gotten up and walked to the Carolina Kid poster just in time to see through the edge of the glass the bus woman drive off in Tom Zucold's panel truck.

"Woman gone in the truck," The Grip said to Tom Zucold.

"Known it," Tom Zucold said.

"You give it to her?"

"She gone pay a hunnert," Tom Zucold said. "Said she need it to get her business done while the bus is laid up."

"Wonder what her business is?" The Grip yawned and scratched like a waking bear. Tom Zucold dropped his hands to his sides and stared at The Grip. Slowly he began to laugh and then it grew to a rolling giggle and finally great belly laughs that brought tears to his eyes and infected The Grip with laughter as well.

"God save us but I don't think you do know what her business is. I can't believe it is one as innocent as you left and that must be part of the plan too," Tom Zucold said as his laughing subsided. "But it is sure hard to take."

"What is her business?" The Grip asked.

But Tom Zucold, in spite of his laughing had not slipped out of the sour mood he had fallen into during the night. He merely waved at The Grip and turned away from him and that was how they went to work together in the Bowie Garage.

It was warm in the morning and by early afternoon it was uncomfortable. They ate their lunch in hubcaps on the western side of the Bowie Garage because of the shade there. No breeze stirred anywhere. Neither man said a word throughout lunch. Finally, Tom Zucold called to The Grip over the engine, "You pay some attention here, you might can learn something."

"Is it anything I can do?" The Grip said. Tom Zucold hadn't given him anything to do all afternoon.

"Don't know of a goddamn thing," the old man said slowly.

"Outta my hands. Probably always was. Man can't trust nothing but himself hardly, and him." He pointed at the poster on the window.

"Been watching," The Grip said. "Don't seem like I learned very much." He walked over and looked down into the distributor that Tom Zucold had just laid bare.

"Got to look *through* things, boy. Not at them," Tom Zucold said and tugged at something. "Got to learn what connects and how and where. And maybe that won't even do you a damned bit of good outside of the satisfaction that come from trying. Look like most of what you can see is covering up all the stuff you need to see and can't. To me, look like that anyway."

"Seen her in my mind," The Grip said and walked over and looked out the El Dorado window, "out there." He looked back at Tom Zucold.

"Outta my hands," Tom Zucold said.

"What's outta that honkey fool's hands?" Clifton said. He had come in the Bowie Garage like a shadow, sliding past the parts on the floor and Tom Zucold without a sound. "What's happening Grip, man?" He stood still but seemed to undulate.

"Ittis a nigger ain't it?" Tom Zucold said. "Tom Zucold must be going crazy 'cause that is a nigger in the Bowie Garage. You is a nigger, ain't you?" Tom Zucold looked up from his creeper and appeared to hope that Clifton would disappear saying he was not a nigger or anything.

"Huh," Clifton said. Then he raised his two hands, fists balled, above his head and twirled around fast. "Wham bam that I am." Then he leaned over close to Tom Zucold's face and said "Can't you smell me?" He winked at The Grip, who knew Clifton had taken this as a compliment.

Tom Zucold looked hard at the engine and then banged it hard with his ball-peen hammer. After he had banged until black oil spurted onto the concrete, he said "Ain't regular to have niggers in the Bowie Garage. Had 'em in the Army." He sounded weary. "Now we done had two women and a nigger faster than I can finish spitting. Ittis coming apart, is all. Just like Nixon said. Goddamn government behind every bit of it. Been knowin' that right along. World gone crazy slowly. Goddamn Citizens Committee don't think I know they is government and government is behind everything. Tom Zucold been knowing that." The old man sighed over the little puddles of oil then spread his hands before Clifton and The Grip and said "But what can a little man do against the world?"

Clifton held his chin between his thumb and finger, pretending to be thinking hard, but grinning.

"I see you got some goddamn fool opinion on things," Tom Zucold said to Clifton. "Ain't lived long enough neither of you to know shit from shinola and the government paying all of you to have opinions. Ittis a time when people knew to keep their stupid opinions quiet. Now all you damn kids do is think and get paid to think you really thinking something good."

"Nawsuh, Rastus heah don't never thunk up nothin'," Clifton said and giggled. The Grip looked out the El Dorado window because he saw that Tom Zucold was working himself to a pitch and there was surely going to be a lesson, even if it was Clifton that got it.

"Peoples come round your house and mine boy and they want to do what they call 'modernizin' and that means fix up your place so it look some place they seen in Cincinnati or *House Beautiful*. And when they done it you won't be living there no more, nor me, cause we ain't modern enough or beautiful enough. But it ain't a goddamn thing wrong with what we got. Still you notice ittis that peoples can't stand cars and parts and such when they want to modernize. Worst thing of all is let a chicken in your yard. Drive 'em goddamn batty, each and every one. But a man got a right and a duty to keep some things same as always. Tom Zucold ain't against progress at all. Let them modernize they own places. Ain't nobody comin' round here and sayin' Tom Zucold got to get rid of his processees, not nobody with more than bird turds for brains." Tom Zucold stood up and puffed his little chest out, adding what little there was of bulk and height on him to his argument. He stuck a dead cigar into his mouth, clamped his teeth, and pulled loose a slickly frayed piece of tobacco which he quickly spat onto the floor.

When he saw Tom Zucold pause, Clifton saw his chance and edged over toward the yawning front door. Then he saw Tom Zucold's eyes follow him and he said, "I'd like to stay man but my momma is terrible bad when I ain't where she be lookin'. Be cool, Grip." Then he was into the light and gone and The Grip wished he had gone with him. Tom Zucold lifted his arm as if to call him back. "Clifton's momma hard," The Grip said. He had never laid eyes on Clifton's momma, a thin, sweet woman who had never said a harsh word to her youngest child.

But Tom Zucold was launched and ignored Clifton's departure as he railed on. "See ittis them that want to modernize and them that wants to gouge money. Onliest peoples change things is rich anyway. Ever see any poor peoples changing anything? No power to 'em. Any way you cut it what them peoples wants in here is a goddamn burger palace where they makin' everybody look like clowns and fools in they uniforms. Man just got to look round. They build you a house and it won't have no goddamn windows for the wind, bet me. Look round. Ittis a goddamn four-lane road where was a pond with nice bluegills and a quail or two on to the side and up the hill a nogoddamngood cousin who wouldn't work but might could chew you arm gone with he's terrible jokes. Road don't even go nowhere yet. Look round. Ittis a goddamn subdivision, what all of 'em call it, bunch of houses shoved up shoulder to shoulder, with a shitload of peoples done moved in who don't know nobody's family much less each other and they all goddamn glad your place look just like whatever it was they seen in Cincinnati." Tom Zucold was wheezing now as he spit out his words, but The Grip had to admit to himself that the old man was rolling.

"Seen it coming long time ago. Thought ittis part of the plan, maybe, possibly. Tom Zucold said it wouldn't probably be as bad as it turned out. First fucking thing a man know they come to he's door and say you got to pay six hunnert and hook onto this and then they come and say you got to pay a thousand and hook onto that. Tom Zucold say where was they when his mommy and daddy need them? When he need them, for Christ sake? But now they done come again. Man say gimme. Man say government say gimme. All of them say gimme or get. Tom Zucold seen it happening. Ittis fucking being human is what it is. Man want to be nobody, be like a nailhead in a board. Want to be modernized and you got to gimme so you can get modernized and be like nobody in Cincinnati. Don't none of them open his mouth and say this is Slim Keester speaking. Say this is the Committee and you got to gimme or get. That is why they want what *was* all tore up and moved away. If peoples started living with what was they'd have to take a look at what is and will be. Can't stand that with they pitiful hearts. But ittis why we got to hang on, boy. We is the hope. We is continuity, programming, ready for Freddy. It is us against the fucking Citizens Committee because the Citizens Committee is us."

The Grip had been getting drowsy until Tom Zucold seemed to shout the last part. Then he jumped up in the air. But Tom Zucold was not finished. He pointed the dead cigar at The Grip and went on.

"Goddamn peoples don't understand we got to live in the past. Ittis all the Bowie Garage is, see. You going to take aholt to things soon, Grip, and all this gone be yours. That's if I can win enough to keep it away from that Citizens Committee. Why we betting everything on *him*." Tom Zucold jerked his head toward the wall that separated them from the poster of the Carolina Kid. "He is the hope, see. He what everybody got to have, even Clifton cross the street and even the womens, something like him, even when ittis clear that hope ain't no more than a piece of meat walking round and slowly turning to shit. Which is all a man is. Maybe." At last Tom Zucold was finished with his speech and he sank down on the creeper and began panting with what little breath still kept his tiny body inflated.

The Grip knew that the old man would no more than stop panting before he would leap directly up, for The Grip saw the woman cross the front yard and enter the Bowie Garage, though she was more shimmer of light than woman.

"Things sure is changing. Look like the Bowie Garage getting democratic and liberal and all in full color too. Seen the nigger," the woman said as Tom Zucold landed on the floor after shooting up at the sound of her first word. She grabbed his hand and pressed some bills into it. "Six twenties there, old Tom. Sharing the wealth, you might say. Besides this is fertile ground for business, this Chapel." She leaned against the pearl fender of the bus.

"Say business," The Grip said.

"Evil," Tom Zucold said. He tapped a wrench impotently on the concrete. "Evil and trouble and worse all of it her kind knows."

"Well listen here," the woman said and tapped Tom Zucold on the head with the tip of her finger. Then she looked at The Grip and said "I take men up in my bus and I confess them."

"Hot ain't it?" The Grip said.

"Hottern hell," Tom Zucold said.

"Which one of you's the dummy and which one is the mouth?" the woman said and laughed.

"Ain't hot's it going to be," Tom Zucold said.

"Say business," The Grip tried again.

"Didn't say yet, sweet meat," the woman answered. She moved toward him and put her red fingernail hard on the bone in the middle of his chest. It hurt but he didn't want to show it. "Woman don't like to let it all out at once, see. We got all the time in the world, pardner." Her voice was oozing out of her like oil now.

"He ain't fuckin' got all that time," Tom Zucold said about The Grip. "Man coming in a week now, nearly." He pointed again at the wall that hid the poster.

"Well looky here, then," the woman said, sounding a little harder to The Grip. "Got time for a drink, ain't we, boy?"

"He don't drink," Tom Zucold said. "Besides you just fooling with him."

"I don't fool with nobody that don't already want me," the woman said and there was no mistaking the hard edge to her voice now.

"I want you," The Grip said simply.

"No you don't," Tom Zucold spat and dropped something that clanked. "You just think you want it. Ittis nothing but trouble beginning to end." Tom Zucold stood up then and looked right into the woman's Pontiac Grand Prix almond eyes and said, "Look like after a hard day's work and more them than you might could count, woman might leave this one alone. Ain't enough though, is it? Look like you just itch to know ittis one left in the world, don't it? You ain't a dime worth different from that one in Paris. I ain't mean to push her out that window but by God she deserved it. Made me pay big, did that."

She ignored the old man who was now trembling. She moved herself up against The Grip and rubbed him. She was soft against his lean, programmed body. "You got a cigarette sport?" she purred.

"He don't sport and he don't smoke," Tom Zucold said flatly.

"They never do, do they?" the woman said absently.

Without warning the woman kissed The Grip on his lips with her cool, thin mouth, then turned and disappeared into the bus.

"Say they," The Grip called after her. Then he said, "Got Gatorade. You want some Gatorade?"

Just as suddenly as she had left the woman returned, this time smoking a pencil-thin brown cigarette.

"Don't do that in here," Tom Zucold snapped, "else we all gone be blown off the earth." He pushed the woman toward the open door and The Grip walked after her. Then she walked all the way around the Bowie Garage and knocked at the El Dorado door. The Grip went back and rolled the window down.

"How big are you?" she said when she saw The Grip lean down to the window. "Big as you are must be a hell of a big. . . ." She grinned over The Grip's shoulder at Tom Zucold.

"Say big," The Grip said. He saw that her eyes were oddly shallow.

"Bet you could tear one from arch to asshole, pardner," she said, then reached through the open window and touched his cheek. Her skin was very cool. "All the locals had the pleasure, I suppose?"

When The Grip did not answer Tom Zucold said, "She mean has The Grip fucked all the women round here." He whammed something with a hammer.

"Crude Tom," the woman said. "Old as you are a person would have thought you might have wore off some of that crude."

The Grip had begun to feel that this conversation between him and the woman was not between them at all. But then who was it between? He had tried to think about connecting and about looking through things, just as Tom Zucold had told him. Now he turned. He looked at the engine. He looked at the bus. He looked at Tom Zucold. He even looked at Clifton's place across the street. Nothing connected with nothing. He could see through nothing. His mind was as blank as the surface of one of his steel shots. He opened his mouth to say something but it died in the darkness there.

"Incredible," the woman said behind him. He turned and saw that she had walked into the lane and now turned back toward him at his thirty-foot marker. She began to walk closer to him. Suddenly her hands fell to her side and the glittery blouse she wore parted down the front and the halves pulled wider. He saw it. Poised and proud, there it was, a wonderful and even a magnificent tit. There were no blemishes, none. The nipple was perfect and a pure Camaro burgundy. It hung there before him like a dream, a thing he had only seen in magazines and in dreams, only it was real now. His heart beat loudly in his ears. It came toward him slowly. He started to reach out for it. Then it was gone. The blouse was buttoned. He stared down the lane at the white stick.

"Getting dark in the Bowie Garage," Tom Zucold said behind him as he snapped the toggle switches that caused the Cadillac high-beams to blaze down from the rafters.

"Course, it don't make a frigging bit of difference so far as I can tell. A man is a goddamned half-ape and half-asshole and ain't anything he can do to change that and about all he can manage is to spout off until ittis time to put he's money down and take a chance. Come on you sorry gorilla, we got to watch TRUTH OR CONSEQUENCES." Tom Zucold was speaking softly now and The Grip knew that somehow the woman was gone.

"Getting darker by the minute in the Bowie Garage," Tom Zucold said, even though the Cadillac lights were almost as bright as the sun.

Bob Barker, his three-piece Brooks Brothers suit showing taste, his anonymous American face radiant as a fog light, said he would be right back after a message of importance. It turned out to be five messages about new style tampons, a fake-meat dog food, an electric company scrubbing a river, a thick pizza, and a can of something that made cars go easier. In this one there was a woman who leaned into the engine well of a Cadillac. She wore a dress that fluttered and showed her rear end from one angle and her tits almost popping out from another. She was pouring the can somewhere.

"Lookit that shit," Tom Zucold snapped from his Thunderbird chair. "Show just how crazy things is. First thing is, Cadillac don't break down on no highway. Second, woman got no more idea what she looking into than what she pouring out. Just like people though. We gone see 'em, too. They pull over and pop they hoods and gone be pouring a can of that stuff and don't even know where to pour. Look like something might jump out and help 'em. Wouldn't know the true thing if it bit them on the ass."

Clenched like a fetus in his brown GI blanket, The Grip rolled and tucked and tried to keep warm in the hard early morning chill. Somewhere a voice went on saying *wire* and he began to dream about the barbed wire he had never been able to crawl under in basic training, the wire that SSGT Davis had finally cut for him.

"Fire, Goddamn Grip, get up," Clifton said. It was like the night itself was shaking him since Clifton was very black suddenly.

"Say fire?" The Grip sat up and yawned. He rubbed his eyes and looked around. "Clifton?" he said. But now there was no Clifton, no anybody but himself.

"Holy mother of monkeys," Tom Zucold said at just that instant. He burst through the door from the Bowie Garage and was also suddenly no more than a part of the inky blackness in the room. "Hell, goddamn, ittis a fire you fur-lined asshole. Get up, general quarters, battle stations! War might could done have started. Fucking Citizens Committee! Tom Zucold ain't thought they'd go so far but—ain't you up yet you baboon?"

"Zzhah?" The Grip said, sucking in his breath as the overhead banks of highbeams flared hard. He looked around vaguely and saw no fire in the house. Then he stopped at the poster of the Carolina Kid. At its edges he saw it was not morning yet. "Still dark," he said.

"What the fuck you expect at four thirty in the morning?" Tom Zucold said from just the other side of the door to the Bowie Garage. The Grip thought he had seen the tiny man leave, a kind of glow on his body, but he was not sure as he stretched, yawned, and swung his great feet to the floor.

"Ittis a fire in the processees," Tom Zucold shouted from outside. "Woman said. Better get your butt in gear if anything mean anything to you."

When he had jammed himself into his fatigue pants and combat boots, The Grip found Tom Zucold at the Bowie Garage's overhead door. The little man stood rigid, a silhouette, his baseball cap pulled down tightly on his head. He seemed to be waiting for the empty maw of the bus to jump forward and gobble him.

"Ittis your Corvette, son," Tom Zucold said when The Grip stood next to him. They faced west where the clay ruts went to the back of the Bowie Garage, to the processees, to the lane where The Grip put the shot. "Corvette is only plastic and plastic burn right smart. Wind come up too maybe and ittis gone north to the processees. Got the Oldsmobile hearse and the '56 Starchief and look like the Galaxy ain't got a chance. Never touch that mother-humping Jeep though. Ain't figured out why."

Another light such as The Grip had never seen, a hot and jittery yellow light that was like that he remembered from the putting lane only more lively, boiled over everything. Tom Zucold had not mentioned that the fire was also in the small pines and even had burned some of an oak that stood beyond the flaming core of his Corvette. The firelight was yellow and orange and red and it crackled and hissed. The heat was bearable but uncomfortable where the two of them stood. He felt an impulse to turn and run into the darkness that was cool and solid behind him.

"Pray ain't no help," The Grip said. He was unsure what he should say but this sounded right to him.

Tom Zucold stepped off the concrete ramp to the garage and

quick-marched to the edge of Yorktown Road. The asphalt and the trees were all lit clearly now by the brilliant firelight that had turned everything to a kind of negative of itself.

"Hey you niggers," Tom Zucold shouted. Then again "Hey you."

Out of the corner of his eye The Grip saw movement and looked up at the bus windshield that was no more than ten feet from where he stood. At first he wasn't sure what he saw, then he knew it was the woman. She sat tall in the driver's seat and she was slowly combing her hair with long, sparking strokes. Her face was full of orange firelight, almost a Pontiac Firebird tangerine, and her hair seemed almost liquid fire.

"You niggers," Tom Zucold shouted again. The Grip looked at the darkness across the street, startled by Tom Zucold, then back at the bus window. Now the woman was gone. He wondered if he was dreaming.

He looked back across the road at Clifton's house. Though the porch was starkly empty it appeared there was a light at the door. Then a light seemed to be at the window, then there was no light. The Grip thought this was as strange a night as he had ever lived through.

"You niggers call them fire trucks," Tom Zucold called into the darkness now. "Know you listening and know you got a telephone."

A thick voice spoke out of the darkness then and said, "Done call them fire. Mens say dey sorry 'bout yoh cahs. Say dey be heah dreckly. Bout a hour maybe."

"A hour ain't no damn good. You call them back and say they best get they asses out here," Tom Zucold spit at the darkness. He waited for an answer but none came so he turned on his heel and marched back toward the Bowie Garage, veering toward the source of the fire at the last minute. The Grip followed and stood behind him as they tracked the fire. The Corvette was now only a hot pile of melted metal, as even the flames had moved on. The Grip stared at what was to have been his way out, his way forward somewhere. Then he saw Tom Zucold had moved around the Bowie Garage toward the line of processees, where the fire had been pushed by the wind. He glanced back toward Clifton's house and saw the reflection of the fire on the tin roof and in the glass windows. Then he saw it was not reflection at all. The fire had somehow leaped Yorktown Road and Clifton's house was in flames. The Grip bolted toward the flames in the processees where Tom Zucold stood, a tiny shadow.

"Clifton's house on fire," The Grip said.

"Nigger's house ain't worth burning," Tom Zucold said.

"House is Clifton's," The Grip repeated, "he maybe need help."

"No time to save his house, is bigger things at stake," Tom Zucold said. He pointed to the Ford Galaxy that was still popping and the Buick Apollo which had burned out and was now ghostly in the firelight. The Grip looked back at the darkness where he was certain that Clifton's house was searing apart. "Besides ittis possible you seen a diversion tactic. Illusion you might say. Germans done that in France. Seen it myself."

The Grip was confused now. Had he really seen fire in Clifton's house? Someone had spoken to Tom Zucold from that house, he knew. But he had heard no one cry fire. It had been still except for the flames. Had he seen them?

"Willys gone. Might can stop it here," Tom Zucold went on. He had sold the Willys cheap to Trooper Drilling and it had left a hole in the line of processees. That and those that had already burned made a kind of firebreak. "But we ain't got time to waste. Got to move," Tom Zucold added. He bolted to the Futura that was next in line, climbed in and released the hand brake with a clunk. Then he climbed out again and shouted, "You gone push the goddamn thing or not? Ittis all up to you."

It took The Grip only a second to heave the car forward so that it rolled into the center of his putting lane. When he turned he saw that the fire was nibbling along the ground and he understood that it was feeding on the years of oil that Tom Zucold had dumped. He hoped that it would burn out because the next vehicle was an old cement mixer that Tom Zucold had got free. Some fool had let the cement harden, probably for a nooner Tom Zucold guessed, and it

76

was as heavy as a battleship nearly. The Grip could not have moved it in a hundred years.

"You hear that?" Tom Zucold said.

The Grip listened hard and heard the faint whine of the sirens. Then they were growing louder and all of a sudden he heard the trucks coming down Yorktown Road. Tom Zucold ran in front of him. When they reached the edge of the road they saw that Clifton's house was no more than a pile of blackened rubbish that spit occasional flames and smoked heavily. Clifton and his momma and some other people stood in the yard watching. Tom Zucold ran to the first truck that had stopped and climbed up into the window. The Grip could see that he was talking to the fireman who drove. Almost instantly Tom Zucold started waving his hands and shaking his head. He pointed to the Bowie Garage and then to Clifton's house. The Grip looked around and saw that the fire behind him had also begun to die out. He listened to the crackling voices from the truck radios and wondered why they didn't snake out the hoses and spray the little fires that were still burning. Then he saw Tom Zucold jerk back from the truck window and fall on the ground. The Grip wondered for a minute if he was crazy. It had looked like the fireman punched the tiny man.

"Go fuck yourself," Tom Zucold said as he jumped up and gave the fireman the finger. But the fireman had already begun to drive off down the road toward Chapel and Tom Zucold was left by the side of the road, the whirling red light bathing him as it passed. The Grip stood alone, stunned.

When Tom Zucold came back to the Bowie Garage, he said "Ittis Citizens Committee on them trucks. Don't surprise me none neither. Motherfuckers ask did we want to pay the fire tax now. Said none of them niggers done paid it and didn't a fool like me want to pay up for both. Said go shit. Said Tom Zucold can't win. Said boys go shit. Man laugh. Said son you ain't nothing but shit done bleached out and the son of a bitch hit me."

"Say it is the Citizens Committee?" The Grip asked. Was that who they were, he wondered now, those firemen? He stared into the closing darkness of the morning sky. He had thought maybe it was a bunch of fat ladies who played cards of an afternoon. Was it, then, firemen who came in the night? He tried to imagine faces. Without faces, they didn't exist. They weren't anybody. After a while he found he was watching the sparks of light that drifted up above Clifton's house. Then he saw that Clifton and his momma and the other people were gone. It was still again. Had he only dreamed it all? He couldn't have just dreamed it. There were those sparks and there was smoke still streaming up from the hot spots. He had felt the heat and seen the light.

"Don't matter none to me," Tom Zucold said. He sat on the small barrel by the door. "Get this old you learn to expect whatever you get. Learn to depend on Number One, youself. That's the main plan. Always was."

"What plan?" The Grip said.

"Fire sure burned the shit outta that Corvette," Tom Zucold said.

"Say plan," The Grip repeated. He knew that Tom Zucold would not explain. Maybe the truth was that he couldn't explain. Maybe the truth was that nobody ever explained because nobody ever really knew what the plan was. Maybe there wasn't any plan but people had to think there was to keep from going crazy. Maybe the plan was that everybody was going to go crazy sooner or later.

"Woman say she was smoking a cigarette. Say she couldn't sleep and then she seen it, that fire in the Corvette. Say she hollered and hollered." Tom Zucold hesitated and The Grip could hear him breathing heavily. The light of the fire was gone entirely now. It was starting to be a pale blue in the world.

"Woman say that," The Grip said matter of factly.

"Look like Tom Zucold might have done it. Possibly. Maybe. Could have throwed a cigar in them weeds maybe." Tom Zucold sounded as if he had a weight on his back. The Grip knew that the old man was forever throwing his whipped cigars into the weeds. One of them certainly could have still burned. Tom Zucold had told him that being a property owner meant you could do things nobody else could. Tom Zucold liked to throw cigars and take a piss wherever he was standing when he was outside.

"Tom Zucold done it?" The Grip asked. He was staring up into the sky that was getting lighter quickly and it looked like he was asking the sky itself. There was no answer at first and then he thought he heard something. He strained and listened harder. Yes, there was a voice.

"Possibly. Might be. Could have been," the voice said. Then it stopped and laughed. It was a voice full of luck and wealth and pleasure and The Grip knew at once that it was Bob Barker disguised as Clifton and saying "Ain't he a prize, though."

The Grip had tried to sleep but had kept drifting in and out of dreams that confused and frightened him. He had imagined the black-suited firemen who were the Citizens Committee attacking from the trees. He had imagined Clifton's face burning and his Corvette collapsing into ash. He had dreamed he was running after Promise Land's pink Harley but he could never catch it. When he got out of bed again Tom Zucold was disassembling some part of the bus engine. Tom Zucold told him he wouldn't say he was sorry. The old man kept saying that all day. He said it when they ate and when they squatted by the bus engine and while The Grip winched the processee out of his lane. The Grip even heard Tom Zucold say it to Trooper Drilling when the black cop pulled into the mouth of their driveway.

Then it was night again. Time seem to have speeded up on The Grip. He felt lost and emptied. He had counted on that Corvette and it was gone. At least, The Grip thought, the old fool had been right about one thing: you could only depend on yourself. He was lying in bed now. It had been quiet for more than an hour and he knew that Tom Zucold thought he was asleep. He watched the tiny figure creep out of his bed and climb into the Thunderbird chair and leap up and grab hold of the rope. Tom Zucold, he knew, was as naked as an orphan baby. Up to the three-fourths point the wiry little body went, then it slid back down. Up and down, up and down. Except for the sound of his breathing, that huh-huh panting, Tom Zucold climbed in silence and in darkness solid enough that sometimes even The Grip could not see him. But he had had enough, he was angry and hurt. At last The Grip sat up, then said "Shitfire." Then he walked out into the night that was white with moonlight.

When he passed near Tom Zucold's dog he heard the low rattling snarl. It would be easy, he thought, to wring the dog's neck. Like a chicken. He had seen his mother do a chicken once. The blood squirted, he remembered. He stepped to a tree near the corpse of his Corvette and started to piss on it. When the woman touched him it scared him so that he turned quickly, tumbled on an old rim, and fell into a small spruce. "Goddamn, goddamn," he said falling. Then everything went black.

After a little bit the blackness faded. His head hurt and when he reached his hand to his forehead he felt a flap of skin. The cut was wet and ragged but not deep. He grasped the skin between his thumb and two fingers and yanked hard. His forehead felt like he'd put out a cigarette on it. He was still lying on his back. The spruce smelled clean and also a little charred.

Then something cold touched his cheek. He jerked his head away and said "What? Say what? Who?"

"It's me," the woman said. "Merci. You all right?"

"Where you?" The Grip said. So much had happened that seemed to him like a dream he was not sure of anything now. Maybe it wasn't really her.

"Here," she said and put her hand against his cheek. She had kneeled beside him.

"Godalmight Jesus," The Grip said.

"Not exactly, pardner," she said and giggled. "I didn't mean to scare you. Sorry about that fall. Are you hurt?"

"Ain't hurt," The Grip said, then said it again. "Ain't hurt." He was trying to push himself up and seemed to be held by something he could not see.

"You don't want to move too fast and hurt yourself now, you dumb ape," the woman said. She was pushing down on his chest.

"Ain't no ape," The Grip said and pushed her arm away, then forced himself up. The woman stood too.

"My mistake, I'm sure," she said as she lit a cigarette so that her face was briefly again Pontiac Firebird Tangerine. Then she held the lighter toward The Grip so that he thought she meant to burn him and leaned back.

"Be still," the woman said. "You're bleeding some." She looked hard at his forehead then said, "Come into my bus and I'll fix you." When she offered him her hand he took it without thinking and followed her to the steps of the pearl bus that seemed to radiate an inner light because of the moon's reflection. Then the woman went inside and called to him to follow her. As he stepped up a soft light came on.

It was a very strange bus. There were no seats in it and there was a turnstile like he had seen at movies, though it didn't turn. He started to climb over when the woman said "Sorry, I forgot to release it," and the bar turned. Then he stood at the back of the bus where a red velvet curtain hung between two walls. The woman called from the curtain and said she was almost ready. But The Grip had turned and was now staring at the domelike ceiling. It had a thick paint like the outside, except it was black as the sky and there were silver stars. Except the stars were pictures of men's faces and there were too many of them to count. It made him dizzy to look at so many faces.

"Admirable gentlemen, all," the woman said behind him. "My life's work."

"Say gentlemen?" The Grip said, thinking of the Montgomery Ward catalog he had scoured. He wanted to be a gentleman and dress like those models.

"Indeed," the woman said. "You'd be fortunate to count yourself among that crowd. My record is known in all the best places. I'm one who can handle things. Now let's get that head fixed."

The Grip looked at the windows to see his wound but they showed nothing in the weak light that seemed to come from nowhere particular. He stepped to the curtain, parted it, and stepped into a room where everything was the cool pearl color of the outside of the bus.

"Jesus," The Grip said.

"Won't help," the woman said. "Was only a fool carpenter anyway." She stood at a tiny silver sink and poured a red liquid onto a cotton ball. "Sit there on the bed. It's the only place where I can reach you."

The Grip sat on the bed that filled most of the room at the back of the bus. The bed was soft as the air itself. He saw that the woman lived here for there were drawers built in the walls, a small refrigerator, a regular-sized color television, and a large console beside the bed. It looked like a Buick Riviera console but it was larger. It had toggle switches, gauges, screens, buttons, holes for glasses and holes to plug things in.

"Lower your head, monkey," the woman said in front of him. When she touched him it felt sharp and cold and he jerked away from her.

"Jesus," The Grip said. "Jesus H., what is that?" The woman had a hook for a hand. While he pointed at it the hook dropped a sash at the woman's waist so the halves of her red robe parted and the magnificent tit was once more revealed. The burning on his head spread to his belly.

"That's a hook," The Grip said numbly. "You got a hook for a hand."

"Don't let me fix your head you be one sorry cat," the woman purred. She reached slowly forward with the hook that held the red stained cotton. The sting he felt was mild and distant as he stared into the depth of the burgundy nipple. Then he drank from the red glass that she handed him and still he did not cease to look upon the perfect nipple.

"You dig that?" she said.

How could a man not like such a creation, The Grip would have asked had he had the words to articulate his feeling. He did not know that the woman meant the drink she had handed to him. He stared at the magnificent tit until he felt himself beginning to go down in it, as if it were a lake or stream.

"It's my special brew," the woman said. "Mostly sloe gin and stuff, terrific relaxer, know whatta mean? I call it Bloody Merci, if you can believe that. Better than Gatorade, maybe." The woman turned away from The Grip and he could no longer see the magnificent tit. He felt as if he had surfaced.

The Grip stood up and bumped his head on the roof of the bus. Then he stooped over and said, "Might better get off here. Didn't sleep much last night." He yawned. He saw the woman do something with her hook and a cigarette so that a balloon of smoke went up.

"It isn't time, man," she said flatly.

"Time," The Grip said and thought he heard it echoing. He felt extremely heavy now, his body seemed to have no muscles, and he sank back to the bed.

"What it's all about Jack," the woman said. "Time is money. Tempus fugit. Got to make hay while the sun shines. My business, you dig?"

"Binuh?" The Grip said. His tongue was very thick in his mouth, his vision seemed blurred. He was getting sleepy.

"I knew you'd ask. That's all that is required, is that a man ask. Get them out and let old Merci in, what I say. Dig it, brother, my business is to do the slowest, sweetest, most outstanding trick in town. Ain't nobody gone say I don't know my business. People everywhere say I am a artist." The Grip heard her speaking but understood nothing. He was floating deeper.

The woman looked down at his face, then said "Good. Stuff works every time." She flipped a toggle switch and the light went pink. Another switch brought country music from the center of the bed.

"Muse," The Grip slurred, then slept.

"Got it, pardner. Use it all the time, just like department stores. Some of my colleagues say it is a needless expense but I want to be remembered. I'm sure you can see how it is," the woman said as she pulled the curtain shut and picked up a knife. "Results count, what I say."

The woman sliced up the inseam of The Grip's fatigue pants, then cut to the zipper and peeled them away. Then she cut his undershorts away and his undershirt. Finally she kneeled between his great hairy legs and covered his crotch with her face. For a few minutes she said nothing. The Grip snored heavily and did not move.

"Well goddamned," the woman said at last, getting up and washing her face in the sink. "Must been too much. You piss ant," she said to The Grip. As if in answer he coughed and then snored on.

"I'll fix you so's next time you'll want some time," she said.

She opened the refrigerator and took out a can of Cool Whip and slowly spread it all over the hair on The Grip's body. The Grip snored. When he was well covered the woman set a small silver pail on her console and from it she took a long curved razor that she began to draw over The Grip's body. Hair and Cool Whip were swept away in gouts until his large body lay pink and clean as a baby's. Then the woman flipped another toggle switch and turned two dials until a shattering electric rock music came out of the center of the bed. Then she hit a switch that made the bed tremble and as she did this she backed away from the bed and gave a shake that left her standing utterly naked. The Grip had still not moved or begun to wake up. She watched him quietly for a few minutes while she smoked another cigarette. Then, with no word at all, she stood between his now hairless legs and swung her hook up in the air so that she brought it down with the steel curve slamming into The Grip's breastbone.

The Grip exploded forward like a circus teeter-totter, his forehead driving into the woman's nose so that it mashed and shattered before she had moved even a fraction of an inch. Already his great athlete's lungs had involuntarily responded with a scream that stretched his thick lips in a horrible scream that echoed up and down the bus. But she heard no scream, for the force of his blow that had spread her nose also flung her against the specially constructed steel drawers and this left her unconscious on the floor of her home. For his part, The Grip was stunned and dizzied for a few moments but the pain in his chest was so severe that he did not attend to that of his forehead and instead stood up to relieve it, only to ram his skull into the steel roof of the bus and fall again dizzied on the bed where acid rock boomed.

After what seemed to him a very long time, The Grip rose to a crouch and stepped over the inert woman on the floor, noticing her stainless steel hook as he passed. How had he missed that before? No answer came to him as he made his way to the other side of the velvet curtain where a hidden door led to her disguised toilet. He snapped on the light and stared at himself. There was an ugly bruise in the middle of his forehead and a bump on the top of his head. He splashed his face from the sink, wiped, and looked again. He remembered taking the drink from her hand but everything was fuzzy afterward. Even now, as he watched himself in the mirror, something was wrong. What was it? His body felt itchy and when he looked at himself he was cleaner and pinker than he remembered. What was it? He felt uneasy but still he waited for the answer to come. Nothing came. He felt silly. Outside the door there was a moaning. The woman was crying softly. Then she started to wretch. Now he felt trapped by the tiny toilet. He pushed open the door and bolted for the front of the bus, climbing the turnstile, and lumbered down the steps into the night air that was astonishingly cool.

He had gone only a few steps when he saw there was a strange light coming from the wall of the Bowie Garage. He stopped and looked at it. It wasn't a strange light at all. This was the window occupied by the poster of the Carolina Kid. Only there wasn't any poster now. The full overhead beams of their house flooded through the window that he had almost never seen until now. Then he saw the rope swing by and saw that Tom Zucold was hanging on the rope and looking out at him. Almost in that same instant he understood what was wrong. Now it was not Tom Zucold who was naked in the world but himself. He had only to walk in the light to see that he was naked even to the hairs of manhood.

"Woman ain't normal, ask me," The Grip said. He sat on the radiator of the bus where he had been sitting most of the morning. He had done some weak puts in the lane but his heart had not been in it so he had come in to sit with Tom Zucold while he put the GMC motor back together.

"Ungodly hot in here," Tom Zucold said and took a turn on the ratchet wrench so it squeaked tight. He had mentioned the heat often, as if The Grip had not noticed it, though his fully buttoned long-sleeved fatigue shirt was a deep green with sweat.

"Woman slicked me clean as pickle," The Grip said tonelessly.

"Probably get hotter too," Tom Zucold said. "If it was some thunder we might have a hope for rain. Ain't heard none though."

Between their conversation which was hardly more than a chant, the only sounds in the Bowie Garage had been passing traffic and Tom Zucold's tools. He was working rapidly, mechanically, and it looked like it wouldn't be long before the engine was done and put back in its place. The Grip watched quietly and felt himself grow depressed without knowing why.

"You ain't the first one by a long damn shot," Tom Zucold said. "Ain't likely to be the last neither." Then he stood up and looked at the engine for a few moments. "Got to go to Carmines for a head gasket. Things done come to push and shove."

It was like a dream to The Grip, only it wasn't a dream. A kind of pressure like a river, a force, a flowing and he was in it. It did not move fast but seemed fast sometimes and sometimes seemed to hold him still. He listened to Tom Zucold's panel truck rumble out of range, then he felt it. He felt it get stronger and though he told himself to sit tight on the radiator it had him. He got up and went out to the putting circle and got off three puts, all short and weak. It had him there, too. Mockingbirds jeered across the lane and for a minute he wished he were a bird and able to just take off in the sky. He thought suddenly of Promise Land's pink Harley and the wind howling at him, but even that wasn't enough to shake him loose. So he turned and went with it, entered the flow, and found himself stepping up into the bus. The sun was like liquid butter outside but in the bus it was cool and dark and music flowed softly from the rear.

"C'mon back here, hon," the woman said. He couldn't see her but somehow she had seen him. He parted the curtains.

"Time's money, man. Everybody got to pay these days, what with prices all the time going up like they do. You dig?" The woman had not yet looked at him. She held a hand mirror in front of her face that had an X bandage across her nose and she was slowly pulling a brush through her hair. She was wearing the red robe and it was loosely tied so that he could see the round edges of both tits. He felt himself going hard and his mouth was dry.

"Ain't got any money," he said finally. He forced himself not to look at the hook that held the handle of the mirror.

The woman continued to look into the mirror but now she flipped another toggle switch and the music shifted to country. Another switch and the pink light filled the room. "Think hard about that money, now." Her robe seemed to open just the tiniest bit more and The Grip felt light sweat on his bald scalp. He was bent slightly under the roof and his back was getting stiff. His legs ached.

"Carolina Kid coming soon," The Grip said.

"Shit," the woman spat. "If you'll pardon my French. Think I don't know 'bout everything CK does." The woman looked up at him and smiled. She was, he thought, still beautiful in spite of the blue tinge to her eyes and the big bandage.

"Sorry I did that to your face," The Grip said.

"Don't give it a thought. Woman in this business got to take what comes and what comes like as not is worse than this. Time's money though kid. Think about money." She resumed brushing her hair.

"We programmed to bet it all on the Carolina Kid," The Grip whined.

"All of what?" the woman said. "Merci just saying think about it."

"It ain't all mine," The Grip answered. "I'd give it to you if it was mine. Want some."

"Hell I could be blind and see what you want boy. Nothing's free, you understand?"

"It was free last night." He meant to stand firm but he was weakening and he knew it.

"Last night, last year, same to me. That is the past and it don't mean nothing. Besides you didn't get anything last night did you?" The woman giggled and tried to grin around her bandage.

"Ain't all mine," The Grip said again.

"We wastin' time, dude." She stuck the mirror beside the console, stood up and yanked the robe off with her hook. The Grip saw all of her and swallowed hard. "You want something in this life, you got to reach out and take it. It is right here, what you want sweet meat, just for the taking and all you got to do is promise me his share of the bet. He ain't nothing to you anyway. Old man about to croak and you just a drifter don't know one end of the road from another." She shook her head so he could smell the perfume of her hair and then with her hook lifted one of the magnificent tits. "You want to suck on that good, don't you hon?"

"Know it," The Grip said.

"Well what are we waiting for? That old man be coming back soon. All you got to do is say yes. Hell, just nod your smooth head at Merci and you almost done." She sat down on the bed and edged herself backward until she was lying full length, her legs just slightly parted.

"Thief," The Grip said, as if he wanted to see how the word felt in his mouth. He wanted to move forward, to lie on the woman, to feel those fine tits. His hands seemed to itch. But something kept him rigid. "Thief mean something," he said.

"C'mon to Momma sweet meat," the woman said and licked her lips slowly. He let his eyes move over those magnificent tits, each better than the one before, and his chest ached bad. Finally his mouth opened to say the word that meant everything but the sound both of them heard was not his voice at all. It was another voice shouting outside the bus. It was shrill and ugly and squeaked like a Volkswagen's brakes.

"Is it anybody in this crate?" the voice said.

"Be goddamned if it ain't getting too hard to make it in this business," the woman said. She sat up and slithered to her red robe. As she coiled it around her shoulders she said "Time's money, son. Yours is up."

"Ain't him," The Grip said. "Ain't Tom Zucold's voice."

She flipped the toggle switch that cut the music and then cut the pink light. "Expenses like to kill a working woman, sweet meat." Then she reached her hand to his cheek, touched it lightly and said "We'll try again sometime, somewhere baby. Go see who's at the door." She pushed him through the red velvet curtain and drew it tight.

As he slid past the windshield and down the steps of the woman's bus, The Grip saw a bright green Chevrolet Estate Kingswood wagon parked behind them. Its doors were all open as if people had bailed out in a hurry. He blinked at the hot sun and walked around to the other side of the bus where he saw three people standing. All three stood with their backs to him and all were watching Tom Zucold's dog Midnight because the dog was stretched to the end of the chain and snarling.

"Yo," The Grip said when he had got up close to the three people so that they jumped.

A sandy-haired man not much older than The Grip took a step toward him and stuck out his hand. When The Grip showed no inclination to shake it, the man said "Hello. We thought maybe it wasn't anybody here."

"Here," The Grip said and watched the man. He wore black shiny pants and some shiny white shoes with little tassles that matched a shiny white belt. His shirt was a shiny white with a black alligator at the left tit and the man had on a blue scarf at his throat. On his nose were a pair of sunglasses that were dark at the top and clear at the bottom. In the middle of the glasses the man's eyes looked tiny and clear as marbles.

"Of course, you're here," the man said and snapped his fingers. "But you aren't the one, don't you see. We're looking for *him*."

"Him?" The Grip said.

"Why, uh, the owner of this establishment? Mr. Zoocold? A small, dirty ruffian of a fellow? Very difficult to talk to, as I recall. Perhaps you've seen the man?" When The Grip did not immediately answer, the man said, "Oh dear me. Do I have to deal with these types?" He seemed to be talking to no one. Then he said "Do you think you can remember where I might find him?" The man took a dollar bill out of his pocket and held it in the air between them so that it fluttered to the ground when he let it go.

The Grip ran his hand over his scalp which prickled in the sun and wiped the glaze of sweat on his fatigue pants. He hawked and spit on the dollar bill, then said "Tom Zucold ain't here." He hawked and spit again, this time at the edge of the man's white shoes, causing the man to jump backward and say "Now see here, you."

"Ain't how you say his name neither," The Grip said. "Say Zuck as in Fuck."

"I beg your pardon," the man said. Then he coughed and gathered himself and said, "The point is we simply must speak to him about this awful mess." He swept his hand out to indicate the grounds of the Bowie Garage. "I mean we have some new proposals you see and well I. . . ."

"Can't say," The Grip said, cutting the man off.

"Well I never," the man said. He slapped at the back of his head and held his hand before him to show a bloody smear and a smashed mosquito which he then wiped off with a handkerchief trimmed with lace. "Well, well," he said, "can you tell us when the old man will return?" He bit the words off precisely and said them loudly as if he were speaking to a child.

"Can't say," The Grip said. He was watching the woman who had left the threesome and had edged around the side of the Bowie Garage. Before she was out of sight he saw Promise Land wink at him.

"What's your name, young man?" the old woman now said. She scolded him with the words as she half-stepped, half-slid forward until she stood even with the young man. She was so old she trembled and her dark blue silk dress, Plymouth Satellite Blue The Grip thought, played in and out of crevices and hollows all over her. The dress was covered with white dots. Her white skin, in the few places it showed, was covered with brown dots. As usual, it was her face that caught The Grip's attention. She looked like bones overlayed with too little skin and the skin had a peculiar blue tint, in spite of the dusty makeup that had been haphazardly applied. The lips had got lost under a blur of hard red lipstick that turned the mouth into an oval like a target. The eyes were almost black and bulged like a frog's. The nose was scarcely more than a bump on that face but from it protruded several black hairs. The hair on her head was a mass of tight white coils with a straggly loop here and there and all of it held down by a round blue cap with some plastic berries on it. The woman was sucking her teeth as she peered at him.

"Didn't say his name, Grandma," the young man said. He had apparently decided to start all over again, thinking maybe that The Grip simply had not understood what was going on. He held out his hand again and said "My name's Cotton Muddleman." The hand was frail and damp looking, like the young man himself. "My Daddy's G. N. P. Muddleman. He owns the bank and the real estate agency and he's a judge. You might know him?" Both the hand and the questions hovered with no reception.

"Say that name again?" The old woman said cocking her head to hear.

"Well," the young man said as he looked at his hand. Finally it fluttered back to his side then reached for a pack of Virginia Slims and held it out to The Grip while Muddleman said, "Care for a cigarette?"

Cotton Muddleman got one of the cigarettes in his mouth and puffed it in little snicks. Then, from a cloud of smoke, he said, "And this is my sister Promise Land, half-sister anyways." He turned to point out the woman who wasn't there, then said, "She done it deliberately. I know that."

"What's that name again, sonny?" the old woman shrieked. She had slipped behind her grandson and cowered as if she feared The Grip would strike her.

"This is Grandma Homer," the man said. His voice squealed almost as bad as that noise from the telephone receiver when you left it off too long, the kind of voice that could hurt a man into violence if you heard too much of it.

"What's his name, boy?" the old woman wheezed.

91

"He didn't say his fool name, Grandma." The man was getting edgier and meaner. "Maybe he don't even have a name.'

"Good golly," Promise Land said as she cleared the rear of the bus and came toward them. "He's got a name. Tom Zucold calls him The Grip. Isn't that cute?"

"Gip, Gip?" The old lady sounded like a bird. She clung to her grandson's shiny white alligator shirt, staring at The Grip intently.

"Damn it all, grandma," Cotton Muddleman whined as he tried to pull away from the old lady and did not. "That's pretty cute, all right," he said and turned toward The Grip. "Still and all Mr. Grit, we want to talk turkey to that old man that owes my daddy three months' back payments. Daddy likes to see people do right but when they don't he sends me out to kind of remind them, you see. This old man here is kind of touchy so I got Grandma Homer and Promise to come along. Sort of like a committee you know."

"Say Committee?" The Grip asked heating up quickly. He had been feeling that voice against the bones of his ears like a chalk screech.

"Tell Gip to get his kit and kaboodle together and get along somewheres else," Grandma Homer hissed to Cotton Muddleman.

"Say Committee?" The Grip said, his face getting red.

"Well, sort of a committee," Cotton answered, spreading his hands and starting to say more.

The Grip's fist exploded against Cotton Muddleman's eye, catching bones above and below, and would perhaps have done serious injury to the little man except for the film of sweat that Muddleman wore. Although The Grip's knuckles slid viciously past the eye, the blow was still strong enough to lift Cotton Muddleman out of the dust and dump him back in it, howling as he fell.

"Jesus Christ," The Grip screamed as pain ran up his arm. Hurting, he whirled and flung his fingers downward as if to shake fire from them but the effort carried his hand into the steel fender of the bus where they struck with a hollow meaty sound.

"Goddamn," The Grip said. Then, "Goddamn, goddamn, fucking goddamn." At last he lifted his hand to see the split flesh between the two middle fingers and the blood that oozed onto his fingernails.

"I seen it," Homer Muddleman shrieked again. She was becoming hoarse but kept up her noise while she hopped from one foot to the other in her agitation and kicked up little wedges of dust. "No eyes sharper'n mine. I seen it and everyone knows I seen it."

"Promise, please help me. Were are you, Promise?" Cotton Muddleman cried from the dirt where he had risen to his hands and knees and where his glasses hung from one ear, lenses shattered and frame bent askew. "That ape going to kill me, don't you see Promise?"

"Jesus," The Grip said and spat out blood he had sucked from his hand. It was all happening so fast that his head was spinning. What should he do now? What should he say? He'd thought the Committee was just a bunch of card ladies and Tom Zucold's nightmare. Then they were firemen who wouldn't put out a fire. Now this was them. Why wasn't anything what you thought it was? Why did all the people he knew seem out of control?

"People keeping a pigpen and a eyesore and everybody see that and add on to it a violent act by this big baboon and I don't know what all," the old lady was saying when she gasped so loud that everybody thought she was going to choke to death.

"He don't like to be called a ape or a baboon," Merci said as she stepped down off the bus in her red robe. "He liable to bust somebody else you go on like that."

"Aghh, aghh" the old lady said, pointing at Merci.

"Eyesore," Cotton Muddleman said then stared at Merci's red silk and the white curves within as if he had been stunned.

"Seen it, it is it," the old lady gasped, recovering herself. "You is it ain't you? Old people know things and I'm old. Don't nobody get too close 'cause it is no telling what that thing can do." The old woman retreated a few steps and took up a position halfway between the bus and the station wagon, where she swayed and hissed.

"They'd put this whole town in the zoo back in the city," Merci said. She put her hands on her hips and stood so the sun burned off the tips of her black hair.

"Do tell?" Promise Land said. She had been standing on her tiptoes to see through the smoked glass of the bus windows but had seen nothing. Now she walked up to Merci and circled her, observing carefully, and said, "You a revivalist?"

"Who wants to know, Little Miss Muffet?" Merci said. Her mouth was no more than a slice in her face.

"This is Promise Land," The Grip said. "Got a motorcycle."

"So you're the one," Merci snarled. "The competition. You clean as Pat Boone nearly." The Grip saw that it was so, for Promise Land wore a white turtleneck jersey with several strands of gold chain and a powder blue wrap-around skirt, rimmed with white, and penny loafers. She was the very same as those women he had seen in Tom Zucold's Montgomery Ward catalog, the women who were obviously the best and what you would order if you could order them.

"Watch it, Promise. It is dangerous," the old woman shrieked again.

"Cotton, why don't you crawl on out of that filth and help Grandma over to the car? Put the air conditioner on. It's too hot out here," Promise Land said. She had not stopped looking at Merci, who now had her arms crossed at her chest.

"You a revivalist?" Promise Land said evenly.

"I confess those who need it."

"For a fee, you might say."

"They contribute to supporting the spirit," Merci said. "I don't see what business that is of yours, however."

"I bet it is some gospel," Promise Land said. "But you are right. It really isn't my business." She nodded her head toward The Grip and said, "But he is."

Merci laughed and said, "You don't look like a fool."

"Never taken for one yet."

"Watch it, Promise. That Mr. Grit working for her look like," the old woman said as Cotton Muddleman dragged her into the car. The Grip watched him shut the doors, one after another and then disappear into the wagon.

"What do you want with him?" Merci asked. The Grip thought

94

she was beginning to look older, tired, and thought it must be the sun.

"Question is what does he want."

"Watch them, Promise," the old woman shrieked. They all turned and saw her head protruding through the open car window. "Sin and lechery and wickedness. I seen it. I'm a witness," she screamed and then began to choke because Cotton Muddleman had started to raise the window on her throat.

"Maybe you got time to wait around 'til he finds out what that is but Merci got to work to live. He don't anymore know what he wants than he was born The Grip," Merci turned abruptly and climbed into the bus. Then she stepped back down and stuck her head into the air and said, "You want to come along with me, Grip? I'll give you a job and good money and some outstanding fringe benefits. You can drive The Confessional." Her teeth, when she smiled, seemed golden.

The Grip stood halfway between the two women. It felt to him that the whole of his life had constricted to this one moment. A mockingbird jeered far off but it was strangely silent where he stood.

"Tom Zucold is my friend," he said at last. "He got a whole bunch of dreams still. Dream ain't nothing much unless it is somebody to tell it to."

"Them kind of dreams kill a man, like as not," Merci said from the darkness of the bus. "Don't believe me ask her." Then she withdrew into the bowels of The Confessional and The Grip stood alone with Promise Land.

"I got to go, Grip. They are waiting."

The Grip looked into her green eyes and felt his stomach drop. He felt light and quick. "See you sometime?"

"You are sweet, I will say that. I guess so." She brushed a few golden hairs out of her eyes and said, "Look like we don't have any choice, though we always do. You might be one those men who gets on a road and can't stop 'til he reaches the end. It's funny isn't it, like my professor over at the community college says, you look up and see the people and the things around you and you wonder how it all happened just like that, not like the people in other places. Do you see? Isn't it profound? I mean did you ever wonder how you came to be here and not say in North Carolina? Gosh, that just wigs me out, you know?" They had started to walk toward the car but when they reached it Promise Land had kept going, following the ruts around to the lane in back, and The Grip had followed her.

"Tom Zucold," The Grip said.

"What do you mean? What about Tom Zucold?"

"That's how I got here. Tom Zucold brought me in his panel truck," The Grip explained. They had stopped walking and both of them stood in the circle that was his putting ring.

"Oh," she said. She was looking out over the lane where the white stick gleamed against the dark green of the grass. "Kind of pretty here, isn't it. Except for those wrecks, of course," Promise Land said.

"Not exactly wrecks," The Grip answered.

Ignoring him, she said, "My place is just over that way by the river," and she pointed to the east of the lane, just over the classic 1949 Ford.

Just then The Grip thought of Tom Zucold and he said "Committee."

"Nightmare," Promise Land said. "That old man is just plain crazy and he thinks there is some kind of vigilante committee that is going to come take his land away. Just a nightmare."

But The Grip heard only that the old man was crazy, for at exactly that point the El Dorado door was whisked open and a person lunged forward with a monkey wrench that struck the big man's head even as he turned to face his attacker. The blow came at precisely the place where he had gouged away skin in his fall and he began instantly to bleed. He crumpled to the ground, stunned and dizzy, but mostly unhurt.

"I got him, Promise, I got him," Cotton Muddleman screamed in joy.

"Gosh, you're a stupid bastard," she said and swung her handbag so that it caught Cotton Muddleman in his unharmed eye like a punch, sending him back through the El Dorado door into the Bowie Garage where he fell against the nearly completed GMC engine of The Confessional. "Even for a half-brother."

The Grip had been dreaming that Tom Zucold was telling him the stories of his life. Tom Zucold's stories were always very sad and always about something bad that happened to him but The Grip was always happier when they were being told. But in the dream Tom Zucold's strong voice kept running things together so that The Grip could not separate pictures of a too fat rider on horses at Bowie Race Track from pictures of the spiffy sergeant who drove and fixed General Happy Arnold's staff car in Paris. These were pictures The Grip himself had made up when he heard Tom Zucold tell the stories, not actual photographs, but they were perhaps more detailed and more real than ever. There was also the picture of the woman who'd got Tom Zucold cashiered and the woman who'd screwed the horse at Bowie and the woman who liked to hang from a rope at Fort Belvoir. There was even the woman who handed Tom Zucold his discharge and winked and the woman from Fort Leonard Wood who held the baby in her arms and told the captain it was fathered by his first sergeant. In his dream, now, The Grip followed the two of them out to the drill field where Tom Zucold was marching recruits back and forth, showing his instructors how to do it right. He felt high blazing sun on his own bare neck and the cool sweat on his brow. Then they were walking on past the troops who stood at parade rest. They entered the Missouri woods beyond and came onto a lane where a single stake painted white stood at the end. The captain tied Tom Zucold to the stake and the woman started piling sticks at his feet. Pretty soon the captain bent down and snapped a lighter and flames began to lick up.

"What was his last words, Cap?" the woman carrying the baby asked.

The Grip did not have to guess what Tom Zucold would say. He always said the same thing when each story ended: "Life been one royal screwing after another and it ain't done yet." He waited for the captain to say those words but the captain's turned head said, "He say hut, hut, hut."

"Hut, hut," The Grip said waking. He felt the flames that were burning Tom Zucold begin to spread over his own face. The heat was intense and he could almost feel it shaking him as it tried to consume him.

"Hut," someone said. The Grip knew this was not his own voice. He opened his eyes and saw the not-a-nigger child. Its eyes were partially crossed and the flesh of the face looked like it had been diced with a knife and sewed together carelessly. In places it truly looked melted. The child was tugging on his arm and kept saying "hut, hut."

The Grip blinked. Something burned in his nose. He half-rolled on his side and then felt the headache. It was like he had been stabbed in the head. Then he felt the sting in his nose again.

"Smoke," he said. The melted face of the child pressed down to his ear and said something that sounded like "ow" and then again "ow." Then it pulled on his arm and said "hut, hut."

He knew now that he was not dreaming. This was a real fire. He lifted his head and saw that the sun was high and furious. Then he saw that the grass along the ditch beyond his lane was smoldering. The wind was blowing the hot sour smoke toward him. But it was not a big fire yet and he could stop it from engulfing the processees this time. He raised himself from the putting cycle and dragged Tom Zucold's garage hose out to the fire. It was not until he had seen the ground soaked and the fire dead that he noticed the child was gone.

"Hut," he said. "Hut." Then he knew what the child meant. He was hurt and she had known it. But for her, however, he would have been hurt much worse.

He coiled the hose carefully at the side of the Bowie Garage and went in for a Gatorade. At first he hadn't seen it but now he saw that the Carolina Kid's picture was once more taped to the window. He saluted it casually, then went to the lane and sat on the bumper of the cement mixer. The grass at his feet was red and brown, burned out from the first fire, what there was of it. He felt restless and confused. He was alone. There was only the sound of the mockingbirds jeering him because he was on their land. He drank quietly.

After a few minutes he saw that between his boots there were two ants, one black and glistening and the other a reddish gold. They darted and circled at each other. One moved forward and the other moved backward. In the area between them there was a tiny piece of something white and each appeared to want it but not if it meant a fight with the other. The Grip watched them for a long time. They were patient and evenly matched. The black one was stronger but the red one was quicker. Finally, his attention wandered and he leaned back against the pursed snout of the cement mixer and looked up into the flawless blue sky. It was the same color as Promise Land's skirt and it, too, was a wrap-around.

Why was he here, The Grip suddenly wondered, remembering Promise Land's questions. Why should he stay with Tom Zucold after all? There were problems coming, he could see that. It wasn't the money, was it? There wasn't enough money to be won. But if he left, he thought, where would he go? And how would it be any different there than here? Did that mean life was the same everywhere? Did it mean life was always the same even in the old days?

So many questions without answers made his head ache where he had been hit. He felt dizzy so he laid his head against the grill of the cement mixer and closed his eyes. From some evening when they had watched TRUTH OR CONSEQUENCES, Tom Zucold's voice came back to him and was saying, "Grip ittis not many things a man knows will help him get through this world. Ittis what he don't know and got to try and find out will do it. One thing is that the world is like a oil pan sitting in the weeds a long time. World slowly filling it up with rust and grit and shit and one day you gone step in all that. Can't miss it. Programmed that way. What a man got to do is figure how to miss that pan the next time. Which he probably won't never do."

The Grip opened his eyes and stared at that flawless blue. Was the world no more than a pan of shit in the weeds? He kept seeing

Promise Land's ocean green eyes and her smile that was full of angels. He knew what she would say, that everything was going to turn out all right. He could almost hear her saying "Gosh."

When he glanced down between his boots he saw that both of the ants were gone and the white thing was gone. The only thing left was the grass that was red and brown and horribly dead.

Tom Zucold banged the potbelly, hollered for the rangotang to wake up, and began to fix breakfast. The Grip was slow to climb out of bed after a night of restless sleep that had finally settled, deepened, and held him. He ate without speaking and listened to Tom Zucold repeat all the deep-sea stories of ancestral fools that Billy Carmines had told the day before. Tom Zucold also said that he was certain he'd have the bus job done before noon and that'd be a goddamn weight off his back. The Grip got up from his chair, all that re-mained of his Corvette, and went out to the lane to begin his stretch-ing and putting. He felt that he had aged many years but maybe he would feel his old self if he had a hard workout with the shots.

"Goddamn Bozo," Tom Zucold said to the poster of the Carolina Kid. "Boy needing you bad. Act like he pussy whipped already."

The Grip flexed and pulled and stretched. His muscles ached and tingled from disuse but slowly he felt himself come around. The lane was filled with a thick mist but he was not concerned by it. The crisp morning made him feel good. Soon he was winging the steel balls into the mist. His body began to feel like a thick rubber band that snapped and yanked just as he wanted it to. Then he en-tered a new state of mind and found himself dreaming as his rhythm carried him easily through the shotputting motion. He could see the woman in his mind. She was stepping toward him down the lane. She was bad looking now, old, her skin wrinkled and cracked, hair dirty and frizzled, her eyes blued as if with bruises.

"What kind of man are you?" the woman said like a hiss.

He heaved the shot and heard himself say in his head "A man

that—" He stopped. "A man that is looking for—" He tried to hear it again, hefting the steel ball and waiting.

"What makes you think you're real? Is anybody here real?" the woman hissed.

He did not answer. The woman had stopped now and stood still in his head just as she stood midway in his putting lane. She twitched once, a kind of body shake, and the red robe pooled into the mist. There were those magnificent tits again. Even at this distance they froze him. Then they began to wither and the fine white skin turned yellow. Then she was herself again before he could blink.

"Magic," she said. "Come on to Merci. All you must do is ask. They asked me everywhere and you can be one of them. You can drive my bus and see all the world. Got 'em eating out of my hand. Got Shriners in Raleigh and Elks in Richmond and Knights of Pythias in Wheeling."

"Can't go," the small Grip in The Grip's head said. He released a strong put that was quickly swallowed by the mist.

"Know your name, too. Could say it, you dig?" Her words seemed to him weaker, as if she were fading out. He knew she did not know his name.

"Can't go, Carolina Kid coming soon," Tom Zucold said.

"Shit, he ain't nothing but a thief and a asshole like all the rest," Merci said. Oddly now her voice seemed closer, amplified. "That old fart is dead all the way through, only nobody wants to see it. Tom Zucold is filling you with all them lies he been believing in since he seen it wasn't nothing that would save his ass and you eat 'em up just like everybody else."

"Save him from what?" He had stopped putting now and stood flatfooted in the putting circle.

"From it, asshole. The end, rottenness and decay and stink in the ground. From what your daddy is and your daddy's daddy and his and his and his."

The voice was strong now and too close. The Grip turned and saw her through the El Dorado window, her hand and hook waving in the air as she screamed at Tom Zucold who was standing calmly in front of her. Both were at the fender of the pearl bus where the engine hung from the hoist right over the engine well. She wasn't talking to him at all.

"Wasn't for him," the woman screamed and pointed toward the wall between her and the poster of the Carolina Kid, "I wouldn't have no business to do at all. You sawed off little shit, don't you know that everybody wakes up humping and scraping the bed one day and scared as fools and got to do something, only it ain't anything to do. Then he come along and say bet on me. And fools do. He got the biggest, richest farm in all of North Carolina and it takes a city full of cash to keep all them servants and hangers-on and kids and bodyguards and creeps that he has got. Where you think they come from? Probably you didn't know that he has a full-time big band dance orchestra and a country western one too? He pays for all that with your life, Jack."

The Grip watched the woman stop for a breath. Then he saw Tom Zucold had been arguing with her and he had gotten to the point he could not talk any more. Tom Zucold opened his mouth to speak but no words came, so he hauled back and delivered a right cross right in the center of the bandage that the woman had on her nose. Her scream rattled the El Dorado glass. The Grip could not hear Tom Zucold say "Bet me" but he knew that he had said it. He opened the door and went in. The woman was crawling to her feet and cursing.

"Woman back," Tom Zucold said matter of factly.

"See her," The Grip answered. He reached for a grease rag and rubbed the sweat from his forehead.

"She be leaving today, though."

"Probably best thing," The Grip said.

"Ask if you could go with her and be her driver," Tom Zucold said and popped a dead cigar into his mouth. "Go with her if you desire, but she is a killer for sure. Ain't no sweat offn my ass neither way."

The Grip could see that Tom Zucold was trembling with rage. He was so angry and so out of control that it amused The Grip and he started to tease the old man.

"Woman got a lot of money."

"Shit."

"Good luck and good looking."

"Double shit."

"Man could go places with her and that rig," The Grip said and grinned. He saw the woman duck into the heart of the bus.

"Bet me if you ain't a double-cheeked pink-skulled full-of-shit gorilla," Tom Zucold said. "You ain't seeing things no better than if you was swinging from them trees out there and—well ittis out my hands." The old man turned and climbed up onto the busbumper and looked into the dark well.

"Grip was just teasing," The Grip said.

Tom Zucold looked back over his shoulder and said, "Woman say the Carolina Kid been fucking Promise Land since she was a girl."

"Say what? She say what?" The Grip nearly jumped forward at the old man.

"Said Carolina Kid been fucking your girl," Tom Zucold said into the engine well. Then he looked back at The Grip again and grinned, "Teasing you, too."

They took a break for fish and grits and while Tom Zucold cooked it up The Grip stood before the poster and looked over each detail again and again. After a few minutes, The Grip stepped back and said, "He is coming. What time we leave for that Moose Hall."

"Leave at the right time," Tom Zucold said as he handed The Grip his hubcap of fish and grits. "Don't, we have to hang around with them Moose fools. Ittis one thing to belong and another thing to hang around with them fools."

Tom Zucold climbed up into his Thunderbird chair, strapped himself in, and looked over at the poster. "Truth is he going to heft our lives up like they was BBs and maybe put us farther'n you can guess." Then he took a big forkful of grits. Around the figure, it seemed to The Grip, there was some kind of ominous and wonderful glow that he knew could have been sunlight but didn't seem like sunlight.

"By God, he coming," The Grip said.

"Man, and I thought I was one quiet dude," a thick voice said. Then Trooper Lionel J. Drilling's wide black face appeared in the door to the Bowie Garage. "You done heared me coming look like. Mind if I come on in?"

Tom Zucold waved him in and asked if he wanted some fish and grits. The Grip had seen Trooper Drilling several times but they had not actually met so he stood up from his Corvette chair and stuck out his big hand and said "The Grip, pleased to meetcha."

Trooper Drilling received his hand and with his left hand pointed at The Grip and winked at Tom Zucold. "Big cat, ain't he? You the one that heaves them shots so far, huh? Used to run the 440 myself. Getting fat as a hog now though." Trooper Drilling pulled back his hand and went into a stance that The Grip thought was a modified parade rest. He watched Trooper Drilling as the man chatted idly with Tom Zucold about the weather and about Yorktown Road and the killer tree and even Clifton, his nephew. Trooper Drilling wore the blue and grey Virginia State Police uniform and he glittered all over. His shirt was studded by a chrome name badge and a chrome chain that connected to a chrome whistle. He had a wide black leather belt with chrome bullets and a .38 Special that was chrome. There was even a bright strip down the side of his trousers. When The Grip looked up he saw that the man's face glittered blackly and the Smokey Bear had a band that glittered. Trooper Drilling was not as tall as The Grip was but the thickness at his waist and in his shoulders made him appear a pretty big man. He smelled of strong shaving lotion that The Grip had always smelled in Army locker rooms.

"Say you was in the Big Red One? Whooee, don't that tie it though," Trooper Drilling said. "Me too, sure as I'm standing here. Got out down to Fort Bragg." Trooper Drilling took off his hat and shook out his Afro and talked on with Tom Zucold. The Grip was thinking about the match to come and the Moose Hall and paid little attention to them.

"Good to meet you, Grip. Be cool, hear?" Trooper Drilling gently slapped The Grip on the arm then he waved to Tom Zucold and he was gone. The Grip heard the big engine start up and then the siren come hard as the car raced away.

"Look like he onto something big, don't it?" Tom Zucold said. "Hee hee, the man just like to race and run that siren. Well let's see what's in this letter he got out of our mailbox."

The Grip watched Tom Zucold's face shift under the dirty whiskers until it set into a hard angle and the eyes narrowed to dark beads. "It is the battle order," he said at last. "Them bastards gone find they bit off more than they chew. Say they gone throw me off the land for nonpayment. From some asshole name of Alvah."

"What is it?" The Grip asked, though he was sure he knew.

"It?" Tom Zucold shouted. "It is it. The order. Tom Zucold seen enough of them to know. He ain't ascared one bit, neither. Goddamn them we gone be ready though. It is getting near and them ain't with Tom Zucold had better clear they ass off the decks."

"What we gone do?"

"Do?" Tom Zucold said, looking baffled. "Do? We gone fight. What else?"

"Carolina Kid coming in three days." The Grip spoke carefully as if his words were matches near gasoline.

"Think I don't know who coming and going round here?" Tom Zucold exploded. He had forgotten his seat belt and he was jerking against it, his face turning dark red. "Think I need a frigging gorilla to tell me what I been knowing night and day?"

"I ain't a gorilla," The Grip said quietly.

Suddenly Trooper Lionel J. Drilling's wide smiling face appeared in the door and said, "Say man I clean forgot. Promise Land asked me to tell you she coming by tomorrow to take you on a picnic. You dig? Say, keep them strings tight." Then the face was gone. The

Grip looked back toward the Thunderbird chair but Tom Zucold was not in it. He was shooting up and down the rope, puffing hard, mumbling about getting programmed.

The Grip had never been on a picnic and did not know what one was. Tom Zucold told him that it was when you went out in open country somewhere and you ate. The Grip had sense enough to realize that Promise Land would certainly come early and he was ready before eight, though she did not show until just before noon. What surprised him was the banana yellow Volkswagen convertible that she was driving. He had naturally expected the pink Harley-Davidson.

"No law says a woman can't have however many vehicles she can afford, is there? I can afford more than a few." Promise Land was more beautiful than any of the times before. Her golden hair was gathered under a red bandanna and her green eyes sparkled. She wore a burgundy T-shirt that said WASHINGTON REDSKINS over her breasts and under that the word *when.* Below her shirt she had on white short shorts that showed a fine golden fuzz on her thighs. She also wore running shoes.

It was not easy for The Grip to fold his massive frame and body into the tiny car, even with the passenger seat fully back, but he wedged himself in eventually and felt almost a part of the car. He bounced and bottomed with each ripple in the asphalt. It was a much harder ride than he had on the pink Harley but with the top down there was, he thought, a similar feel to it all. It was partly the openness, he knew, but also the delicious sensation of somehow riding the edge of danger—as if you were actually controlling a machine that could easily kill you rather than riding inside of something that was as automatic as the elevator. As they rolled down Yorktown Road he leaned his head back on the seat. The telephone wires were full of birds that exploded when the chattery car went by. Crickets and katydids buzzed in the ditches and fields. Once, in the road ahead, he saw a smashed turtle still alive and trying to crawl to the safety of the ditch. When Promise Land finished it, leaving only a dark red smear on the pavement, she gave no sign she knew what she had done. He did not want to watch the road after this and kept his eyes fixed over the dark green fields. The air smelled clean and salty.

"Makes a person feel really alive," Promise Land said.

"What did you say?" The Grip said. He was beginning to feel more confident and sometimes he had become slightly more articulate. Now he felt a sort of glowing inside himself and he knew that it was radiating outward. It was a form of power and he had never had it before. It was there, though, he was sure.

"I said you feel alive on a day like this and in a car like this. Why I bought it," Promise Land said. "Let's get some music." She snapped on the radio and dialed until she landed a clear station and rock music blasted out.

"I don't feel like that today, do you?"

The Grip shrugged his shoulders. He rarely listened to music since Tom Zucold did not allow it and his preferences were pretty much unformed. He liked music, however, and would gladly listen to whatever type played. She dialed slowly and soon came on another clear channel. This time a man with a harsh nasal voice was singing about being a carpenter and asking a woman if she would have his baby. Then he told the woman that he had given her his onliness. The Grip listened closely to the song, fascinated with what he was hearing. Was that how it happened, he wondered. Did you ask a woman if she would have your baby? And if she said yes, did you pay her something? It was a kind of business deal? And this onliness, what could that be?

"I just love Johnny Cash, don't you?" Promise Land said now. She was humming along with the song even though the song was over.

"What is onliness?" The Grip asked. He said it very quietly because he somehow felt shy.

"You'll find out," Promise Land said. "Lots of people don't, goodness knows, but you will." She went on humming the song, her golden hair flying out under the bandanna. The Grip saw that she watched him out of the corner of her eye.

"It's hard to explain, you see," she said. "It's a little like your soul—if you believe in souls—and a little like your personality. Oh gosh, I can think of twenty reasons why it isn't like either. Isn't that a riot? Well, let's see. It's like a whatness of a thing, if you see what I mean. What makes an elephant is elephant onliness, if elephants have that. I don't know about that, of course. But for you, there is certainly an onliness, a youness." She watched him again to see if he understood. He thought he saw what she meant.

"The trouble is that whoever wrote that song just said something very pretty, very nearly poetic even, except that it isn't true, I don't think." She smiled at him and he noticed that they were driving very fast, the curves coming at him at a frightening speed. He was pushing his feet hard on the floorboards but it was doing no good.

"Yes," The Grip said for no reason he could see.

"I just don't think that you *can* give your onliness away. Not really. I mean Lord knows enough people have tried it, haven't they. And there's no shortage of testimonies about people in love for fifty years. More. You know that. Even in this time of virtually infectious divorce. Still, here's the thing I think: if there really is that secret essential you down there under all those layers of skin and bone and fluid and personality, the chances are that it is always and permanently alone. You can't touch it. Nobody can touch it. A person maybe can see it in herself but you couldn't touch it in me. I couldn't touch it in you. It follows, don't you think, that you couldn't possibly give away what you can't even touch?"

The Grip wasn't sure he should have asked. He had set Promise Land off and she was having a whale of a time explaining. Still, what she said did make sense to him. He couldn't quite see how it mattered or what good it did anybody to know what she had said, but it made sense. He watched the thick pines fly by him at an awful rate.

"Why you're afraid of my driving!" Promise Land said and laughed. She laughed a lot and The Grip liked her for that. It made him feel easy around her. "I like to go fast, don't you?" She did not slow down at all.

"I hadn't thought about it," he answered, being careful in what he said.

"Gosh, if you don't go fast, where's the fun in going?"

He watched her naked arms on the steering wheel. Like her legs and her delicately featured face, her arms were solidly tanned. But he was really watching her fine breasts, which were held taut and outlined against the T-shirt by the way she held the wheel. He knew that she kept looking at him out of the corner of her eye. This time she caught him looking at her and he blushed. She laughed again and passed a truck loaded with chickens in crates. The smell was awful.

"Where's the hooker?" she asked.

The Grip was looking at a red roof in the distance and he ignored her. Maybe she would think he had not heard her and wouldn't ask again.

"Where's that friendly brother of yours?" The Grip asked her.

"Poor stupid baby. Cotton means well. He thought you were attacking me. He—well, he's got the weak head from his mother's side of the family. He's all right, though. Really, he's harmless. Terrified of women, of course. I think the only girl he has ever had lasted less than a week. Lots of jokes around about that, of course. Some people never forget, you know? Everybody takes care of Cotton, have to. Daddy gives him real estate to sell and then sends him customers. You know he's a major in the Guard? It gives him something to do but honestly if there was ever a war—. I am sorry he socked you, though."

"OK," The Grip answered. "I'll get him someday."

"I bet you will, but not too hard, please? He just can't take very much. Now listen, where's the hooker? I saw the bus go by yesterday and looked for you but you can't see much, you know." Promise Land brushed hair from her eyes and braked the car. "This is called the Point. I brought you down here to get some clams for our picnic." She pulled the car up to a square white building and stopped. The air smelled of salt and drying fish. "So where's the hooker, for Pete's sake?"

"Her name is Merci?"

"Merci? Did you say Merci?"

"Said Merci," The Grip said flatly. He looked at Promise Land's thighs that were as smooth as a baby's bottom except for the golden dust of hair. For the first time he realized that she was a tall woman. It was, he thought, odd the way she had of being so different every time he saw her, as if she could change to be whatever she wanted to be. He forced himself to look away from her and saw out over the water a gull drop a fish from its mouth and then go for it again.

Promise Land got out of the car and shut the door and laughed, then said, "Goes to show you can't tell a thing by some names doesn't it?"

He watched her walk up some short steps into the white building. Her rear was beautifully even. His throat was tight and the sun was hot on his head and its prickly covering of hair.

When Promise Land came back to the car, The Grip said, "She is gone."

"Who? Oh. You mean the hooker with the bus." Promise Land wheeled off down the road where they had come and wound the little yellow bug up in every gear.

"Well I wouldn't bet too much money on that," she said.

Soon they were nearing the Bowie Garage and The Grip wondered if she had changed her mind about the picnic. But then she downshifted and deftly whipped the little car to the right. The Grip barely had time to see the sign that said Emmaus Road. The road was bumpy and hurt him at the speed she took but they passed under a canopy of trees so thick that the shade and the cool air made it feel like night. He smelled the moss and fern and damp ground and it seemed that he was descending in a cave. Then they slid around a curve and burst into the light.

"That's my place over there," Promise Land said and pointed over the steering wheel. "Daddy gave it to me when I finished high school."

Suddenly they were in what was very nearly a different world. The trees and fields and grasses were more intensely green. It seemed to The Grip that the birds sang louder and more sweetly. Azaleas grew alongside the road and there were thick clumps of both blue and white hydrangeas. He smelled the long vines of honeysuckle and smiled. It felt to him as they rode along, more slowly now, that nothing was or ever could be out of place, distorted, unhappy, or lost here. Already, had anyone asked him, he would have said that he felt he was becoming a gentleman.

"Those are my horses over there. I love horses as much as anything in the world," Promise Land said. He saw two clusters of horses in the distance, most of them brown and shiny but a white one and a black one were also there. Abruptly they turned to the left and entered a rutted dirt road. There were wooden fences on both sides of the road and The Grip understood that the two clusters of horses were separated by this road.

"Is is is it here?" He stuttered because Promise Land was still driving very fast and the car was shaking him very hard.

"Well a little farther," she answered. "Down by the river. A quiet place that I like to go to."

"Which side is yours?"

"Both sides all the way to river, most everything you can see," Promise Land said and waved her arm in a great circle.

She stopped the car at a gate across the road and got out and moved the wire gate back, then drove through, then replaced the gate. The Grip watched her move with admiration not only for her beauty but also for her efficiency and her authority.

"You do that right smart," The Grip said and surprised himself.

Promise Land shifted the banana Volkswagen and rammed her running shoe down on the accelerator so the engine chattered and the car leaped forward through the ruts. They came to a small tree-hidden bridge that crossed a slow creek and virtually leaped over it, then came down with a bounce that slammed The Grip's teeth together so he had to check to be sure some of them weren't broken off. The woman laughed and continued to ride hard.

"Where are you from?" She had to holler to be heard above the engine.

"Here," The Grip said. He clung to the little handle on the dash and to whatever else he could grab, although there was no way that he could have been thrown out. "Bowie Garage." He shouted above the noise too.

"No, no," she said. "I mean before you came here."

The Grip saw a small knoll coming at them and he steadied himself as the car went into the air and thudded back to earth. When he let his breath go, he said "Ocracoke. In North Carolina."

"Yes. I know that country. Splendid place, too. I've got some family there so I guess it's part of me." She smiled at him, her unpainted lips beautiful against her perfect white teeth. They wheeled around a turn, she shifted down, and pulled quickly between two large loblolly pine trees. Almost as quickly she had shut off the engine and leaped out, saying "here we are finally." Then she was off running to a grassy spot over a little hill. The Grip was left to wedge himself out and it was less easy, he found, than wedging himself in. When he reached the crest of the hill, he saw the most serene place he had ever been in. Promise Land had spread the blanket in a grassy area beneath some sycamores and not twenty feet away the river lapped peacefully at the bank. Actually, it was not open river, for he could see that in the distance, but a cove.

They ate slowly and without speaking very much. The biscuits she had baked herself were delicious and the corn on the cob was fine. He had five pieces of her fried chicken and ate a plate of sliced tomatoes. He had never in his life had an apple pie that was so good and he washed it down with ice cold tea. While he ate, Promise Land told him that the river was called the Chapel River, and the name meant something sacred. It was a fine river from up in the trees but if you got close, The Grip discovered, the water had a faint grey tinge to it. Still the smell of the ocean not far away made him restless.

At the end, Promise Land poured white wine into two small silver goblets and they drank slowly. He could hear fish jumping in the cove. Promise Land said they were mullets, probably. After a while he lay back on the blanket and felt the wine warm his body. There was a fine cool breeze which moved over him like a fingertip. Somewhere near a quail kept calling "Bobwhite, bobwhite." Under him the earth felt solid and he thought maybe he could even feel it turning enough to start drawing the tide out.

"Golly, it's perfect here."

The Grip did not answer her. He kept his eyes closed. What could he add with words, since words would never capture the sense he had in him of this place?

"Do you want to row out in the water a little? I have a boat just over there." Her voice was almost distant because he was so content. He twisted grass in his fingers. When he opened his eyes she was standing with hands on hips, waiting for him.

"Sure," he said.

He rowed with deep, confident strokes. It was a small boat with stout oars. One thing he had learned growing up in Ocracoke was how to row a boat. They faced each other and he pulled wherever she pointed. There were little creeks that ran off the cove and first he pulled her in one of these. That turned out to be a bad idea because of the mosquitoes, though he had also flushed an elegant white crane. She was pleased about that. Then they went around the edge of the cove out to the river itself. The oars dripped when he drew them from the water and small silver pools spun themselves into the wake that left the water unblemished not far behind them. Then he dipped the oars back in and pulled easily so the boat shot forward. It was cool on the water and Promise Land hummed one song after another.

"Let's not go in the river OK?" she asked him. Her voice was dreamy and fluid. "Let's go back toward the shore." He turned the boat as easily as he had rowed it, then drove it forward. They had gotten about midway across the cove when she asked to go in another direction. He slowed and started the turn, when abruptly she stood up. At just that minute he had dug an oar in deeply. He watched her scream and topple into the water almost as if it were all happening in slow motion. Her head went under and then popped right back to the surface. He grabbed and missed but heard her fingernails clawing the side of the boat. She went under again, then once more she surfaced.

"Icandim," she tried to shout, "Icandwim," then she was under a third time and The Grip realized she was trying to tell him she couldn't swim.

He stood up and catapulted himself out of the boat but his head never went under before his feet hit the gooey muck on the bottom. He stood up and the water was just over his belt, about four feet he guessed. It was easy to pick up Promise Land, his hands curled under her armpits, and lift her coughing and sputtering into the light. Even as he held her out of the water, she thrashed and slipped out of his grasp and back into the water. He matched her wiry strength and slipped his arm under her arms and across her breast, then held her tight. She coughed and gagged, then cried, and finally relaxed. He saw that the boat had drifted off with the turning tide.

"Gone walk us back," The Grip said. "Don't be afraid. Won't let go." Maybe he could do it and maybe not, he thought. It was nearly fifty yards to the nearest shore. That would be easy if it stayed the same depth or got shallower. But this kind of water often had holes you never saw until you were in them.

"OK," she said.

He took one tentative step and felt the muck under his boot. He did not fall but slid a little. He took another step, then another, and was getting the feel of it. Once he hit an old oyster bed and it was just like walking on a sidewalk until he hit a hole on the other side and both of them went under. But the hole was not a large one and he had soon got them through it. They were close enough to shore now that he knew he could let her walk. She would not cut her feet, not with those running shoes. Still he did not let her go. And when they had stepped up onto the ground she stayed in his arms and he carried her to the blanket.

"I'm sorry that happened," she said and shook her hair. It was drying quickly in the afternoon sun.

"What did you do?" The Grip stripped off his fatigue T-shirt and the sun warmed his broad back. Then he sat down in the grass and began to pick at the mud-covered laces of his combat boots.

"I thought I saw a snake," Promise Land said. "It was silly. I nearly got us both drowned."

The Grip knew that was wrong. You could drown in water that

deep, of course, but it would be hard as long as both people could stand up. Still, he said "Check." He did not look at her but faced the cove. The sun beat against his chest hotly and he was glad. He heard her rustling behind him but went on trying to get his boots off. When he had done so, he heard her say "Stand up, please."

She stood naked in the sun, her wet clothes piled beside the blanket. Her hand was reached out to him. He shivered just a little and felt the blood rushing and the flutter in his stomach. He saw already that Merci's tits, which he had imagined magnificent, were but ridges by comparison. Before him were firm and flawless globes that seemed to breathe warmth as he saw them. The nipples were the color of freshly wet sand and were absolutely smooth. But it was just so everywhere he looked. She had stepped from a magazine. Or at least he would have said that if asked. How futile the other woman seemed in memory now! How could he have imagined she had been perfect?

He took her hand and she led him back away from the water to a small glen in the pine trees. The ground was covered with a thick bed of pine needles and there were only the frailest spears of light dropping through the roof of trees. It was cool and dark and sunken in the ground like a nest. She kissed him lightly on the lips and he tasted the salt of the water again. He felt quick and glad and he thought that he loved her. She pulled him down on the bed of pine needles and he listened to a distant chainsaw razz and whine, razz and whine.

When he woke she was leaning over him and she kissed him again lightly. He could see that the tide had gone out of the cove and knew he had slept some time. She lay down in the crook of his arm and they looked up into the starlike darkness of the pines and talked softly. She told him she had divorced her first husband because he gave her no children. She had divorced the second because their one child was born sick.

"No that wasn't really it." She was almost inaudible, whispering. "We never really got married. The first one was a semi-pro baseball player. Not very good either. A pitcher with a curve that went flat and no fastball so's you'd notice. That boy was wild, too, I mean.

Guess that's why I loved him, that wildness. But he couldn't tell when to quit and he kept going from bad teams to worse, always on the road. Probably he's getting knocked out of the box somewhere right now. Me, I got to have land, home, freedom—gosh, I don't know what all. So he made me a free woman. His name was Butch Land. So my name is?"

"Promise Land," he said. "My girl."

"Well not so fast there, you." She sat up and shook out her hair. She was dressed now and he felt exposed. "We got to take plenty of time, son." She stood up. "Gosh, I'm late now, speaking of time. You ready?"

On the way back to the Bowie Garage she asked if he would like to see her barn and horses. The Grip did not care if he did or did not see a horse but this meant more time with her so he said he'd like that. On the way he told her the Carolina Kid was coming.

"I don't keep up with concerts much anymore—if that's what you're talking about."

"Ain't a concert," The Grip said.

"I used to go to fights, but I haven't been in years. He a fighter?"

The Grip told her that the Carolina Kid was the best hustle pool player there ever was. He told her all that Tom Zucold had told him and she listened with interest. But she said nothing. Somehow he had hoped she would say something, though he did not know what. For a moment, she seemed annoyed.

It took only a few minutes and they were parked before an enormous barn. There was also a white truck there and Promise Land said that was the vet, Dr. Garton. "C'mon," she said. They walked inside and The Grip saw there was a great grey horse standing between two people. A yellow light shone down in a large pool. Then The Grip saw that a third person stood at the rear of the horse and this man was holding the tail of the horse. The air stank of urine and manure.

"Let me see," Promise Land said, walking straight to the man at the horse's rear. The Grip followed her. She took a yellow glove from the man and tugged it on and without hesitation plunged her arm into the horse's rear end. He watched her face tighten and strain as if she were looking for something with her hand. Then she was pulling her arm and pulling the glove off.

"Too early," she said to the three people. None of them spoke.

The Grip followed her to the car, wedged himself in again, and off they flew. His brain stung from the raw odor of the barn and from Promise Land's shocking coldness with her horse.

"Is your name really The Grip? I can't believe that," she said after a while. They had not spoken very much after leaving the barn. He did not answer until they pulled into the Bowie Garage.

"I don't have a name," The Grip said. "But I love you."

"Nameless or not, we'll meet again. I'm glad you saved my life and I'll try to return the favor." Then her car nosed forward and she turned it around in the front yard. When she had stopped again, she said "I hope you all win that bet on the Carolina Kid because Daddy wants his payments. I heard him say so to Cotton yesterday. Come here." The Grip leaned down and Promise Land kissed him, then accelerated away.

CHAPTER IV

The Moose Hall

Tom Zucold had worked furiously to complete repairs on The Confessional and had done it in record time. As he had said, this job was by the hour so time really was money. But The Grip thought it must have been more than that, for the little man seemed increasingly possessed by a force that was clearly there just as it was indescribable. Then the woman was gone and it was quiet in the garage except for the squeak of the rafters as Tom Zucold sent his wiry body up and down the rope. He no longer seemed to care that The Grip watched. He was getting programmed. It worried The Grip. The old man hardly talked anymore, his face was dark and set all day long, as if he expected any minute to be attacked from behind the oil drum. Life settled very quickly into a pattern that was tense though pleasant enough. The Grip went into his lane and put shots until he could no longer lift his arms. Between the shots he watched for the melted face of the child and tried to analyze what he had or had not done correctly. Tom Zucold, ignoring the processees because he said there was no time right now to restore them, sat in his Thunderbird chair and calculated odds on various sums of money they might muster for a bet until he heard brakes or car doors in the front yard. He repaired a Peugeot short in the steering wheel, did two minor tune-ups, sold a pair of wheels from the burned-out Galaxy, and overcharged every customer while he complained to each loudly of heart attacks he knew to be imminent. His arms hurt so he could probably work better with his feet, he claimed. The Grip knew this was the result of all that rope climbing. He said nothing. Once he heard Tom Zucold say it was the Lord's punishment to saddle him with a gorilla who couldn't spit and turn a phillips screwdriver at the same time. The Grip said nothing.

Promise Land came by one evening just before dark. Dogwood bloomed so white along the roads that it looked like lights in the trees. She couldn't sit still any longer, she hummed. He climbed up on the rear of her pink Harley and they took Yorktown Road to Route 17 and drove over the Coleman Bridge to Gloucester. It had been warm for several days and the bugs began to ping at their faces, leaving small welts that stung. They rode for hours and tried to talk but gave up because the throaty exhaust of the big motorcycle drowned out every other word. When she dropped him off beside the killer tree, she tilted her face up to be kissed and in the darkness seemed to him as luminous as the dogwood. Their helmets clashed when he went to kiss her and they laughed easily, then removed their helmets and kissed. She told him she would see him again soon, then sped off before a truck whose brakes shrieked in protest.

"Think you got a chance to claim that stuff, huh monkey?" Tom Zucold had said when he walked in. The old man was standing in his Thunderbird chair and toweled himself off. He wore nothing but a jock strap and the film of light sweat that told The Grip he had been at the rope again. For a minute he stood and watched his room-mate. At seventy, Tom Zucold still had a hard, lean body. His tight strings were impressive under the sparse white hair that remained but his skin was as pale as tissue paper and almost as transparent. The Grip saw bright veins bulging and the knobs of bones poking at the taut skin so that he thought of a misshapen onion he had once seen his mother pull from her garden.

"Hear me, don't you? Ittis many a man gone after that piece and thought it was his and swish swish she was gone. Nothin' left but a good smell," Tom Zucold had said. The Grip said nothing.

"She ain't what you think, boy. Take everything you got, soul in-cluded, and you be left with the memory." Tom Zucold jumped up the rope, hung, then said, "And it might start out beautiful, but then it won't talk to you and soon it start to sicken and pop ittis dead. Just warning you to keep your mind on him because he is comin'," Tom Zucold said, nodding at the poster he had retaped on the win-dow. The Grip said nothing as he heard Tom Zucold grunt and fart his way two-thirds up the rope.

"You ain't gonna make it," The Grip said, having drained the last of his Gatorade.

Tom Zucold hung at the two-thirds point, his stringy muscles pop-ping and his joints creaking, his old asshole whistling. He threw his head back, then looked into the hole where The Grip had seen moonlight. He seemed to be waiting for a word or a sign. Suddenly he released and slid down the rope in three quick jerks.

"Know it," Tom Zucold said. He stood again in his Thunderbird chair. "Ain't none of us gonna make it. Get old that's one thing you sure of. Another is that I gone take them Committee bastards with me. Getting programmed. Better start doing it yourself."

The Grip moved to sit down in his Corvette chair and saw that it was gone. "What'd you do with my chair?" For an instant he was certain the old man had sold it. He would do anything for more money to bet on the Carolina Kid. Of that, The Grip was certain.

"Go look in the truck," Tom Zucold said, then leaped up on the rope.

"Fuck you," The Grip said flatly.

The force of it knocked the old man off the rope, or seemed to since he dropped like a cat onto his feet and said "What the hell you say?"

"Works fine," The Grip said. He pushed the button again and made his chair swivel around so he could look out through the back of the truck. All the buttons Tom Zucold had installed worked fine. The seat turned and rose and fell and went forward and backward.

"Known it," Tom Zucold said. He sat in the driver's seat, still wearing only a jock strap, and stared ahead at the back of the poster on the window.

The Grip also looked out of the narrow windshield. He felt ashamed of himself and wanted to say something. Where were the words? They sat for a long time and said nothing.

"Shoulder sore," The Grip said at last. It wasn't much, he knew, but it was something. "Too many puts probably."

"Any man that sling them sixteen-pound balls all them hours got to be hurtin'," Tom Zucold said just above a whisper. Then, brightly, "But it is a good hurt. A man's hurt."

There seemed no place for The Grip to take the conversation, though he tried. He could talk about Promise Land. There were things he wanted to ask the old man. What did it mean to love a woman? How did you know you loved somebody? How could you tell if she loved you? What was an onliness? After you fucked somebody once didn't that mean you could do it anytime? But he could imagine no way to bring these questions up and, anyway, Tom Zucold didn't seem to like the woman very much.

"The woman pay cash?" The Grip said, making it barely a question.

"Paid every cent of it. Bitched the whole time, too. Done this to me," Tom Zucold spit. He lifted his beard and showed his neck but the wound was invisible in the dark of the truck.

"Don't see nothing."

"Don't see nothing? You motherhumping baboon, look ahere," Tom Zucold said and leaned a little toward The Grip. "Woman like to cut my throat with that hook of hers."

"Too dark," The Grip said.

"Sucker's there, though, and you can thank me it ain't on your neck," Tom Zucold said. "Woman said we ain't seen the last of her. Said we owed her."

"Don't owe nobody," The Grip said.

"Don't go too goddamn far there, champ." Tom Zucold lit a dead cigar he had left on the dashboard with some matches. Its rank aroma hovered in the cockpit like the stench of a dying thing. "But you right about her. Don't owe that bitch a damn thing." Tom Zucold drummed on the dash with his fingers.

"It don't make sense to me, not any of it," The Grip said.

"Ain't nobody ever said that it did. If it was any sense into the whole nine yards, Tom Zucold wouldn't put up every nickle he can beg, steal, and earn on a bet on a pool hustler he ain't actually seen. Think about it."

"Good seat," The Grip said and pushed the reverse button.

"Good as any for watchin' but you ain't going to watch, you going to be assdeep in it."

"It?" The Grip asked.

"It?" Tom Zucold barked. "It is it. What's out there, you Promise Land. All of it. Life, what the hell else?"

"Fuck you," The Grip said, only gently now, with a kind of affection.

"That it will. What I been trying to show you every way I can."

They were quiet then. They sat and watched the back of the poster, both hunched in the dark like animals frightened of the man in the window but hungry for what he might give them.

"Time, goddamnit Grip," Tom Zucold said suddenly. "Got to get ready. We go tomorrow. He comin' tomorrow night." Then he was out of the truck and in the Bowie Garage and The Grip sat alone.

After a few minutes he got out and gently closed the door. Tomorrow, he kept thinking. It was going to happen, then. He was coming. He tingled all over and the air made him jittery. It was like a dream. But he was coming tomorrow night. The Grip walked past the Bowie Garage and around toward the putting lane, then down the lane until he stood beside the white stick. He had not meant to come here, but here he was. He touched the stick and said "tomorrow" and then drew his hand back. He looked up into the sky that was as black as the inside of an engine at fifty-five, except for the stars that bristled. Then he said "Love."

As if in answer a voice said "Comin' oh my God comin' " and then it said "Hunh, hunh, hunh."

It was near the cement mixer, The Grip thought. But he found no one there and moved around to the rear but again found nothing.

"Hunh, Hunh, Hunh," the voice said again, nearer now.

There, he saw it, a flash of white. It was in the pile of old tires that Tom Zucold kept beyond the processees. He had forgotten the tires. He climbed over a litter of engine blocks and saw feet lift in the air, then realized that it was a man on top of her.

"Wait, wait," the girl's voice said and then "Oh now, Clifton, baby, now."

"Hunh, hunh, hunh," Clifton said, his body falling in tune with the noise he made, rising between.

"Oh, oh, oh," the girl said.

"Comin'," Clifton said.

Suddenly Tom Zucold shouted "He is coming!" The Grip looked at the El Dorado door and saw the tiny man outlined by the light behind him. Then Tom Zucold raised a rifle and fired it at the sky.

"He coming for sure," Tom Zucold shouted again and slammed the door shut.

The Grip looked back at the tires and was startled to see no one there. Tires lay stacked in a black heap but there was no one fucking on them. Had there been anyone? Had he only imagined Clifton and the girl? He rubbed his eyes and walked back to the Bowie Garage. Cotton Muddleman's younger sister Hope, an exact duplicate of his older sister Promise, watched him from the ditch that bordered the Bowie Garage.

"How come Clifton's fucking Hope and that's fucking Promise?" she whispered and grinned.

The drive from Chapel to Virginia Beach took a little over an hour and The Grip cradled the accumulated money in a locked glove box from a Mercury Marquis. They parked the truck behind a low brick building which was next to the Moose Hall and walked around to Atlantic Avenue. Tom Zucold took a card from his wallet and slid it in a slit in the door so that something buzzed and the door opened.

They stepped into a large and dimly lit room in the center of which was an oval bar that shone in the light. A few people sat at the bar sipping drinks. Tom Zucold stopped at a table and signed his name in a ledger book. Then a man in a white waiter's coat stepped up and said, "Look like you boys come for some action," as he read over what Tom Zucold had written.

Tom Zucold muttered something unintelligible in response and stepped toward the bar, popping his baseball cap on as he did so. He had already put on a clean blue workshirt and a yellow and black checkered coat that he had gotten out of a processee. His slacks were green gabardine.

"Hey old man," the white waiter coat said, "he got to sign too."

"Signed for him. Ain't blind is you." Tom Zucold neither slowed in his steps toward the bar nor gave any sign he intended to.

"Says NN here, must be it," The Grip heard the white coat say behind him.

Tom Zucold was ordering two tall beers when The Grip asked him what NN meant. "Ask them damn people for Jax but they ain't got any. Woman I knowed once love Jax. Got us Coors." He stopped and looked up at The Grip. "NN is Not Now. Or make it any damn thing you want, just so's it gets us in the party." He swept the two tall cans off the bar and said over his shoulder, "Let's go."

Tom Zucold weaved them around the bar and through a cluster of people and they entered a small room that was hardly bigger than their house and certainly darker.

"Kitchen," Tom Zucold said simply. He waved his arm to indicate that The Grip should stay close.

There was a small pool table in the middle of the room and a naked bulb hung over it. A stove filled one end of the room, with adjacent sinks, and seemed almost bigger than the pool table.

"Look like a toy to me," The Grip said.

"Believe what you see," Tom Zucold said, "and when things is over you tell me who's the toy shooter and who ain't."

They circled the room then sat on the stove because it was wide and solid and close to the action that was coming. At the other end of the room someone had set up three rows of chairs and it looked like there might be a little standing room. Above the last row, on the wall, there were shelves of cans which bore no labels and gleamed in the light.

"Early. But we got the best seats in the house," Tom Zucold said.

"None of them is too hot," The Grip answered. They climbed up and settled in and for a while they sipped the beer and said nothing. It was peaceful in the room and they could hear the crowd noise getting louder by the bar. There was also a country band playing something in a distant room.

"Hillbilly stuff all right," Tom Zucold said.

Suddenly there was loud cheering and a greater sound of feet moving.

"Some fool woman taking off her clothes like as not," Tom Zucold said.

"Promise Land got a sister," The Grip said. It was not a question.

"Say that again," Tom Zucold answered and swallowed a big mouthful. "Most of the people in that town done give up on her long ago. Seem like she just won't get out of they way. Girl is named Hope, if you can believe that. She and her sister is just woman, can't help way they is. That boy, though, he is the biggest goddamn timewaster it is." Tom Zucold spit on the floor.

"You seen him yet?"

"That fool Cotton?"

"The Carolina Kid."

"Too early. Resting probably. Part of being programmed," Tom Zucold said. He got up off the stove and stretched. "He don't want to be all trampled on by these Friday night drunks. I'll get us a couple more."

The Grip had seen pool tables in the Army, more pool tables in more pastel-colored rec lounges than any man in his right mind would ever want to see. He had seen soldiers cleaned on them and seen soldiers cold-cocked onto them. Everywhere the track team had traveled there had been pool tables and rec lounges and loud soldiers. He had even slept on a pool table once. It was, therefore, with at least a little experience that he noted this table was worn badly at both ends. Looking closer to check the level of the thing he was startled to see a pair of flashy white pants, not just flashy but sequined. They walked around the table and stopped between The Grip and the table. Then they bent over and sighted the same line that The Grip had been taking.

"You in my line," The Grip said in what he hoped was an accommodating voice.

"What say pardner?" the man said as he turned to see who had spoken. He was tall, though not as tall as The Grip by six inches, and he was solidly built, though The Grip outweighed him handily. His face was bright and fresh and anonymously handsome, with a froth of very light blond hair falling over the grayish eyes. He wore a T-shirt that said in electric blue letters: SURFING USA and LADIES WANTED.

"Said you in my way."

"What way was that exactly?" the blond said, eying The Grip carefully. He took a white comb out of his pocket and stroked it twice backward through his hair, though it had no discernible effect. A yellow mustache dropped at the corners of his mouth and it rose with each chew he made at a wad of gum.

The Grip slid his combat boots onto the floor and started to heave his body after them.

"Hey, hey, just a kick, good buddy. A joke, man. I seen you looking," the blond said just a little too quickly and shoved his hand out in front of himself. The Grip ignored it and it fell away.

"You hear about the big match tonight?" The blond shifted to the side and pretended to relocate an invisible ball on the table, which he then pretended to shoot and for which he pantomimed a drop into the pocket.

"Yes," The Grip said.

126

"Question is will this Carolina cat show up," the man said. It was, The Grip thought, like hearing a mannequin talk, the man was so flawlessly dressed and groomed. He might have stepped from a men's fashion magazine. When he spoke there was a flash of pale white teeth and pink gums.

"He'll be here," The Grip said with quiet confidence.

"He better be," the man said and spread his palms up and apart as if he were waiting for someone to slap them, which in his imagination someone did so that they flew down and away and the man twirled on his white shoes to face The Grip. "You know this Carolina Kid? You ever seen him shoot?" There was, The Grip saw, a single droplet of clear sweat glinting at the man's temple.

"Never seen him but he'll be here."

There was an immediate relaxation in the stranger's posture and the comb flew once more through the fine hair. The man strutted to the other side of the table and said, "Baby, he better be here because there is a big beachload of dust going down."

"We betting everything we got on him," The Grip said.

"On that old man?" The stranger took a few steps back as if he just had to get one more look at this unbelievable fool, then said, "Soldier I'd think a few strokes before I'd do that rash deed. People say this dude Graham is one outtasight shooter. You might cogitate and ponder before you lay down against him."

"Ain't betting against. Betting for. Betting for the Carolina Kid," The Grip said. He watched the stranger blink, then wave at him as if he were inexpressibly dense, and slide out of the room.

By eleven o'clock the small room had rimmed with people and it was very hot. The air was thick with stale smoke. The blond stranger had been shooting pool for some time with a red-faced man who was called Turkey and said he shot for the honor of his hometown of Churchland. A woman kept appearing in the doorway and saying "She sent you another Wild Turkey." The man drank each of the shot glasses as they came. It was surprising to The Grip since he was winning easily though he missed a lot of shots that it looked like he should have made. Tom Zucold whispered to him that it won't nothing to it. That Turkey was just getting hustled. Anybody could see that the other one had all the moves, all the style, had been bred to it. Besides, Tom Zucold whispered, peoples said this was Pupil Graham, the big one who'd been brought in to shoot with the Kid.

The Grip paid closer attention to the blond stranger. It was funny but the man looked like everybody and nobody. You'd see him in a crowd but you wouldn't remember him. There was something about him that was unpleasant, too. Still and all, the man was open and friendly and it was obvious the crowd liked him, joked with him, and even wanted to touch him. Beyond all this, the man shot effortlessly and the balls seemed bound to obey. When he missed, The Grip thought, it was all but deliberate. But he disguised it by talking to someone or pretending to slip on the slick floor. The Grip knew an athlete when he saw one, though, and this was a professional.

The Grip began to grow bored with what was clearly a charade and shifted his attention to the increasing crowd. There was a man in the far corner who made subtle signals with his hands and eyes. The Grip was fascinated with this little man and yet though he watched closely he was unable to decipher the effect of those signals. No one seemed to pay the slightest bit of attention. The man sat on a velvet cushion that was thick as an arm and he bounced a lot. He had fine long fingers and a grey goatee. With him was a woman that nobody would remember if they saw her every day for a week. Now and again she would stand up and the man would hiss, "Sit down Plum Lee." Or she would start talking and he would spit, "Shut up Plum Lee."

"Strange bunch of people in this world," Tom Zucold said in a low voice, "and this ain't the strangest, if you can believe that."

The Grip thought he could believe almost anything now, at least after the time he had already spent with Tom Zucold and after the things he had learned. Now he felt that he was near the middle of something like TRUTH OR CONSEQUENCES and soon he was going to be swept up in it. He was interested, there was that of course, and it all made him feel that life was busy all around him, in places and ways that he had not known. Or that most people did not know, for that matter. But he also felt on the edge of losing control. It was like being that girl who got whirled beyond the rainbow, being caught by something that was going on with or without you and certainly without giving a damn about you.

He looked back at Plum Lee and the odd little man who seemed to have gotten into a full-fledged argument and were now shouting at each other. He stared so intensely that Tom Zucold asked him what the hell was so interesting. The Grip was not actually answering anyone or anything when he said "Odd, odd."

"Hell he ain't no odder bout anyone else," Tom Zucold said, watching the fight subside and the combatants settle into their seats. "Look like a supply officer I knowed once. Man was scared shitless, college professor. Supplied this and supplied that and got his ass right where he wanted it. Life work like that for some. Long run, though, ain't worth it. Little bitty fellow, he was. Wore cavalry boots with lifts. Wrote poetry that'd make an aunt gag."

The Grip was looking at the woman while Tom Zucold talked. But there wasn't a whole lot to see so he scanned the rest. One woman had a face full of red splotches like a big leech had kissed her a lot. There was a man with an enormous black dog that drooled on the man's foot. Way in the last row, in the corner, he saw Billy Carmines and told Tom Zucold that he was there. Billy Carmines was Tom Zucold's oldest and best friend, even if that meant sometimes being no friend at all.

There was a big ponytailed hippie who leaned against the door and had a Gulf Oil shirt with a patch that said *Mano*. Next to him were some people who had plastic nametags pinned to their collars. The only one that The Grip could read said DeMott. Off to the right The Grip saw an old man leaning against the wall and tilting back a big beer until it was drained. Then the man slumped under a row of cabinets full of glasses and dishes and closed his eyes until the beer settled. Even in the poor light The Grip could see the old man was tough-fibered and wiry, a farmer. His skin was the color of bacon fried and he wore bib overalls that seemed even now to carry enough tools for a homestead.

At this man's elbow there was a boy, a young boy whose hair had all been cut off except for a thick tuft atop his forehead. Like the old man, the boy wore bib overalls. He had no shoes and his feet were dirty. While the old man appeared patient, even placid, opening his mouth only a fraction to speak to the boy, the boy himself jumped, jiggled, shifted, turned, scratched, grinned, frowned, and otherwise kept up a continuous motion. It took The Grip only a few minutes to understand that the old man was futilely trying to explain to the boy how pool was played.

"But Firp," the boy said, jamming his hands into his deep pockets in his exasperation, "how can he tell which way the ball is gone go when he done hit it the other way?"

"Boy I swear you don't know nothing," the old man wheezed. He opened his mouth far enough this time so that his absence of teeth showed. There was also the twinkly glitter of a few gold fillings.

"Boy, a man know where it is gone go because he done put a spin to it. Like marbles, don't you know."

The boy looked back at the table and his eyes seemed to blink with his recognition. "See that blue stuff there? It is chalk. Man rub his pool cue in that so he can get some purchase on the ball. Make the cue do what he want so the ball will do what he want. Then he shoot them other balls to one side or another, maybe top or bottom, to where some go in a hole and some sit right where he wants them to. It is pretty as you please," the old man said with a wet puff of breath.

The Grip and the boy watched the man named Turkey stroke a clean shot that was supposed to drop a red ball in the far corner but did not. Instead, the white ball dropped in the side pocket and Turkey put it back on the table, saying "Shit luck."

"Don't look like he know too much to me," the boy said loud enough for everybody to hear.

The glittery blond man was leaning over to sight his shot when the boy spoke and he looked back over his shoulder and squinted at the old man.

"Boy don't mean you, mister," the old man said. "Mean him. Just a boy asking damnfool questions. He be quiet later on."

The blond stranger pulled his cue back and stood away from the table. He grinned around the room to let everybody know who was in charge and said, "May be. May be. But I ain't want to hear no questions anyway. Just tell that boy to watch close and he gone see how things are. See everything he need to know. Tell him to keep a close eye, see, 'cause what happen here might not happen again just the same." Then he leaned back to the table and almost automatically nipped one ball into a side pocket and another into an end pocket and left the white ball right where he had found it.

"Shut you mouth for you catch a fly," the old man said to the boy, then spat into a dixie cup.

The Grip got up without a word and went out by the bar and took a left where Tom Zucold had told him and went in the door that said DUDES and had a painted cowboy winking. When he got back and had settled on the stove again, he noticed that Tom Zucold looked tired. Everybody was buzzing and talking so loudly that he almost didn't hear Tom Zucold say "He be coming soon."

Then Tom Zucold slid down onto the floor and said "Time." The Grip did not so much hear the word as he saw the lips move. He watched the little man move through the people to a shadow of a man who was scribbling in a notebook near Plum Lee and the odd man. The shadow nodded and someone out near the bar called the blond stranger. Tom Zucold came back and hoisted himself onto the stove.

"Check," Tom Zucold said.

"Say check?"

"Check," he repeated.

Suddenly the people stopped talking and the blond stranger came back into the room, glittering brighter than ever. He leaned over toward the man called Turkey and said, "Son I need the table now."

"You win it, you got it," Turkey said.

The only sound was the kathunk and kaplop of balls striking and falling as the blond stranger efficiently cleaned the table and pocketed the two dollars thrown into the center of the felt. The Grip saw the man was programmed.

"You see her?" Tom Zucold hissed into his ear. "Goddamn me. I known it. You see her?"

"See who?"

"Her? Who you think? Merci, the bus woman. That's who," Tom Zucold said and stuck his agitated finger at the door where the woman had come to stand. Then she was moving off behind Plum Lee, taking a seat that a man had offered her, filling the room with a gaudy false smile.

"See her," The Grip said, his stomach feeling light.

"Unlock the glovebox. Ittis time," Tom Zucold commanded.

A deep and very loud voice shouted from outside the door to the kitchen of the Virginia Beach Moose Hall, "Who's the asshole playing me tonight?"

"Ittis him, ittis him," Firp's boy shouted in the suddenly quiet room. "I would'a knowed him anywheres. Look Firp."

People who had stood in and around the doorway now peeled silently away and there stood the Carolina Kid. He eased forward as if he weighed nothing and stood to one side of the glowing naked bulb. The face was the same, The Grip thought, as that in the poster if you could trust this dim light. Then he wasn't certain it was the same, it seemed to change as he watched it. But there was no question in his mind that this was the Carolina Kid. It was odd, though, the face betrayed no age whatsoever. You couldn't tell how young or old the man was. It seemed perfectly itself, composed, yet restless and even perhaps troubled. There were fine scars at the hairline but the skin was tanned and healthy. The nose was surprisingly red on the tip and he held it up a bit, as if he were impatient. But it was still the eyes that held The Grip and everyone else. They were blue and deep set but it was a blue for which he had no point of reference, no catalog and no ocean, not even Promise Land's blue eyes. The nearest he could imagine to them was the blue of scorched metal. But the eyes, so amazingly deep, seemed bottomless and sealed while they exerted a pressure on what they beheld.

"Huh," the man named Mano snorted, "He look ordinary as anybody to me."

The Grip did not take his eyes away from the Carolina Kid, who was now scanning the room. He wondered what he had expected. Had he thought the Kid would not show at all? Had he expected exactly what was there on the poster? Tom Zucold had said the Kid would change with the times, would not be what they might think. Still, there was a vague disappointment as he surveyed the man they would bet it all on. He wore a blue banlon shirt that did not open at the neck and matching blue-checked banlon pants. He had on white patent loafers with two gold tassles on each one and he wore no socks at all. The skin that The Grip could see at the end of the pants was an angry, chaffed red.

"Izzat him?" Plum Lee wailed. No one answered her so she added, "Look just like my old grandpa. He's the one that's a wino in Cleveland, you know?" Then the others were talking and each thought he looked another way. Could he, The Grip wondered, be different to each person? Wasn't there something he was that everybody could agree on and speak out? If not, what was this thing that Promise Land called onliness?

"Didn't think you'd make it, Pop," the blond stranger said just then, stepping out of the corner and offering his hand under the dim light.

"Name's Graham. Pupil Graham. My friends call me Pill," he giggled. "My daddy was a druggist see." There was a cheery buoyancy in Graham's voice that seemed to melt away when the Carolina Kid stepped to him and took the hand and held it.

"Know you, don't I boy," the Carolina Kid said. Graham squinted at the Kid, looked down into those eyes as if something was terribly wrong, then looked at the doorway as if for a signal. Sweat broke on his forehead and he pulled his head back. "Know your people too, don't I," the Carolina Kid said in that big voice that could rattle windows, only softly now.

"Some people said you was too old, Pop. Said you couldn't get out and keep your thing going." Pill Graham's voice quavered as he tried to bluff his way through.

"At's him ain't it, Firp?" Firp's boy said.

The Carolina Kid wheeled sharply to face the boy and the old man. His face flushed and tightened, the muscles in his exposed forearms rippled and knotted. The room breathed one slow breath. The Kid stepped forward and put his hand on top of the boy's head and said something that sounded like a growl. Then he looked into the crannies of the old man's face and growled louder. A man with a gold earring in his ear stood against the wall and laughed.

"Firp you can't do it. You promised," the boy said as tears fell onto his cheeks. "You brung me all this way and you been promising ever since I was born, right along regular, that you'd show him to me. Tell him he can't just kick us out this way," the boy said.

"You shithead," Billy Carmines hollered at the Carolina Kid.

Firp moved out from under the cabinets and raised himself up taller than he had appeared, then took hold of the boy's arm and said, "No use boy. It is done. He got the say to it." The old man stepped forward and dragged one leg. Then just as abruptly he stopped and reached a dirty envelope toward the breast pocket of his overalls. Before it reached the pocket, the Carolina Kid's hand snaked out and caught him by the wrist.

"What's this you got, old man?" the big slow voice drawled.

"Peoples always said you was a great one for teaching the kids dude, so let the little prick and the old man stay," a hard voice said. The Grip knew instantly it was Merci but everyone looked at her. The man with the gold earring laughed again.

The Carolina Kid spun around as if he had been slapped and faced the woman. "Why you cocks—," he whined. Then he burped a great rolling thunderous burp and he lifted his arm to point at her and said, "You urp urp whore urping urp." Instantly the Carolina Kid's face flushed and puffed and he seemed suddenly much older and fatter. He fought for control of his anger and his belching at the same time, then let out a thunderous burp.

"I ain't forgot that time in Memphis. And you was supposed to be dead," he said, his arm shaking like a divining rod that had just hit water.

The woman laughed so even the dim light sent sparks off her

black hair. "Some just ain't the dying kind, you dig? Why don't you just shoot or get, CK. You're only proving that smart people already know, words ain't deeds and it's deeds you take to the bank."

"Got that right," the earring man said.

"Shoot shithead," Billy Carmines said.

"Why you scabbed up bag of evil and pus, I'll—no. No I won't." The Carolina Kid looked back over his right shoulder at Pill Graham, then back at the woman who looked like she'd just got a big dividend check.

"Pilgrim, the best thing you can do is pray. Nine ball, cash down, in ten minutes." The Carolina Kid had turned and was through the door before Pill Graham stopped nodding his head.

"Ain't he got a nerve," Plum Lee said and sniffed. "Act like he's God hisself."

"Shut up Plum Lee," the odd man said and gave her a playful slap on the cheek.

"That lady got his number, look like," Turkey said. Heads nodded in agreement.

"Don't be fooled boys," Merci said, blowing out a mouthful of smoke. "They say you can get a powerful lick from a dead rattle-snake if you don't look to what you're doing. All CK ever did was play his game and he is still around. Some not."

"Used to be darlin'," Pill Graham said, "used to be around. Hadn't played this boy yet." His white comb whipped through his hair three times while heads swiveled and nodded and whispered in the room.

Ten minutes passed and then fifteen minutes. The room grew thicker with bluish smoke and the noise hurt The Grip's ears. He could hear many of the spectators swearing that the Carolina Kid wasn't coming back, that he had seen what he'd have to beat and made a quick re-treat. He wanted to stand up on the table and shout that it was a lie but each passing minute made him less certain. The back of his fatigue T-shirt was wet with the sweat that rolled off him. People were shuffling and arguing and there was almost a fight between one of the men with a plastic nametag and *Mano*.

"Peoples getting tight," The Grip said to Tom Zucold as he wiggled on the iron stove. He knew it was only the tension but the metal under him felt hot.

"Something's wrong," Tom Zucold said.

"Say wrong?"

"Been drinking."

"You ain't had that much," The Grip said softly. "I been watching."

"Not me, ape," Tom Zucold snapped, "Him."

Pill Graham was strutting around the table nervously. He kept looking at the door. His face had gone from a confident grin to a mask of creases that scowled anxiously. He stopped at the far end of the table, took a cue up and slammed it hard on the cushion.

"You people think I wouldn't play that old bastard anywhere in the world and beat him like a drum? Think I don't know what's going on? He ain't shakin' me with this old crap of making me wait." There was a film of sweat on Pill Graham's face and it shone on the curve of his nose.

"Settle down Pill baby," the shadow said from its position by the door.

"Right, man," the odd man said. "You in charge, baby."

"Man sound like he scared, don't he," Tom Zucold said at just the instant the room fell silent. The Grip felt the entire room telescope on the two of them. Heads turned to each other and whispered, eyes still on Tom Zucold and himself.

"Shoot," Pill Graham said in a voice full of false confidence. "Now is that something or not, you folks?" He swung his right arm in a wide arc and pointed it at them so The Grip felt he had just been introduced by Bob Barker.

"Something," Tom Zucold said and sipped his beer.

"See that old Carolina Kid, well he was around before my momma even knew where babies come from, got him many a trick." Pill Graham grinned and chalked the cue in his hand very slowly. "Like he'll leave a man to wait and wait and that man maybe will be looking for a sign or a word and none come. He wait and he wait and

136

suddenly somebody start putting a whisper in that man's ear, and it shake him up bad while he waiting. You folks see anybody here that might be planted for such a trick?"

All the eyes in the room turned on Tom Zucold. Tom Zucold tilted his tall can and finished the beer, then calmly set it on the stove behind him. The Grip heard everybody breathing.

"You sure are something, Pilgrim," Tom Zucold said. "But maybe not enough."

Pill Graham threw his hands up in the air so the cue fell clattering to the floor, then he said "A believer! Can you believe that?"

It was uncomfortably quiet in the room. Then the woman said, "I have put my money on Pill Graham. You people got any sense you will do the same."

"Evil talks," Tom Zucold said in a whisper so that only The Grip heard it.

"Let the woman talk. Sound like she knows things," the odd man said.

"It isn't none of my business here people. I'm just a working woman trying to make a buck. How about a cigarette there chum?" Merci took a cigarette from the man wearing the nametag that said DeMott, lit it, and puffed. She grinned at The Grip and winked.

"Course I told you about CK so it is only fair to tell you everything, I guess," she said and brushed a bit of ash from her black silk pants.

"That's right, only fair," a man said.

"Pill Graham here is been to the war. He is a veteran. The man has seen and smelled death and puke and the gizzards of babies. Been wounded bad, too. Fact is that he ain't even got a heart that is a real heart. Got a kind of machine in there. Sucker just ticks on and on. Man with a heart like that, how can he lose? CK just cannot do anything, you dig?"

"He ain't got any heart at all," Firp's boy said.

"Might can do something," The Grip said, astonished to hear his voice in his mouth.

"He jogs five miles a day. Drinks carrot juice. Goes to Kiwanis meetings. Is president of the high school booster club. Ain't but twenty-eight years old," Merci said, ignoring The Grip. "Got a regulation pool table in his recreation room and he practices on it most every night. He is prime, a prime dude."

"Something to that, Trucker says, which is me," the man with the earring said, barely opening his eyes as he leaned against the wall. "Course everybody chickenshit anyway, prime or not. Where's that other fucker?"

"Bullshit," Tom Zucold said. "He coming tonight."

"Well it ain't never meant much to me anyway," Plum Lee said and got up and moved toward the door. "Hope it isn't anybody gets my place. I got to tee-tee."

"Who'd want it?" the odd man said and slapped her on the butt.

"What the fuck is a tee-tee?" Trucker said and shook his head.

Out of the corner of his eye The Grip saw the man with the Gulf Oil shirt that said *Mano* step in front of him. The man was thick and dirty and had long greasy hair.

"Got a cigarette sport?" *Mano* said.

"Don't pay him no attention," Tom Zucold said. "Remember, you promised to stay out the pen for six months anyway."

But The Grip's attention was already gone. The look on *Mano*'s face was one The Grip had seen often in the Army, the deep pupils that darted sideways just to be sure what was there, a kind of intense maliciousness that seemed to pack itself tight under the puffed flesh.

"Don't smoke," The Grip said, choosing his words carefully and feeling a little tingle of danger at the base of his skull.

"I'd ask for a drink but it's only pussies like to lap up that cat-piss you got there." *Mano* did not laugh or even grin. He was trying to insult The Grip into a false move. The man wanted a fight and The Grip knew that he would not stop.

"You this Graham fellow's sister?" Tom Zucold snapped. "He ain't gone win no matter what you put out."

"Hey man," *Mano* said, his threats muted now by the laughter of the people in the room, "*Mano* don't give a fat rat's ass who win."

138

He thumped his chest and turned to face those still laughing. "You assholes just a bunch of losers, know whatta mean?"

Tom Zucold knew things. The Grip had always been impressed with what the old man knew and he hadn't ever been able to see how he knew things. Without a hint, Tom Zucold had known *Mano* was going to turn and throw a punch. When the punch came Tom Zucold met it with a cast iron frying pan that had been hanging on the wall. The first sound was meaty and soft. The second was *Mano*'s scream and the third was more laughter. *Mano* went out to the bar cursing and holding his hand.

"Just like a cartoon," Tom Zucold said solemnly. "Why don't they ever learn?"

A telephone rang out in the bar. Then there was the sound of breaking glass. Suddenly there was a commotion at the door and The Grip thought that *Mano* was back with real trouble.

"Jees, what is it?" Firp's boy squealed from the corner.

"Hope it ain't what I think," Tom Zucold said. His eyes were trained on the door and he was as frozen as a hawk.

It turned out to be only a couple of drunk Moose regulars, they claimed, who had heard there was a pool table in the kitchen and thought they'd just shoot a few games.

"More pilgrims," Tom Zucold said thoughtfully. "Not what I thought. Not yet, anyways."

"How much time now?" Pill Graham called over the table to the shadow man at the door.

"Forty-six minutes."

"Give," Pill Graham said.

The room slowly fell into attentive silence. You could hear ice cubes click in bourbons with water. Pill Graham and everybody else watched the shadow man place a leather case on the green felt. He unlocked it with a key that looked like gold. When the top of the case went back and the man lifted out a section, the people made an audible insuck. When he had lifted out the second piece they released their breath. Then the man assembled the pool cue and held it to the light and sighted it. Satisfied, he removed the case and rolled the cue on the felt. That test, too, the cue passed.

"Balanced," the man said and handed the cue to Pill Graham, then sank back against the wall where he'd emerged. Holding the cue to the light again, Graham resighted.

"Well kiss my ass," the Carolina Kid barked into the room. Everyone looked up to see him standing in the doorway, a dozen faces behind him pressing to see what was going on. The Kid wore the same shoes and no socks but now he wore only a pair of yellow boxer shorts and a fishnet T-shirt with them. His face was redder than ever and his eyes looked pink.

"I knew it. Goddammit I knew it," Tom Zucold snorted.

"You motherfuckers think you go'me," the Carolina Kid said, swaying backward. He held a glass half full of whiskey in his right hand and as he lurched he slammed it down on the felt table. He looked surprised when it did not break and leaned against the cushion to look closer at it. He laid his head on his forearms for a moment, his feet pushed behind him in an obvious attempt to keep himself upright. When he raised his head, his eyes were glazed and he was drooling a little.

"Mean fucken trick ast me." He was speaking into the table. "Steal a man's cue that is got best friggin' balance inna world is low, man. Thass low."

"Jesus, he's drunk," the earring man said.

The Carolina Kid pushed himself back from the table and swayed upright then looked at the man who had just spoken.

"Thass cute, that earring." He grinned broadly and waved at the people bunched in the corner of the room. "Ain't that cute? Les give him a round of hands." He winked at the man with the earring. "I know who you are, Grit."

Pill Graham started to unscrew his pool cue.

"Think I don't know you, too, you slimy cocksucker?" the Carolina Kid shouted, turning so fast that he slipped to one knee but managed to hang onto the table. "Think I don't know who stole my cue?" The man pulled himself upright once more and said, "Thass all right though. Can play with any ole stick." He stumbled toward the wall rack of cues and took one down to sight it.

"Ain't that hell, him drunk," Tom Zucold said through wire-tight jaws. His skin was Cadillac Ermine white and he was clenching the stove with knuckles that paled of blood.

The Carolina Kid was sighting his stick in the air when he swayed and passed out on the floor. Or seemed to have passed out, for he was once again pulling himself up by the table and then standing with the table as leverage.

"All you peoples here can't beat me now or never and that ain't no piss in the boot," the Kid slurred. "Ain't that the gospel, Merci baby?" He looked up at the woman and she blew him a kiss and laughed.

"You," the Kid said to Pill Graham who had retreated near Tom Zucold and The Grip and who now watched his drunken opponent across the table, "you think you such a hot shit. Beat yous daddy and yous daddydaddy and don't know who all. Testin' me f'Christ's sake. Testin' me. Ain't no hotter shit'n any the rest and I gone beat you like a beer headache. Yessir, I gone—"

The Carolina Kid had seen the old man in the corner and his boy. He blinked and shook his head and looked again. He seemed to be standing more upright and swaying less.

"What's wrong with him, Firp?" the boy said, tears welling over the bottoms of his eyes and staining his cheeks. "He ain't like him, not like you said."

The Grip wasn't sure but he thought that the Carolina Kid had flinched as if he were stung. He raised the arm that had been so weak and planted it hard in midair, his finger aimed at the old man Firp. The Grip saw with surprise that it was a gnarled finger and hand, an old hand, as if this were a man of the dirt or the machine, not a pool player. The voice came again, the deep strong voice that was like a windhowl, and said, "Get that fucken kid out of here or you'll wish in Hell you never heard your name said."

The boy ducked behind Firp's great overalls and could hardly be seen. Firp put out both of his big hands as if to ward off a pressing force and said, "We going, Mr. Carolina, if that is who you is. Don't say no more. No call to scare a poor boy. No call. And he come a long way to see you."

The old man turned and hugged the boy to his belly and started to shuffle toward the door. When he had reached it, he stopped and said, "Don't think folks won't hear about you neither. Me and him and his children's children gone spread the word on you buster. Down to Zuni, Virginia, you won't be much higher than a mound of pig shit." Then the old man and the boy were lost in the darkness beyond that room.

For only an instant it was thickly quiet until the Carolina Kid picked up a pool cue and flung it like a spear into the cabinet where the old man had stood. Dishes shattered and spilled onto the floor.

"Thass how much I care what you peoples say. Thass how goddamn mush," he said, swaying backward, suddenly drunk again, or at least less controlled. "What do you people know about anything anyway? Not half of it, not a fraction of it. Fuck around all your life and think nothing gone ever happen to you and wantin' somebody always to carry you, come along and save your bacon. Yeah, go and shake you heads. I seen it and you know thass the truth. Want me to carry you ass right now. Think I ain't sick of you bellyachin' and you stinkin' piddly towns and backrooms that always stink of vomit? Think I ain't up to my ass in your miserable dreams? I ain't carryin' you bastards forever. Hear me? Hah? I can't do it no more."

The Carolina Kid leaned back against the pool table and swept up the glass of whiskey and took it all in one swallow. When he glared at The Grip, his face had the same fixed, pained, raging expression The Grip had seen on shotputters at the point of maximum effort.

"Don't look like you might can play this evening, pardner," Pill Graham said quietly.

"Maybe it is the night to send the old fart back to his mountain for good. The only thing left of him is the memory," Merci hissed. Her voice cut through the room like a saw's whine.

Slowly the Carolina Kid rolled himself over so that he sat on the cushion of the table and faced her. For a long time he just looked, as if he were thinking of something to say or trying to understand where he was. "Maybe it is time for some true confessions in that bus of yours, Pretty. Maybe we can get to that when I have cleaned this young pilgrim. What do you say, Pretty? Come on and gimme some kind of answer now—I got to pee quick."

The Kid never stopped watching the woman as he rose and backed toward the door which someone now had shut. He reached his right arm up and drew his forearm across the length of his mouth, wiping drool and whiskey, still waiting for an answer.

As if it were a slow-motion film, The Grip knew what was going to happen even before it did happen. He saw the Kid's elbow rising, backing, meeting at its apex the full impact of the door which Plum Lee had just then pushed, sending the emptied whiskey glass sailing directly across the room where it shattered on Tom Zucold's forehead, which was just that instant delivered of the protective baseball cap, letting the blood instantly rise and slide into the white whiskery eyebrows. He saw, almost simultaneously, the Kid himself, spun by the force of this blow, carom off the table and, clutching the fractured elbow, fall moaning at the feet of the odd man. It amazed him that he could see it all as if he had designed the whole action.

"I hope I didn't hurt nobody," Plum Lee said as she breezed in and took her seat.

"Jesus Motherfucking H. Christ," the Carolina Kid said to the elbow he cradled in one hand.

Tom Zucold peeped out from under a handkerchief he had whipped from his jacket, the white cloth already mostly red, and said "It is broke? Is the sumbitch's arm broke?"

The Carolina Kid looked up then, grinned and said, "Bet your ass it is broke. Gimme a drink will you friend?"

"Ain't never seen anything to beat it," Tom Zucold said. He sounded almost proud. He lowered his handkerchief and saw that the blood had stopped. It was, after all, a shallow cut. "Somebody give the chief a drink," Tom commanded, and somebody did.

The Kid took the plastic cup of whiskey and knocked it back, then moaned a little.

"Maybe you should try later," Pill Graham said. Until then he had stayed back in the shadows of the corner.

"Fucken A, son, let's play," the Carolina Kid said. He slowly forced himself to straighten out his arm. "Look at that. It ain't broke, just bunged up. Gimp, maybe, but the Kid gone play. Fucken A. And he ain't playin' for nobody but hisself." He stopped and looked around the room. Then he said, "Hopin' you peoples hear that. CK don't play for naught but hisself from now on until."

"But you can't do that," The Grip blurted. He hadn't meant to speak. He didn't know he was going to speak. He wished he hadn't done it. But he knew what he had said was true. They were just donating their money if the Kid took that attitude.

"Who you?" the Carolina Kid asked.

"Who is he?" the Carolina Kid said to Tom Zucold.

"Ain't nobody."

"Somebody," Merci cooed from the background.

"He a friend of Pretty's?"

The Grip saw that the Carolina Kid was about to go again and he leaped to his feet but he was too late and it was too far. The Kid's head hit the floor with a thud. He had passed out cold.

"Well that ties it," Tom Zucold said as he slid to the floor. "I ain't putting a nickel on that asshole. Even if I did wait all my life to see him just once. Make me hot, whoo."

The Grip had already kneeled down and taken the Carolina Kid into his arms. He was not quite limp and he was not entirely unconscious. He kept mumbling as The Grip lifted him.

The odd man stood on his chair. He was only a few feet from The Grip. He seemed to be speaking to the Carolina Kid and he said "You can't do this. You got to play. You will play because we got all these assholes' money and we gone to win it. That's the agreement you made."

"I guess that makes me king of the cats," Pill Graham said off in the corner.

The Grip would think to himself later that it might have been all right if the odd man had not said anything just then. Or if Tom Zucold had not heard what the odd man said. Or if Tom Zucold had not been pushed just that little bit too far by what the odd man said. But it was possible that nothing could have changed what was already happening when he cradled the Carolina Kid in his arms so that the dim light threw their shadows onto the wall in the form of a cross that became a spider as soon as Tom Zucold leaped up and grabbed the odd man by the throat and started to bang the odd man's head against the wall. Then there was the sound of glass breaking and of furniture cracking. There was the soft smack of flesh against flesh and the gusts of pain. The Grip saw them coming at him and being flung from him when he swung the Carolina Kid around like a weapon. He knew it couldn't be so but he thought he had heard the Kid tell him to twirl and he thought the Kid's body had gone rigid in his arms, but he could not be sure in the heat of the brawl.

It was almost over when the pool cue knifed down out of nowhere and struck The Grip's right eye so that he saw a bolt of lightning and tumbled backward to strike the base of his skull against the pool table. He saw the room start to spin and saw the Carolina Kid's face rising away from his own until he thought it was a shot he had put. He tried to watch it as it flew up and arced and then it was gone and everything was black and he could hear the surf of the ocean breaking not far away.

"He waking up," The Grip heard a small voice say.

His eyes were open now and it was dark. He was afraid and sore and he didn't know where he was. There was a small pale face hovering over his own and he thought at first he was staring at the poster of the Carolina Kid.

"Kid's going to play." The Grip spoke slowly through swollen lips, then let his eyes close again. "Soon."

"He waking up, Firp. Hurry. He waking up."

The Grip's eyes opened again and the face was gone. There was only the black night and off to one side a blue flourescent moon. He blinked, feeling a sharp pain at the corner of his right eye, then saw that it was not a moon at all but a street light.

"Where's the Kid?" The Grip said to the light.

"He's here," another voice said, then a large shadow fell across him. "Don't try to move yet cause you hurt. You hurt right good and we taking care of you."

"Ain't bleeding no more, Firp," the boy said behind the old man. "Maybe he wants something to drink."

The Grip groaned.

"Take time, boy," Firp said. "Him took one hell of a beating. Look like they was after him way they all got on him. Man can't stand too much, any man." The shadow that spoke kneeled beside The Grip and then lay its head on his chest like it meant to sleep. The head made a gentle pressure on his chest that was nevertheless enough to pop The Grip's mouth open in a little involuntary cry of pain. His chest felt on fire.

"Sorry, sorry," the head said as it moved back quickly. "Heart beating good now. Sound strong." The shadow stood up and stepped out of the light.

"Wonder he can talk," the boy said.

"He can talk all right," Firp said, "but it must hurt some. Maybe he ain't got anything that important to say right now."

The Grip parted his lips again and tried to speak. At first the words came out as little yips and hisses. His tongue felt thicker than usual and it hurt. With it, he felt little shreds of flesh on the inside of his cheeks and he tasted blood.

"I'm all right," The Grip said at last. He lay very still.

"That's the wonder of it," Firp said and leaned down to look into his face. "They like to stomp the pure shit out of you. Hadn't a been for that pool player coming to like that we'd be carting you home in a box. God only knows how he come to swing that pool cue so good. Funniest damn thing you ever saw, them people getting swatted that way. Ain't that so, boy?"

The boy nodded and rocked on his heels in the dark and said something that sounded like "Mmmm unh."

"Room was jumping for sure," Firp went on. "People getting knocked on they head and blood flying so and I don't think that Kid had no idea who he was hitting. Just hitting, look like. Boy here ain't got any sense and broke loose of my hand and run back in there. Don't know how he didn't get hit."

"Firp come in after me," the boy said proudly, "and it was mostly over then so we drug you out here."

"Dumb luck is all I know," Firp said.

"Boy you sure do look awful," the boy said.

"Hush boy," Firp snapped.

"Well he does, don't he?"

"Where's Tom Zucold?" The Grip moaned.

"Who?" Firp asked. He kneeled again and laid a cold wet rag on The Grip's lumpy forehead.

"Old man," The Grip whispered.

"Oh him. That started it all," Firp said and started to laugh. "Lord didn't he grab aholt that man's throat now."

"We got him too," the boy said. "Got him yonder in the back of his truck."

"Hurt," The Grip said and lifted his head as if to rise up.

"Guess you do hurt, all what they did," the boy said.

"Not him, boy. He mean is that old man hurt," Firp said sharply. "He ain't hurt, don't worry. Not on his body anyways. Look like something maybe inside though. Said he don't want to talk to nobody. Come out here when it was all over playing and he seen you laying here and walked right to that truck. He didn't say a word. I went over there and told him you's hurt and we made you comfortable. He say he didn't want to talk none."

"Firp say he probably too hurt to talk. I don't like him none," the boy said.

"Finished playing?" The Grip groaned and pushed himself up with one hand so that he was half sitting. His chest felt like someone had dug potatoes in it, the pain sharp and spreading. It was hard to breathe, as if someone were sitting on him. His head throbbed and his face ached.

Firp leaned over him and looked hard. "Hold on there. Didn't I tell you them fellows crucified you? I said the old man was all right. Didn't say nothing about you. Might be they fixed something in you for life that a ordinary old man like me can't tell about."

"TV say don't never move the victim," the boy said importantly.

"Then how you gone help a man, answer me that?" Firp snapped right back. "What if he lying in the road from a wreck or got throwed by the tractor? You just leave him there?"

The boy shrugged in the darkness, then turned and went to the truck.

Firp kneeled beside The Grip again and said, "Boy a good boy but he don't know any more than he got a right to. Telling you now, you got to rest up and lay down. We here with you."

The boy was back. He reached toward Firp and The Grip saw a gleam in the blue light.

"Here, drink some of this," Firp said. He put the mouth of a bottle to The Grip's lips.

"Keep some back Firp. You need it to get home on," the boy said.

"Hush boy. He need it a whole lot worse than an old man."

The Grip was sitting upright on the concrete now. It felt warm from the afternoon sun. He pushed his thick tongue against one of his front teeth and felt it move. It hurt. There was no tooth to push beside it, only a slick hole and a tendril of skin. He felt around with his tongue and found only one tooth broken off, its edge sharp and surprising. He took the bottle and tilted it to let the liquid in. It came with a searing at lips, tongue, and gums, then with a spreading heat as it passed down and into his body. He blinked back water at his eyes and sniffed where his nose started to drip. After the initial shock, the heat of the whiskey made him feel a little better so he drank harder and felt his face flushing.

"Firp made that medicine himself," the boy said. He seemed to The Grip to be hovering at the edge of the darkness like a moth.

"Stand up," The Grip said, his voice hard and low, and handed the bottle to the old man who handed it in turn to the boy. "Got to stand up. Ain't gone lay down no more."

Together the old man and The Grip took a deep breath and shuddered and began to push his great body upright. The Grip's legs seemed stripped of muscle but slowly he felt the strength coming back and then he stood, the old man's arm at his waist and his tobacco breath in his face.

"Be OK," The Grip said but he made no move to stand on his own.

"Man sometimes need a good kick. Mule done it to me once. Then a man need somebody to help him see how he might can stand again," the boy said.

Firp laughed. "Listen at that wise old man telling things."

The Grip tried to take a step, felt his legs buckle, and was held up by the old man who seemed as strong as a tree though he hadn't looked it.

"Sometimes the first is the hardest," Firp said.

"He mean the first step," the boy said.

"Boy where'd you learn to be so lippy?" Firp hissed. Then he jerked his head and said, "Get it ready."

It turned out that Firp meant for the boy, whose name was Bob, to open the rear gate of the Ford Ranger pickup with the camper shell that they had come in. The Grip made Firp help him over to the back of the panel truck where Tom Zucold sat staring at the night, but Tom Zucold would not speak. After a while, Firp helped The Grip sit on the tailgate and fixed him a sandwich of bologna and mustard and then gave him a cup of scalding coffee. Bob told The Grip it was what they always had when they went fishing and that was almost all they ever did.

"Playing finished?" The Grip said between mouthfuls of the sandwich that burned the inside of his mouth.

"Ain't much to tell, is it boy?" Firp said over his coffee. "We done got you out of there and time we seen you was gone live that shooter was near done. Man come roaring out and say that old fart too drunk to win, say that young fellow name Graham was cleaning him out. Anyways, they long gone now."

"Wadn't no good anyway. I'm glad I didn't have no bet on him," the boy said with obvious bitterness.

"Ain't so sure. Maybe this is just a bad night. Man can have a bad night, boy. He been around a long time. Got a lot of pressure on him."

"What pressure? He don't care about nothing but him. Said so didn't he?" the boy said.

The Grip looked off in the darkness and chewed his sandwich as he tried to let it all sink in. There was such a distance between the man on the poster and the player he had seen. It wasn't the man's fault. They had all come together because of the man but he owed them nothing, not when they saw what he was. He hadn't asked them to bet on him. He had even told them he was playing only for himself.

"Carolina Kid lose?" The Grip asked almost in defiance of the logic he had followed out in his head. Something wasn't connecting. He and Tom Zucold had bet everything on a match that was over and he had not even seen it. Was that how it was for everybody? Would it always be win and lose and not even see what happened?

"Man say he lost every single game," Firp said as he lit his pipe. "Funny thing is, man said he was all that drunk and yet it look like he knowed exactly what he was doing. Like who he was gonna hit with that cue, now I think about it."

"Lost everything," The Grip said absently.

"Everything," Firp echoed, looking hard at The Grip through the cloud of pipe smoke, looking as if he expected to see something that he had seen before.

"He was a pure disappointment," the boy said. His small voice was heavy with regret.

"Don't be too sure things are what they look like," Firp said, keeping his eyes fixed on The Grip. A small cloud issued from his mouth, then another and another.

"You give that old man the bottle I told you to give him?" Firp's voice was lower and firmer, almost as if it belonged to another person. He watched The Grip carefully.

"Shoot, he never even said thank you. Some manners, ask me."

"He just tired, Bob. Everybody is tired. Hard to keep carrying on when you are tired. Just like that player saying that he ain't gone carry nobody any more, say they got to look out for theyselves. He knows none of us can keep on much without everybody else helping out some. He tired. Probably wouldn't have said that last week and likely won't say it tomorrow. Just squeezed that's all. Everybody gets squeezed."

"Lost," The Grip said. His mouth was open and slack and his great body slumped over so that his head hung down. He was sitting on the tailgate now and staring into the asphalt of the parking lot. It didn't matter where he looked because everything he saw or could see except Firp's face was black. Before him, sitting in an aluminum lawn chair, Firp watched him, his own face blued by the streetlight and gleaming.

"Squeezed," Firp said evenly.

"Lost," The Grip said.

The Grip drove the panel truck down Atlantic Avenue, slipping almost soundlessly into and out of the blue puddles of streetlight. There was hardly anyone out this late and he drove slowly, his bulk hunched uncomfortably in the hard seat. Tom Zucold sat in the Corvette chair and glared at the dark fronts of stores as they passed. He had not said a word since The Grip had told him to get up front in the Corvette chair.

He slowed for a cat that stopped in the middle of the road and did not know which way to run, then shifted, and ran along smoothly. He was surprised the truck was so easy to drive. He had driven trucks in the Army but not regularly and had not driven much for longer than he could remember. He liked the pleasure of the wheel and the shifting except that he hurt and the memory of their money kept intruding. Oddly, though, the lost money did not seem all that important to him. In fact, he wondered why it didn't cut deeper than it did. There was even a kind of cheeriness that he felt building inside of him and he made certain to keep it repressed. He began to think about the flat shine of puts whistling up in the air.

"Whoa," Tom Zucold shouted suddenly. The Grip was so startled that he glided silently on before remembering to apply the brakes.

"Goddamn asshole monkey, stop this vehicle," Tom Zucold shouted and hit him in the face with his baseball cap just as he had touched the brake pedal.

"You see it? I seen it. Right back there," Tom Zucold hissed as he turned in his seat and rose to his knees and looked out the window. "There it is. Goddamn me if that ain't it. Back this baby up, if you can do that."

"What is it?"

"It is it. Her bus. What she call it, The Confessional?" Tom Zucold was leaning out the truck and waving The Grip backward even though the car was still. He dropped back in. "What the hell you waiting for? Let's go."

"Ain't gone do any good."

"The hell you say," Tom Zucold said. "I been thinking all night and I see how it all fits." He was leaning out the window and waving furiously.

"You old fart, she didn't beat anybody. He did." The Grip was talking to Tom Zucold's backside and he wasn't moving the car. He hurt all over. "Don't you know when to quit? What can you do now? Leave that bus be." He didn't know what Tom Zucold intended but it couldn't be good and whatever it was he'd be in the middle of it.

Tom Zucold turned around and dropped back into the Corvette chair and for a few moments said nothing. The truck idled comfortably and there were no cars anywhere.

"Who do you think sponsored that Graham? That means put up the money? What the hell made that Kid get drunk on the one time he can save me? They in it together, bet me," Tom Zucold said to the front windshield. He waited then and finally said "Money."

"Money?"

"Her biddnes. Goes where the game is. Ain't no game, she make one up. Them two play for her, look like. Ittis old as spit." Tom Zucold's face was almost as black as the night and looked cramped when it turned to The Grip.

"Money?"

"They done took it. All we had, don't you see nothing? They take away everything you got. Time is money. They done took time from Tom Zucold and next thing they want is his land. Fuck 'em. Just like a woman too. Back this goddamn thing up."

"How you know?"

"Some things a man knows, is all. Like knowing a woman has done fucked another man on you. You just *know*. Move it, boy."

"Wasn't our money to start with," The Grip said. He wanted to reason with Tom Zucold but he was tired and he hurt and it was apparent to him that the old man was a knot of poison now. He would listen to no one.

The Grip got it in gear, slid left down a dark street, went left twice more and eased up behind The Confessional that was parked before a closed taffy parlor.

"What are you going to do?" The Grip asked as he turned the lights off.

"Ain't much a man can do look like," Tom Zucold barked and flung the door open, then stepped onto the sidewalk. He eased the door shut and leaned in through the window. "Course if you programmed right it is always something inside you they can't fuck. Don't anybody know that better than that fake drunk pool player. It's like a carburetor, boy. Turn them jetscrews this way and then that way and get it all clean and then turn them some more. Get it tighter and cleaner and you figure out the right spot sooner or later. You just can't sit and wait for them screws to move theyselves. It is the plan."

Then the old man was gone from the window. He opened the rear door of the truck. Reaching under a tarp, he pulled out a gallon paint can and large brush.

Within minutes a large hand holding up its middle finger had appeared on the back end of the pearl bus. The Grip had pulled the panel truck up close so that Tom Zucold could stand on the bumper to work and each stroke of the thick black paint hurt him almost as much as he knew it would hurt the woman whose bus it was. Then he watched Tom Zucold draw lines and clumsy figures of men's genitals and women's mouths—the same kind of stuff he had seen in every bathroom he had ever been in while he was in the Army. It was crazy, pure craziness.

"That's the plan, soldier," Tom Zucold said as The Grip drove off into the darkness, his baseball hat with STARS on the front jammed down tight on his head.

CHAPTER V

Blue Moves

He had been better programmed even than either of them had thought, so it took The Grip only a few days to shake the soreness of the beating and in a week the bruises were only a memory. It was June now, early in the month, with that fine special softness that June near the Atlantic Ocean always brings. The nights were humid and warm and felt like velvet if you took a walk or went riding. Where the pines were thick there would be a cold patch of air and in the mornings the dew was like a silver paint on everything. The birds sang deep in their breasts and baby rabbits appeared in the putting lane and teenagers roared by the killer tree all day long and late into the night. But there was also in early June the chance of extremes in that fine weather, late frosts that nipped the vegetables or sweltering heat and drought that drained the water reservoirs.

The Grip could not remember feeling better in his life, tighter, more tuned and happy. But he felt that something was about to explode. It was a sourceless fear and he was able to dismiss it most of the time. He found work to do in the Bowie Garage, plugs to wire-brush, parts to strip from or add to the processees, oil changes, even the few minor repairs that Tom Zucold had begun to trust him to do. When he was free of these duties, he went to the lane and began the laborious process of working his puts back to the level he'd attained before the Moose Hall. Tom Zucold managed to do enough business, primarily because of his padded prices, to keep occupied. But it was clear to both of them that the Bowie Garage had died and was merely lingering in nervous spasms. Neither of them seemed for a while to have an idea that there was anything to look forward to. Life seemed stopped in its tracks.

"We can hope things'll get better," The Grip had said one afternoon when there had been no customers at all.

"Hope?" Tom Zucold shot back. "Thought you seen what Hope amounted to out there in them shot tires."

The next day, early enough that Tom Zucold did not have the main overhead door open for business yet, Promise Land showed up with her pink Harley and asked Tom Zucold to check it out and clean it up. She had decided to sell the motorcycle, she said, and buy a glider plane.

Tom Zucold circled the motorcycle warily, peering through eyes that were surprisingly red, and touched it here and there to see if it would respond.

"Hmmm," Tom Zucold said. He circled it again. "Yep," he said. He honked the horn and touched the chain and said "Uh oh."

"Well, whatever it is, Darling, please fix it up. Got to run, coffee at Mrs. Evans' house this morning. Grip, we *must* get together again soon. See you, sweetie." She blew him a kiss and jogged back to Yorktown Road where the Chevrolet station wagon and Cotton Muddleman were waiting for her.

"Poison," Tom Zucold said. He was looking at the Harley but The Grip was certain that that was not what the old man meant.

When she picked up her motorcycle the next morning, nearer to noon this time, Promise Land picked him up as well. They rode most of the day, stopping in the later afternoon at Buckroe Beach and walking alone for an hour. Then it was time for dinner and they ate hotdogs at the Amusement Pavilion, the music of the merry-go-round just behind them. Men boldly looked at Promise Land when they walked past and some whistled, waiting cautiously until they were far enough away that the big fellow with the woman couldn't possibly suspect. But he did. He tensed with anger. The angrier The Grip got the more it seemed she bubbled and shined and made herself obvious. He wanted to touch her again, to hold her, to hide her from all those eyes. She wanted to be seen, to dance and sing, to bloom in the light.

"I love you," The Grip said when he uncoiled from the pink Harley and stood in the front yard of the Bowie Garage.

"You said that before," she answered above the rumble of the engine, "but it's always nice to hear."

He looked at her bluntly and for what seemed like a long time. He felt that there were words which could say what he felt, even though he did not himself know exactly what he felt, and he would wait for them. He thought that surely they would come if he was patient.

"Yes?" she said. He did not answer.

"Look Grip, I like you a lot you know? But love is serious. I don't know if there is such a thing. You're trying to say something, I can see that. But I won't be able to answer when you do say it. Remember what I said about onliness? It's that onliness which makes love so impossible, don't you see. It keeps us separate when love tries to bring us together. Oh God, I'm sounding like a Baptist seminary student." Promise Land sighed and looked across the road at the ruins of Clifton's momma's house.

"I know," he said.

"No, you don't," Promise Land said, louder than she had meant,

"That's the problem. You don't know. All you know is what that warped old man wants you to know. Listen there's a kind of special you inside yourself, a kind of tiny faceless you that nobody can touch even if they want to. If they could get to it, maybe real love could happen. Do you see?"

"Mine ain't never been touched," The Grip said. A mockingbird jeered in the silence that fell between them.

She looked at him in the darkness and he could barely see her face, even with the reflected light from the motorcycle. Then he saw her lean to him and he leaned and she kissed him.

"Listen, I have to go. I'll be in touch—maybe you'll get yours touched." She laughed and waved and then rumbled off down the road.

It was toward late afternoon in the crease between the afternoon wanderers and the home-from-work traffic that Tom Zucold looked up from his creeper and out from under the Pinto whose gas tank he spent half an hour admiring. He liked any car named after a horse and as a boy he had a special fondness for pintos. The woman who'd left this one had read about a gas tank recall on Pintos, had dropped it off and told him to fix anything he saw, no matter what the cost. For more than half an hour he had lain there looking at the crud-covered tank and its seams. There was nothing to do and he would do nothing. Except that he would charge her a cool twenty-five and mumble about statistics and seam analysis. It had made for a very pleasant time lying there remembering all the horses he had ridden. That is until he heard it.

Then he saw it. He lifted his head and banged it on the under-carriage so that crud dusted down into his eyes but he saw it anyway. He had been waiting for it. Expecting it. He scooted forward on the creeper and leaped to his feet. The big crowbar was right where he had put it, just inside the door, and the 12-gauge Winchester Pump, Model 12, was right beside the bar if that was needed. He had taken the precaution of loading the shotgun.

By the time the woman stopped the bus in front of the door, the crowbar had made deep dents in both front fenders and one in the hood for good measure. Then he stood by the driver's side while the woman nearly pulled off her hook trying to get the little window open. He could see that she was livid. Her eyes were bugging out and she seemed to be panting.

"You sawed-off little sack of shit, what the hell are you doing?" Tom Zucold grinned as she called him every name he would have been able to think of and a lot he had not imagined. She waved her hook at him and threatened to sue for damage. If that didn't work, she said, she'd find a way to take it out of his hide. She raged, she pleaded, she reasoned.

"Knowed you be back," Tom Zucold said at last. He stood with his arms folded at the chest like a proud grandfather. The crowbar hung from one hand.

"What the hell you expect you moron?" She looked at him incredulously. "You owe me a new paint job at the least and I mean to see that you pay. You might think it is all right to stick it to a lady but you don't know this lady, Jack."

"Try me," Tom Zucold said. He had exhausted his patience.

"There's ways old man. Don't think there ain't."

Tom Zucold walked up to the window where the tight face was thrust out at him, whipped back the crowbar, and smashed the first window behind her. Then he stepped back and said "Get."

When she glared at him and did nothing, Tom Zucold smashed the next window and then another. By then she was grinding the gears and whining the bus backward into Yorktown Road. Probably somebody would come flying around there and kill her, maybe themselves too, Tom Zucold thought. The thought did not affect him. It merely passed.

He was back on the creeper under the Pinto when a voice said, "Busy day there chief?" It was a thick voice, a man's voice, but he didn't recognize it.

"Trooper Drilling by God," Tom Zucold said cheerily when he had gotten off the creeper. "How's that car you bought off me."

"Well now that car is a whole nother story, Colonel." Trooper

Drilling had gotten in the habit of calling Tom Zucold Colonel. He knew that Tom Zucold liked this rank. "Yessir, a whole story. Don't get me wrong, here, you understand. Gone make that honey hum. Yessir! Right now, though, I got her jacked up behind the house. Keep them tires from dry-rotting, see. They do that so easy make a man's head spin."

Tom Zucold agreed that tires did dry-rot quick in the humid weather and it was a good idea to jack it up like that.

"How about something to drink, Troop?" Tom Zucold thought it was a better idea to stay on the right side of the law as long as you could. Besides he liked Trooper Drilling anyway and more than that he was nervous whenever Trooper Drilling had his hand resting on the chrome-plated pistol at his waist. Trooper Drilling liked to rest his hand on the pistol a lot, in fact all the time except when he had something to drink or eat in his hands.

"Don't drink on duty, Colonel. Not off duty either, unless I have to. Circumstances might dictate that, you understand. Will take a Gatorade if you got one. Puts that liquid and salt back into your system, way I heard it. Scientific drink, they tell me. Man big as me sweat a lot when he ride around in that cruiser so he got to drink a lot of the right stuff."

Tom Zucold had already gone into the house to get one of The Grip's Gatorades because he knew it was what Trooper Drilling liked best of all.

"What can I do for you today, Troop?" Tom Zucold sat on the bumper of the Pinto and watched Yorktown Road.

"Not much, I reckon, Colonel. Heard tell the town said it was too many accidents at that tree out there. Said they might send a crew out to cut the sucker down." Trooper Drilling spoke with a melodramatic staccato delivery of words. He kept his lips as still as he could, apparently suspecting that the information he had come to deliver might be overheard by the wrong person.

"What tree?"

"Of course no question of where I heard this. You understand. I can't reveal my sources." Trooper Drilling was staring at the top of a great elm while he spoke. He wore his Smokey Bear hat and his reflector sunglasses and he seemed to be entertaining an idea that he hadn't decided on yet.

"What tree you talking about, Troop?"

"Come again, Colonel?" Trooper Drilling looked down out of the sun and great blank eyes that held only tiny Tom Zucolds looked at Tom Zucold. Then he grinned, drawing his pale brown lips slowly back over an enormous set of white teeth.

"Your tree, Colonel. That killer tree at the road there," Trooper Drilling said and gave the faintest jerk of his head to show the direction.

"Cut my tree down?" Tom Zucold said. He was baffled, as if it was simply beyond the pale of comprehension that anyone would want to cut down a tree in his yard.

"Probably send a crew and a truck when the occupants are out," Trooper Drilling said in that stuttered delivery. He had resumed staring at the top of the elm tree, his posture upright, correct, and rigid. Once again he appeared to be gradually allowing himself to reveal something whose entirety he knew or guessed. "Probably won't come after dark. Mens don't like to work less they get stout overtime. Union gets into it. Probably won't take them long to zip through that sucker. Chain saws is quick, whoeee."

A truck whipped by the curve, its brakes squealing. A motorcycle followed and then a convertible full of teenagers that skidded slightly and righted itself. Tom Zucold heard one shout, "Christ, a cop."

Trooper Drilling never lowered his head or looked aside. "Don't think they gone ask if they can do it. They thinking that that tree killed, maimed, and injured enough peoples already. Might could be right. On the other hand that tree be yours. You understand."

Tom Zucold felt as if somebody had switched on a lightbulb. Suddenly he did understand. It was exactly why Trooper Drilling had come. *It* was coming. The war. He saw it as clearly as he saw his own fate. It was only a matter of time. They would try to evict him. Take his land. Take his cars. Attack. Burn. The tree was just the first step. The woman was part of it. Oh yes. He saw it all now.

Wasn't it just the way Tom Zucold had told that hulking ingrate he gave home and board too? A man had to be prepared, programmed, because nobody was going to do it for him. He'd believed all those years in that goddamn drunken hustler. It would cost him, had cost him. Not just money. He might have seen things differently, done other, and better. Now there was himself and whoever he could recruit. Tom Zucold's mind raced. There was so little time. He was so vulnerable. So much to do.

Trooper Drilling drained the Gatorade. He relaxed now, having delivered what he had come to deliver. He dropped his gaze from the treetop, then said, "Heard you mens lost all your money to that pool player. Too bad, that's for damn sure. Wisht it was something Troop could do." He waited for Tom Zucold to answer but the old man said nothing.

"Been seeing that fool boy that live with you running around with Promise Land. Dude is got it bad, seem like. Take one look at that face and you say 'Oh shit, oh shit.' She just like always, got a dozen after her if she got one. She promise 'em and grin 'em and smackey mouth 'em but she don't never stay with 'em. Woman remind me of them giggly girls always getting caught in the back seat of cars. I don't mean to catch 'em, you understand. Thing is that Promise Land is different. She a cold one. She freeze the balls off a boss rabbit. Know just what she doing all the time and whatever it is you can bet it do her some good. Course you know that good as anybody."

"Bus," Tom Zucold said when he stopped hearing Trooper Drilling's voice.

"Seen it," Trooper Drilling answered. "Look like rocks done fall on it. Woman say she come here to get her motor fixed and you beat the shit out her fenders. Troop say Lady you hear what you saying? Say how a man gone figure he can fix a motor by beating up fenders. Say that's crazy Lady. She said probably it wasn't a whole lot in this little burg that wasn't crazy and I said maybe maybe. Woman say she ain't give up yet. Say don't hurry. Hang in there Colonel, got to hit the road."

But Trooper Drilling did not move. Instead he lifted his Smokey

Bear hat and ran his chocolate fingers over his close-cropped Afro and sang a few quick words in a high falsetto voice. Without looking at Tom Zucold, he said "That Stevie Wonder is super fine, just super fine."

"Somebody ought to kill that bitch," Tom Zucold said to the concrete.

A car braked around the curve and a horn honked.

"Hey Momma," Trooper Drilling shouted. Then, "You talk about killing somebody. That stuff there will do it to you like that." He popped his fingers and sang a little more.

"Shoulda killed her," Tom Zucold whined.

"Bound to tell you, Colonel, that put you in a whole world of shit." Trooper Drilling laughed gaily. "Course the world ain't much more than that any way you look at it some say. Not me, though. Gimme my woman, some Stevie Wonder, and a good bust—that lights my fire. You understand."

Tom Zucold got up and walked slowly into the Bowie Garage, stripping his clothes as he went. When he reached the Thunderbird chair he climbed it and leaped onto the rope and started jerking his way up.

Trooper Drilling stood in the door and watched silently, his broad face stretched wide in a grin. "You some old turkey," he said softly at last and then was gone. When he backed the patrol cruiser onto Yorktown Road Clifton was nailing a sign in the yard before his momma's burned-out house. The sign said FUTURE SIGHT OF CHAPEL GARAGE. Trooper Drilling rolled down his window and raised his hand in the thumbs-up salute.

"Later, man," Clifton said and went back to pounding the sign in the earth.

The television was on in the house and The Grip saw that Tom Zucold was already strapped into the Thunderbird seat. He had canted it forward and his eyes were tightly focused on the black and white screen. The Grip got a Gatorade and sat down in the Corvette chair. He fidgeted and tried to get comfortable and then gave up. It

163

hadn't felt right since they had taken it out of the panel truck and brought it back into the house. Even so he was glad to sit down. His body still shook from the pounding it had taken on Promise Land's Harley. They had ridden all afternoon, all over hell and back, sailing and roaring hard because something was wrong with her. He had asked her but she refused to say. Twice they had almost been run into, once by a truck carrying a load of chickens whose feathers swirled after them and once by a schoolbus.

"It's something wrong," The Grip said when he got off the motor-cycle on the far side of Yorktown Road. She wouldn't even go on the Bowie Garage property.

"Nothing is wrong," she said out of the side of her helmet, facing up the road firmly.

He started across the road, his boots scuffing the asphalt.

"Tomorrow night," she said.

He turned around at the edge of the road. She still faced up the road. "Tomorrow night we'll go to a drive-in movie. It's X-Rated. Eight sharp." Then she accelerated and sped into the dwindling light.

"Don't know no drive-in movies," The Grip said and walked to-ward the Bowie Garage.

He did not buckle himself into the Corvette chair. He was restless and did not want to strain against the restriction. He watched the commercial without comment while the Man from Glad wrapped a lady's meat and stuffed it into her refrigerator.

"Who's winning?" The Grip said. He did not know even what game was playing but would not have cared anyway. He had been silent all day on the bruising ride and he felt sociable. He wanted to talk.

"Story ain't done yet," Tom Zucold said.

"What's the prizes?"

"Man win two tickets to Disneyland," Tom Zucold wheezed and loosened his seat belt. "Said he ain't got nobody to go with him."

"He can find somebody if he look."

"Might, might," Tom Zucold said. "Man find most anything if he look hard enough. Could be he won't want what he finds too."

There was a raw edge to Tom Zucold's voice. It was in the way he said the words, somehow without buoyancy, a flatness that seemed final. The Grip had heard it coming ever since they'd left the Moose Hall. Tom Zucold had always liked it when people won tickets to Disneyland. He joked about how Disneyland was probably no different than the neighborhoods them people lived in already. Tom Zucold thought it was wonderful that TRUTH OR CONSEQUENCES set up like a clearinghouse to send the fools right to what was foolish as anything, their own dreams. Probably they were getting just what they deserved, Tom Zucold often said. But his tone was different now, and it made The Grip uneasy.

"Ain't anything worth having look like," The Grip said. He said it without force and he knew it. He wanted Tom Zucold to feel his support but the support wasn't there. For his part, The Grip had little idea what Disneyland was except that Tom Zucold had described it as full of kids with melted candy on their faces and shit in their pants and women with curlers on their heads and cameras around their necks. It had fake ponds and fake woods and fake animals and you couldn't tell that the people who wandered around inside were not themselves fake.

Another commercial came on. While The Grip watched a dog chase a cat he heard Tom Zucold maneuvering the Thunderbird chair. He watched one more commercial, then at the third one got up and went to the open commode and pissed noisily. Out of the corner of his eye he saw that the window was dark and it startled him. Every time he looked he was startled to see only the window and what was outside, not the poster of the Carolina Kid. Tom Zucold had stripped it away the night they came home from the Moose Hall. The Grip had not watched what he had done with it.

The Grip went to the window and looked into the darkness outside. There was nothing to look at except the road that was empty under the streetlight and that sign in Clifton's yard. Yet something did not seem right, something was different.

"Might rain tonight," The Grip said, returning to his seat. Tom Zucold pushed the button that moved him back into his forward lean before the television. The Grip sat down heavily and grunted. This time he buckled up.

Bob Barker stood in the center of the screen. His suit was shiny and splendid and he gestured to two men who looked ashamed and fidgeted. Barker handed each of the men some money and walked them offstage. When Barker turned and spoke into the camera, light flashed from his teeth and made a halo around his sleek hair.

The camera cut to a man in a gorilla suit. The Grip saw the tennis shoes right away and knew that it was not a real gorilla. The camera followed the gorilla to the stage door through wooden props, where the gorilla stopped and mugged and did a softshoe dance, then followed him into an alley and out onto the street. At the corner, the gorilla boarded a bus and rode off. Bob Barker flashed back on the screen where he stood talking to a middle-aged woman with hair piled high on her head. She wore a short skirt, boots, a field jacket and had a whip in one hand and a net in the other. She looked silly and she knew it.

Then the camera panned to the audience. All the people were jumping up and down and waving their hands in the direction of Bob Barker. Their mouths were wide open and they screeched silently and The Grip thought of a nest of starlings he had found as a boy. The little birds were jammed in the nest, almost overflowing it, and they were hairless, ugly creatures who seemed more mouth and hunger than anything else.

The camera cut once more to Bob Barker whose lips barely moved and then the gorilla was again on the screen. There was a crowd around him and he stood in a public fountain. He was waving handfuls of bills but nobody was taking any. A little white boy was swinging a long stick at the gorilla and some black kids were throwing rocks at him.

"Man come to the Bowie Garage today while you was riding," Tom Zucold said. He did not speak loudly but in the silence it was enough to make The Grip jump a little. When he turned he saw that Tom Zucold wore the baseball cap with STARS on the front. Oddly, the little man looked like a duck.

166

"What man?" The Grip asked politely, though he had already turned back to the gorilla who, now desperate to escape an increasing number of violent children, had lumbered out of the fountain and grabbed a woman jogging past. Money blew across the pavement like green leaves with the children scrambling after it. The Grip watched the woman screaming and struggling. He saw her knee strike the gorilla in the crotch so that he tumbled to the pavement and clutched at himself.

"Black man. Trooper Drilling. Black as the ace of spades, too. Ain't his fault, though. Happen to anybody. Man can't make choices much. Nice fellow."

"What did he want?" The Grip remembered the one. He smelled of locker room aftershave and he laughed too much. He had bought the Willys for a hundred dollars and Tom Zucold had even told him the engine was seized.

"Said the Committee gone come take down that tree. Gone cut down that tree in the front yard. Clear as can be what that means. Means the Bowie Garage gone to come under fire. Next thing is a paper that say cease and desist and get your asses out."

The Grip watched as a motorcycle cop rode up over the curb and came to a halt beside the gorilla. He slid off the cycle, leaving its lights winking and whirling, and knelt beside the gorilla. Instantly the gorilla rolled over on his back and reached up and pulled the cop on top of him. The cop broke free of the gorilla's embrace, yanked his nightstick and began flailing at the gorilla's head. From both sides of the screen then people began to attack the cop, some throwing stones, some sneaking up to deliver a kick in the rear end. Astonishingly, the lady jogger catapulted out of the crowd and leaped onto the cop's back so that he swung wildly. The gorilla rushed to the camera, his face mashed and widened in the lens, then took off his mask and revealed a man with a beard and no hair. His face, too, was mashed and widened by the lens and he kept looking desperately back at the cop with the jogger on his back and shouting something in the camera.

Suddenly, another cop appeared. He was dressed exactly as the first cop except that he wore no motorcycle. He started toward the camera, his arms waving like the gorilla's had, then went back toward the cop now on the ground under the weight of the lady jogger. He too had a nightstick and The Grip watched as he struck the first cop in the helmet. He looked hard and there it was again. The nightstick bent. It was only a rubber nightstick. The second cop turned and grinned at the camera. As he did so, the first cop shucked the lady jogger off his back and jumped up and struck the second cop in the helmet. The Grip could hardly believe his eyes. Now the gorilla tried to get between the two cops and part them but both cops were swinging nightsticks and it was impossible to tell who they were swinging at except that the gorilla had fallen to the pavement a second time and he lay still.

The camera cut back to the studio audience. The people sat huddled in their seats, some clutching each other's arms, all of them wide-eyed and open-mouthed. They, too, couldn't believe what was happening and were truly horrified.

"Get so close ittis hard to see what you seeing," Tom Zucold said. The Grip realized that Tom Zucold had been talking right along and he glanced at the old man but went back to the screen in front of himself.

The camera went to Bob Barker for just a second. Barker was bent over facing the camera, his hand to his mouth, and there was a man with a head-set microphone holding Barker's arm. A woman on the other side of Barker was gesturing for someone to come to her. The camera cut back to the street but a crowd had gathered around the fight and all you could see was a circle of backs and the face of a kid who kept hopping up into the camera.

"Go to jail," Tom Zucold said. "But what the hell good is it to be alive if you ain't willing to go to jail for what is important."

The Grip turned at the mention of jail and saw that Tom Zucold had maneuvered the Thunderbird chair so that he lay stretched flat under the hanging rope, as if he were a patient laid out for surgery. The little man looked blue in the television light and he spoke in a monotone to the ceiling. The Grip would have been shocked if this

168

were the first time he had seen Tom Zucold behave this way, but it did not shock him now. Tom Zucold had not been the same man since the Moose Hall. The Grip knew that he had not only grown sharper, more edged, but he behaved in an increasingly bizarre manner, and he seemed more depressed, darker, intense. He did not talk much anymore but when he talked it was either about riding those horses in Maryland, horses that had been fed to nameless and long-dead animals generations past, or it was about the Committee which somehow controlled everything and lurked everywhere. It seemed to The Grip more and more that the old man could not tell what was actually happening from what he imagined was happening. He had thought about this enough that he had tried to explain it to Promise Land.

"Problem, no question of that," she said. They were sitting at the foot of the blue-green Confederates in the War Memorial Park that overlooked the James River. "But, gosh, there's another problem too. If he thinks something is happening and it really isn't but he still thinks it so hard that he does something in response, then isn't what he thinks is happening really happening?"

The Grip blinked at her and then looked out at a man tonging oysters near the James River Bridge. He could see the man's arms opening and closing like pincers and he knew they were working tongs on the bottom. Tom Zucold had told him about oystering. But he had never actually seen the tongs and could not really see them now. He hadn't seen the oysters scraped up or the silt spread on the bottom. But he saw it all in his head and it seemed real enough to him.

"Oh, it is a thorny one, isn't it," Promise Land said. "I'll have to spring that one on my professor. Oh I probably didn't tell you I was taking evening classes—just to stay ahead of things, you know? Anyway, I've got this guy in Philosophy 52A and he—"

"Like my father," The Grip said.

"I don't think you're listening. You're not interested in my class one bit are you," Promise Land said, starting to pout.

Riding home on the pink motorcycle The Grip had decided there really wasn't any difference between what was happening and what you thought was happening. You just did what you could and what you had to and, if you were lucky, you didn't ask any questions about the rest. Then he had thought how hard it was to tell why a man did what he did or was what he was. There was so much you never saw going on and all you could know was that if you were alive you were sooner or later going to wake up and see that you were alone inside, no matter who was around, and the world would look crazy to you and all you could do then was try to hold onto somebody and try to find some way to keep the craziness controlled. The one thing The Grip was dead certain of was that craziness was catching.

"Say jail?" The Grip said.

Tom Zucold pushed the button on the side of his Thunderbird chair and raised himself up slowly in the blue television light so that he might have been a corpse sitting up. Deliberately, he unbuckled himself and stood upright in the chair.

"Life is a jail, ape." Then Tom Zucold sat down in the chair, as if he had remembered something he meant to do. He buckled himself back in and hit the button until once more he lay flat under the rope. He seemed to ignore TRUTH OR CONSEQUENCES.

"Cop say that tree done got three people he know of. Say it got some maybe while he was in Vietnam, can't tell about that. I said it got three while he was gone. More people killed by that tree than by the Viet Cong, I told him. He say well they just want to cut it down and save they sons and daughters look like."

"Say jail?" The Grip said, trying to steer to conversation back to where he had lost it.

"Tom Zucold told him thanks. Didn't say nothing else. Can't tell but what he got a loose mouth and it is ears everywhere. Fact is that tree ain't but a first step. They after me, Grip. They after me and the Bowie Garage and onliest thing stop 'em is money and we done lost it all. Just like dominoes look like. Get that tree, then another one go and another one. Then it'll be the processees and then the house. Man can't run from his own dirt."

The Grip did not know what to say. Tom Zucold was beginning

170

to cook. He was not talking in that monotone any longer. Something was about to happen. He felt the pressure building and though he wanted to say something that could defuse the old man, what could he say? He glanced back at the television screen as if some answer waited there but saw only a thin girl washing her hair in a heavy rain.

"Maybe sell them processees?" The Grip said. It was just a gesture, a sudden dart thrown blindly. Had he thought what he was saying he would have seen this was futile.

"Tom Zucold ain't gone sell a fucking one of them babies," Tom Zucold hissed. He hit the button hard and the Thunderbird seat slowly whirred upright. The Grip saw the old man's forehead was dark under the baseball cap. The eyes were sunk in the head. "They gone have to kill me before they taken the Bowie Garage. Ain't going to no goddamn jail neither. Man's garage is his castle. Got roots here."

"Maybe you could talk to them," The Grip said as he watched Tom Zucold step down from the Thunderbird seat and snap on the blazing highbeams. His stomach felt sour and tight even though he hadn't eaten.

"Give you some time, if you talk to them." The Grip had no idea what Tom Zucold would talk about or to whom he would talk. But surely words were at least harmless, he thought.

"No time for that shit. Never was. Time is always for moving up and flanking and cutting down. Time is for killing. Same for every man and he can't change his part. If he rich and got the power he is the mover. If he the little man he is the moved. Ittis evil, all there is to it. Evil ain't nothing but greed. That Committee don't give a gnat's turd about my tree or about my processees. They thinking shopping centers and cash in they pockets and golf courses and flowers and zoos. Ittis women behind ever bit of it too. Always was." Tom Zucold had climbed back into the Thunderbird seat and buckled in as he snapped out the words like an automatic lug wrench. Now he was sapped and he sank, breathless, into the naugahyde.

"Jail?" The Grip said. He felt very tired, his body heavy. He had tried to understand what Tom Zucold was talking about but all he understood was the anger. It wasn't true that women were behind it all, he thought. How could Promise Land be behind anything?

The Grip watched the television again and saw that the gorilla was being led up the wide steps of a gray stone building. The helmeted cop on the motorcycle was pushing him and behind them another helmeted cop pushed the cop who had the rubber nightstick. All of the cops grinned into the television camera. The gorilla had his head on and The Grip couldn't tell if he was grinning. Then the camera cut to another camera and Bob Barker stood inside the door with a black microphone in his fist. He was laughing and waving the foursome forward. Studio lights gleamed off the badges and bullets and pistols.

"Ain't going in no damn jail," Tom Zucold said then. "Been in them bastards enough to know to stay out. Man get to be my age he might as well go in the ground as go to jail." Tom Zucold hawked hard and deep but he made nothing come forth.

On the television Bob Barker stood before stage curtains and suddenly they opened. There was a woman and a little girl standing and the little girl had on a blindfold. While they stood there, a cop brought the gorilla on stage behind them and then unlocked the handcuffs on the gorilla. Bob Barker took the little girl's hand from the woman and motioned the woman offstage. Then he put the little girl's hand in the gorilla's and went behind the girl where he took off the blindfold. The little girl looked forward into the lights and squinted, then looked at the thing holding her and and burst into tears. She tried to pull away but the gorilla would not let her go. The gorilla began to touch her chest and to tap his own. The little girl screamed and yanked at her hand but it was no use.

"Ittis all right, ittis the father," The Grip said to the television. But the little girl did not hear him and the gorilla bent close to her to tell her something and she screamed harder. Then The Grip saw a puddle of liquid at her feet and knew that she had wet herself in terror.

"Help," The Grip said and leaned toward the little girl.

"Help? You fucking ape, who gone help anybody?" Tom Zucold

172

spat. "They gone try everything and it come down to push and shove and we won't get no help but ourselves. Think I don't know what game is going on? Think I don't know that whore Promise Land wants everything it is, you, me, the world?" Tom Zucold unbuckled and nimbly leaped down and put himself between the television and The Grip.

"Listen here, soldier. Pussy done turned around many a good man and you ain't the first lost it for Promise Land. But you can tell her it ain't going to happen here. Tom Zucold gone defend his country!"

The Grip was so shocked by Tom Zucold in his face that he did not see the gorilla unzip and did not see the girl scream at the man who was not her daddy at all and he didn't see Bob Barker hustle the two of them off camera as he announced that both of them had won a case of Dreamwhip.

"Ain't true," The Grip said.

"Shitfire, monkey. I'm telling you."

"She don't want the Bowie Garage," The Grip said. He stood up and towered over the wiry little man. "Ain't no committee. You just crazy."

"Godalmight, Jesus, boy. You ain't her people and I ain't her people but her people is the enemy. Signs is clear. They got three chances to screw us good: good, better, and best. She ain't nothing but a woman and can't help herself. See, they like that. Got their own reasons for what they decide they want. Everything ain't got a explanation. I admit that. But facts is facts and you got to face them. Fish don't fly and rocks don't fuck. Bet me."

The Grip turned and walked to the window and stared out into the dark. He had felt that if he did not move he would strike the old man. His head was pounding now. He felt himself being caught up in the old man's passion and he knew that it was crazy. He hoped that something out there would push back with the kind of authority the poster had once had. There had to be something to control whatever it was that was overwhelming both of them.

"Promise," The Grip said, watching his lips move.

"Ain't saying to stay if you don't want to. Saying you got to get your head clear, get programmed," Tom Zucold said. The Grip heard him snap off the television.

"Promise is beautiful. She is good," The Grip said, as if he were testing the words.

"She ain't nothing but a woman. Gone do you wrong every chance you give her. Got a strong smell between her toes and got warts where you ain't looked. Programming only thing gone save you long enough to get some revenge. Revenge is having something. Tom Zucold got this place and ain't leaving. That's it, Jack." Tom Zucold snapped off the highbeams so that they died crackling.

The Grip lay in bed, his GI blanket pulled tight under his neck. A car bulled through the curve in Yorktown Road and he listened to it until there was no more sound. When it had approached he had seen the headlights spray in through the window and had seen Tom Zucold's rope hanging dead still. He had lain sleepless for hours as he tried to figure out what was happening. The Bowie Garage was the nearest thing he had to a home and the old man who was without doubt crazy as a loon the nearest thing he had to a father. But he knew that he was going to leave. It was coming. The question was why and how.

"Got a plan, if you want to stay," Tom Zucold said gently in the darkness.

"What plan?" The Grip felt almost as if he had spoken out in a dream.

"We might can move all them processees into a circle around the Bowie Garage. Plenty of them. Put them suckers end to end like the cowboys done to the Indians. Be a fine breastwork. Then we get us some guns and we kill anybody that come over."

"Say kill?" The Grip said. He listened to his breath whistle as he tried to keep it steady. He had never killed anything, really. Not tried to kill and done it. He'd been a good shot but it had never occurred to him that he would really shoot at somebody. He hadn't had to do that. SSGT Davis had taught him to shoot and he had said any man that couldn't kill must be a pussy. But The Grip had started to put very well then and he had been assigned extra training duties with the shot. SSGT Davis said he was an artist with that steel ball and artists didn't have to kill anything but themselves.

"Got that right, son. Death ain't nothing. Not if you lived, it ain't. If you lived any you done already smelled it and it ain't any worse than bus fumes."

"Everybody live," The Grip said.

"Monkey, don't you see at all? Most people don't never live. Truth be told most people ain't got sense enough to know that it is something inside you that is precious delicate and you got to be risking it all the time or you forget it is there and it just dry up on you. That's what you can't let anybody fuck with. But if you know it is there and you know what it is and you taking care of it so it talks your heart to thumping now and again, then you know what death is and it ain't half bad."

It was goddamn funny, The Grip thought just before drifting off to sleep, but Tom Zucold sounded a lot like Promise Land and neither one of them seemed to know what was real the way he did.

He woke chilled, his blanket kicked to the floor, and his bladder felt as if it was going to burst. When he had finished peeing in the dark, he saw that it was raining and the northeast wind blew gusts against the thin walls of their house. He went to the window and saw that it was gray outside and realized that it was morning. Tom Zucold hadn't banged his pan, though, and it was too still to be anything but night in the house.

"Tom Zucold awake?" The Grip said. When there was no answer he walked to Tom Zucold's bed and found it made smartly in military fashion. For just a second The Grip wondered if Tom Zucold had been the one to pull out first, but the idea was absurd. Then The Grip saw the service order pinned to Tom Zucold's pillow. He unpinned it and held it in front of him but could not read it in the gray light. He stepped to the panel and toggle switches and made the Cadillac highbeams blaze like the lost sun.

GONE TO CARMINES JUNK STOP STRATEGY TALKS STOP RECON-
NOITERING SUPPLIES STOP INVENTORYING TROOPS STOP ACCEPT

NO MORE MISSIONS STOP STAND BY STOP WILL RETURN ASAP STOP COLD FISH RATIONS AND GATORADE AVAILABLE STOP SUSPEND ALL COMMUNICATIONS WITH ENEMY AND PRIORITY COMMUNICA- TIONS ALL OTHER PERSONNEL STOP SEND NO TWX WO AUTHORITY COMMAND HQ STOP SSGT T. ZUCOLD 4500 BGPV

The Grip read the message from Tom Zucold three times and after each reading he was more convinced that Tom Zucold had got stark raving mad. What other way was there to describe it? He was afraid and his stomach swirled. He felt like soap spinning around on top of the water that was plummeting down a bathtub drain: the weight of being crazy would take whatever was near wherever it went. He sat down in his Corvette chair and put his head in his hands and tried to think. Then he got up and walked to the El Do- rado door and looked out into the lane. He thought maybe if he could just do some putting things would look clearer to him. It was raining lightly now and the wind had dropped but the lane was sop- ping and he knew that all of his puts would slip and squirt and slide without force or focus. He walked back toward his Corvette chair but passed it and went on to the window. He saw nothing in the yard except a gray 1955 Chevrolet and puddles of rainwater. He went one more time to his chair, snapped on the television and sat heavily.

Cartoons were on the television and The Grip felt himself fleeing into them, absorbed by the phony violence and the hysterical chases between dogs that weren't dogs and cats that weren't cats and people who were strange animals that weren't really animals. He liked to watch the aardvark who never quite caught his ant, but it was the panther he liked best. Tom Zucold would have been angry if he saw The Grip watching anything besides TRUTH OR CONSEQUENCES. He felt guilty as he looked at the panther chasing something that re- sembled a dog. Then, without knowing he was going to do it, he raised himself from the floor and tuned in the color and was de- lighted to see that the panther was pink. The animal the pink pan- ther chased was brown and the sky was blue. The grass and the trees were green. It was all so simple. It was just like life, The Grip thought. Except it wasn't life at all. Nothing ever happened the way it looked on television, though it was clear people hoped that it would.

"Hope," The Grip said to the television set. Hope, he remembered Tom Zucold had told him, was off fucking whatever came along in the bald tires. He stood up and turned off the television and listened to the rain hissing on the tin roof.

After he had eaten his cold breakfast of fish and Gatorade, working to keep each swallow down and swearing to himself that he was going to leave and not knowing where he would go, he pulled out the Montgomery Ward catalog and pored over the pictures of men in suits and men in sport shirts with bright colors. In each picture there was a beautiful woman somewhere near and she was smiling at the men though they didn't look at her. None of them, he thought, was as fine as Promise Land. He looked at the hunting gear and the fishing gear and the stereo record players and after a while just flipped the pages as if there was some kind of secret to it all and maybe it would just jump up if he kept looking.

He was looking at the women in underwear when he heard a motor start. It coughed and then caught and roared. But it wasn't Tom Zucold's panel truck. He went to the window and looked into the front yard. It was a 1955 classic Chevrolet and someone was in it.

The car had been hunched up in the rear with huge black tires. It was painted a dull gray and he knew this was industrial primer. There were no door handles and no Chevrolet insignias. In fact there was no chrome on the car at all. Tom Zucold had taught him about such cars. Kids couldn't stand the cars being normal, Tom Zucold said, because they were normal and they hated it. So they changed everything around and put all their money into sinking the headlights and smoothing the hoods and welding on wings and flares and such until you couldn't tell what the hell kind of car it was. Then they painted it up like a cheap whore and put some silly name on the rear fender and at night they crept slowly around the drive-ins and gas stations just so people could see what a mess they had made of a perfectly good piece of equipment.

"Make me hotter than hell," Tom Zucold had told him.

But it wasn't Tom Zucold in the car. It was Clifton. The Grip went to the big overhead door and raised it and walked in the rain to the car and got in. The passenger door seemed to pop open on its own but he knew that Clifton had pushed a button or pulled a lever or something.

"Ain't this something?" Clifton had a radio playing in the car and the volume was up so high The Grip barely heard him. The car seemed to be rocking with the noise of the music but it was actually Clifton rocking in the driver's seat that did it. Clifton had on black silk pants and a black shirt, also silk, that opened almost to his waist. He was wearing sunglasses that completely hid his wide eyes. A cigarette sent a thin wire of smoke to the roof from Clifton's fingers that curled lazily at the steering wheel. The steering wheel was a chain that had been welded and chromed.

"This baby look sharp. Sharp as a tack," Clifton said. "Look like she will dance and dig out mothuh."

"Yours?" The Grip said. The bucket seat that he sat in was wide and thick and covered with long white fur. It was more comfortable than his Corvette seat.

"What you think, white boy, that my momma got a 'heritance?" Clifton threw his head back and laughed. "Think Clifton done got hissef a summer job them government mens be begging to give to us 'norities?"

The Grip reached for the radio and casually turned it down. The car stopped rocking and he could hear traffic hissing around the curve of the road.

"What you do that for, mothuh? Think it was you that stole this piece of junk?" Clifton's shouting seemed extremely loud with the radio so low. "Nawh, can't be you. White folks don't steal nothin'— they just lets niggers' house burn down."

"Didn't," The Grip said weakly.

"Didn't my ass, brothuh," Clifton said and looked at The Grip. "Seen you over theah and you ain't brung no hose cross the street has you? Shitting me you ain't." Clifton dragged hard on his cigarette and rolled the window down to throw the butt out. "Coach see me smoking it gone be my ass."

"Didn't mean to," The Grip said.

"Sheeet, don't sweat it bro. Momma said you done what you could. Said can't expect much from anybody and nothin' from white folks anyway. No sweat, man. Let's hear some sounds, baby." Clifton turned the radio back to ear-splitting level.

They sat in the dwindling rain for almost an hour, the car rocking and the music blasting. Clifton smoked and wiggled and snapped his fingers and made occasional comments on the singers. The Grip, feeling glad to be with someone, sat in silence and watched the water run down the windows as he had when he was a boy waiting for his mother to come home.

"Stole it," The Grip said finally, ending his silence.

"Man, it was the easiest thing I ever done. Got it from a gas station and gone before you could wink your smooth browns. Woman with me, one fox if ever it was a fox, say Clifton you the coolest. I say, true true. I didn't even tell her it ain't got but a sewing machine for motor. Shit on it, phony fucker."

"Phony?"

"If you can dig it, that ain't nothing but a sick six under the hood. It look good, dig it. Look like ain't nothing can bear it. Seen them like this that sound so fine and shine so good and they just lick that road. This thing? It need a hill to do the speed limit."

"Why'd you put it over here?"

"Troop say he will say he found it here. Troop related to me somehow."

"Let's go."

"Go where, fool? Think I want to spend my young years in the damned jail? You must be crazy." Clifton looked at the window and hummed. Then he stopped and slowly turned his head, grinning wide.

"You said go? You did say go, I believe?" He laughed and kept laughing so that The Grip laid his head back against the bucket seat and let laughter come rolling out of him until there were tears on his cheeks and his chest hurt.

"Pull the son of a bitch out," The Grip said gaily.

Clifton had the car halfway in and halfway out of the drive when he stopped and said he couldn't see for the rain. The Grip got out and shut the door and had just turned to see what traffic might be coming when he saw Tom Zucold's panel truck start to slide. It slid its rear end toward the ditch, righted, then slid toward the road and in what seemed to The Grip like slow motion eased nose-first into the killer tree. Clifton rolled the Chevrolet back to its original position and drifted noiselessly off in the rain.

"Who the hell move my customer's car in the drive like that?" Tom Zucold snapped when The Grip yanked open the truck's passenger door.

Sunlight speared through the nickle-colored clouds just after noon and by early afternoon the sky was bright blue with only a few scudding streams of grey. The wind had shifted and blew out of the South steadily though not strongly and by dusk it had become a hot day and promised to be a warm night. It had taken them most of the afternoon to pry the left front fender of the panel truck away from the wheel and then change the tire that had been slashed. Oddly enough Tom Zucold had not raged as The Grip expected him to and had in fact seemed cheery. From time to time The Grip heard him humming "My Old Kentucky Home." There had even been time for an hour of putting the shots, though each put left the steel shot buried in the soggy lane. Twice The Grip thought he had seen the not-a-nigger girl's face in the trees at the ditch but when he had gone to find her he had seen no one.

The Grip listened to the creak of the rafters that came from Tom Zucold's rope climbing as he splashed his body and toweled off. He shaved quickly and put on his last clean fatigue uniform.

"Mr. Grip," Tom Zucold said from the two-thirds point of the rope, "the truth is that you smell like a French bordello."

Promise Land's banana Volkswagen beeped in the front yard and The Grip started out the door then stopped when Tom Zucold said, "Keep it tight, things go right." When he looked back, The Grip saw Tom Zucold staring at the tiny hole in the ceiling, sweat gleaming slickly on his wiry arms that were stretched tight.

Promise Land was programmed for the movie. She had brought a huge bag of popcorn and a dish of pizza and a six pack of Budweiser tall cans. All was stashed under a blanket in the back seat. "No sense in paying what they charge at the movies. There ought to be a law," Promise Land said. "It's outrageous."

When it was over all the popcorn and pizza was gone and only one beer remained. And all The Grip could remember was that the movie was called something like Blue Moves. There had been some kind of explanation about making a blue movie but he had seen nothing blue about the entire matter. On the contrary, everything seemed to have been flesh pink. All he could be certain of was that it was a movie whose only story was fucking. If there was anything else to life except that it was not known to the people in that movie. People did it on the stairs in houses and did it on the lawns where there was a party going on. Then a man and two women did it in a swimming pool. Then two men and two women made up combinations on a tennis court. After that there was a ski lodge and a room full of people and each person did something to another person. Some people did two things and three things at a time, things which left The Grip with a hard crotch and an open mouth.

After a while no matter what the people did, it bored him. He thought about a circus he had seen once while he was in the Army. He remembered the elephants peeing, splashes of water and yards of pink flesh. Then he began to look around at the cars in the parking lot of the drive-in. How strange it seemed to him, the cars parked like hundreds of dead or dying processees, the dark night silence that held them, even the toneless voices of the naked people on the screen.

"What does it mean?" The Grip asked Promise Land. They were the only car on the road as far as he could see ahead or behind. The only light in all that darkness, he thought.

"Doesn't mean a damn thing, I guess," Promise Land said. "It's just life. Going on everywhere, even if nobody sees it. It's, well, it's energy, you know? I think it is just wonderful that man has come far enough that he can use art and philosophy to make a movie like that, don't you? I mean it *shows* us us. Heraclitus and Plato and Masters and Johnson and Bob Dylan. I mean it's all in my notes, if you'd care to look. We don't have to mean anything anymore and that's why we can show it like it is. Isn't it exciting to be alive?"

Promise Land was so excited that she was giggling and going faster and cutting the curves on Yorktown Road so that The Grip had his great feet once again jammed at the firewall. He watched her whipping the steering wheel with one hand while she tuned her radio with the other.

"Wow," Promise Land cooed. "That's Janis Joplin. Talk about somebody who really knows. Listen to that: Freedom's when you got nothing left to lose. Doesn't that just about say it all, I mean doesn't it?"

"When you got nothing left to lose, you dead," The Grip said, but the banana Volkswagen was roaring through another turn and the woman on the radio was screeching and Promise Land heard nothing but what was in her own head.

"Talk about your portraits of the human condition," Promise Land said as they sailed into a straight stretch of the road. "I really loved that part where the people pretend to be naked puppets—you know the part I mean? They walk down that long road together and eat dinner in a stranger's house and the strangers get up and go with them and they go down into a swamp and build huts, you remember? And the black guy comes and strings up a light bulb? Wasn't that fabulous? You remember?"

The Grip remembered. It was a black and white sequence, almost another movie inside the movie, and the black man brought light and people started wearing clothes. Then there was a woman on a hospital table and she had her legs wide apart and the man dressed as a doctor pulled down a light bulb on a cord like the one The Grip had seen at the Moose Hall. The Grip thought he meant to hold it close to the woman to see what was there but the man had actually put it into the woman and turned it on and the woman's face looked radiant with happiness. When the doctor removed the light all the people in the room were standing beside her bed and clapping their hands. It had made him sweat while he watched.

"I bet you never saw anything like that," Promise Land said.

"I didn't understand the story," The Grip said. He was almost shouting.

"No story to it. That's the beauty of it, the truth. Things just happen all the time. One thing happens and then another thing happens and things happen at the same time. It's like my professor says, we don't mean anything. We don't have to mean anything. We don't even exist, if you think about it."

"Could slow down some," The Grip said. The little car was going so fast that they had jumped off the pavement at least twice. He was packed in hard and felt as if he were wearing the Volkswagen. Once he had looked up at the stars but they were going by so quickly it made him afraid. He felt more certain that he existed than of anything else.

"You think life isn't like that, don't you?" Promise Land whined above the engine. She did not let up on the accelerator. "I bet you think people don't even do those things. Oh boy, the stories I could tell you, let alone that it was people doing those things on the screen. I bet you always liked baseball didn't you? You know what, baseball players are maybe the worst of all. They're about as smart as rabbits and they do the same things most rabbits do. Except rabbits don't read comic books."

The Grip couldn't see what baseball players had to do with people who pretended to be puppets and who walked naked down a road and didn't do anything but fuck each other and then fuck some cows and goats afterward. And farmers and businessmen and housewives with children in their station wagons drove right on by and paid no attention at all.

"Them freaks ain't normal. Worse than TRUTH OR CONSEQUENCES."

"It's all relative, though. That's in my notes, too. It's relative and existential. It's normal. Freaks are normal. You and me. Put yourself in front of a mirror some time and take a good look. You are a freak because you're so big and you can't hardly talk and you don't know anything. You think everybody's got to be one way or the other and it's got to mean something. I'm a freak because of my name. And that old man you live with, well, take my word he's his own kind of freak. But nobody asked for what they got. Who do you know that has the life he wants?"

Trees hung darkly over the road as they flew along and The Grip thought they looked like hands reaching out of the darkness. He could only hear a part of what Promise Land said and what he heard made very little sense to him but he was glad she was there. He liked to look at her face that was tinted green by the dashlight and was full of quick-changing expression as she talked. He liked the smell of the perfume she was wearing and though he was afraid of her driving he even liked the sense of tearing through the darkness with her.

She surprised him when she pulled into the yard of the Bowie Garage and turned off the ignition.

"Ain't a freak," he said, his voice too loud so that a dog started barking somewhere and Tom Zucold's Midnight ripped off a series of snarls.

"What? Oh that," Promise Land said. She had gotten out of the car already and was stretching beside it. He saw the outline of her slender body and wanted badly to hold her to him. He had wanted to touch her during the movie but what was up there stopped him. He couldn't say why, but it had.

"We can spread it out back there where you throw those balls," Promise Land said, and dumped the blanket in his lap. Astonished, he silently watched her open the front of the little car and then hold up yet another six pack.

"Don't want to die of thirst, do you?" She giggled and struck off in the darkness beside the Bowie Garage.

When he had pulled himself out, The Grip squinted at the dark and tried to find her. It was like trying to find her in one of his dreams but he knew the yard and the lane so he went blindly ahead. There were, he knew, only so many places she could be waiting.

He found her standing beside the white stick. The moon was coming up now and it glinted off the Edsel's grill. He laid the blanket down and smoothed it out. The night was warm and damp as breath.

184

She sat down and spread her dark skirt carefully to her knees. She wore a white cotton turtleneck that made her breasts seem large in the moonlight. Without a word she patted the blanket and told him to sit down.

"This is where you do it, isn't it?" Promise Land said briskly. "I mean you throw those big steel balls at this stick don't you? And you do that hour after hour?" She sounded as if she could hardly believe it.

"Right here. Stick is a world record."

"Talk about freaks," she said and whistled softly. "You ever wonder what a grown man is doing when all he does is throw steel balls until he can't lift his arm? You ever wonder what kind of job that is?"

The Grip said nothing. His face began to feel hot.

"How far do you throw it?"

"Stick is seventy-five feet," he said. He waited, then said, "I ain't hit it. World record if anybody hit it." He felt a flutter in his chest, as if the air was too thin to work in his lungs.

"Well, son, you will. You will hit that record." She half-turned to him and pushed him onto his back. Her hair fell over him and it smelled like honeysuckle and mint. Her perfume was sweet but he had never smelled anything like it. He looked up and saw the big dipper. It was the only constellation he could ever find.

"That's the big dipper up there," he said, the words squeaking in his throat. His mind was whirling with images from Bob Barker to SSGT Davis to the men in the Montgomery Ward catalog. He saw faces and bodies flash into his head and disappear as if carried by a black flood.

"You got to relax a little, son," she said and shook her head so that her hair tickled his face. "You're so tight I can feel myself trembling when you do."

"Am," The Grip said smartly. "Am relaxed."

Her mouth came out of the darkness and covered his and it felt warm and wet like oil on a dipstick. Her lips made a good seal so that whatever passed between a man and a woman in a kiss passed between them. He wiggled his toes in his boots. Her tongue came into his mouth then, surprising him, and seemed to play on his teeth. He did not know what to do until he put his tongue into her mouth and she sucked on it lightly. Then he did this to her. Then he reached for her tit and found it floating just under the turtleneck like a lump in a pillow, only firmer. He hefted it as he hefted his steel shots, then toyed with it in his fingers, rolling the nipple so that it hardened. All the while, he wondered if this was what he should do. It was like a part of himself had stood back and was attempting to discover if this was the appropriate action to take with a tit. And the part that had stood back seemed to whisper that it was absurd, the whole business, for though it pleased him to be holding the tit he might as well have been holding a mockingbird or a warm pear. The tit did nothing at all. What good could it be?

Abruptly Promise Land broke the kiss and sat back away from him. "It was just a kiss, mister whatever your name is. I swan," she said. Or at least that was what he heard.

"Look like nothing what you think it is," The Grip said after a minute staring at the stars.

"I swan," she sighed in exasperation. "You still on that? It's downright immature, you know? I mean this thing men have about everything having a meaning. Even that professor—and he is a really smart man I guess—is always trying to find out a meaning. It's right there in my notes, too. He was talking about this monomaniac guy, some Greek I think, that elected himself to go on a trip and go hunting and had to drop down into some underworld and come back with some stupid message. It was getting pretty boring and I started to draw a picture of the professor in my notebook and he said Miss Land, can you tell the class what the meaning of this journey is? I liked to jumped out of my seat—call on a person like that. You could have a heart attack. Well, I said some things have a meaning but not everything does and just because a person takes a trip I didn't see why that had to have a meaning. He said this trip was one that everybody took and I said maybe so but it was news to me and by

186

this time he was standing right at my desk and he saw the picture and he said I could come to his office after class. You bet I could see what that meant all right."

"Beer," The Grip said. He lay flat on the ground and he felt the rain that had fallen seeping up through the blanket. It felt wet and cool and he wondered if this was what it felt like when you were dead and buried.

"Now you're talking," Promise Land said. She popped the top of a Budweiser and pressed it into his hand.

"It's fun and all listening to that professor but I swan," she said and popped a beer for herself. "Life is just what it is. A person ought to try and have a good time, don't you think? A person should do what seems right for a person to do. Like you and those balls. Ought to throw 'em until it don't feel good to you anymore. That's what I say anyway."

They each drank their beers without talking, slowly and comfortably. He stared at the big dipper and listened to crickets. Maybe she was right, he thought. She was certainly smart. But still, things did have meanings and it was important to try and find them. Tom Zucold had taught him that much at least. He thought about touching Promise Land's tit and how she had got angry. The meaning of that was that she didn't love him, or that he had done it wrong. He thought about what he had done but he could not see how it had gone wrong.

"Well, didly poot, why not?" Promise Land said and popped another beer.

"Say what?"

Instead of answering him, Promise Land pulled his face over and laid her mouth against his. She was shaking just a little bit and her mouth tasted of Budweiser. Somewhere a dog was barking faintly. Then she took his hand and put it between her legs and he felt her silk pants. He rubbed the pants for a while and slipped a finger under the tight seam and she opened her legs automatically, as if he had hit a button. His finger slid easily and she clamped her legs on his hand so that he could not move it. As she held him he felt her hand touch the front of his pants and unzip him. Suddenly she jerked back from him.

"You're wearing a goddamn jock," Promise Land yipped. "I can't believe it. Is that a jock or not? I swan."

The Grip did not answer. What could he say? It looked to him that all those men in the Montgomery Ward catalog were wearing jocks. Why else did their crotches bulge so? So he had worn a jock. It was the one part of his wardrobe he was never without. SSGT Davis had warned him that a man with a dirty jock or without a jock at all would never hold records.

"Am I right? You are wearing a jock aren't you?"

"Yes," The Grip said. He searched furiously for an explanation. He could find none.

"Well take the damn thing off," she said, her head turning toward the processees so it almost seemed her voice had come from the Edsel. The earth was colder and wetter now and he shivered. He could not believe he had heard her say that.

"What kind of invitation do you want?" Promise Land stood up abruptly and The Grip felt his stomach tighten.

"Shit," The Grip said softly. He had lost it now. He felt small and stupid and large and ugly and he shivered though he was hot. But Promise Land did not leave. She stood above him on the blanket and grinned.

"You got a second chance, son. Three and you're out."

He stood and dropped his fatigue pants and had one leg over his boots and off when the second leg caught and he toppled to the ground. His cheeks flushed hotly but he pulled himself up and got the other leg free. He kept his back to Promise Land as he pulled off his GI shorts and then his jockey strap. He was shivering now.

"OK," The Grip said. But when he turned Promise Land was gone.

"Hey, over here. It's the best place in the world," Promise Land cried from the back door of a four-door Desoto sedan. The Grip could not actually see her but her hand waved from the darkness that held her voice. His combat boots sounded thick as he padded over to her.

"I got made in the back seat of a car like this," Promise Land said sweetly and pulled him deep into the darkness. "Long time ago. They don't make back seats like this anymore. Pity."

He got in and sat down on the prickly seat that rubbed his naked skin. It smelled faintly of gasoline and strongly of mildew. He pulled the heavy door behind him and it shut with authority. But Promise Land pulled away from his grip and went out the other door, nimble as a weasel, and clambered atop the huge car's hood. Even without much of a moon and through the cruddy windshield The Grip could see clearly enough. Promise Land kneeled down and peeked in at him, then sat back on her heels and stripped off her turtleneck and her brassiere. Her breasts hung slightly in the darkness, just white enough to be visible and to make him suck in his breath. He felt light-headed. Without a word Promise Land stood and dropped her skirt and wiggled out of her panties that seemed to glow with moonlight. She was stark naked.

"Boy, pay attention. This is your night," Promise Land crooned as she bent over to look in through the windshield, her breasts hanging like ghostly pears.

Suddenly Promise Land leaped into the air so The Grip saw only darkness through the Desoto windshield. Then she hit the hood with a buckling racket. Almost immediately she did it again, this time kicking her legs apart and shouting.

"Gimme an R," she shouted above the metal's clatter.

"Gimme an I."

"Gimme a P."

"Put them together and what you got?"

"Shithead! Shithead! Shithead!"

As quickly as she had climbed up on the hood and begun to jump and shout, Promise Land scooted back into the big Desoto. Midnight was tearing the darkness apart with snarls and Tom Zucold had hit the Cadillac highbeams, but The Grip heard and saw nothing except

Promise Land. Her skin was cool but electric when she crawled on his lap.

"I love you," said The Grip.

"Throw them balls hard as you can and get us a record," Promise Land whispered and kissed him.

Tom Zucold seemed to bang the big iron pan right by The Grip's ear and he woke slowly, grudgingly from a dream he neither wanted to leave nor could remember as soon as he had left it. Sunlight streamed full and golden through the window and he blinked at it. He had been sleeping only a few hours since Promise Land's banana Volkswagen finally clattered off up Yorktown Road. In spite of himself, he felt cheery as if his life had taken a good turn. Lying in bed, wrapped in his brown GI issue blanket, the fine smell of Promise Land still in his nose, The Grip had no obligations, no responsibilities, no debts, no wounds, nothing to prevent him from feeling he stood at the first step up a long ladder that was not only his future but his beginning.

"Best get your ass up and get the area policed," Tom Zucold barked. "If you still in this outfit."

"Sunday," The Grip moaned.

"Sunday all right, but that don't mean piss to the troops in the field. Ittis time to move."

The Grip stirred and smelled bacon. There had never been bacon in the Bowie Garage. Not since he'd lived there anyway. He sat up and pulled his blanket close. The whirr of the Thunderbird seat told him where Tom Zucold was.

"Intelligence working while you asleep," Tom Zucold barked. "Ittis all here." Tom Zucold snapped a newspaper taut in his hands and held it up to the light.

When he had made his way across the room, smelling Promise Land as if she were beside him, The Grip looked at the back of the paper and saw black headlines. He couldn't read them but he didn't have to. They announced new wars in places he didn't know existed and disasters in places he had heard of but couldn't locate. He never read the newspaper because there was nothing he could allow in his life.

"Looks the same as always."

"Lord if you wasn't a monkey I'd ask you to deliver me from monkeys in my house," Tom Zucold said. Then he snapped the paper shut and turned it around and snapped it taut. "Look at this," he barked. "Look right goddamn there in the society section."

The Grip saw it then.

"You seein' it now ain't you, ape?"

"See it," The Grip muttered through tight lips. There was a picture of Cotton Muddleman and his grandmother and a dark-haired woman the paper identified as Molly Mae Midget. They were all standing in front of what the paper called Chapel's eternal flame. In the middle and in front of these people stood Promise Land. She wore a flowered dress that had a lace collar at the neck and a wide-brimmed hat that extended almost over each shoulder. Underneath the picture, in big black letters, it said PROMISE LAND CHAIRS COMMITTEE.

"Mule get hit in his head he know ittis time to move. Tom Zucold know it too," Tom Zucold barked. "See that woman there known all along. Read it and see what she said. Know what it means? Can't mean no damn other thing."

The Grip heard Tom Zucold jerking at his seatbelt but he was reading what the paper said. Promise Land was the new president of the Chapel Garden Committee. Vice-presidents were Molly Mae Midget and Cotton Muddleman. Mrs. Homer Muddleman was historian and sergeant-at-arms. Mrs. Land, the report said, promised to do her best to make Chapel the cleanest, loveliest, most desirable community to live in anywhere around. She planned to work hard with Mayor Billy Carmines to see that the town kept up its historical monuments and kept out undesirables. She believed that tourism would pick up whether they liked it or not and that steady growth was controllable. The paper said the charming Mrs. Land was widely known for her community service, her stable, and her pink Harley-Davidson motorcycle.

"Don't say anything about the Bowie Garage," The Grip said at last.

Tom Zucold tipped his baseball cap back on his head and said, "You think they gone draw you a picture? Jesus don't have to say no names. Ittis there just like I knowed it would be. Been knowing it right along regular. Bet me. But ain't nobody gone take a old soldier like Tom Zucold by surprise. Spit in hell first. Bet me."

The Grip searched the faces in the picture for some kind of clue. Cotton Muddleman squinted bluntly at the camera, his glasses helping to hide his watery shallow eyes. He looked as frankly puzzled as ever. Mrs. Muddleman regarded the camera as if it were about to strike her and seemed no more possessed of a clue than did her grandson. Molly Mae Midget, a woman who appeared about the same age as Promise Land and who was too plump for the tight pants she wore, had her eyes closed and her mouth open. The Grip stopped at Promise Land. There was no doubt that it was the same woman whose smell lingered in The Grip's nose and yet the picture made her look very different. He would never have picked her out as someone who would jump up and down naked on a processsee. Why, he wondered, were people never what you thought they were?

"But I am programmed. Bet me. Look at this," Tom Zucold said. He threw another section of the paper at The Grip. When The Grip had picked it up, he saw that it was the classified ads and one ad was circled in red magic marker. The Grip moved his lips as he read it to himself.

"Say the damn thing out loud," Tom Zucold said.

"Wanted. Weapons. Any size caliber, age, type. Ammunition also. If it shoots we will take it. Reply Box 71, Chapel, ASAP."

"Supply Corps handled that," Tom Zucold said and grinned.

"What does it mean?"

"Apes in the house for Christ's sake," Tom Zucold barked. His face pinched up and darkened. "Mean Tom Zucold going to lay holt to every weapon he can and any aggressor son of a bitch and his kin that attackts this post gone meet his maker. Just like the Constitution says it got to be."

The Grip sniffed the air. It smelled rank suddenly. "Something burning?"

"Godalmight," Tom Zucold said and hit the Thunderbird seat button to bring him upright but he was already upright and it merely chittered under him. "We done burned the bacon."

"I don't know," The Grip said as Tom Zucold finally released himself from the seat belt and darted to the burning bacon.

"Don't know what?" Tom Zucold said. A trail of smoke followed the tiny man out of the Bowie Garage into the lane. After a few minutes Tom Zucold returned and without a word, as if there had been no burning bacon and no pan, climbed into his seat and buckled in.

"What the hell don't you know?"

"Guns," The Grip said. He still held the want ads in front of him as if he had continued reading to see what else might be for sale.

"Know," Tom Zucold said as he tilted himself slightly back and clasped his hands under his head. "Ain't nothing to know. Commencing immediately all troops under Yellow Alert, Condition 2, which means everything but open fire. Can't open fire except under Condition 1. You gone have to inform all troops that we start circling up the processees soon as morning chow and KP is done. No kind of way we can know what heavy stuff they might bring up right off."

Tom Zucold did not appear to be watching The Grip but when The Grip stood before the open commode and pissed loudly, the old man said, "That is if you staying in the unit. Might be she done sabotaged your mind and you be leaving."

The Grip finished and zipped up and glanced at the Champion Spark Plug clock. He saw but paid no attention to what time it was. His head seemed suddenly thick and he was acutely aware that nothing made any sense. He could not remember when there had been sense to anything he did. He turned and went to his bed and started to lace on his combat boots. Then he stopped and looked at Tom Zucold's head and the back of the Thunderbird chair.

"Ain't any troops but you and me, old man." It was the first time that he called Tom Zucold anything but his full name and he spoke with deliberate firmness. But Tom Zucold gave no sign that he heard or understood the test that The Grip hoped was in his words.

"Where you getting any money for them guns? If you find any," The Grip said flatly.

"Don't you worry none about that. The Lord provides for them that helps themselves even if the Lord ain't nothing but a monkey," Tom Zucold said, the buoyancy in his voice clear as he hit the Thunderbird chair button and turned himself around toward The Grip. He had a dead cigar jammed in his mouth now and he spoke around it.

"Ain't spent thirty years in this man's army for nothing. Know better than to field a broke unit, got a reserve treasury." Tom Zucold waited for that to sink in.

"You likely to get in trouble, you know that," The Grip said. "Could get us killed. And it ain't nothing but you crazy as hell." The Grip hadn't wanted to say it but there it was and if it hurt the old man, well then it hurt him.

Tom Zucold hit his button another time and put the chair in what he called the launch position. He unbuckled and dropped to the rug. His back was ramrod straight inside his coveralls and his chin was tucked tight against his chest. He stood directly in front of the television set, just to one side of The Grip's Corvette seat.

"Chance we got to take, son. Men that mean business willing to get killed for it." Tom Zucold hit the rug on his palms and knocked off twenty-five push-ups, the last ten straining and gagging because of the dead cigar in his teeth. Then he bounced up and slid into a parade rest position.

"Got to get strings tight for the hand-to-hand," Tom Zucold grunted. "All business with the civilians got to be restricted, too. No women allowed." Tom Zucold whipped into fifteen quick jumping jacks. Each time his feet cleared the rug he clapped his hands and yelled "Kill" and each time he hit the rug his face turned redder and darker. His hair began to look bleached.

"Can't give up Promise Land," The Grip said, feeling out of control of his destiny. He spoke as calmly as he could but it shook Tom

194

Zucold so that he came down on the side of his ankle and toppled to the rug. But he bounced right back up, then reassumed the parade rest position.

"No choice," Tom Zucold said. "Promise Land is the enemy. Paper said it clear. She the worst enemy of all. Just ain't what you think she is."

"Then I love the enemy."

"Man in a war zone got no business loving the enemy. It's subversive," Tom Zucold said. "Against regulations, too." Suddenly Tom Zucold let out a piercing scream and assumed what was apparently a karate position from which he unleashed a series of violent hand gestures at an invisible enemy. Each time he jabbed or sliced he shouted "Kill" and finally delivered a smashing kick to the side of The Grip's Corvette chair.

"Love can't listen to no regulations. Love her anyway," The Grip said. He knew now that it was futile. There would be no reasoning with Tom Zucold any longer but he had to try.

Tom Zucold started to run in place, slowly at first, lifting one knee and then the other, then accelerating. He panted right away and the darkness in his face had bled out. The Grip wondered how long the old man could take it and glanced from feet to face and face to feet.

"Well, you pays your nickel and takes your chance, soldier," Tom Zucold wheezed between lifts of his legs. His eyes looked dimmer now, his face a terrible pale.

"Better take it slower old man," The Grip said gently.

Tom Zucold was pumping hard when they heard the oncoming raw squeal and grind of brakes, then tires skidding, then the smack of metal and splash of glass against the killer tree.

"Son of a bitch, ittis another one," Tom Zucold said and keeled over on his face in a dead faint.

CHAPTER VI

Onliness

Monday morning just before noon Trooper Drilling wheeled into the front yard of the Bowie Garage and touched his siren lightly to announce his coming. The Grip had just finished gathering his shots into the Havoline box and he stood in the putting circle while he mopped off sweat with his T-shirt. He had put steadily and well for nearly two hours and he felt cleaned inside. Mockingbirds jeered back and forth across the lane but he ignored them as he drew on a clean olive shirt. The thickness and pressure that had been in him when he was wakened was gone now. He walked through the Bowie Garage and saw that Tom Zucold had taken Trooper Drilling over to the killer tree. Trooper Drilling held a clipboard and made brisk notes with a silver ballpoint pen. The patrol cruiser's red bubblegum light whirled silently.

The Grip walked up behind them and stood listening. Trooper Drilling turned and nodded the brim of his Smokey hat to acknowledge The Grip's presence but went on talking to Tom Zucold.

"Trooper Wren got all the details, of course. Got 'em right here on his report. Just that I'm the kind that likes to double check everything, you understand. Say it was lucky that woman was so fat else she be dead. Wren say she look like she was her own airbag. Say them ambulance boys could of used a crane." Trooper Drilling chuckled at his joke but Tom Zucold nodded solemnly.

"Had to pry that door right off that Toyota," Tom Zucold. "You can see the skid marks, what little of them it was."

"Was to Buckroe Beach with the kids yestiddy," Trooper Drilling said and handed Tom Zucold the end of a tape measure. "They lettin' black people in there now. Used to be a beach for each one of us, you understand. Times has changed since we was young. Stick that right on the tree, Colonel."

Trooper Drilling pulled the tape to where the skid marks began on Yorktown Road and then wrote something on the clipboard.

"Don't look like this tree known anything 'bout color," Trooper Drilling said as he walked back. "That old lady last night black as my ass. She related to some of my kin, somehow."

"Everybody's related somehow," The Grip said. It seemed to jump out of his mouth and he was a little embarrassed when both Trooper Drilling and Tom Zucold stared at him as if he had just shit in front of them.

"Promise Land say that, anyway," The Grip said. He blushed nervously and added "But nothing mean anything. She said that too."

Trooper Drilling and Tom Zucold looked at each other and then back at The Grip. As if to cover the awkwardness of the moment, Trooper Drilling said, "Yessir, had me a day off and took them kiddies to the beach. Great day, too. Then old Troop Wren told me this morning it was another one hit that tree and I said I'd just zip on over and see wasn't nothing missing from the accident report. You understand."

They walked past The Grip and entered the Bowie Garage. When The Grip went into the house Tom Zucold had buckled into the

Thunderbird chair and Trooper Drilling was sitting in the Corvette seat.

"Damn if I know how they do it," Tom Zucold said. He had his baseball cap jammed on and a black nub in his teeth.

"Hard to say 'bout that, Colonel." Trooper Drilling puffed on a cigarette that he held between his thumb and finger, then ground it out in the rug. "Leastways you can't figure it statistically. Say you can, but I don't believe it. Speeding, dope, booze, that gets 'em. But then it's a bee gets on they nose or some damn thing. This one easiest enough, though."

Tom Zucold hit the chair button and whirred forward. "Say what?"

"That fat lady just zooming on that gospel music. She headed to church, you understand. Mt. Emmaus Chapel of the New Reformed Holy Spirit, said on the report. Seen it happen before. The Lord got with her so awful hard she done jammed that pedal to the floor and got the tape deck all the way up. Ecstasy, you understand. Ain't nothing like it. Hadn't been for the Lord putting that tree right where it is to slow her down, probably driven right through somebody's house and killed maybe four, five kids. Just sitting down for breakfast, they eyes not hardly open, smelling like warm puppies, and bam. They just gone quick as you can blink. Happen. That's one way to see it seem like."

"You a religious man, Troop?" Tom Zucold said, his eyes bulging.

"Got to be, got to be, Colonel. In this business anyway," Trooper Drilling said. "And this is my religion," he said and patted his chrome pistol.

"I see, yes," Tom Zucold said. "How 'bout something to drink, Troop? Get the boy something to drink, Grip."

"Don't drink much, can't afford to," Trooper Drilling said, "but I will take one of them Alligators if you got one handy."

"He mean Gatorade. Give him one, Grip," Tom Zucold said, then tilted his seat slightly backward to a more relaxed pitch. "Uh, say Troop, you hear any more about that Committee coming to cut down my tree?"

Trooper Drilling stood and stretched and said he had heard nothing more. He sipped the Gatorade and said at least the woman wasn't killed so she was not likely to make the papers and that was good news for the tree. Then he said, "That sure is some fine chair you got, Colonel. Must be great for watching them Redskin games."

Tom Zucold's face had darkened just a little and he said, "Is. But might not last. Can't tell on that yet."

"How's that, Colonel?"

Tom Zucold told Trooper Drilling all about the Citizens Committee and the picture in the paper and how Promise Land was this monkey's girl friend and was just using him to get information about the Bowie Garage and after all it was her and the woman's goddamn greedy family that had come sneaking around when he wasn't even there and it was all tied in with the whore in the pearl bus and the motherfucking Carolina Kid who got his money and left everybody else to suck eggs and the upshot of the whole thing was that nobody was going to take his ass even if he was seventy-year-old because he had been around and he knew a conspiracy when he seen it and he by God had seen it and he wasn't going to be shucked off his land, no sir, and had him a plan and would take a plenty of them before they could get him.

"Push done come to shove," Tom Zucold said loudly. He was straining against his seat belt, his face swollen red. "Man can't make but a few choices and it all come down to who he stand for. In this garrison a man stand for he's buddy or he don't stand at all."

The Grip knew very well that Tom Zucold was talking about him but before he thought of anything to say Trooper Drilling spoke.

"Colonel, I have got the message." Trooper Drilling stood in a relaxed parade rest. His hand rested on the handle of his pistol. His face slowly drew tight and The Grip could see that he was thinking hard.

"Way it is," Tom Zucold said. He sat bolt straight in the Thunderbird chair and his arms waved as if he were describing the sky. "Survival is all. Military man know what is what, why I'm telling you. Can see what everything mean, even a bird feather that done fall out. They fuck you and fuck you and fuck you and the time come you got to say stop here. If you a man."

The Grip could hardly believe what he was hearing. It was insane.

Yet Trooper Drilling seemed taller and harder with every word, nodding, his fingers curling around the pistol.

"They done got Miz Sexton's farm, Colonel," Trooper Drilling said, biting off the words with authority. "Didn't think nothing of it 'til now. She done sold out and gone. Rumor say it gone become a shopping center."

Tom Zucold looked as if he had been struck in the mouth. He pulled the black plug from between his teeth and snapped, "Mrs. Sexton's farm? Border the back of the Bowie Garage? Shopping—Goddamn I seen it coming, know it, you all know it. Goddamn it—"

Tom Zucold hit the Thunderbird seat button and spun around so he could look out the window. He was silent for a minute. Trooper Drilling looked over his shoulder at The Grip and grinned.

"They gone put that new garage over there, too, ain't they. Same people," Tom Zucold said. "Your people done sold out too ain't they."

"Can't say for sure, Colonel. Sound like that be right, though. Might be. Can't say, you understand."

"They wantin' the Bowie Garage bad," Tom Zucold said. He spoke softly now and still looked out the window.

"Like to have me a garage, truly would," Trooper Drilling said. "Ain't nothing better'n being a Trooper. Just exciting as hell. But a man like to have his own place, where he got his tools and he can fix something or not as he take a mind to do. Wisht it was something I could do to help out, Colonel."

"Tom Zucold thinks he needs an army," The Grip said in disgust.

"Got a army," Tom Zucold said weakly.

"In your head maybe," The Grip said quickly.

"Maybe it is," Trooper Drilling volunteered.

"You turning too?" Tom Zucold whined.

"Maybe it is something I can do to help, Colonel. Things looking grim."

The Grip stood at the El Dorado window and gazed over the lane at his record stick. It was a clean, hard evening and the sun seemed

200

to fall in the west at an unusually slow pace so that the light fell across the lane and held for a long time. Ordinarily such a light made him feel comforted, as if he was where he belonged and had done what he was supposed to do. But this evening he did not feel comforted at all. He felt thick and awkward and confused and helpless. He felt restless as if he should be leaving but had no idea where he should go.

Mockingbirds jeered and insects chattered while the light slowly went red. The Grip did not hear them because he kept hearing the conversation between Trooper Drilling and Tom Zucold. All afternoon he had tried to find something to distract himself from whatever it was that had hold of him. He had wirebrushed some Ford spark plugs. That did not work. He had tried to remember stunts from TRUTH OR CONSEQUENCES but they had bored him. He had taken the Montgomery Ward catalog to the back seat of the Desoto and had skimmed the pictures but they were nothing more than lies. For a while he closed his eyes and thought of Promise Land and that was all right but he couldn't shake the nagging suspicion that somehow she was, well, what Tom Zucold thought she was. In the end Tom Zucold's crazy declaration of war kept ringing in his ears.

Trooper Drilling had turned and looked at The Grip and then said, "Seem to me there's always some can't make up they minds, you understand. Man like me can't afford that. Cop got to be ready. Got to act. Got to do it just like that," and he snapped his fingers and drew his pistol. The Grip had flinched just as if he had been shot and Trooper Drilling had laughed, then holstered his weapon.

"Every day a war for me. War 'cause I a cop. War 'cause I black. War 'cause I the kind of man I is. Got to know what is real and what ain't if you like me. That is to say, a Troop can't cruise around guessing who right and who wrong, what is and what ain't. No time, you understand. Got to know in his heart what is real and what ain't. I know the Bowie Garage is real, if you can dig that. My kind of place, see what I mean."

Tom Zucold clapped his hands in the Thunderbird chair and whistled.

The Grip felt stung and annoyed. Did Tom Zucold think he was not loyal? Hadn't he told Promise Land he could not leave when she had said that it was obvious he ought to escape that crazy old man? Wasn't his day a war, too, a war just the same as Trooper Drilling's? Wasn't everybody's? But wasn't it smart to think about things some?

"That 'zactly why I can see the Colonel need some experienced troops to help get things right. 'Zactly why I'm going to take my vacation and bivouac at the Bowie Garage. Man got to lend a hand to his bro when it's a clear and present danger. Learned that a long time ago in the Masons. Someday when I got my garage, maybe it'll be me that needs help, you understand."

Tom Zucold had taken Trooper Drilling out on a tour of the processees and the perimeters of the Bowie Garage. The Grip walked around the house and tried to think of home. Outside he could hear Tom Zucold chattering and occasionally breaking into song about the wild blue yonder. He could not get over how Tom Zucold had unsnapped his seat buckle and scooted down to Trooper Drilling and kissed him on both cheeks. On *both* cheeks! Tom Zucold said that was how Napoleon commissioned his officers. It made The Grip sick to his stomach.

The Grip backed away from the El Dorado door and entered the house. Tom Zucold clung halfway up the rope and his strings were popping with sweat. It did not appear he would get any higher.

"Time," Tom Zucold wheezed.

The Grip looked at the Champion Spark Plug clock over the open commode and said, "Just after noon." But it could not be just after noon. He looked at the long red second hand. It wasn't moving. The goddamned clock had gone haywire and stopped. He stared at the moon face of the clock until it seemed to become a kind of face staring back at him, a mute and mocking face which somehow threatened him. He felt pushed and defenseless like a child before a bully. He could leave. He could turn and flee before the bully, maybe try to outrun him. His mother had told him to do that. Suddenly the face of the clock became the face of his mother, screaming and drunk, only silent as in a dream. It was hard to tell what she was saying but she was raging and it had something to do with time, he was late, too late, like his father, and it was just too goddamn late.

"Home," The Grip said. Then "Home?" But the clock face did not answer. It didn't work. The black hands were frozen and the red hand drooped.

"Broke," said Tom Zucold at The Grip's waist. "Goddamn time is broke. Ain't nothing the way it used to be."

Anyone who did not know the Bowie Garage would have imagined that its business was steady and profitable during that week. At least it would have seemed so from Yorktown Road, for Tom Zucold had the garage lights on early and late every day and there was always a car in the garage. Only The Grip knew that Tom Zucold worked without stopping on the processees. When he did take a few minutes away from pumping air through gas lines and patching old tires he spent them on repairing weapons. The Grip put his shots and mostly stayed out of Tom Zucold's way.

He was in bed when he heard thunder early Friday morning. It crackled and boomed and he drew his blanket up around his neck. It smelled of mildew and reminded him that he hadn't seen Promise Land in quite a long time. He had seen Clifton hitchhiking on Yorktown Road and Clifton had said she was fine, had been out scouting for a glider plane. Clifton said she told him to say she missed The Grip and would be in touch.

A series of thunder cracks came then and The Grip shuddered. They came again and then again and he realized that something was knocking on the wall.

"Goddamn, man, I been left out in the rain most of my life but this takes the goddamn cake. Goddamn," Trooper Drilling said when The Grip finally opened the El Dorado door and let in the soaked man. He was wearing fatigue pants, but not the camouflage type, a field jacket and an Australian bush cap. Dog tags jingled at his neck when he slapped his wet duffle bag on the concrete floor.

"Didn't expect you so early," Tom Zucold said, yawning in the darkness of the house.

"Come undercover," Trooper Drilling said as he stripped off his bush hat and slapped it against his legs. "Wife let me off 'bout a mile up Yorktown Road. Come down through the bush. Lassie couldn't find that track."

"But you don't go on vacation 'til tomorrow," Tom Zucold said.

"Got sick," Trooper Drilling said and chuckled. "Wife gone call me in sick when time come. Be sick the whole vacation look like."

"Best thing is that you move that Corvette seat out in the Bowie Garage and lay your sleeping bag in front of the television."

"Man it gone make me happy being back in the saddle again," Trooper Drilling said. Only then did The Grip see that the Trooper was wearing his chrome-plated pistol. And when he turned to go after the Corvette seat, there was a bayonet shoved inside the Trooper's boot.

By midmorning The Grip and Trooper Drilling had moved the classic 1949 Ford into place against the right flanking bedroom wall. It was necessary to hitch themselves into tandem ropes like a couple of mules but Tom Zucold kept a firm hand on the reins and they pulled evenly. The rain fell easily after the thunderheads had passed and they were grateful for it on their faces. Trooper Drilling said that they were lucky the old Ford still had some air in its tires and The Grip told him that Tom Zucold and he had managed that on their own. It was not luck. In fact, the problem had not been the tires and moving the car but rolling it over on its side so the under-carriage formed a solid breastwork. The Grip had finally to attach a pulley to the roof overhead and he had been able to do it without the wasps swarming. It had been no trouble after that to heave the Ford on its side, wheels turning slowly in the air. Once they had found the method, putting the Desoto at the left flank wall was a breeze.

"Got my first piece in one like this," Trooper Drilling said as he drew the rope tight through the pulley above the Desoto.

"Piece of what?" The Grip asked as he prepared to push at the bottom of the car. The Trooper laughed and did not answer.

Tom Zucold strutted anxiously as they put the Desoto in its place and then casually said they would have to make some adjustments since the cement mixer obviously had to go between the two cars.

Both The Grip and Trooper Drilling bitched caustically about this change in the plans. Tom Zucold grinned. It was the right and privilege of every soldier to bitch and he knew that when the bitching was most intense things were getting done.

"Gone have to retract that Desoto and put that mixer in there, then slip that Desoto up against it," Tom Zucold said as he studied the terrain. Then, anticipating his troop's questions, he said, "Hard to figure what artillery can do until you got your bunker built. Then ittis clear." He puffed on a black stump and his baseball cap was low over his eyes. "Now Tom Zucold see what that motherhumpin' mixer come to the Bowie Garage for. Always wondered. Go right there," he snapped and whipped his arm straight out like a fake Nazi salute. He paused just a second then strode forward and passed through the El Dorado door that shut with an expensive, solid sound.

"War is a bitch, ain't it," Trooper Drilling said.

The Grip would have sworn that it would take no less than three days and a small army to move the dead mixer, but he would have been wrong. He would also have been amazed at what two men under pressure can accomplish. They spent the rest of Friday forcing some air into the mashed tires of the great hulk and jerryrigging a winch on the trunk of a gumball tree. By Saturday dusk they had managed to pull and wiggle and push and slide the dead weight into the slot Tom Zucold had designated. They had all but torn the rear end out of the panel truck and had burned through the ropes twice. Finally the old mixer heaved over on its bloated belly like a dinosaur with a heart attack. Trooper Drilling stood at the open window of the El Dorado door and hollered that he couldn't see a damn thing and couldn't even get the door open for the monster. Tom Zucold hollered back from the lane that this was perfect according to specifications. Tom Zucold then marched into the Bowie Garage and ordered Trooper Drilling to take five with the other troops.

"Say Grip, man, that was some day, you understand," Trooper

Drilling said as he leaned against the Edsel with The Grip. Trooper Drilling lit a cigarette that was shaped like a submarine and puffed and held his breath and pushed it toward The Grip.

"Don't smoke," The Grip said.

"Hawaiian stuff, bro. Paco lolo. Have some."

"Why you doing this?" The Grip said sharply. He had been wanting to ask all day.

Trooper Drilling took another big puff and closed his eyes and very, very slowly let a stream of smoke from his mouth.

"I could move that mixer by muhself, dig it," Trooper Drilling said. He studied The Grip's face for a moment, then looked off at the sky.

"Man, he against them. They coming. They always coming. They been coming ever since they come after my daddy and they always gone be coming. I can't stop it. You can't stop it. We can't stop it. But that old dude in there, he done slid right on past all that. He think he can stop them and it make me feel some better just to let it seem like I gone stop them, too. Ain't real man, is illusion—just like that television and them movies. You dig?"

"But who is *they*?"

Trooper Drilling took another deep puff and stayed on it. After a minute he said, "Nobody. Anybody. Everything. Say man you sure you don't want some of this stuff? Knock you back good."

The Grip asked again who *they* were.

"They? Well bro, gone tell you. *They* is whatever get between you and who you think you is. It'll get at you like a smell and you can't run from it and you can't hurt it away. First thing you know everything you lookin' at ain't what you really lookin' at. It's always something coming at you and most times you handle it but time come it all flow together and it bigger, stronger, more, and stead of seeing light you see dark, stead of feeling open you done closed, stead of throwing that ball for a record you trying to get it in the air."

They stood silent for a few moments while The Grip tried to understand what Trooper Drilling said. It almost made sense. Then

Trooper Drilling asked did he know why he was staying with a crazy man.

The Grip did not know and honestly said so.

It was too late for TRUTH OR CONSEQUENCES when they marched into the darkness of the Bowie Garage. Both men were clammy with cold sweat and stank and could hardly stand with fatigue. The Grip went to his bed and sat on it. Trooper Drilling sank to the floor and lay on his back. The Grip was surprised to see that the television set was on, though there was only a fuzzy glow of light showing. He watched as Tom Zucold set up a packing crate before the television and put some papers on top of the crate.

"Be at ease Troops," Tom Zucold said smartly. "Chow call coming soon but we got a priority briefing here."

"War is sure a bitch," Trooper Drilling said happily. He got up and placed his cot perpendicular to the television screen. The Grip came over and sat beside him. Trooper Drilling turned to The Grip and said, "I sure hope the chow stinks. Situation like this it ought to."

"Don't worry," The Grip said.

"Gentlemen," Tom Zucold said as he tapped on the packing crate with a broken radio antenna, "While you have been erecting breastworks, Command has requisitioned a map of the area. Can't fight a war without a map. I'll put the map up now."

Tom Zucold took one of the papers and taped it with masking tape to the glowing television screen. The Grip leaned forward and saw that it was a crudely drawn sketch of the Bowie Garage and its ground. Trooper Drilling also leaned forward attentively and nodded each time Tom Zucold touched one of the area's topographical or strategic points of interest, such as the killer tree, the curve in Yorktown Road, the houses of civilians across the road, the putting lane, the rear ditch, etc. The Grip slowly began to drift with the official flow of words and was barely able to hold himself upright until the briefing was completed and the chow call made.

On Sunday Tom Zucold ordered The Grip to commandeer and procure a band saw for special military usage. The Grip passed the order on to his junior in service, Trooper Drilling, who crossed Yorktown Road when he had ascertained no traffic was near and borrowed one from a civilian who also gave him a kiss on the cheek and a pickled pig's foot.

Working under the close supervision of Tom Zucold, The Grip cut an old peeling sheet of plywood into four squares and then, with a can of orange day-glow paint that had been abandoned in the cement mixer, he painted four signs that said OFFICIAL: WAR ZONE. Trooper Drilling quickly nailed the signs to trees along Yorktown Road and hung one on a pine at the end of The Grip's putting lane.

When the signs had been hung and when Tom Zucold had inspected them, he ordered The Grip to have Liaison Officer Drilling report to the Thunderbird chair. Trooper Drilling, it turned out, was asked to supply an opinion as to the legality of such signs, not to mention the security breach they might represent.

"I couldn't say for sure one way or the other," Trooper Drilling reported in both situations.

"What I want to know is can I shoot 'em legal if they come past those signs," Tom Zucold said. He leaned against the seat belt.

"Colonel," Trooper Drilling replied, removing his motorcycle helmet, "that is a thing you will need to check out with a lawyer. They don't teach a cop nothing to do with that. We just answer the horn and keep the peace."

"No time to reach the Adjutant General," Tom Zucold blurted.

"If I wasn't sick I could call the station and find out, but you know how it is, Colonel," Trooper Drilling said.

The Grip listened to Tom Zucold discuss why it was not necessary to call the state police in such matters and watched a caterpillar cross his boot. He was not aware at first that it was being dragged by an ant.

"Old business," Tom Zucold said abruptly. Then he climbed down and stepped briskly to his post before the television and snapped it on. "You troops give me your attention here. Command done had a strategy meeting and here it is." He pointed to a new line on the map taped to the screen.

208

"It's a line," The Grip said.

"Trench," Tom Zucold barked. "Command want it dug all around the Bowie Garage. But we only gone dig on the flanks at first. No sense in giving away the plan."

It took The Grip and Trooper Drilling all day Monday to make two trenches three feet wide and four feet deep. The last foot was dug in mud and filled quickly in with water. Trooper Drilling said Command probably didn't figure on the Chesapeake Bay.

Tuesday morning Tom Zucold said Command had given the troops furlough time in the yard. He had noticed that both The Grip and Trooper Drilling were lethargic.

"Command knows a troop's need better'n a troop," Trooper Drilling said.

The Grip had feared that he had lost his edge with the shots. Then he found that he had lost maybe ten feet of his lane to the cement mixer. He paced restlessly and inspected each of the shots.

"Go on and heave them suckers," Trooper Drilling said.

The Grip moved the record stick as far to the end of the lane as he could without going into the ditch. When he paced it off he found he had about seventy feet and he had never put it that far anyway. But he was still thinking about the ditch when he coiled and whirled and let the first one go. His lack of concentration caused it to shoot off to his right. When it thudded harmlessly on the ground he knew it would have taken out the Desoto steering wheel if they had not moved that processee.

"Woooeee, heave them mothuhs," Trooper Drilling said. He had climbed up on the huge front tire of the cement mixer and he puffed one of those funny cigarettes as he looked down on The Grip's puts.

The Grip felt himself growing cleaner and stronger with each put. He had missed this. He put one after the other and each one sailed a little farther. Still, he could not entirely shake himself from the feeling that what he did had no function, no meaning, that even if he got the record, it would count for nothing.

After supper Tom Zucold and Trooper Drilling told war stories, each one delighting the other with a story that was more gruesome and horrible than the last. Both men had apparently seen indescribable combat and though all the stories contained lost heads and mangled limbs they were always about fools who had done the stupid thing they'd been trained not to do. The Grip had only stories of throwing the shot and that one time in Baltimore, so he had kept quiet. Neither of the two men noticed him when he got up silently and crawled in bed. Or if they noticed him neither said anything about it.

The Grip slept badly, tossing and throwing off his blanket, waking to drag it back. He dreamed and was shaken by the dreams but when he awoke he could not remember what he had dreamed. It seemed that Promise Land had been in them but he couldn't say that was true. When he sat on the end of Trooper Drilling's cot for morning briefing he was groggy and fought to stay sitting upright.

"Sleeping on post is bad business son. Get a man shot in combat," Tom Zucold said, and gently tapped The Grip's head with the radio antenna. The Grip shook his head and tried to pay attention.

"Today's mission men is to get the Studebaker Hawk," Tom Zucold said as he pointed his antenna. He added "Here." The Grip saw that he meant to butt the Hawk against the Desoto.

"Second run," Tom Zucold said, "We'll lay in the green Edsel here." This meant that the Edsel would front the Hawk and there would be a solid line of processees on the side of the Bowie Garage. "That should cover our southeast flank. Now then," Tom Zucold said sipping from a cup of steaming coffee, "bring up the Galaxy and Apollo on that northwest flank and we'll have our asses covered jake."

"Any questions," Tom Zucold said and went smartly to a parade rest. When there were none, Tom Zucold said "Dismissed men."

The Grip and Trooper Drilling had become practised at their jobs and the work went quickly. They had the Hawk and the Edsel both snug in their berths by noon and Tom Zucold said they could take a little extra break with their lunch. No one had said anything but Trooper Drilling and The Grip had begun to eat apart from Tom

Zucold. Tom Zucold had not said lunch, but Enlisted Mess. The troops ate sitting on the balded tires by the putting lane.

"Colonel," Trooper Drilling said while they hitched the winch to the Galaxy, "Colonel it look like a car heaved up on its side thataway make a breastwork just high enough for a man to shoot over."

The Grip nodded in agreement.

"Course, the Colonel have to have a box or two if he gone do some shooting," Trooper Drilling added quietly.

The Grip jerked his head up from the rope he was threading through the Galaxy. It was true. Why hadn't he thought of it? Obviously only Trooper Drilling and himself were tall enough to shoot over those cars. But Tom Zucold said nothing. After a while he said he had some errands to run and left The Grip in charge as Officer of the Day.

When Tom Zucold returned, backing the panel truck to the Bowie Garage's big overhead door, he hollered "Gimme a hand, troops." He popped the two wing doors in the back open.

"It's guns, man," Trooper Drilling sang beside The Grip. "It's load-'em-up and blow-'em-away for sure. Out of sight."

The Grip could see that it was true. There was a small arsenal spread on the floor of the panel truck and Tom Zucold stood behind them like a tiny demon. The Grip was astonished and though he felt a quick heaviness in his spirit there was also an excitement and he wanted to hold one.

"Four M-16s, three Enfields, stout and true. One Winchester Model 12 pump twelve-gauge, deadly on squirrel, rabbit, possum or other small game, such as women. One Ithaca double barrel, twenty gauge, one barrel defunct. One J. C. Higgins single shot .22, stock cracked but repaired with good electrical tape, sniper potential. One Colt revolver, facsimile of the old Navy Colt, fires perfect on alternate shots, trigger loose. One regulation zip-gun, sawed-off tubular steel with heavy-duty rubber band. One USA Coast Guard flare gun. All weapons carrying three rounds ammo or more." Tom Zucold beamed as he ticked off his weapon inventory.

"Jesus H.," Trooper Drilling said and moved forward past The Grip. He lifted the big-mouthed flare gun, cocked it open, and said, "What the hell caliber is this mother?"

"That is a flare pistol, US Coast Guard regulation equipment," Tom Zucold answered. "Excellent weapon for repelling boarders or other enemies at close range. Burn a mortal hole if a man get him a close enough shot. Now you troops snap to here and get these weapons unloaded."

The Grip and Trooper Drilling spent most of Thursday cleaning and doing what repairs they could with the weapons. Some of the pieces gleamed in the corner by the open commode and The Grip couldn't help feeling a little surge of pride. He glanced at them all during TRUTH OR CONSEQUENCES. Tom Zucold had arranged them along the wall, at neat intervals, so that they were stacked like the remnants of an ancient war for which there were no longer any survivors to bitch or reminisce. The entire bedroom had that banana smell of gun solvent, a smell that Trooper Drilling said was sweeter to him than the smell of pussy. It was, Trooper Drilling claimed, like being on a big football team that knew it couldn't lose. Or like getting that pussy you never thought you'd get in a hundred lifetimes. The Grip remembered all that talk about teams and pussy from the Army. It was, he guessed, what men deployed against the enemy, boredom and death.

"Goddamn, I ain't been this happy in a long time," Trooper Drilling said.

On Friday Command sent the order to extend the main redoubt trench all the way up to, but not including, the primary corridor entrance to the Bowie Garage. According to Command scuttlebutt no one had yet ascertained the vulnerability of that entrance or the probability of frontal assault. Command, Tom Zucold, halted what and when it wanted and it started up what and when it wanted.

"Same old fucking story. Make a man want to quit this goddamn army. Same old hurry up and wait, hurry up and wait," Tom Zucold said as he dismissed the troops and sent them to their mission.

"Get this sucker done like they say and time we get back to bunks that fucking Command gone change its mind and back out we gone go," Trooper Drilling said as he and The Grip slogged up shovel after shovel of dirt.

When they returned to the Bowie Garage, sure enough Command had sent down its decision. The redoubt would be extended before the primary entrance to the Bowie Garage. It had been declared vulnerable and critical. Command congratulated all troopers on work completed so far with no casualties and zero defects. The troopers slogged back out and linked up the pincers of the redoubt, then settled in for evening chow.

They ate quietly, each man alone with his thoughts in his own way. They were bone weary and ached from the digging but each was ready, if called upon, to give more of himself. The Grip leaned against a two-by-four wall support and tried to remember what the Bowie Garage had been like when he first came. It was all so far away, another life it seemed. He tried to focus on the lane he had built and the processees in a neat line. He remembered the excitement of waiting for the coming of the Carolina Kid and wondered where the Kid was now. There was so much darkness in his mind. They had transformed the Bowie Garage into a formidable fortress and he knew that any assault would surely mean severe casualties. It was a little like playing war with toy soldiers and chunks of wood and brick. It really was that easy to shove a fort into place and occupy it. But what did all this have to do with what they had lost at the Moose Hall? Would a battle, a war change anything? Why did nothing ever connect as it surely ought to, as Tom Zucold had once said things connected—if you had the right angle of vision? The Grip closed his eyes and yet he could not shut out the pressure that was like hearing the pin pulled on a grenade. *It* was ahead— only he didn't know what *it* was. The closest he could come to it left him smelling Promise Land and shivering with a kind of vague terror.

Tom Zucold rapped on the wall of the Bowie Garage and announced it was time for the evening briefing. The Grip opened his eyes and stared at the broken Champion Spark Plug clock. A spider crawled on the clock's white face.

"Command has noted we ain't got proper visibility," Tom Zucold announced. He had assumed the now familiar parade rest position before the television screen. His voice was firm and authoritative, but not harsh. It was not loud but it filled the house. The Grip wondered what would have happened if Tom Zucold had been taking the poster test but he knew there would be no more poster tests. Neither The Grip nor Tom Zucold spoke as Trooper Drilling belatedly put his cot into place and made room for The Grip to sit down. Then Tom Zucold patiently outlined what the Intelligence boys had come up with.

"Command gone have our asses we don't shape up," Tom Zucold snapped. "Any damn fool ought to see what we never seen, men. We standing too close to what we seeing, so we ain't seeing it. Got to back off and fan out and expect the unexpected."

The Grip had no idea what Tom Zucold was talking about and after a while it didn't matter because he had drifted off to sleep with his eyes open. This was a trick that all soldiers have mastered during their service. The Grip watched Tom Zucold's mouth move and from time to time he nodded assent but he was watching Promise Land, smelling her, feeling the softness of her, wondering if she was at home thinking of him.

The Saturday morning briefing was just what The Grip knew it would be, a repeat of the one he had slept through. Trooper Drilling told him that was sure as hell the army, everything done double and triple. The whole briefing had consisted of outlining preparations for a night attack.

It was raining in the yard, a soft drenching rain that was common to this terrain in early June. The Grip knew that seeds in the fields were starting to burst open and the fishermen who lived only a few miles away would be mending their nets in the wharfhouses. Everything you looked at was feverishly green. He boosted Trooper Drilling into the biggest pine tree at the apex of the curve in Yorktown Road. His shoulders hurt from Trooper Drilling's hard combat boots but he said nothing.

"Man this gone light up somebody's life," Trooper Drilling said from the darkness of the pine limbs. He was carrying a string of headlights and a roll of thickly insulated wire, plus some wire cutters, some electrical tape, a hammer and some U-shaped brads. He went up easily, pulling himself through dead pine needles and snapped branches, and The Grip admired the skills that a man got from the Green Beret training. Even the rain did not seem to affect Trooper Drilling's ability to motivate in the tree. His feet stayed as snug on the bark as a locust's.

By late afternoon they had the headlights stripped from all the processees and had installed them in a dozen strategic trees, splicing lines and running them carefully down the trunks and underground to a main switch inside the Bowie Garage. The evening light was a solid gray and might have been sufficient for a trial run but Tom Zucold said they would wait until dark.

"It ain't no telling but that they will attackt at night when they think we least expecting them," Tom Zucold hissed. He stood straddling two stacked tires in front of the Bowie Garage, a tiny colossus, and faced the gumball tree where The Grip helped Trooper Drilling to the ground.

"Bastards and devious gooks, ever motherhunching one. They known to send mass attackts, human waves screaming and scaring the shit out people. But by God we gone be ready this time."

They waited. Trooper Drilling said it was Saturday and Tom Zucold said that Command known that. Trooper Drilling said they might as well watch the end of the football game on television but when they turned it on all they got was College Scoreboard. They waited. At last Tom Zucold positioned The Grip at the primary entrance and Trooper Drilling at the El Dorado door. He counted down to lightup and pulled the switch.

Rain was still sweeping the yard like a fine snow and it caught the flood of flaring light everywhere they looked. Instantly the whole world had turned a silver glittering. Midnight leaped at his chain and bit the air and snarled viciously. After a few minutes the civilians across the road edged warily onto the porches and stood, arms folded like Indians, whispering among themselves.

"Post number one, report," Tom Zucold said.

"Check," The Grip answered, giving the agreed signal.

"Post number two, report."

"Check," Trooper Drilling said.

"Hey Uncle Troop, them your lights?" Clifton shouted across the road.

"That's unauthorized communication. You gone be in the deep shit boy," Tom Zucold shouted back. He strode out into the splendidly sparkling world and made a quick tour of the yard, then whipped back inside the Bowie Garage and plunged everything into a wet darkness.

The Grip remained at his post. He could see the figures on the porch across the street. They were outlined against their house lights and he could hear them talking. He wanted desperately to call out to them, to warn them that *it* was coming, only he didn't know what *it* was and he did not want to betray Tom Zucold. He forced himself to watch the edge of the trees, half hoping there would be something he could call out in a report. There was nothing, not even the face of Bob Barker that somehow he was sure was hidden just behind the darkness.

They worked on, laboring against what would not come and what Tom Zucold insisted was nearly upon them. The Grip woke and dreamed and slept thinking about *it*. *It* had him and clutched him as surely as an undertow off Cape Hatteras. Time passed and he and Trooper Drilling began to move in accordance, with the greased harmony of two transmission gears.

Tom Zucold saw that it was necessary to construct observation posts. The order came down from Command and it sent The Grip and Trooper Drilling back to the trees. This time the order specified counter-stealth and Trooper Drilling first blackened The Grip's face with ash from the long-destroyed Corvette. They slunk out through a mist that hung over Miz Sexton's soybean field. It was easy to find and requisition the supplies that Command had dictated. Chapel was a sleepy suburban town whose fields were rapidly being sliced up into plots by developers taking advantage of the military presence at Langley Air Force Base and Fort Eustis. The town was full of half-built spec houses that sat funerally quiet along the creeks. They commandeered two-by-fours and pine planks, sheets of tar paper and plywood, two kegs of nails and some industrial wiring. Hour after hour they slipped noiselessly along the ditch and into a stand of poplar, then around the edge of a reedy swamp. If The Grip had not outranked and overruled Trooper Drilling, they would have moved through the swamp itself. Nevertheless, Trooper Drilling alerted him to taking care of their trail. No one saw them.

"You see that?" Trooper Drilling hissed on the last run. He had taken cover behind a fallen pine log.

"Didn't see anything," The Grip said beside him.

"Over t'other side of that hydrangea. Didn't you see it? Look like a face? Small, ugly, like a child?"

The Grip looked hard now at the hydrangea but its thick clusters of blossoms all began to look like faces. "Ain't nothing, let's go."

They moved out. The Grip heard Trooper Drilling behind him, coiled in the industrial wire, say, "Something over there on Promise Land's ground."

On the tenth day of Trooper Drilling's vacation, tired but also a little exhilarated from their surprising accomplishment, they constructed three observation posts, two in pines at either edge of the Bowie Garage's front flanks and one in a gumball at the rear perimeter. The Grip had done most of the actual carpentry work, discovering with pleasure that he was quite adept with his hands in spite of Tom Zucold's early doubts. Trooper Drilling was content to pass up the planks and the tools and stand wary guard below. When The Grip had completed the last of the front stations he sat back and looked down the two straights of Yorktown Road that fed into the infamous curve where cars so often squealed. Except he saw that there would be no cars squealing for a while. They couldn't because traffic had both picked up and slowed down.

"Look like them civilians calling everybody they know to watch," Trooper Drilling said cheerfully.

"Might be a trick. Be wary," Tom Zucold called.

Below and in front of him The Grip saw that a kind of garrison of civilians had formed during the day. People cruised slowly in every imaginable kind of car, even on tractors. The yards were full of spectators. It was clearly impossible for anyone to attain enough speed to squeal around the curve so long as this parade continued.

"Crazy, all them people," The Grip said when he had descended. "What can they want?"

"They don't want no more than anybody else," Trooper Drilling said. He waved to someone who waved back. "Related to her somehow. They just want to be famous and rich and sexy. What else is it?" He giggled.

"They trying to see and be seen, bro," Trooper Drilling said.

It was hard to miss them. The crowds came all afternoon, the cars winding slowly around the curve, music blaring from convertibles, beer cans tinkling onto the asphalt. At one point The Grip saw Trooper Drilling sprint across the street and talk to a man that The Grip knew owned the big pink house on the end. He worried that Tom Zucold would see this and accuse Trooper Drilling of being AWOL but the old man was busy inside the Bowie Garage and Trooper Drilling scurried back without trouble.

"Them bloods getting into it," Trooper Drilling said.

"Say *it*?"

"Dude owning them two houses there say he gone take advantage of the good thing. Say he called in sick at the shipyard. Gone rent out space in his yards for them that want to watch. Quarter for standees, fifty cents for sittees. Get a dollar for plastic lawn chairs."

The Grip watched the flow of the crowd, its buoyancy like that of a holiday crowd. People sang and chatted and strolled. Once he saw Tom Zucold bolt from the primary entrance to the Bowie Garage out to the edge of his ground and holler at a woman who had curlers in her hair. Maybe, The Grip thought, Tom Zucold figured the curlers were some kind of new communications gear. If he did, he had kept it to himself. If he didn't think that, The Grip sure as hell wasn't going to plant the thought by asking why he had rushed out and hollered. He felt the need for control more than ever, for whatever *it* was he knew that time was short and *it* was coming hard.

Still he couldn't stop watching the spectators as they watched him. Women with babies came and some men in suits, obviously on their way home from work. Some teenagers in T-shirts and cutoffs gathered and punched each other on the arms and made crude jokes very loudly. One particularly looked like the Carolina Kid. The Grip had climbed up into the observation post now, more to escape being seen than to see, but the boy spotted him and held up a sheet that had printed on it SHOOT THE LIGHTS OUT. The boy grinned but soon tired of holding up the sheet and sat on it. He was not the only one with a sign. In fact they seemed to be popping up everywhere. The Grip saw one that said TOM ZUCOLD'S A FOOL and another that said DON'T LOSE YOUR GRIP and another that said CARMINES FOR KING AND PROMISE LAND FOR QUEEN. He was trying to figure out this last one when Tom Zucold once again roared up to the edge of Yorktown Road.

"Goddamn freaks," Tom Zucold screamed. "You think ittis any fun in this? You think life is any fun? Ittis goddamn sweat and blood, that's what. Go home, if you got a home. Leave a man alone to do what he can."

The Grip watched Tom Zucold through the pine needles and saw him whipping his pants with the radio antenna. He was surprised to see Tom Zucold abruptly about-face and rip back into the Bowie Garage. But he was more surprised at the round of cheers and clapping that followed the old man across the street.

When The Grip came out under the closing darkness and entered the Bowie Garage he felt that something had changed, accelerated, fixed itself. He ate his fish and grits quietly while Trooper Drilling and Tom Zucold swapped old stories. He was not surprised when he saw the map illuminated on the television screen and he was not surprised to see that the Champion Spark Plug clock was still broken. But he stared open-mouthed when he saw the poster of the Carolina Kid mounted between the clock and the open commode.

They passed the next week as if it were a nightmare. The Grip felt constantly on the edge of an explosion and increasingly wanted a way out. But there seemed no way short of outright betrayal and there was the chance that nothing would happen after all. And there was also the lulling comfort of camp routine. During the mornings The Grip put the shots until his body tingled and ached nicely. Trooper Drilling cleaned and recleaned weapons, sometimes practising a quick draw with his revolver, and always pumping Tom Zucold for information about how to run a garage. Each night as soon as it grew dark Tom Zucold sent his troops into the trees where they would stand to their battle stations. Tom Zucold counted by the thousand until he felt they had had time to secure, then threw the switch that flooded everything with an eerie brutal light. There was always a response from the spectators that Tom Zucold called "freaks" and usually it was cheering. While they waited for this moment the spectators entertained themselves by chanting and singing all sorts of songs, including gospel and dirty. From time to time The Grip would gaze over the faces and wonder who the people were, what they did, where they lived, but usually he just listened to them. Their faces were like a nest of baby birds, always open and always making noise. Tom Zucold said it was worse than the squealing tires had been, if you could believe that.

The Grip knew that if they could have easily seen him they would have been nasty. He had heard them call him a monster already. But he was well camouflaged with his fatigues and was nearly invisible from the road. When he grew bored with the spectators he looked down on the Bowie Garage. It sat like a hump on the ground, blacked out by Command order. Sometimes even as he watched the house he could hardly believe he lived there. Or that anyone lived there, for that matter. So far it had seemed almost sane in the trees while the madness in the house gathered strength and seemed to close in.

Once Tom Zucold had nearly choked in the Thunderbird seat. They were watching TRUTH OR CONSEQUENCES and the stunt was that a man had to stuff himself in a telephone booth with as many women as he could. Bob Barker had said the man could win a brand new Ford Pinto. But it wasn't clear just what the man had to do except be smothered by those women. Right in the middle of Bob Barker's attempt to explain, Tom Zucold leaped against his seat belt, his mouth full of fish. Clearly, The Grip thought, Tom Zucold only meant to jump to the floor and forgot his seat belt. He grabbed the tiny man, freed him, and began to pound his back. Tom Zucold thrashed in his grip and his face turned dark red.

"Think he just trying to get a word in," Trooper Drilling said calmly.

When The Grip finally released him and he had caught his breath, Tom Zucold said he seen it in the stunt. They were boxed in the Bowie Garage. It was clear to him that the Committee knew their weakness. The Committee wasn't going to make a costly frontal assault. Tom Zucold said the attack would probably come by air, just like the helicopter ships in Vietnam.

"That happen," said Tom Zucold, "we dead as ducks on a pond." He looked up into the roof beams. "That happen onliest chance we got is your shooting, men."

"Can't shoot," Trooper Drilling said almost absently.

"What's that? What's that?" Tom Zucold said, snapped back into the house.

"My vacation 'bout over, Colonel. You understand," Trooper Drilling said. He was sitting on his cot and he grinned. He did not seem unhappy at all.

"Vacation?" Tom Zucold said.

"Over. Troop got to go back to the force. On the payroll. Troop can't be here when the shooting starts. Just the way things are, way the cake splits."

"Where the hell you going?" Tom Zucold was visibly shaken.

"Out there," Trooper Drilling said. "I got to know what is real and what ain't. Told you that, Colonel. Back into the world."

The Grip had seen this coming but he had hoped it wouldn't happen. Trooper Drilling was as crazy as Tom Zucold, only in a different way. Trooper Drilling had been playing war just as if he'd been a child. It was as if he had gone away to a kind of war camp. But Trooper Drilling was a cop. And he was a killer. He was reality itself, having no choice in what he did, offering no choices to anyone around him. Why wouldn't he be happy? Everything was clear and his path was obvious, no anxiety, no hassle, no complications. If there was an assault on the Bowie Garage, The Grip saw immediately, Trooper Drilling would be leading the charge.

"Out there," The Grip said like an echo.

"Hadn't counted on desertion," Tom Zucold whined.

Trooper Drilling looked into the brown leather of his hands and said, "No choice, Colonel. Got to stick with the law. Ain't like it hadn't been fun, though."

"How come you stayed a week past your vacation?" Tom Zucold said. He sounded hard and suspicious now.

"Been sick. Ain't you noticed? I done took five sicks."

Tom Zucold stood still for a moment. Then the red drained from his face and he looked smaller than ever. He walked to the light switch and flipped it but no one could see any light since it was just early afternoon. The old man said no more. He climbed into the Thunderbird chair and tilted it so that he could stare up the rope and after a while fell into a sleep that was light and restless. The troops did not receive an order from Command that night but they went into the trees anyway.

The next morning Trooper Drilling and The Grip were up at dawn, the pan banging hard and loud. There was a briefing before morning chow and Tom Zucold stood on a packing crate to announce the formal order transferring Trooper Drilling out of the garrison, effective at 2300 hours, no advance pay provided, no per diem given, no travel orders cut. Embarrassed a little, coughing lightly, Tom Zucold took the occasion to extend the entire camp's gratitude for a job well done. And he hoped that Trooper Drilling would certainly convey Command's appreciation for his wife's part in the covert operations which had made it possible for him to be with the Bowie Garage.

Trooper Drilling stood before the packing crate when Tom Zucold asked him to say a few words. He hitched his pants and said he was a man of few words but he felt privileged to serve with the Bowie Garage. He said something The Grip missed about a far, far better thing and then something about freedom and then said "The onliest thing I got to say at this point in time is that I hope the Colonel gets all that he got coming. He one tough sumbitch."

Tom Zucold was tough but his voice cracked a little when he spoke of the Intelligence reports and The Grip thought he might break. But the old man toughed it out and kept going.

"Command maybe in trouble," Tom Zucold said finally. He stepped down off the packing crate and peeled the rug back, a gold Cougar XR7 rug, and pulled his radio antenna to full extension. Then he drew a rough diagram of the Bowie Garage in the dirt.

"Air attackt is got to be anticipated. Command figures here," he said, and stabbed the dirt. He hesitated just an instant and then stabbed the dirt again and said, "But could be a naval attackt here."

"Say Navy?" The Grip blurted in disbelief.

"Said Navy. It might could come here when night make us blind," Tom Zucold said and stuck the radio antenna in what represented the ditch at the rear of The Grip's putting lane. "Seen pontoons in a dream last night."

"Ditch ain't but three feet wide. Me and Troop jump it with ease," The Grip said.

Tom Zucold was stonefaced. "Helicopters could come down on the Bowie Garage any time they like," the old man said. He ignored The Grip's naval intelligence.

By early afternoon The Grip and Trooper Drilling had wedged the eastern end of the ditch shut with a processee.

"Right where that Rambler belong," Trooper Drilling said.

"Ain't a Rambler. It is a Gremlin," The Grip said.

"Won't ramble no more neither," Trooper Drilling answered.

Trooper Drilling checked out when it was dark, creeping out along the deep shadows just as he had come in. When he was gone, The Grip felt his absence. He had watched until he could no longer see the Trooper's outline, then he marched into the bedroom, passing

Tom Zucold who was on his way out to check perimeters once again, and stood directly before the poster of the Carolina Kid. He felt drained like an oil pan, the heavy sludge all that was left. He confronted the poster. Nothing, he thought. It revealed nothing. He went to the window and looked at himself. His hair had grown in to a soft black brush. His eyes looked dark and sad. He tried to smile and then let it die. He thought that he looked smaller and older. He waited for some answer. Finally he watched the thick lips part to say, just above a whisper, "Fuck it."

He climbed the tree. It was the tallest and highest tree in the camp and he had built a sturdy station in it. Tom Zucold had made him wait an hour after Trooper Drilling departed, to confuse the sentries the old man said and make it look like they were still at full strength, and as he climbed he was aware that the crowd across the street had been alarmed by the wait.

He climbed, thinking about Tom Zucold's craziness, a madness to which he had so far reluctantly belonged. The moon did not lack much of achieving its fullness and, riding high in the clarity of that June night, it made his leaf-spotted fatigues shine when he crossed the open ground between the Bowie Garage and the observation tree. The catcalls and whistles from the darkness still stung in his ears.

"See 'at big bastard? Like an ape. See him? There he goes," one hollered.

"Where, Alfred?" a woman's voice demanded. "Show me, dammit."

He reached up for another branch and something fluttered out of the tree. Trooper Drilling had said probably bats. The sack of steel shots that he had strapped to his back pulled him heavily. He adjusted the clanking sack for a more appropriate center of gravity, then he pushed off again with his boot. He groped limb after limb through the double darkness of the night and the thick weave of the sycamore among the pines. Then the M16, which he had strapped snout up on his chest, caught in a fork of small limbs and turning to see what had happened he jammed a twig in his eye. He brushed it away and rubbed hard, though the resin seared. He felt close to falling and knew that if he continued to rub the eye he would fall. He clenched a branch above him, holding hard with both hands, and hung motionless like a bat. After a while the burning in his eye stopped and he climbed higher.

"There it is. Don't you see it?" a voice in the darkness said.

"I don't see nothing, Cotton."

"It's right under the tree house. That son of a bitch."

The Grip saw a handlight's beam dart in the limbs above him. He stopped climbing and waited for the light to catch him full in his face, then stared.

"Jesus, will you look at that?" A new voice said.

"Is that the one we kin to, Cleveland?" a thick female cried.

"Must be. Has got a black face ain't it."

The Grip thought of the ashes on his face and then of Trooper Drilling. His station was no more than twenty yards away. The Grip missed their whistle code.

"Sonofabitch is got a gun," a child said.

"Hush your mouth, Charity Mae," someone answered shrilly.

He climbed more quickly now and soon eased over the edge of the observation platform. The shots on his back clanked and pulled toward the darkness. He heaved everything to the middle of the planks and another light played past him.

"Damn Go-rilla, if it ever was one," someone said.

He eased the bag of shots to the edge of the platform, then placed the M16 in a crotch of limbs. It sat up and ready to hand just as if it were in a gun rack. Then he flipped the rope of seat belts around the trunk and belted himself in tight. He saw the shadows of people across the street, clear in the moonlight, as they milled around and waited for something to happen. Their voices were a low hum, idling like a tight Chevrolet.

After about an hour there was some kind of disturbance and The Grip heard glass break on the asphalt. He could see the shadows scattering but little else. Then there was a siren and he saw the bubblegum light coming down Yorktown Road. He knew it was

Trooper Drilling even before he stepped smartly from the cruiser that sent its red light cascading into the darkness.

"Who you think you are man, telling me 'bout disturbing the peace? You pigs eat shit," a voice spit. The Grip heard something that sounded like a pumpkin dropped. Shortly thereafter he saw Trooper Drilling helping somebody into the back seat of the cruiser and saw the door shut.

"Calling in reinforcements, case anybody else thinking about disturbing the peace. Peoples got to be cool, you understand," Trooper Drilling said over the cruiser's microphone, then he turned around and roared off toward Yorktown.

"Power to the people," somebody said. "Look like them cops think they own everything. Old man over there knows what's what. Get him a buncha guns and say ole buddy walk your own ass on down the road." The Grip couldn't be sure but he thought it sounded like Billy Carmines.

"God don't love drunkards and brawlers and whores. Beware, beware," a reedy voice piped off in the darkness.

"Izzat the preacher?" a child's voice said.

"Now hush your mouth, Charity Mae," a woman said quickly.

There was a stir among the shadows now as they settled back into their waiting. Someone asked if anyone had seen the thing in the trees and someone answered that maybe it was eating since everything had to eat sometime.

"Got to shit too," the child said. The Grip heard the woman slap the child and heard the child wail.

"Better pray fore it's too late. He comin'," the reedy voice said.

"I done paid for four hours of sittin', preacher, and that's just what I'm gonna do and if He come before that He gone have to wait," somebody said and everybody laughed.

It made The Grip feel good to hear them laugh but in just a little bit he felt the hostility crowding back. The voices hummed louder and were edgier and The Grip knew that the shadows wanted action. A car came down Yorktown Road from the northwest, its mufflers razzing and popping, and he thought it would surely crash into the shadows but at the last minute it downshifted and squealed around the curve, leaving some of the shadows screaming. His eyes still burned some from the resin and he rubbed them.

When he heard the shadows make a big noise like a suction, he knew that Tom Zucold had flipped the light switch. He opened his eyes. Midnight snarled and leaped against the chain. The whole world seemed to have turned to a white eyeball under him and he saw the darkness like an ocean surrounding the world. In the center of the white world the Bowie Garage squatted darkly with the overhead door raised so that it looked like the entrance to a deep hole. When Tom Zucold marched smartly out of that hole, the crowd once again sucked in its breath and was silent except for a squeal and someone saying that the lady had fainted.

Tom Zucold was impressive, even The Grip would admit that. Instead of his coveralls Tom Zucold wore the brown uniform of the United States Cavalry. He strutted in lustrous brown boots that ended at the knee and in which were tucked crisp riding breeches that had only a slight bag to them. These were a lighter brown than either the woolen campaign jacket or the leather straps that neatly crossed Tom Zucold's chest. The shirt and tie were a faint beige at the neck and The Grip was shocked to see that the old man had shaved his straggly beard. Ribbons colored red, yellow, blue, purple, and green dangled silver medallions at the left coat pocket. There were gold hashmarks on the sleeves of the coat and gold master sergeant's chevrons. The Grip guessed that Tom Zucold had never demoted himself when the Army had demoted him. Below Tom Zucold's hip hung a holster with an ominous black revolver. The only thing which was not regulation U.S. Cavalry was the baseball cap with STARS on the front. The Grip did not think this diminished the tiny man's impression of bold authority.

Tom Zucold made his way unhurriedly and confidently up to the front perimeter of the camp, swiping his breeches all the way with the radio antenna that seemed electrified in the blazing lights. It appeared and disappeared, making the only sound in the darkness, as Tom Zucold strode up to each of the observation stations and pretended to talk to troopers on duty, troopers The Grip knew did not exist. Slowly the tiny man worked his way back to the yawning mouth of the Bowie Garage then came to attention facing the shadows. He stood and let himself be absorbed by each of them, then swiftly clicked his heels together, executed an about face, and sank into the darkness. Abruptly the lights went out.

The Grip knew his part and he waited now. The shadows were hissing and humming but he ignored them. He held a steel shot in his hand and knew by the heft of it that it was only average. He stood shakily, not quite upright, and went into a half-coil. He could not pantomime his motion on the platform so he concentrated on tightening himself into a knot of muscles and then releasing, in this way warming up as much as he could. He had told Tom Zucold it was dangerous to try it at all but Tom Zucold insisted it was part of the calculated risks inherent in any operation. He tested the give of the planks by trying a light bouncing uncoil and heard the wood whine. It had to be. He set himself into a tight coil, took a slow deep breath, then half-spun into his putting motion and released the shot hard at the darkness. In his mind he saw it spin like a blue star, watching it arc and then begin to plummet. With a great ringing of steel it struck the Galaxy amidships. He knew before it had left his fingers that it was a good punch put, though not a great one.

"Oh God almighty, what was it?" a voice quick with terror howled.

"He coming, you sacks of shit. He coming," the preached howled.

"I can't see a damn thing and done paid for it. Did it start yet?"

The Grip listened to Midnight's wet streaks of vicious barking and to the few who had broken for their cars, filled with whatever dread they could imagine. Suddenly, in the moonlight, Tom Zucold stepped out in the lane behind the cement mixer, channeled a round in his M16 and took aim on the brightest star in the sky. At the report of the weapon a woman in the crowd screamed, then another woman screamed that someone had been shot.

"Over there, see 'em. By God it's hundreds of them. I ought to

228

know. I run enough frigging films of Korea at the National Guard," Cotton said.

"Yeah, damn right," another voice answered. "Seen 'em and I ain't waiting any more."

The Grip heard the feet thudding out into the darkness and the slamming of car doors and the roaring of engines. He watched the lights sail off up and down Yorktown Road. He knew that Tom Zucold, according to orders from Command, had quietly locked the El Dorado door, glanced at the star he had not wounded, and was about to flip the light switch again. Suddenly the world was once more a lake of light and Tom Zucold stood before the mouth to darkness.

"Command here operating by Geneva rules. Any wounded gets picked up only by Red Cross. If I'm lyin', I'm dyin'. By order Headquarters."

Then Tom Zucold was gone. The Grip had to hand it to the old man. The operation had gone exactly as Command ordered. He imagined that now, off duty temporarily, Tom Zucold had hung up his brown uniform and leaped onto the rope to the roof.

"They trying to kill that fine little man," a weepy female voice said.

"Shoulda taken you home hours ago, Homer. Let's go."

"Them yeller sons of bitches is attackting," a child shouted.

"Charity Mae don't you hush up I am gone wear out your bottom."

"Here come the cops," somebody said in the darkness. But The Grip had already seen the three cruisers coming, their red and blue bubblegum lights livid in the distance, sirens wailing. Somehow he knew the one coming from the other direction would be Trooper Drilling. It used no siren and long before it would reach sight of the remaining crowd, the bubblegum lights went out. Then the headlights went out, too, and The Grip lost sight of the cruiser.

"You in the tree," a voice said.

"You in the tree, listen here," a voice said. The Grip had been dozing and at first he thought it was his mother talking. Then he knew it was Clifton's momma. He did not answer because Tom Zucold said it would be a violation of military law.

"Troop say for me to tell you he want to talk to you. Say you can come down and come over to his car. Call it Field Headquarters."

The Grip hesitated, then decided he would have to answer. "Tell him I can't leave my post. Desertion."

It was quiet for a minute, then the woman said "OK. But don't go back to sleep yet."

"Check," The Grip said.

He heard Trooper Drilling dart across the road and shoulder past a pine. "You thinking like a soldier, man. I understand." Trooper Drilling stood against the sycamore trunk. The Grip could see nothing in the darkness.

"Check."

"Cousins taking in a bunch of dust on you tonight. This go on we gone have enough for Troop to open up his own garage. You hear?"

"Check."

"Didn't come about that though. Got me a SWAT team all set up. That's a bunch of cops out in the trees and they loaded with gear and ready to fight. I got them all over, you understand. Ain't had so much fun since Gunfighter Village over in Nam. Thing is, see, you got to give up." Trooper Drilling paused to let that sink in. When The Grip did not answer, Trooper Drilling said, "You got to tell the Colonel he surrounded and you got to come out with hands in the air and surrender. That what the Trooper manual say. Myself, I don't think he gone do it, probably not anyway. Got to ask, you understand."

The Grip felt the presence of *it* as he had not before. It was like a fog in which you couldn't breathe, a pressure at the throat and chest. He knew that whatever *it* was time was getting short now.

"You gone kill him."

"Naw, man. We try to wound him a little first. See that stop the mother, can't do nothing is what we hope. But can't let no war go on like this, you understand. Law don't provide for it. Colonel understand that. Man like me don't like to kill nobody, you understand. Just a job like any other one. Got to protect the peace."

"Check."

"Now you can cut and run any time you like. Don't figure you for that but it takes all kinds."

"Say what?"

"Thought you wouldn't do that."

The Grip could smell the acrid smoke of the funny cigarettes that Trooper Drilling liked.

"Colonel like you," The Grip said sadly.

"Shoot, man. I like that Colonel too. Man got a job to do though. Just like he got to fix them cars. I sure do look forward to getting me a garage. Lookit here, I make you a deal. You stay in that tree and don't shoot none I won't let nobody shoot you. Man got to watch out for hissef first thing."

The Grip didn't answer. What would he say? He felt overwhelmed by the madness he had feared. He was treed, trapped, cornered and helpless. He stared into the darkness where the Bowie Garage hulked quietly. He knew there were armed men out there but he could not see them. He had been trained by his country to fight and now he was in the middle of a war that was insane and he was being asked not to fight. He didn't want to fight, he wanted to run. Only Tom Zucold was depending on him.

"Troop, radio says it want you," Clifton's momma said softly.

"Tell it I coming. Listen here, Grip, you think about it. Tell Clifton's momma and she get word to me. Only don't take too long, man. Time short." The Grip heard Trooper Drilling pass into the darkness.

"You hungry?" Clifton's momma said.

He didn't answer.

"Got a few steamed crabs left. Sold right many but look like it tapered off now. Too late, seem like. Could throw some up and you might catch them."

"Ain't hungry."

"Well, well," Clifton's momma said. "Sorry I ain't got no beer left. Damn bunch cleaned that out."

"Check," The Grip said.

"When he be coming?"

"Who coming?" The Grip answered.

"That old man, fool. Trooper Drilling say they gone flush him out and catch him in a crossfire. Said it to the radio. Don't want to miss that." Clifton's momma was breathing loud enough for The Grip to hear her.

"Hope he coming out soon. That crowd getting mean, look like. Say they ain't gone wait forever. Hope they do, though; we making a good living now," Clifton's momma said. "They eat 'bout anything you throw to 'em."

"Don't know," The Grip said wearily. "Don't know a damn thing seem like."

"Huh," Clifton's momma said, "Ain't no cherry in that. You just like everybody else. Hope something happen though. This waiting bore the legs off a person."

"Check," The Grip said.

"Well listen, I got to go get them chirren in bed. Boy it time for you to do some thinking, aks me. Course it ain't none of my business. Still and all that Troop a hard man. Wouldn't want to tangle with him. He related to me somehow."

Then the old woman was gone and he was alone. He watched the emptied straights of the road and listened to the humming of the shadows until slowly he fell asleep.

When the rock hit him in the forehead he jerked back and struck his head against the tree. It hurt. He had been dreaming that he was riding in Promise Land's banana Volkswagen and Trooper Drilling was in the back seat. Now he heard Trooper Drilling speak below him.

"Hey man, you hell to wake up," the voice said.

"Ain't figured out what to do yet. He's counting on me," The Grip said.

"Who's that? Be cool, Baby. You hearing me?"

The Grip saw Trooper Drilling's woolly Afro slowly rise over the edge of the observation platform. Only it was not Trooper Drilling's face. He reached automatically for the M16.

"Easy man, take it easy," the black face said and dropped out of sight. "Let's don't be shooting nobody. Ain't good for you," the face said from under the planks. Then it began to rise up again.

"Everything cool, right?" the face said.

"Check," The Grip said, and put the M16 back. He could see that this man was no soldier.

"Dropped the rocks, man," the face said to the darkness of the tree.

"Son of a bitch, don't I know," somebody said.

The black face looked back at The Grip and pushed something shiny into The Grip's face. He knew immediately it was a badge and said, "I surrender. Ain't got nothing to say. Code say I don't have to talk."

"Hey man, this is a Press card," the face said and put the card away. "You can't surrender yet, it's a story here. Things got to happen. Name's White, Mighty White my friends call me. I'm on the news with Channel 3, the Power Play news, dig it. Probably you know me, huh?"

The Grip shook his head and said Tom Zucold didn't allow news.

"Say look man, I'm down here in the swamp covering a missing kid story, a real drag, dig it. I see Trooper Drilling hotting it along the road and I pull him over—we're related somehow—and I tell him 'Man this missing kid stuff is dull, just plain dull baby. Woman by the name of Land and her sister both out looking for this idiot kid.' Troop say that kid always wandering off but everybody know her and she turn up. Man, I said, that is the way and then ain't no damn story and Mighty White got burrs in his threads. Troop say he known a story might be something. Dig it. So here I am, spill baby."

"Say what?" The Grip was stunned.

"Comin' on up, baby. Be cool with that boom-boom now." Mighty White slid himself up over the edge onto the platform. "Say what? Mighty White come out in the teeny-tiny to do you a favor bro.

Gone make you news, make you famous, make folks sayin' your name. Dig it?"

He had perched on the edge of the platform and The Grip saw now that he was a small man like Tom Zucold. The Grip started to ask what he wanted but the man raised a hand that glittered with rings and stopped him. Suddenly there was a silver and black microphone held up to the man by a hand that disappeared. Then someone was cursing and breaking branches and a light like Tom Zucold's highbeams began to blaze. It rose beside the platform like the sun. The light was so intense that The Grip could see nothing.

"I fall out this tree I am going to sue that frigging channel for every mother-fucking cent they got," a strange voice said. It seemed to come out of the light.

"You got him focused, Jack? How's this audio level?" Mighty White seemed to be talking to The Grip but he had no idea what about. He tried to stand up, found his legs were numb, and fell back onto the planks.

"Hey man," Mighty White said to him, "Be cool. Be famous. Your own special divine Mighty White is here. We ain't shooting yet."

"Say shoot?" The Grip said, his anxiety showing.

"Off limits," The Grip said. "Station is off limits."

A branch cracked below and a voice said, "Christ in a tree."

"Listen pal, Mighty White ain't got a shitpot of time. I am gone make you famouser than Bo Diddley. Just look at the sun over there and answer my questions. Hell, a monkey could do it."

"Say what?"

"Jesus," Mighty White said. "First they give me high school baseball, then a wonder name Promise Land that can't locate her kid, and now this. Put that gun in your lap, monkey."

"Say Promise Land. You saw her?" The Grip snapped.

"Yeah, I seen her. What's it to you?" Mighty White was uncoiling his microphone.

"I love her."

234

"Hey you don't think Troop set all this up just to get on the air, do you?" Mighty White said to somebody below.

"Well it's something 'bout a woman don't have only one child and that one be an idiot. Course it was pretty odd with both that woman and her sister Hope. Hot puss, that Hope. Come on strong. I said Sweetheart, White is my name, but she didn't get the joke. Say you ain't the father of that kid is you, I mean it ain't nothing personal man."

"He ain't the father," a voice said below the tree. "Research said it was somebody named Zucold. Supposed to have died already."

"Your name ain't Zucold is it?" Mighty White said, opening his notebook. "You ain't dead anyways. Listen, you guys down there ready?"

"Hurry up, will you?" the sun said, "this sumbitch is killing me."

"OK baby, speak right into the 'phone, and not too loud. What's your name and why are you in this tree?"

"Tom Zucold's baby," The Grip said. He was trembling now.

"You too? Then your name be Zucold, ain't it?" Mighty White had set the microphone between them and there was a small black box beside it. The reporter was scribbling in a notebook.

"Name The Grip."

Mighty White snapped off the microphone and said "Look baby it's near midnight and I ain't got time for games. Nobody named The Grip."

"Somebody named Mighty White," a voice giggled behind the light.

"Fuck you," Mighty White said and snapped the microphone back on, "Say that name again."

"Tom Zucold call me The Grip."

"Tell me your regular name, baby. Say it slow."

"Name was Tomson. Billy Luke Tomson."

"Now we getting somewhere," Mighty White said. "Where you from?"

"Tom Zucold's."

"Jesus," Mighty White said and shook his head. "Aksed where you from Jack."

"Right here," The Grip said. "Tom Zucold's."

"Who the hell is Tom Zucold anyways?" Mighty White said and looked up.

"Own the Bowie Garage. Having a war," The Grip answered.

"Oh, I see, I do see," Mighty White said and scribbled furiously. "He trying to kill you cause you love this Promise Land. That it?"

"Ain't gone kill me, might kill them."

"Who in God's creation is them?"

"The Committee. Them." The Grip nodded at the darkness where the shadows had camped for the night.

"What committee you talking about, baby?"

"Ain't no committee," The Grip said.

"But you said he might kill them," Mighty White said.

"Is. Tom Zucold crazy."

The light cackled and somebody said, "Oh wow, a double wow man."

"OK, OK. This Tom Zucold is crazy and he owns this property and he is having a war with somebody and you are in love with the woman that had his mongoloid kid and you work for him. Have I got that right?"

"Don't work for him," The Grip said. "Live here. Family."

"Then why are you carrying that gun?" Mighty White said.

"*It* is coming."

"It?"

"Tom Zucold say we got to shoot when *it* starts." The Grip heard the light laugh nervously. "But I ain't shot anybody. Don't plan to."

"Hey Mighty, how 'bout wrapping up huh?" the light said.

"You in the Army, baby?"

"Was, was a shot-putter," The Grip said.

"OK, OK," Mighty White said as he wrote faster and faster. "You trained to kill, can see that. Lover's triangle, can see that. Look like the Viet Nam veteran syndrome, can see that. Everybody being thrown off they land, I can work that in. This gone be a hot one,

236

baby. I'll make you famouser than Stevie Wonder. Thing is what does the old man want, what angle?"

"Say what?" The Grip said. Then, "Can't say."

"What the hell do you stay up in a tree all night for, then?" Mighty White was losing patience and the light was trembling and whoever held the light was laughing.

The Grip blinked at the light and tried to think of an answer. A lime green Corvette sailed in his head. He saw the pages of the Montgomery Ward catalog and the gentleman in it. He saw steel shots, one after another, fly off into the distance. But nothing that came into his head was an answer to Mighty White's question. He was still asking himself "Why?" and hearing no answer when he saw the television crew pack up and drive off. He leaned back against the tree and was almost asleep when he heard Clifton's momma's voice.

"Troop say you can go to sleep now. Say that radio tole him them cops got to go look for a missing child."

The troops did not return the next day. Trooper Drilling stood in the shade of the tree and informed The Grip that his supervisors said they would do nothing until something happened. It seemed there was always some other disaster about to claim their attention, something worse and in progress that the troops had to attend to. But Trooper Drilling was glad to report that the girl had been found, alive and well, and he personally would attend to the war at the Bowie Garage. The Grip listened and nodded but did not speak. His mind was on Tom Zucold.

He had tried to tell Tom Zucold he was quitting but it seemed there had been no good opportunity so it never quite got out. They had watched TRUTH OR CONSEQUENCES at evening chow but he hadn't been able to get interested. Do it, do it, a voice in his head kept saying. But he hadn't done it. In the middle of the program Tom Zucold had leaped from the Thunderbird chair and gone to the window, crying "She coming. She coming."

It was so like the old days when Tom Zucold had cried "He coming" to the poster of the Carolina Kid that The Grip's heart had stirred with hope, only to sink when he understood Tom Zucold said "she."

"Merci coming?" The Grip said. He had no idea why she would come back.

"Promise Land coming. Know it. Been knowing it."

He wanted to scream at the old man. He wanted to punch his face. But he knew the old man was just crazy as a bedbug. He went heavily back to his station in the tree. Maybe, he thought, it was military discipline. Maybe it was loyalty. Maybe it was nothing. Maybe words meant nothing. Maybe nothing meant anything. He was tired and he felt the pressure of waiting for *it*.

On the next day he again found himself unable to tell Tom Zucold he was leaving. They sat now in their chairs, chow finished, and waited for TRUTH OR CONSEQUENCES.

"She coming," Tom Zucold said flatly.

"Who?" The Grip said.

"Promise Land coming," the old man repeated, as if he were not talking to anybody really, as if the words were echoing around in his head.

"Bullshit. She ain't coming near you old man," The Grip said nevertheless.

"That's insubordination. Put him down for insubordination, Trooper," Tom Zucold said. The Grip looked around but there was no one else in the room.

"Man say she got a kid that's yours," The Grip said. "It is that not-a-nigger-girl, ain't it."

"Children can't be allowed in the combat zone," Tom Zucold said.

"It don't matter to me if it's yours. Promise Land's same to me."

"That's life," Tom Zucold said blankly.

The Grip stepped over to get a Gatorade and found there were none left.

"That's war," Tom Zucold said. He stared at the grinning face of Bob Barker. "Anything worth having is worth dying for."

238

"Ain't that some shit," The Grip said. "And a man without roots is a dead man, ain't he." He felt malicious and when he mocked one of the things he had so often heard Tom Zucold say, he felt good. But it didn't last. He couldn't be sure if Tom Zucold had even heard it, or if he had heard whether he had understood it. He walked out into the front yard, leaving the old man alone with TRUTH OR CONSEQUENCES. He was angry now. Everything was falling apart He felt on the verge of something, some purpose maybe, some beginning when they had gone to the Moose Hall. Tom Zucold had been almost a father to him. Now it was all turning to shit. He did not want to die because Tom Zucold was crazy and he did not want to kill anybody either. It seemed so simple—all he had to do was to léave. Why didn't he just do it, then?

Because it will kill him if I leave. Or Trooper Drilling will kill him.

And it will kill him if I stay.

He climbed up to his station once again. It was still daylight now, but it didn't matter if they saw him. It almost seemed to him that nothing mattered anymore. He settled down and looked at the yards across the road. People had left their litter everywhere, like a kind of scum. Beer cans shined among the take-out chicken boxes and flattened popcorn boxes. There were wadded pieces of paper everywhere. He had never imagined that people were such pigs. And not only because they were filthy but also because they were brutally ugly. Didn't they seem to drool for blood? Didn't they look for the least sign of violence with an excitement that made a man sick? Sometimes they threw things up to him and hoped he would eat it while they watched him. They called him names. When he did not respond they turned on each other. There been more than one fight.

The Grip watched them filter back for the evening wait. Many of them were regulars. Soon there was a line for the steamed crabs and another for the cold draft beer.

"Hey Grip, give 'em hell boy," said a fat man wearing an olive T-shirt that said GRIPPER.

"You think he'd really shoot somebody?" a girl in shorts said.

"Bet your ass honey. A man don't go in a tree with a gun lessn he mean business." The Grip recognized this boy's voice. He often played frisbee with members of the crowd.

Another night passed and then another. Nothing seemed to change and The Grip was once more in the tree. Everything was running together. He had not told Tom Zucold anything. It was hot now, in the nineties, and The Grip thought it must be Friday because the crowd was exceptionally large. They were arriving earlier and he saw that some of them were drinking from bottles. One shouted up and asked him how much he weighed but he did not answer. He never answered them. He had begun to feel that he was like a man standing outside a zoo. Let the animals jabber, he would not try to understand what they wanted.

"See there, it live in that fucken tree practically," a voice said.

"Call to it again and see don't it say something."

"That man is a goddamn hero, lady, and don't forget it," a girl said.

"Charity Mae I am warning you," her mother said from a chaise lounge.

"Some truth to that," somebody said.

"It don't look as big as it did on the television."

"Mighty White say he just a victim of Veet Nam. Say he trained to kill and he just got to do that."

Darkness fell and the voices chattered on like shadows in a dream. He heard them and did not hear them. Cars whipped by along York-town Road. It had been the same every night. Once some boys had thrown a bag of dogshit on an old lady's lap. Another time somebody had stuck a bare ass out of the window as the car passed. Some old women had driven by and shouted obscenities at the crowd. The Grip could hardly believe what people were actually like. Suddenly Tom Zucold's tree lights came on and The Grip flinched. Nobody else seemed to react, having grown used to it now. There were a few squeals and somebody said, "I swear that gets me ever time," but mostly the people hummed and went on doing whatever they were doing. He watched patiently.

"Hey Grip, you up there ain't you man?" It was Clifton. The Grip couldn't see him but he knew who it was.

"Check."

"They pouring in tonight, ain't they. Look like it gone be standing room only."

"Momma say to come and aks if you want a beer. I tole her you wouldn't want none, being on duty and all, but she say go aks anyway. Say to tell you that we wouldn't be nothing without you."

"Check."

"What the hell that mean bro? You want a beer or not? Momma say I could climb up there and watch whatever it is you watching while you drink one."

The Grip told Clifton that he was grateful but did not want a beer and he heard the boy slip off in the darkness. Then he was back.

"Grip? You still up there man? Trooper Drilling say to hang loose. He say his radio done tole him Promise Land's kid is lost again. Say he just got a feeling it is about to happen."

"It? Say *it*?"

"Troop done tole Momma he reckon he be in the garage business soon. Say maybe he build a lane in the back for throwing them shots. Look, time is money man. Later."

"Say *it*, Clifton?"

It was inside him like a darkness, like a worm that slowly had eaten away until now it nibbled at the nerve ends. He realized that *it* was the same as Trooper Drilling's *they*. The thing was that what Trooper Drilling had described was outside, even if it didn't have a shape that you could see or touch, but this was inside and outside. *It* was something that surrounded a man, a craziness. And craziness was like a disease that just kept growing and making sores you couldn't tell you had until the thing that was you, *onliness* Promise Land had called it, was seeping to a black crust. Just thinking about it frightened him so much that The Grip had to hold on to the edge of the platform to keep from being washed bodily out into the ocean of darkness.

He had almost got to feeling able to let go of the platform, had steeled himself to climb down and walk into the Bowie Garage and turn in his M16, when he heard the car squeal around the corner at Rooster Smith's store and then begin to accelerate down the long stretch leading to the Bowie Garage. Through the branches he could see it coming, highbeams on, barreling hard, and after a while even saw that it was either a Camaro or a Pontiac Firebird, perhaps a Trans-Am. It took only a matter of seconds but seemed forever as he watched.

"Stop," he cried out involuntarily.

But the car had already passed the point of no return and though he knew it was not possible he thought he could see the terrified look on the faces of the two teenage boys. Suddenly the car was fishtailing, the lights flashing from one side of the road to the other, the tires smoking and screaming, and at the last instant it appeared the car might actually find that magical line and howl through the curve and off into the darkness.

The Trans-Am, for that was what it was—an ocean metallic blue, caught the killer tree broadside, sending smoke and sparks and gouts of dirt and bark everywhere. The sound of the collision was composed of glass shattering and tires bursting and metal shearing and the solid deadliness of a thunderclap. The force was so great that the engine ripped from its mount and decapitated the reedy-voiced preacher, then took a passing chunk of meat from Charity Mae's thigh, sending her into a bloody sprawl.

Immediately the shadows screamed and wailed, scattered from the sight of what was an unknown terror come out of the darkness, and begged mercy from a God that was nowhere to be found.

As if it were a reflex action, the tree lights came on and bathed the carnage in a hot glare. Tom Zucold smashed the bedroom window with the butt of a rifle and fired. His first shot struck the still spinning left rear tire on the Trans-Am.

"You goddamn gooks, take that," Tom Zucold shouted. "You ain't taking me alive." He fired another shot, a small spurt of flame leaping from the snout of the M16. The Grip could not see what this round struck.

"Cease fire, cease fire, Colonel," Trooper Drilling shouted from behind his cruiser. "We got bad casualties here. People killed, people injured."

"Past talking, time for shooting," Tom Zucold said and fired off another shot, this time striking the roof of the cruiser.

"Oh God," somebody wailed among the litter of bodies across the road.

"Sumbitch can sure shoot," another voice said.

"Speak to me Charity Mae," her mother crooned. The Grip could see the woman sat on the ground and cradled the limp form of the child.

Just as abruptly as he had turned on the lights and started to fire, Tom Zucold put the lights out and ceased fire. There was an eerie silence which was broken only by the soft sobbing of the injured and the crackling of Trooper Drilling's radio. Trooper Drilling himself had already trotted down the road to put out flares for the traffic. The left rear wheel of the Trans-Am had stopped spinning and there was no sound at all from the clot of metal held upright by the killer tree.

The Grip edged over to the side of the platform. He kept saying "Oh God, oh God, oh God." He was shaking badly. He lowered his left leg and felt for a branch to step on, found it, let his weight come, and slipped. He grabbed at the last instant for the platform but connected with the bag of shots so that they slid off the platform and yanked him away from the trunk.

He was lucky. He knew that much. The bag of shots had fallen free of his hand and clanked to the ground. He had struck first one and then another limb on his way down. The second one had caught him in a kind of cradle of branches. His arm ached, his back throbbed, and he was certain that his ankle was broken. At the least, a bad sprain. Still he was lucky. He was alive.

The Grip pulled himself to a sitting position. He could not move but he could see everything. He did not know why the lights in the trees were blazing again. Across the road people in nightgowns were attending to people who lay in the grass. At least two were covered completely with blankets. He could see that three or four others had bandages. Some stood back out of the flare of light, solemn and disbelieving, pale blue as ghosts. Then he blacked out.

He jumped at the acrid smell in his nose and Trooper Drilling, restraining him, said "Take it easy now man. Just smelling salts."

"What happened?" The Grip said.

"Just what you'd expect look like. Pressure build up in the cooker it got to go off, you understand. Look bad to me. Probably get worse too. Listen, you lean on me and we'll get you back on the ground."

He was not far above the ground. Still it hurt with each bump. Finally he sat in the grass, the cool dew feeling welcome.

"You sure make a lot of noise," Trooper Drilling hissed. "Man big as you fall it seem important." He laughed as he crouched beside The Grip.

"I hadn't shot nobody, Troop."

"That's too bad. Time yet though." Trooper Drilling sounded as if he meant what he said. He pulled his revolver from its holster and said, "A man ought to—" then stopped.

"Ought to what?"

"Listen," Trooper Drilling said.

He heard the soft sobbing across the road and very faintly heard sirens. But that seemed to be it. Then there it was, voices, low, angry, even snarling.

"In the Bowie Garage," The Grip said.

But there was no need to wonder any longer for now Tom Zucold began to bellow, "I knowed you was coming. I seen you in the newspaper. You ain't gone take it all again. I knowed you was coming."

"Lookit," Trooper Drilling said quietly and pointed to the bedroom window.

There at the window, barely above the sill, stood the not-a-nigger girl. Light from the Cadillac highbeams flowed over her melted face and made it gleam as if it were wet.

"I'll get her out the way," Trooper Drilling said and started across the open ground in a running crouch. He had gone only a few steps when he heard the crack of a shot, but not this time Tom Zucold's M16. Trooper Drilling hit the dirt on his belly and the not-a-nigger girl darted into the darkness beyond the garage as quickly as if she had been a small deer.

"Godalmight," The Grip said. He forced himself to stand on the ankle that seemed broken, then tumbled to the ground. He got up again and hobbled until he came to a small limb. He used this as a crutch and went forward toward the yawning overhead door opening.

"Jesus Christ, Tom Zucold, ittis me. Ittis The Grip. Don't shoot."

Trooper Drilling leaped ahead of him and waited with his body pressed to the outside wall of the garage. He held the chrome pistol up by his head and it sparked in the tree light.

He had taken only three steps into the darkness inside when he saw the body. It was not anyone he had ever seen but the face resembled Promise Land's. It was a slender woman, young, pretty, with sort of anonymously colored hair. Her legs were splayed out and she had been smashed on the floor by the falling MG engine that Tom Zucold had hung from the roof. It had been connected to a tripwire and Tom Zucold called it his MG Line, the last line of defense. Trooper Drilling had showed Tom Zucold how to set up this Green Beret trick. The Grip had been very careful whenever he had come near the spot. The engine sat, carburetor up, on the woman's chest, as solid looking in its installation as if at any moment someone might hook up the gasoline line and a battery and turn it over. Blood welled out from either side of the woman and looked like an oil spill. The woman's eyes were turned toward the door to their house and when The Grip followed them he was certain he saw a brown-clad figure pull back from the light. He leaned over and looked at the woman's lips. Her tongue protruded just slightly between the lips and teeth, like a bird's he had once seen. He turned away and swallowed the welling saliva of nausea, looking straight at Trooper Drilling in the process.

"That's Hope there," Trooper Drilling said cheerfully. "He's done killed her dead as you please. Ain't no question about that. Known he had it in him, the Colonel."

Trooper Drilling pushed by the hulking figure of The Grip and bent over the body. "That's a four cylinder, ain't it?" He touched the cold metal with the tip of his chrome pistol as if it had to be watched carefully, as if it might attack, then said, "Man don't see too many of these babies."

The Grip had recovered himself enough to take another look. He turned around and said "You say Hope? Promise Land's sister?"

"That's the one bro."

The Grip moved closer to the body. He saw that a trickle of blood ran out of her one ear and shined darkly in her hair. Colorful intestines were trying to push up around the engine's oil pan and Trooper Drilling was slightly rocking the engine on top of them.

"Bet that thing ain't run in years. Could though," Trooper Drilling said. "Man with a garage can make things work."

Trooper Drilling pushed the tip of his pistol under the body's left breast and the breast slid away from the body. It looked like a rubber ball chopped in half by a lawn mower.

"By God she nekkid under it all," Trooper Drilling said as he probed her with his pistol.

The Grip heard the bedroom rafters creak before Trooper Drilling did and moved to the door to the bedroom. Then Trooper Drilling heard it and said, "He's in there ain't he," as he followed The Grip. On his way Trooper Drilling fired two quick shots into the bedroom wall, shooting for but missing the doorway, and would have fired a third round except for the elbow that The Grip timed splendidly to land on the farthest forward point of Trooper Drilling's angular chin. The black man dropped like a sandbag, unconscious instantly.

"Coming in Tom Zucold," The Grip said. "Coming in our bedroom. Don't shoot."

The Grip could not have said which he had seen first or which hurt him more, Promise Land sitting in the Thunderbird seat or Tom Zucold halfway up the rope.

Promise Land had a smile on her face and her blue eyes were open wide. The Grip looked down at her and saw the J. C. Higgins .22 in her lap. Or what was left of it. He picked it up and turned it over. The top of the barrel, just above the stock and rusty trigger, had exploded upward and backward to leave the metal with the appearance of an odd weed. The Grip looked back at Promise Land, sitting so still she might have been waiting for a portrait to be done, and then saw the dark hole, scarcely a hole at all, just above her right eyebrow. He touched her bare forearm. It was cold.

"Didn't shoot her," Tom Zucold hissed. "Shot herself, ask anybody." He hung in the rope, one foot coiled and one hand clutching. The other hand held the flare gun.

"Why?" The Grip said. It was so simple.

"Who knows why? God doesn't know why. Come in here with that whore of a sister, snuck up the lane she said. Said she looking for that idiot kid that wouldn't stay home. The whore pushed its way in while I was watching out the window over there and she hit the MG Line. This one grabbed the gun and say she gone kill me. I said shoot straight cause you ain't taking me alive and that old piece blew up boom in her face. Fell over like she was sleeping."

"Do you know who she is?" Tom Zucold looked pale and harried.

"They sisters. They whores. All of 'em. They all after me. Who the hell are you?"

The Grip had been easing forward, inch by inch, intending to shake the old man from the rope and now he grabbed what he could. Tom Zucold flailed at him with one brown boot but he was too high up to connect. The other boot was locked in the rope's coils. He tried to jerk himself free, pushed and pulled and jerked, but got nowhere.

"Listen it's over, don't you see, it's over," The Grip said as he tried to shake the old man loose.

Tom Zucold kicked out hard at The Grip again. The brown boot missed but the momentum of the wiry body and The Grip's attempt to evade the blow threw The Grip off balance and he fell backward onto the open commode. Tom Zucold looked down on him, his old eyes deep with madness, and raised the muzzle of the flare gun until it was aimed at The Grip.

"He coming," The Grip said as he watched the muzzle shaking. "The Carolina Kid coming, remember?" Tears began to trickle down his massive face but not in fear. He knew that there had been a man in the shell that pointed the flare gun, a man who had bet everything and lost, a man who had been the nearest thing he would ever have to a father.

"He coming," The Grip said again, his voice breaking some now. "Man can't get to the top alone. Some things a man got to have help with. Some things you just got to believe in no matter what. You showed me that. You and him."

The big mouth of the flare gun was bobbing now and The Grip thought that it had started to fall just a bit when Tom Zucold said "yourself" and pulled the trigger. A split-second after that explosion The Grip heard the crack of Trooper Drilling's chrome pistol. Hit in the chest so that some of the medals were torn away, Tom Zucold spun backwards in the air like a struck tetherball and hung in the rope, his boot stubbornly coiled. The Grip looked up and saw the burning heart of the poster of the Carolina Kid. He saw at once that Tom Zucold had never meant to shoot him. It had always been the Carolina Kid that Tom Zucold lived by and that he now meant to die with.

"Hate to do that, you understand," Trooper Drilling said as he ejected his spent cartridges and replaced them from his belt. "What he would have wanted, aks me. Colonel don't take no shit from nobody. He wants to go right and quick, aks me. Too bad about that one," he said and pointed to Promise Land who sat primly still.

"Why?" The Grip said.

Trooper Drilling thought The Grip meant Promise Land. "Why? Cause she and her sister out looking for that kid. Any woman do the same thing. Same as you done, you understand."

The Grip was not sure that he understood Trooper Drilling at all but maybe what he said about both Tom Zucold and Promise Land did have a sort of logic to it. He tried to think it through but his head and his heart were numb. All he could do was sit and stare at the woman who could not be, as he had dumbly expected, his future —or at the man who had been his future and who was already his past. He stared and smelled the foul smoke of the burning poster that seemed to last a terribly long time.

Trooper Drilling stood in the door and grinned at the body under the MG engine. "Ain't a pretty job at all, you understand, but somebody's got to do it."

He had hit the button on the Thunderbird chair and put it into a dive so that now he lay like a patient waiting for a dentist, his eyes fixed on the place where the black rope must surely pass through the black hole in the roof to the black night that blanketed everything. There were no lights on in or outside the Bowie Garage. He could not believe how fast it had happened when *it* finally happened. One minute they were all alive, trying hard to survive the rising tide of craziness, and the next minute it had killed them or hurt them or left them just trying to know for sure that it wasn't a nightmare. Maybe, he thought, that was the worst of it all, thinking what was most real and most final was not real at all. Thinking what was really wasn't. In the end, he supposed, it didn't matter. Not now. Not anymore.

He could see the white-clad ambulance attendants, how delicately they picked up the bodies and the parts, how they joked as they worked. He watched them in his mind as he had watched them in fact, only an hour—or was it two?—before, and they carried Tom Zucold out under the white cover. He would never see the old man again. It was like mailing something overseas. Then they had taken the women, Hope first, and only after they had had to hook up Tom Zucold's engine hoist.

"You all right, Mack?" one of them had asked, stopping with Promise Land on the stretcher before him. He did not cry. He had not even wanted to cry. He only felt light, as if the least breeze would lift him too and send him sailing forever into the darkness.

"They just taking her somewhere. Gone fix her," he had said to Trooper Drilling. He almost believed it. There was a chance to believe it if Trooper Drilling agreed.

"Fuck that shit, man. The woman wasted. You got to face it now and every time you think 'bout it, you understand."

Then he had watched the zombies in white drive off and the silence came flooding in and Trooper Drilling spoke softly and offered him a taste of the funny cigarette and he took it. But that had not helped. He lay now remembering that Trooper Drilling said he would handle everything. The Grip, he said, had no choice. Drafted, he said. Tom Zucold caused it all and there wouldn't be anything but that in the report. Trooper Drilling didn't have any hard feelings about that elbow either because they'd been buddies in the trenches and this counted for something, if anything did, and something had to.

"War is sure a bitch," Trooper Drilling had said as he fingered the point of his chin. Then he said, "Might be good idea if you was to move on, though. Can't tell what them fucking Muddlemans might try to do now."

His legs hung over Tom Zucold's chair and there seemed to be no part of his body which did not cringe with pain at any movement. It hurt to breathe and it hurt not to. It hurt to think and it hurt not to. He didn't care. He tried to focus Promise Land's face in the darkness and he could see her, almost, astride the motorcycle. He could see her in the banana car and he could see the bluish figure beside him in the lane. But he could not see that face, he could not make it distinct so that he could look at it and say that he was sorry. After a while, his head hurting from trying to make it come clear, he fell asleep.

When The Grip woke there was a cold gray morning light falling through the window. The same light winked at the top of the rope. He had been dreaming, something he couldn't remember, something about the Carolina Kid. He hit the button and brought the chair upright and found himself staring at the poster on the wall above the open commode. He felt an intense desire to look into those sad eyes

—had they been sad eyes? why did he never notice that before?—as if could he once look into their depths he would know something true, something unchangeably real. But there were no eyes on the poster. There was hardly any poster, only a charred paper with a derby hat at the top and pebble-grained alligator shoes on the bottom. Tom Zucold's shot with the flare gun had flown true and done its work. The scorched wood on the wall where the Carolina Kid had been made him feel terribly lonely.

He glanced up at the Champion Spark Plug clock. The three hands were as still as the trinity and the clock face as blankly indifferent as the universe. As far as the clock knew time had stopped forever. Then he looked back at the remains of the Carolina Kid. He felt something, maybe time, winding up tight inside him. It felt hot and hard and was a kind of sourceless anger. He stepped down from the Thunderbird chair, buckled on the sore ankle, then supported himself by clinging to Tom Zucold's seat. It hurt badly. Streaks of pain shot up his leg from the ankle. He ached all over. But he knew he would stand. He pushed himself away from the chair and hobbled to his bed, then pulled the duffle bag out from under it. He had never had to use the Ace bandages but he was never without them. He was programmed.

His ankle wrapped so that the flesh above it swelled milkily, he walked to the poster, pulled the remains free, and flushed the Carolina Kid. But it would not go down, the stiff paper resisting, so he left it in the open commode, blackening the water. Rather than halt the dark anger he felt rising in himself, this fed it. He felt that he was going to explode, but he did not want to lose control. Even SSGT Davis had told the troops that a little anger was good—because it pumped you up—but a lot was the worst thing that could happen. It fucked up the focus, SSGT Davis said.

He went to his bed and began to pack his duffle bag. He had no idea where he would go or even that he was actually going. His eyes kept pulling toward the front of the room, then watching the television set. It wasn't on. It just sat there like innocence itself. But he couldn't stand it. The thing seemed to hiss or whisper. Then he saw that there was a wine bottle on top of the set. Beside it was a can of something called Sterno and a paper paint filter that seemed stained. There was also a bottle of hair tonic, half-filled, and a bottle of cough medicine, empty. He walked to the set and stared at the bottles. Then he understood. "War," Trooper Drilling had said, "is a bitch." Tom Zucold had been mixing all this and drinking it on the sneak. It kept him going all those nights of crazy hours. But it had been like a bomb slowly preparing to detonate.

Almost habitually The Grip snapped on the television. Only then did he see that the combat map was still affixed to the screen. He ripped it off and balled it up, then flipped it into the open commode. A man in a suit gradually emerged from the gray haze. He was sitting at a desk and held a sheaf of papers in his hands. There was no sound and no color in the set. The Grip watched the man move his lips and then turn his face away as if talking to someone. Then it was Mighty White's dark face on the screen and he, too, had papers in his hands and his lips, too, were moving. For an instant The Grip thought it was a dream, then that it had all been a nightmare from which he would waken. But at that moment the camera showed the picture of Promise Land that had been in the newspapers, only she was circled in the picture. The Grip quickly turned up the sound and heard Mighty White say ". . . tragic death. More on this after a brief message." Then there was somebody riding a motorcycle and somebody else singing about the time of your life.

He backed away from the television set as more commercials played. Then he stepped on Tom Zucold's M16. Without a thought in his head, his eyes hardened and, instantly alert, he eased down and picked it up. His thumb edged the release and he knew without looking that the weapon had been set on rapid fire. The report of the bullets spraying was deafening but he crushed the trigger until the weapon was empty and smoking and his great arms were shaking on their own. The television screen lay in a million fragments all over the Cougar XR7 rug.

They were shouting out in the yards now. He walked to the window and saw the yards were packed, wall to wall, with what Tom

Zucold had called freaks. Many of them were standing, some jumping to see what had happened. Some had telescopes, some had binoculars, there were even little periscopes as they tried to watch the Bowie Garage. Over to the right, atop the pink house at the end, a camera swung slowly down on him. He could see the lens nosing out toward him.

There were many more of them than before. He watched them as they watched him. He remembered Tom Zucold's crazy fear of a citizens committee that Promise Land had told him didn't exist. Maybe, he thought, she was wrong. Maybe they were the committee after all, all of them, even himself, for as odd as it might be he felt that he was one of them. He understood them, what they wanted, what they were. He looked at the wide, yearning faces. These were what he would have found in the Carolina Kid's eyes, there was the truth—whatever it might be. Tom Zucold was only what they let him be, what part of themselves they allowed to get out and go crazy until it was time to stomp it out, to send in discipline in the form of Trooper Drilling. And he knew that though he was also all of them, he had been set apart and made to know and to be what they never wanted to know or to be. If he walked across the road there would be some who would spit on him, many who would shrink from him, others who already waited for him with malice making them tremble. He listened as if through a membrane grown suddenly thin.

"Can't tell what that monster gone do next."

"Say he dropped a motherfucking car on her yesterday. Girl name of Hope."

"That old man been training him for years and nobody knowed."

"No shit?"

"Town ought not let freaks like that live round here. Ittis chirren here."

"Constitution say people free to live anywhere."

"Fuck the constitution. We the people says what goes."

"Lookit him standing there just so peaceful. Say he put a bullet square in that other uns head."

"Naw, naw. Cop done that. Green Beret man."

"You people don't know shit. The old man put a flare gun between her legs and made him a Grand Canyon— and wouldn't that be something to see."

The Grip turned back into the gray room. It was all the same, the words running together and changing everything until nothing was the way it had been. Maybe, he thought, there wasn't any language that said things the way a person knew things were, knew them inside. Maybe that was why the hum went on across the road, all those mouths moving and tongues slicking, because each of them saw a thing his way and had to believe the others could see it that way too —or else each person was finally alone with a reality he couldn't be sure would stay the same for even another minute. But none of them seemed able or willing to see this. Instead, it was him who was alone, apart, alone, wordless almost. And yet they needed him, he could see that now. They needed Tom Zucold and Trooper Drilling and Promise Land and Hope. They needed what they didn't understand, a story and a mystery, to carry them along on the illusion of their own connection to the fragility and danger of life. They were freaks not because of their size or shape or what they did or what they wore, he saw that now. They were freaks for the same reason that he was, that everybody was, because they stood utterly alone in the world and couldn't tell what was real 'and what wasn't and the only thing they had to help them tell was words.

His ankle hurt worse now and he was hungry. He hobbled over to the Gatorades, but there was none, so took a can of beer Tom Zucold had hidden and a package of Saltine crackers, then hobbled back to the Thunderbird chair. As he ate he listened to the world. The freaks were buzzing so that he thought he could almost see the air currents from their breaths. Then he heard a chain saw razzing somewhere and in the other direction there were faint sirens. He thought of the ambulance that had carted Tom Zucold into the night, its lights mournfully flashing, its sirens screaming. He wondered what its hurry was. The old man was dead. They weren't taking him to the hospital. Then where? He had meant to ask Trooper Drilling

254

but he'd been directing traffic. Now there were other Troopers sitting idly in their cruisers, keeping the crowd disciplined. He didn't feel like asking them. Maybe it didn't matter. Or not enough.

He heard a tapping at the El Dorado door. Then, "Hey shithead, open up."

Billy Carmines was pressed against the back wall of the Bowie Garage when he rolled the El Dorado window down.

"Say what?" The Grip said.

"Tom Zucold said if anything happened I was to give you this." He pushed an envelope through the window. It was oil-stained and wrinkled.

"Listen shithead," Billy Carmines said, "You can stay with me you want."

The Grip nodded. He did not know where he was going but he said "Going. Somewhere."

"Where the hell you going to go? Ain't no different anywhere else. People is all. Just people. Shitheads. Might can use a man like you," Billy Carmines said and flexed his biceps to indicate The Grip's strength. When The Grip shrugged, Billy Carmines said "The old man knowed you was going to go. Said you was the kind that had to go looking everywhere for what was right under your big nose. Said he was gone do what he could to get you ready but look to me like it ain't taken. So long shithead."

When The Grip sat in the Thunderbird chair he opened the envelope and found it contained five greasy ten-dollar bills, a picture of the Bowie Garage, and a picture of the not-a-nigger girl. This picture was wrapped in a service order and Tom Zucold's scrawl on the service order said NAME FAITH. Under this it said WRONG?

The Grip closed his eyes and pushed the button that sent the Thunderbird chair back. When he opened them he was staring up the rope that seemed to sway just a little. He was sure there was some kind of message hidden in what Tom Zucold had left him but he couldn't find it. He had closed his eyes again and was trying to concentrate on the face of the not-a-nigger girl when there was another tapping on the El Dorado door.

"Ain't locked," The Grip called and whirred the chair upright. As big as he was, the height of the chair made him look like a king on a throne.

He couldn't have been more surprised if Tom Zucold had walked into the room. But there stood Clifton. He wore a white shirt and a string tie.

"How do I look man?" Clifton said.

The Grip grunted.

"Got me a job down to Montgomery Wards. Coming up in the world, you might say. Man say the sky is the limit if a boy work hard. Be unpacking clothes and like that. Say you ain't looking too fine, bro." Clifton was looking at the television. "Must be what you was shootin' this morning. That ain't gone stop TRUTH OR CONSEQUENCES though. Tole Momma you wasn't shooting yourself."

"Hope?" The Grip said.

"Yeah you got to have some of that," Clifton said and went to look out of the window. "Momma say hope them people stay some more. Got enough now to get the garage started. But ain't no hope got me this job. Momma done talk to that Mighty White and say he can come see my sister if he help me some. That bro a 'nority with contacts. Bip bam and here I am, 'bout to go to work."

The Grip watched Clifton cross back to the door. It seemed hopeless to talk anymore.

"Say man, I just stopped in to mention the truck. Momma said do that."

"Truck?"

"That old panel truck in your yard? The old man's truck? I taking that dude to work hear."

"Truck is Tom Zucold's," The Grip said. He felt the darkness tightening inside him again.

"Was. That's it. Was. Ain't he told you? Old man sold it to Momma. Said he needed a treasury for his war. If you can believe that. He don't need it no more, do he. Momma say it gone be Clifton's Carriage from now on. Be cool Grip, catch you later."

Clifton shut the El Dorado door solidly. The Grip heard the

256

starter on the old panel truck, then heard the engine stutter and backfire. He looked at the picture of the not-a-nigger girl that was still in his lap. Its face was blank, expressionless, untroubled. When he heard the freaks cheer he knew that Clifton had driven off to work.

"Name not The Grip," he said to the picture. "Name Billy Luke Tomson."

"Ought to hang that yeller son of a bitch killer-ape," somebody said across the street.

"Ought to crucify him," a woman shouted.

He packed his fatigues and his blanket in his duffle bag, then he slipped the pictures and the money down under the clothes. He went out the El Dorado door and stood in the shadow of the cement mixer. The earth smelled damp and rich. None of it made any sense. But then Tom Zucold said it never had. Still he wondered why they wanted to hang him. He had not hurt them. He had not hurt anyone. He had only wanted to belong, to be a gentleman and drive his lime green Corvette, to love Promise Land and make a record put. Was it for that they hated him? He knew that it was not so. What they hated was in themselves.

He lay down in the grass beside the Desoto to see if he could feel the earth spinning. Slowly, ever so slowly, he thought it was taking him around. He closed his eyes and dozed a little. When he woke the mockingbirds were jeering as if something moved in Promise Land's bordering fields. He sat up but saw nothing. His face was hot from the sun.

He went back into the bedroom to get his duffle bag. He was thirsty but there were no more Gatorades. He went to look one more time from the front window. There were only a few freaks now and a lot of trash. A white boy he didn't know was raking the trash in front of the pink house where Clifton's momma and sister rocked on the porch. Trooper Drilling stood in the yard and was talking to the reporter named Mighty White. They seemed to be laughing a lot. A television news truck was parked at the edge of the road behind Trooper Drilling's cruiser.

The Grip turned away from the window and looked at the Champion Spark Plug clock. He was startled to see the hands moving, or at least the red second hand was moving and the clock creaked. He stared at it for a moment as if waiting for an answer. The clock creaked and said nothing.

He told himself to keep going, just keep going. His ankle hurt worse and his back was stiff. He threw the duffle bag over his shoulder, groaned at the weight, and shut the El Dorado door. But when he stood outside in the brilliant sunlight he knew that something was wrong, something was unfinished. He waited now, waiting and breathing and feeling the earth move. After a while he saw the putting motion in his mind. Slowly and painfully the shadow-putter there talked himself through the pantomime put, programming carefully. He watched the coil and the balance and then the uncoiling thrust. He concentrated on shoulder roll and hip turn. He was clean and thorough, machinelike, beyond surprise or love or hurt, tight as a knot, undistracted, entirely becoming himself. When he released The Grip knew that it would have been a world record, the steel ball a full extension of the man.

The Grip watched the light playing in the leaves of the gumball. It flowed full and hard and lustrous in the lane, bouncing off the remaining windshields and headlights, glittering from antennas and windshield wipers and hubcaps and bumpers. He was ready to make the put, the one put he could get off with his battered body. But something nagged at him. Something. Something. He felt like crying now but did not know why. He walked the circular line he had put in the ground for his putting ring.

Then it was there. Inside him. It grabbed and touched and burned him, a small spark glowing. It turned him around. It made his legs move. It made his head feel hot. He felt it pulling him and followed it into the bedroom. He took the matches that Tom Zucold kept above the workbench. But there wasn't enough of the sterno left. He went out into the Bowie Garage and returned with Tom Zucold's can of motor solvent and a jug of gasoline. He poured in a circle around the potbelly stove and then along the walls and then in a line to the

Bowie Garage's workbench. He doused the workbench, then threw the can against the far wall. At last he rolled the window to mid-position on the El Dorado door, struck a match from the outside, and tossed it back into the Bowie Garage. As it began to smoke and the flame worked its way over the rug and up the walls, he pulled on a baseball cap that said STARS on the front. Then he hefted a shot from the Havoline box.

It was not a great shot, not even entirely round. But it was the best of all that he had made. He let it take the shape of his palm and fingers. It felt cold and distant and heavy and deadly. Hefting it made his muscles contract and they ached. There would be only one put. He remembered that first punch put he had made from the tree. He remembered Tom Zucold shaking his head at a man that threw steel balls toward a white stick. He remembered that Tom Zucold had told him this was what he could do. He looked at the shot. Its flame-scorched greasy blue surface reminded him somehow of Merci's tits but then he thought of Promise Land and the hardness came behind his eyes.

"Put the fucken thing," he said. He knew that this was what Tom Zucold would have said. Behind him now the Bowie Garage was crackling loudly and he barely heard the sirens coming.

He cocked the shot behind his ear and took his position inside the putting ring. Leaning into his coil, he closed his eyes and looked for that shadow-putter he had seen before, for that image of pure action and perfect trajectory. Then it came, rocketing in from beyond time, so that he spun and hurtled flawlessly through the motion, muscles and sinews responding instantly and powerfully to the sparks that leaped across synapse and nerve, his body giving everything, heaving the steel ball so inevitably true that nothing could alter its course.

Except that it had. She had. At the last second of his extension, his ankle throbbing as if something had pierced it, falling forward away from the pain, he saw her. Tom Zucold's not-a-nigger girl. Promise Land's not-a-nigger girl. Saw. Knew. Waited. Screamed. And there was not a damn thing he could do.

But he was lucky. She was lucky. The sixteen-pound steel ball flew on a line at the white dress standing in front of the white stick and the face that looked melted spread in wordless terror as it watched the ball coming. But he was lucky. It had been a great shot. The ball struck the soggy ground in front of the child, then skipped, its force spent, and struck her in the left shoulder with a spatter of dirt.

"You could of stopped it," The Grip said on his hands and knees.

She howled when he cradled her in his arms, a wild uncontrollable howl that was more fear than sobbing. There was no blood and as far as he could tell it was not a bad injury. It was Tom Zucold's howling and Promise Land's that he held and now he began to sob too, the tears slipping onto his cheeks to glisten in the sunlight. He saw her hair was coarse and tightly curled, her skin was the color of light coffee and was very soft. Her eyes were solid black. Lifting her he heard the Bowie Garage collapse on itself and crackle. It didn't matter. He hobbled down the side of the lane to the front yard. There was a fireman in a slick black suit and he offered the child to the fireman but the man went on unrolling hose and ignored him. He crossed the street. Trooper Drilling and Mighty White stood laughing as he approached them.

"Help," he said and held the child to Trooper Drilling. But Trooper Drilling made no motion to accept it.

"Tom Zucold's mongoloid, ain't it?" Clifton's momma said from the porch.

"Look like his now," Trooper Drilling chuckled.

"Cat could of been famous," Mighty White said, "could of had it made in the shade." He shook his head.

Trooper Drilling put on his reflector sunglasses and looked at The Grip. Flames were flickering in the glasses. "Could give it to Cotton. Of course he would put it in a room and lock it up 'til it die, you understand."

"She's hurting," The Grip said.

"Ain't we all, ain't we all," Trooper Drilling said.

"Belong," The Grip said.

"What's that, man?" Mighty White said, and brushed something from his white summer suit.

"He want to know who it belong to now," Clifton's sister said.

"Ain't mine child," Mighty White said laughing.

"Sho ain't mine," Trooper Drilling said. He laughed too.

"Somebody," The Grip said.

"Ain't nobody boy," Clifton's momma said at last. "That ain't the worst neither. It don't belong to nobody. Won't nobody take it. It just a it."

"I was you bro, I'd leave it in that fire engine over there. Ain't your lookout anyways," Trooper Drilling said. His hand was nervously rubbing the handle of his chrome pistol.

"It look like it ain't been born yet, don't it. Like it was a tiny thing waiting inside a person," Clifton's sister said.

"Quit that kind of talk right now," Clifton's momma said.

"Must be his, whoever he is," Trooper Drilling said and stared up into the blue sky. "I was him, whoever he is, I'd take it on out of here. Man can't never tell when they coming at him, you understand."

He stood beside the long ribbon of asphalt. He did not know what road it was, where it went to or where it came from. His ankle hurt but not so bad as it had and he knew that he would be able to walk come daylight. There had not been a car or truck in hours. There was only the intersection and the fields that surrounded it. The darkness was like an ocean everywhere and sometimes he thought that he could smell salt water. Above him the stars glittered electrically as if they loved him enough just to shine that bright. He pulled the baseball cap low over his eyes and lifted the Gatorade to his mouth, drained the last of it, then flung it as far as he could. It struck the earth with a dull sound like a small steel shot. He was an outlaw now. He knew that. They would try to find him. It was all right. He would find a town somewhere. He thought vaguely of his father thrashing out in the Atlantic surf, the sound of those girls screaming. Then there was only the darkness of water and the darkness of the ocean and his father felt himself sinking—just as he now felt himself going under. But he wouldn't give up, not yet. Maybe never. He kneeled beside the road and smelled its hair. It slept peacefully in his duffle bag. No, they wouldn't give up.

"Bet me," he said. "Billy Luke Tomson don't give up."